CLEOPATRA'S TOMB

ALSO BY NELLIE H. STEELE

Cate Kensie Mysteries

Shadow Slayers Stories

Lily & Cassie by the Sea Mysteries

Pearl Party Mysteries

Middle Age is Murder Cozy Mysteries

Duchess of Blackmoore Mysteries

Maggie Edwards Adventures

Clif & Ri on the Sea Adventures

CLEOPATRA'S TOMB

A MAGGIE EDWARDS ADVENTURE

NELLIE H. STEELE

A Novel Idea Publishing

For my cousin, Tim
Who always enjoyed a good "G.I. Jones"
adventure movie

ACKNOWLEDGMENTS

A HUGE thank you to everyone who helped get this book published! Special shout outs to: Stephanie Sovak, Paul Sovak, Michelle Cheplic, Mark D'Angelo and Lori D'Angelo.

Finally, a HUGE thank you to you, the reader!

CHAPTER 1

$\mathcal{M}$aggie Edwards pushed through the darkened shop's door. The sound of her heels clicked across the marble tile floor. Sets of unseeing eyes from various locations peered at her. The smell of must filled her nostrils. She flipped the light switch to her right, brightening the room with the overhead lights.

"Good morning, everyone," she greeted her admirers. "Hello, Fluffy." She stroked the head of one. "How are we all feeling today?" She continued greeting everyone as she made her way to the cash register and display case. Owning a combination bookstore and antique shop had its perks. She had multiple friends in the form of exotic antique taxidermy mounts from various locations around the world. She greeted them every day as she opened the shop, a fun game she created to ease any fear that crept into her after she consigned the items.

Maggie had opened her bookstore, Maggie's Books and Baubles Boutique, several years ago following graduation from Aberdeen College's graduate school, putting her degrees in library sciences and business management to good use. She added the antiques component after a few years to make the shop more interesting and inviting. She specialized in unique, hard-to-find or out-of-print books, dedicating a special section in her shop to them. She also carried top-sellers and mainstream books. Her cozy shop allowed customers to browse through unique objects, hard-to-find books and more. It even allowed them to enjoy a cup of coffee and peruse a book before buying it in one of the many comfy leather armchairs scattered around the shop.

Her keys banged against the glass countertop as she dropped them to scan the note on the display case. She rolled her eyes as she read it. It was scrawled in her assistant's handwriting.

Hey—Didn't get to dust and stuff last night, we were super busy. Figured you'd get to it in the morning.
   - Piper

Typical Piper, Maggie mused. What Piper described as "super busy" was likely the arrival of one customer coupled with a few friends. Still, the "Help Wanted" sign in her window hadn't garnered any other more qualified applicants. While Piper may be lax in menial tasks, she excelled in reliability and trustworthiness, allowing Maggie to leave the shop in her more than capable hands.

Maggie completed her opening duties, turning on all lights, opening the register, turning the "We're Closed" sign to "We're Open!" and propping the door open. Though summer waned, the weather remained warm. She also brewed a fresh pot of coffee for her early customers. When she finished these tasks, she began dusting and tidying the shop, since Piper had failed to find the time before closing last night.

After she finished, she checked her cell phone. She found

a text message from her on-again, off-again, at the moment on-again boyfriend, Leo Hamilton. Though the two had dated for a few years, their relationship had been turbulent resulting in numerous breakups and subsequent reconciliations. She often wondered why she allowed herself to be talked back into a relationship with him, but she surmised it was because he usually possessed the ability to bring a smile to her face. Today was no exception.

His message beamed off of the screen at her: *Good morning, gorgeous!*

She smiled as she typed a good morning back. A return message arrived soon after, asking her about her morning so far. She took the opportunity to complain about her less-than-motivated shop assistant. Leo assured Maggie she would manage everything with ease, as she always did.

The morning hours passed quietly, with only a few customers filtering in and out. About an hour before lunch, the daily mail delivery arrived. "Thanks, Mike!" Maggie called as he exited the shop. She filed through the letters, sorting junk mail from important correspondence. Next, she moved on to the packages. One box contained a few office related supplies.

A much-awaited order of books also arrived from the distributor. She sliced the tape sealing the top of the box, as giddy as a child on Christmas morning. New items always excited her. She loved unwrapping the merchandise, rearranging the shelves and setting up new displays.

In her eagerness over the new pieces, she almost overlooked a small box amongst the packages. It clattered to the floor. Maggie picked it up and studied it for a moment. It was a small, nondescript brown box. There was no return address. Her own address appeared to be scrawled in a shaky hand. She set it down on the counter, choosing to open it later when she had finished with the shipment of new materials.

After unpacking the entire box, Maggie closed the shop and stepped out for lunch. She met Leo at a local café for a salad and an iced tea. Refreshed from her lunch break, she returned to her shop ready to redecorate. The overhaul to showcase the new materials took her the better part of the afternoon. Maggie just finished putting the last few touches on the front window display when Piper plodded through the door.

"Hi!" Maggie greeted her. "The new stuff came in! How's the display look from outside?"

Piper didn't respond. She bent down behind the desk, stuffing her bag into the cabinet below the register. Her pink, blue, and green hair bobbed behind the counter. When she popped back up, Maggie shot her a questioning glance. "Huh?" She pulled earbuds from her ears.

"I said, how does the window display look?" Maggie repeated.

"Oh, I didn't even notice it. Good, I guess," Piper responded with a shrug of her shoulders.

"Good you guess? You didn't even spot the major change?" Maggie rolled her eyes and waved her hand at Piper. "Oh, never mind, I'll check it myself." She hopped out the door to glance at the display. When she came back in, she adjusted a few items before she was satisfied. "There, finished!" she declared.

"Great," Piper said in a monotone voice. She waved a finger in a circular motion in the air.

"It might be helpful if you took an interest in your job, Piper. You might even enjoy it then."

"Mmm, doubt it," Piper responded. "Hey, I've got a massive term paper due tomorrow, do you mind if I close like half an hour early?"

Maggie considered it for a moment. "Okay," Maggie agreed, "but don't make a habit of it. You need to learn how to manage responsibilities, Piper. You can't always depend on your boss to let you out of work."

"Yeah, yeah, yeah." Piper held her hands up in defeat. "I won't be in school forever. Soon, I'll just have a job to worry about."

Maggie smirked at her before a startled expression crossed her face. "Oh, shoot! What time is it?"

"Umm," Piper mumbled. She checked her phone. "Four forty-six."

"Oh my gosh, I've got to run! I'm having dinner with Leo and I need to change!"

"You look fine to me." Piper shrugged.

"I can't wear this!" Maggie exclaimed. "They're my work clothes!"

"It's a designer dress and heels. You're wearing more jewelry than jewelry stores stock. Perfect for a date. For you, anyway. I wouldn't be caught dead in that outfit."

"That's because you have no sense of style," Maggie stated. "The goth makeup and all those piercings do not constitute style. Anyway, I need to change. This, Piper, is a day-dress, not a date-dress."

"What? Your dust-covered day-dress won't cut it for the date?"

"Very funny," Maggie answered, a wry expression on her face. She raced behind the register to grab her purse and keys.

"You've got to learn to be more responsible with your appointments," Piper chided.

Maggie frowned at her, rolling her eyes. "See you tomorrow, Piper!" she exclaimed. She slung her purse over her shoulder after pulling on her jacket.

"Oh, boss lady!" Piper called after her. Maggie spun

around, finding Piper waving a small box in the air. "Did you want this? It was on the floor."

"Oh, yes, although I have no idea what that is! It came earlier. Here I'll take it and open it later." She waved her over as she took a few steps back into the shop. She retrieved the package from Piper, stuffing it in her purse, spinning around and dashing out the door.

She checked her watch when she hit the pavement. Yep, she'd be late, she surmised. Before meeting Leo, she needed to change into something more appropriate. If she was correct, tonight could be a turning point in their relationship and she wanted to be dressed for the occasion.

She and Leo had been together for six months this time, making this the longest stretch their relationship had lasted over the years. When Leo asked her to dinner this evening, he told her they'd be dining at her favorite French restaurant and suggested she wear her favorite dress. "It's going to be a big night!" he teased during their lunch earlier. Maggie figured the fancy restaurant, suggestion to dress up and hint about the big night was a signal to expect something great. A smile crossed her face, and she bit her lower lip, a habit when she was excited, as she turned the corner onto her tree-lined street. Despite their tumultuous relationship, Leo was the image of what she pictured in a husband. Tall, handsome, affable, on his way to attaining a prominent position in an illustrious career. He could provide Maggie with the lifestyle in which she'd be very comfortable. A manager of marketing with his international company now, he was in a position to rise in the ranks within a few years.

She made her way halfway down the street to her home, a mid-rise art déco style apartment building. She readied her keys after she pressed the call button for the elevator.

The doors slid open, and she stepped inside, pressing the button for the top floor. She flipped through her phone while the elevator whisked her upwards. One new text message awaited her from Leo: *Looking forward to tonight!* Maggie smiled at the message. She echoed those sentiments. She texted back informing Leo she was running late but wouldn't be long. His next text message made her laugh as she exited the elevator: *So what else is new?*

Maggie unlocked her apartment door and entered her multi-room apartment, tossing her keys and purse down on the entry table. She hurried to her bedroom and en suite bathroom, where she spent a few moments touching up her makeup. She revived her eyeliner, added a coat of mascara and darkened her neutral eye shadow until her dark brown eyes sparkled. She curled her shoulder-length brown hair and added a pearl headband. She tore through her walk-in closet, pulling out several dresses before finally deciding on a baby pink sheath paired with strappy gold sandals.

Maggie pulled on a white cashmere sweater before donning a pearl necklace, earrings and bracelet. She finished by slicking on a light pink lip gloss before hastening to the hall to retrieve her purse and keys. As she shoved her lip gloss into her purse, she noticed the package she had stuffed inside earlier. She pulled it out, tossing it onto her couch before leaving the apartment.

Despite her four-inch heels, Maggie hurried along the sidewalk to the restaurant. She was already late and eager to begin the evening. As she rounded the corner, the restaurant came into view. Its sparkling lights shimmered through the shrubs surrounding its patio dining area. Light music floated through the air as she neared.

Maggie loved this restaurant. An avid fan of the finer things in life since she was a child, Maggie appreciated no expense being spared. The daughter of a prominent doctor and an upper-class socialite, Maggie had never wanted for anything in her life. European vacations, fancy restaurants and frequent parties had filled her childhood.

She pranced to the front entrance, offering a wide smile to the maître d' as she inquired about her table. He led her to a table near the window. Leo waited with a glass of wine. "Hey, you're late!" Leo exclaimed as she sat. "I was beginning to wonder if you were coming."

"It takes time to look this good." She winked at him.

"It's okay, I told you to be here thirty minutes before our reservation. I figured you'd only be about fifteen minutes late then." He grinned at her as he leaned forward, resting his elbows on the table.

Maggie gave him a wry glance as she shook her head. "Then don't complain if I'm not that late." She unfurled her napkin and placed it on her lap.

Leo poured her a glass of wine. She sipped it, gazing at him over the glass. It promised to be a magical night, and she planned to savor every moment. They ordered their meal before settling into a conversation. "So," she said. She traced the rim of her wine glass. "Nice choice in restaurant."

"It's your favorite," Leo responded after he took a sip of his wine.

"It is," she confirmed. "What's the occasion?"

Leo smirked at her as the server delivered their appetizer. "You were saying?" she asked when they were alone.

"Patience, Mags, patience." He bit into a canapé.

She smiled at him, annoyed by his stalling but willing to remain on the hook for the payoff. With Leo unwilling to share his secret, Maggie steered the conversation to the events of her day. She spent most of the meal discussing her new store displays. Maggie possessed the innate ability to monopolize a conversation when it came to discussions about her shop.

After their dessert was served, Maggie pressed the matter

with Leo. Taking a spoonful of her dame blanche, she stared at Leo. "I've waited long enough. Why my favorite restaurant? It's not my birthday. What's the occasion?"

He smiled at her. "Does there need to be an occasion?"

"You're such a tease." Maggie rolled her eyes. "Come on! This is quite a fancy restaurant for no occasion!"

"You'd tell me you're worth it, occasion or not," Leo countered.

Maggie met his stare, giving him an unimpressed look. "All right, all right. I do have a reason for my choice." A smile spread on Maggie's face. She expected an overture about their relationship, perhaps even a proposal. Leo reached into his pocket, withdrawing a small object. Maggie eyed his hand, expecting a small velvet box. She imagined the ring inside. Large and lavish if he selected well, she mused. Instead, she could spy nothing.

He set his closed hand on the white linen table cloth and, after opening it, slid something across the table. A confused expression replaced Maggie's smile. Leo's hand, still covering the object, was flat. Was the ring out of the box?

He snapped his hand away, revealing the object. "I bought a new car!" he exclaimed.

Maggie stared at the object, highlighted against the white of the tablecloth sat a black key fob. "What?" she managed.

"A new car! Remember when we drove past that car lot and I mentioned how much I liked that yellow sports car? I bought it!" Leo's excitement was obvious.

Maggie didn't respond. "Speechless, huh?" Leo said.

Maggie stuttered, "I... I... I don't know what to say."

"How about 'let's go for a ride!'" Leo suggested. Maggie sat dumbfounded, frustrated and disappointed. "What's wrong with you?"

"Are you serious?" Maggie asked.

Confusion crossed Leo's face. "What do you mean?"

"You booked my favorite restaurant, invited me to dinner, told me to dress up, promised a big night, all to tell me you bought a new car?"

"What did you think I did it for?" Leo asked.

"Something to do with us. With our relationship, perhaps?" Maggie conjectured.

"Like what? A proposal?" He guffawed.

Maggie pouted, fluttering her eyelids. "You don't have to make it sound so ridiculous," she muttered.

"Oh, come on, Mags! We've only been together for a little over six months." He slumped in his chair.

"We've been together much longer than six months in the grand scheme of things," she contested.

He snorted. "You aren't seriously mad, are you?"

"I'm disappointed," she admitted.

"How can you be upset? Come on!"

Maggie continued to pout, anger brewing inside. The downside of Maggie's childhood was that it made her difficult when things didn't go her way.

"Mags, things are going good this time. But it's way too early for us to be considering marriage."

"Way too early for you, I guess," Maggie snapped.

"Really? Are you really going to ruin my big moment?"

"Ruin your big moment? I thought this was OUR big moment. You misled me!"

"Misled you? Are you kidding me? I didn't mislead you. It's not my fault you assumed I was proposing! This is a big moment for me… us! It was supposed to be a big moment for us, anyway!"

"Whatever," Maggie said. She threw her napkin on the table in disgust.

"You're being ridiculous!"

"Yep, it's always me. I'm always ridiculous!" Maggie held her hands up in frustration.

Leo rolled his eyes. "Oh, stop. Knock it off, Mags, let's not fight."

"Fine, we won't fight," Maggie said.

"Great! Now, how about a ride home?" He grinned at her.

"I'll walk," Maggie hissed. She stood and stalked from the table.

"Maggie!" Leo shouted behind her. "Fine, have it your way!"

Maggie stomped to the sidewalk outside, crossing the street and veering toward her apartment building. She made it to the end of the block, turning the corner before a yellow sports car pulled up beside her. The car crept along next to her. The passenger window rolled down. "Get in, Mags!" Leo called.

Maggie continued walking, refusing to answer. "Come on, Mags, just get in."

"No," she retorted.

"Maggie…" Leo started.

"Just leave it, Leo."

"Fine." He rolled up the window and sped away. His engine revved as he peeled out from the stop sign at the end of the road.

Maggie shook her head, her annoyance growing with every step. She stormed down the sidewalk, thundering through the door to her apartment building. She continued to poke the elevator button until the doors slid open.

As the elevator glided upwards, she tapped her foot on the floor, agitated. When the doors whisked open, she trudged into the hall, stomping to her door. She shoved her key into the lock and threw the door open. She slammed it shut behind her after entering and slogged to her couch, slumping onto it.

A frown settled onto her face as she recalled the conversation over dessert. She crossed her arms, sighing. The evening had not gone the way she expected or hoped. Why did their relationship take so much work, she mused? They were never on the same page. Another disappointment, another fight with Leo. At this point they were on track for another breakup rather than a commitment. She tossed her purse to the side, throwing her head back onto the pillow.

She closed her mind, trying to shut out the world and her agitation. Within seconds, she popped her eyes open, unable to relax. She blindly reached for her purse, intent on grabbing her phone for a distraction. Her hand hit something hard instead of delving into the purse's lining.

Maggie turned her head, glancing at the object her hand hit. The small cardboard box peeked out from under her purse. She recalled tossing it on the couch before her doomed date with Leo. Her brow furrowed as she pondered what waited inside.

Her head dropped back on the couch as she continued to pout. Did she even care what was inside? Her eyes slid back to the package. Perhaps it would distract her from her misery. She grabbed the box and studied it. The sender scrawled her name and business address in dark ink. No return address appeared anywhere on the package. She turned it over in her hands, examining each side. No other markings existed other than the postage and postage processing. The package appeared to have originated in Jordan.

Jordan, she mused, she didn't know anyone in Jordan. She viewed the top of the box again. The handwriting looked vaguely familiar but she couldn't place it. "There's only one way to find out, I guess," Maggie muttered to herself.

She pushed off the couch, heading to the kitchen for a knife. She sliced open the brown packing tape sealing the box. Packing material filled the inside. Maggie used the knife to push the material around until an object revealed itself.

A tiny gold fleck gleamed from beneath the packing peanuts. Maggie pushed more peanuts away, some of them spilling over the side of the box. She peered inside at the curious object. Gems in red, green and blue adorned the gold item.

With her thumb and index finger, Maggie picked the bejeweled piece out of the box. She rotated the object in her hand, studying it from all angles. It was a gem-encrusted beetle. If Maggie remembered her ancient history, it was a scarab beetle. Who would send her this, she wondered?

She dug into the box again, searching for anything else. At the bottom, she found an envelope bearing her name. Opening it, she pulled a note from inside. She held the golden scarab in her hand as she read the note.

Maggie—I have little time to explain. I have found something... something big. This little scarab is the key to the greatest archaeo-logical find of our time. I can't say more. I don't want to endanger your life and I need to lay low for a while. The stakes are high.

Maggie—Keep this object secret and safe. DO NOT let it out of your sight! When I am able to return for it, I will. Until then, good luck.

Your favorite uncle, Ollie

"Uncle Ollie?" Maggie said aloud. She furrowed her brow. She flipped the page over, searching for more. A blank page stared back at her.

She re-read the note, her brows pinching even on the second read. The handwriting was recognizable despite being shaky. It appeared the note was written in haste. The scrawled handwriting suggested this, along with the overall tone of the note.

Oliver Keene was Maggie's maternal uncle, her mother's brother. A renowned archaeologist and professor at nearby Aberdeen College, Uncle Ollie, as Maggie called him, traveled the world often in search of precious artifacts. Maggie's love of antiques was cultured from a young age by Uncle Ollie.

It wasn't unusual for him to be out of the country. What was unusual was for him to send a precious object to anyone. Was it some kind of joke? She couldn't recall ever receiving even a postcard from Uncle Ollie when he visited an exotic location. She studied the item again. The beetle was heavy. Its gems sparkled in the light. While Maggie worked with antiques at her shop, she was not qualified to determine if an object like this was real or fake.

Whether or not it was, Uncle Ollie had implored her to protect it. Its value to him was obvious. Moseying back to the couch, Maggie spent another few moments studying the golden beetle and the note that accompanied it. Learning nothing else, she tossed both in her purse. She checked her phone, hoping for an apology message from Leo. Nothing awaited her but spam email. Disappointed, she collected her phone and purse and wandered to her bedroom to change for bed. She checked her phone one last time. Still no messages awaited her. She slammed the phone down on the night table before turning out the light.

CHAPTER 2

$\mathcal{M}$aggie padded barefoot back to her room, coffee in hand. She climbed under the covers, pulling her laptop onto her lap. Maggie often enjoyed her morning coffee snuggled under her covers before starting her day. She checked and answered her emails, then scrolled through her social media accounts. Pictures of Leo's new car caused her to roll her eyes. She checked her phone, still nothing. Annoyed, she grimaced and tossed her phone onto the bed.

As she sipped her coffee, her mind turning to the odd object she received the night before. She jumped out of bed and grabbed the object and note from her purse.

She scanned the note again and studied the object. Nothing new jumped out at her. She grabbed her phone, opening her text app. She sent a text message to her mom: *Hey Mom! Have you spoken with Uncle Ollie lately?*

As she waited for a response, she performed an internet search on golden scarabs. She checked a few articles, but learned nothing about the object in her possession. Perusing the images returned in the search, she unearthed nothing that resembled the item from Uncle Ollie. She leaned back in bed, pondering her next move when her phone chirped. She swiped it open, hoping a text from Leo awaited. Instead, she discovered an answer to the question she posed to her mother. *I haven't... the last I heard he was out of town.*

Maggie considered the response. The package had originated in another country, consistent with the story of Uncle Ollie being out of town. But why send it to her? Why the dire warning? Was the object that valuable? If so, why not send it to the museum he worked with to retrieve these types of objects? Or why not send it to her mother, his sister?

Maggie spun the object in her hand. "What is your story?" she whispered to it. "Why are you so special?"

The object remained silent. With no answers, Maggie answered her mother. She texted back: *Thanks! I have a question for him regarding an item I came across. If you hear from him, let me know!*

Her mother confirmed she would text if Oliver appeared on her radar. Maggie swallowed the last sips of her coffee and rose from her bed to shower and dress for the day. As she slipped on her shoes to finish her outfit, she checked her phone again. Still no new messages. Maggie seethed inside, frustrated at Leo's stubbornness.

She grabbed her purse and keys, heading to the store. Her favorite pastry shop was on the route to her shop. She stopped to purchase an éclair, planning to indulge for her breakfast given her less-than-stellar mood.

She unlocked her front door, turning her sign to OPEN. As she flicked on the lights, illuminating the store, her phone chirped. She raced to the counter, dropping everything in a mad rush to retrieve her phone. Her preview screen revealed a message from Leo. She swiped at the screen to open the message: *Good morning... you out of your mood yet?*

A scowl formed across Maggie's face and she slammed

her phone onto the counter. In the process, she knocked her purse over, spilling the contents. The gold beetle clattered across the glass desk. "What a great start to the day," she murmured. She shoved the contents back inside. As she reached the bottom of the pile, the gold scarab commanded her attention, shining against the glass countertop. The item's beauty possessed the ability to distract her from almost everything.

For a moment, she forgot the text, admiring the small object again. She held it up to the light in the store, watching the gems sparkle. As she studied them in the light, something caught her eye. She peered closer at the object. Small etchings appeared inside the gems mounted on the beetle's back. They were too small to make out. After shoving the rest of her belongings into her purse, she pulled open the drawer to retrieve a magnifying glass.

Maggie peered through the magnifier at the gems. She shifted it at several angles but could not distinguish anything. Frustrated, she shoved the magnifier back into the drawer. She stuffed the item into her purse. She would deal with it after completing her morning chores.

Maggie spent over an hour reviewing the sales from the previous evening, dusting, readjusting and tweaking displays in the shop. When she finished, she collapsed onto the stool behind the register. She pulled her laptop onto the counter, opening it. As it started, she checked her phone. Another message from Leo awaited her: *I guess you're not*

It was a reference to the previous message. When Maggie failed to send a response earlier, Leo assumed annoyance still coursed through her veins. His assumption was correct. Maggie considered making him wait even longer, then decided against it. She typed a message back: *Not a mood... if you can't understand why I am annoyed, we have nothing to say to each other at the moment*

She slammed the phone onto the counter, turning her attention to her laptop. Again, she attempted an internet search on golden scarabs and related terms. She turned up nothing. Changing tactics, she called her uncle's office phone and cell phone. Both went to voicemail, but Maggie chose not to leave a message. It wasn't unlike Uncle Ollie to be unreachable even when not overseas. However, the peril hinted at in his note made her concern grow.

The front door's bell jingled, pulling her attention away from the object and its mystery. She greeted her customers and made herself busy while they browsed the shop. The remaining morning hours proved busy with a steady stream of customers browsing the shop. Maggie stepped out for a quick lunch before returning for the afternoon. Her busy day prevented her from studying the mysterious beetle any further. It also kept her from her phone and any messages waiting from Leo. Maggie considered that a good thing since it appeared they were heading for yet another argument.

Piper arrived in the late afternoon to take over her duties as the self-proclaimed "night manager." While it was not the title Maggie gave her, Piper insisted on using it, claiming she did the same work Maggie did all day. Since she was a capable worker, Maggie allowed her to use it, and left the store in her hands for the evening.

Maggie checked her phone as she stepped into the warm afternoon air. She had several unread messages from Leo. She read through them as she began her walk home. The messages began with the assertion that Leo did not understand why Maggie was upset. Another stated if she preferred not to talk, that was fine by him. Still another launched into the usual accusation that her behavior was "ridiculous." He also questioned why she was not happy for him.

Maggie rolled her eyes, deciding to answer him when she reached her apartment rather than attempt to type a response while walking. Why did she continue this relationship? It usually brought her grief. Were all relationships this hard? She shoved her phone into her purse and focused on savoring the day's fading warmth. She enjoyed living in her mid-sized midwestern town. The town offered everything a young woman could want: great restaurants, fabulous boutiques and enough nightlife to keep things interesting. And all within walking distance. With all the amenities of a city and none of the drawbacks, the quaint town, with its tree-lined streets and picturesque shopfronts, represented perfection to Maggie.

She reached her building and took the elevator to the top floor. After shoving her key into the lock, she turned it, not hearing the usual sound of the lock releasing. Confused, she tried the door, finding it unlocked. She figured she must have missed the clicking noise that accompanied the lock's release.

She stepped into her apartment and came to a halt. Her jaw dropped open as she glanced around the living room. The entire room was a wreck. Couch cushions lay haphazardly strewn about. The couch itself was overturned. Table drawers were pulled out and dumped on the floor.

Maggie hurried to her bedroom, finding it in a similar state. Her heart raced, and she felt weak in the knees as she dialed 9-1-1 on her phone. The operator answered and Maggie stated her emergency, assuring the dispatcher the responsible parties were no longer on site.

She stepped into the hall and sunk to the floor to await the police, having been told to touch nothing inside. Within minutes, police arrived, and she recounted her brief story of arriving home to find her apartment trashed. Several officers rushed into the apartment while one took Maggie's statement before they both entered.

Inside, they continued to ask her questions, determining

if she had any problems or issues with anyone or anything valuable. They asked Maggie to confirm, to the best of her ability, if anything was stolen.

She checked several items in the living room, finding everything that came to mind. She moved to the bedroom to determine if anything of value was missing there. It appeared nothing had been taken, only torn apart for some unknown reason. Her drawers were all emptied, shoe boxes were opened and tossed around the room and closet. Clothing items were heaped everywhere.

As she finished confirming the contents of her jewelry box, she overheard shouting from the other room. She hurried to the living room, finding Leo engaged in an argument with an officer at the door.

"Oh my God! Maggie, are you okay?" He peered over the police officer's head.

"I'm fine. It's okay," Maggie said to the officer. "You can let him in."

Leo pushed past the man, eyeing the apartment. "Mags, are you sure?" He pulled her into a hug then leaned back to study her face as she answered.

"Yes, I'm sure. I wasn't here when it happened. And it looks like they didn't take anything." She stepped out of his embrace.

The lead detective on the scene approached them. "And you are?" he asked Leo.

"Boyfriend," Maggie and Leo responded in unison. "Leo Hamilton," Leo added. He extended his hand.

"Ah." He flipped his notebook open, ignoring Leo's hand. "And where were you earlier this afternoon?"

"What?" Leo questioned. "Are you serious?" He turned to Maggie. "What the hell did you tell them? Did you tell them we were fighting? Are you kidding me?"

"You're fighting?" He raised his eyebrows.

"No," Maggie replied. She shook her head at both men. "He had nothing to do with this. We're not fighting. We had a minor disagreement last night. It was nothing beyond what all normal couples go through."

The detective jotted a few notes in his notebook. "What are you writing?" Maggie asked. She peered over the top of the small pad.

"Just basic information. And as long as your boyfriend, Mr. Hamilton, was it? As long as he can account for his whereabouts earlier, we'll be fine."

Leo rolled his eyes. "I was at work. Ask anyone I work with. Tons of people saw me."

The detective took down information about Leo's workplace and closed his notebook. Frustrated, Maggie rolled her eyes again. "You should concentrate on finding who is responsible for this instead of wasting your time with people who aren't."

"Well, we often find, Ms. Edwards, that someone you were acquainted with is the culprit. It's obvious this wasn't about money. You have a number of valuables, but nothing was taken. They were searching for something here. So, I'd venture to say it's someone looking for something specific and figured they'd find it in your apartment."

"How much longer do you think you'll be here?" Maggie asked.

The detective glanced around. "The team's almost finished dusting for prints and photographing everything. They should be finished within the hour."

"Can I clean up then?"

"Sure. Oh," the officer said. He pointed to Maggie. "And you'll have to come to the station at your convenience and give us a sample of your fingerprints. A lot of the prints we pull will be yours. We'll want to rule those out when searching for a suspect."

"I'll make a point of coming tomorrow morning," Maggie answered. The detective wandered away to oversee the last bits of evidence gathering. Maggie assessed the damage, mentally calculating how long it would take to put her apartment back together.

"Mags, about last night..." Leo began.

"Listen," Maggie snapped, "I don't have the time or the patience to deal with that now. I've got to clean all of this up plus the mess in the bedroom. Just leave it, Leo."

"I'll help. I just wanted to tell you I was sorry."

Maggie glanced at him. "Really? After all your texts, you stopped over to apologize? Somehow, I find that hard to believe."

"Well, actually, when I didn't hear from you, I figured I'd stop to talk about it at least..." he began.

Maggie cut him off. "So, in other words, you weren't coming here to apologize, you were coming here to continue the argument. But now you feel bad and you don't want to come across as an uncaring heel."

"Oh, come on, Maggie, give me a break here."

Maggie held up a hand to him. "I just want to straighten up this mess and go to bed. I don't want or need your help so you can leave. I am absolving you of any duty to help me."

"Go to bed? Here? You can't stay here, at least not tonight!" Leo argued.

Maggie considered it. She would feel unsettled if she stayed the night. She imagined tossing and turning, wondering if the robbers may come back to finish searching for whatever they were hunting for earlier. While she hated to admit it, Leo was correct.

"Fine," she said, "I'll clean up, but I won't stay here."

"Good. You can stay with me. I'll take the couch. You can have the bed."

"I'll go to a hotel, thanks," she answered.

Leo dropped his head back onto his shoulders, frustrated by her response. "Are you kidding me? You're being impossible. Can I do nothing right?"

"Yes, I know. I'm being impossible. So perhaps you should leave."

"Come on, Mags." Leo pulled her close to him. "I care about you. I'm concerned. I just want to help."

"I'm still bothered by what happened last night. And I'm not willing to give you a free pass because I was robbed." She pushed him away. "Now, please. I'll be fine at a hotel."

"Well, we could always, I don't know, talk about it? There's a novel idea!" he mocked.

"Yes, that's just what I want to do during or after I've cleaned up my wrecked apartment: talk about why I was upset and listen to you tell me I shouldn't have been and how it's my fault and how I need to grow up and get over it and whatever else you decree to be the case."

"All right, fine. I give up!" Leo held his hands up to signify surrender. "You want to do this yourself? Fine! Go ahead. Have at it, Mags. You keep acting stubborn and one day you will find yourself with no one." Leo stormed from the apartment.

Maggie shook her head, biting her lower lip in frustration. Perhaps she should have given in and let him stay to help her. She had done it several times in the past, but his behavior frustrated her over and over. Allowing him to stay would have buried last night's incident only to be resurrected in a future fight. Then he would accuse her of never letting things go. She pushed the argument from her mind. She had many other things to handle. She wouldn't waste energy on a petty argument.

Maggie spent her entire evening restoring her bedroom. She rehung her clothes, put her shoes back where they belonged, refolded and filled her drawers, shoved her mattress back onto the bed and changed the sheets. Exhausted, she decided to tackle the living room tomorrow. She packed a small suitcase with clothes and other essentials and left the apartment for a hotel.

Maggie dragged her suitcase to her car and drove to the Grand Hotel. The hotel was the best rated hotel in town, which was why Maggie selected it. No stranger to luxury, Maggie preferred to indulge in all the comforts life offered. She checked into a suite, expecting to stay for a few nights until she felt safe enough to return to her apartment.

Maggie unpacked her suitcase and changed, climbing into bed and nestling under the covers. She flipped on the TV before pulling her purse across the bed toward her. She dug into the front pocket, searching for her phone. Her hand hit a cold, hard object. She clasped it and removed it from her purse. The golden scarab stared back at her.

Maggie frowned at it, recalling the note that accompanied it. An idea crossed her mind. "Were they looking for you?" Maggie asked the beetle. She laughed, dismissing the idea as ridiculous. Or was it, she pondered? "We should figure out what your story is, little guy," she said, setting it down on her night table.

She dug further into the pocket, retrieving her phone. She unlocked it, checking her messages. Finding none, she set the phone on the night table next to the beetle. The room plunged into darkness as she switched off the light, nestling into the covers. She sighed in the darkness as she settled back into her pillow. After a few moments, she snapped her eyes open. She searched the darkness for any movement.

The break-in at her apartment unnerved her more than she was willing to admit. She second-guessed her prideful decision to opt for a hotel over Leo's apartment. Her mind wandered back to their argument. She grew annoyed all over again. She turned over to grab her phone to check for messages again. None awaited her. She spotted the beetle next to her phone. Her mind returned to the mystery surrounding the object. She let her head rest against the pillow as she stared at it. Maggie dozed off speculating about the item.

* * *

A shrill ringing startled Maggie awake. She jumped, bolting upright from a sound sleep. Confused, she glanced around, getting her bearings. As her mind focused, she recalled being in the Grand Hotel following a break-in at her apartment. She took a deep breath, relaxing. Only then did she realize ringing still filled the room. She swiveled her head in the direction of the noise. Her cell phone jangled, buzzing and sliding on the night table, signaling a call coming through. Who would call in the middle of the night, she pondered, as she reached for the phone?

"Hello?" she answered.

"MAGGIE!" a voice shouted on the other end through static.

"Uncle Ollie?" Maggie questioned.

"Yes..." The voice answered through static. "... get the scarab?" The conversation cut in and out.

"Uncle Ollie, I can't hear you. The line is cutting in and out. I got the package..."

"Good! Maggie, it's... protect it... worse than I imagined... danger... careful... safe."

"Uncle Ollie, I'm losing you."

"friend... help... important... notes... talk... no one..." The line disconnected. Her phone beeped, signifying a dropped call. Maggie redialed the number, but she could not connect with anyone. The line rang and rang, but no one answered.

Maggie set her phone down, unnerved by the call. She sat in bed, parsing through the few words she made out in the conversation. None of it pointed to anything good. She laid back on the pillow. What was worse than he imagined? Why did the scarab need protection? What was so important?

Her mind whirled with questions. She considered texting her mom but didn't want to wake her with upsetting news in the middle of the night. She had already opted not to inform her of the break-in, finding no reason to upset her. Maggie closed her eyes and took several deep, steadying breaths. With her eyes still closed, she reached to the night table, grabbing the gold beetle. It was cool against her skin. She pulled it close to her, squeezing it in her hand.

"Are you what's causing all the trouble?" Maggie asked it. She opened her eyes. The beetle stared back at her, silent. Maggie stared at it another moment. She needed to find some answers. Uncle Ollie mentioned the word 'notes' in his cryptic call. Was he referring to the note that accompanied the beetle? No, Maggie surmised, he said notes, not note. It was plural. Did he have notes on the object? Perhaps in his office. It was the best place to start her search for answers.

Maggie resolved to check there the following day. Piper could cover the store from lunch on, freeing her up to make the trip to Aberdeen College. With a plan in place, Maggie fell asleep, still clutching the golden scarab in her hand.

CHAPTER 3

$\mathcal{T}$he next morning, Maggie awoke with the golden beetle still clenched in her fist. The gems made indentations in her palm. She placed the object on the night table, wiggling her fingers to release the stiffness.

Maggie stretched as she sat up. The mysterious call from her uncle flooded back into her mind. She must find answers. But first, her morning cup of coffee called her name. She rose from the bed and padded to the coffeemaker, starting the machine for her morning cup. When the process completed, she snatched her cup and raced back to bed, sliding under the covers.

She grabbed her phone from the night table. Swiping it open, she checked her email. She found nothing important there. No text messages awaited her. She opened her recent calls, dialing the number Uncle Ollie called from last night. It rang several times with no answer.

Maggie disconnected the call. She received no answers from Ollie over her morning coffee. With no information gained, Maggie climbed out of bed to prepare for her day. After showering, applying makeup and pulling her hair into a ponytail, she slipped a dress over her head, donned a pair of heels, a necklace and earring set. She stuffed her phone and the golden scarab into her purse and left her room, heading to her shop.

Maggie spent her morning dusting the store and rearranging products. Piper arrived just before lunch, and Maggie left her in charge of the store for the rest of the day. She strolled to the hotel, retrieved her car and drove the short distance to neighboring Aberdeen.

Maggie eased her car into a spot in the visitor parking area, gazing at the collegial buildings surrounding her. She recalled fond memories of her college and graduate school days. She wandered among the buildings, crossing the green to a small building that housed her uncle's office. While Maggie didn't have keys to his office, she knew where she could get them.

She climbed the building's central stairs to the second floor. Navigating to the main office of the Department of History and Classics, she popped her head in the door. She found a familiar face sitting behind the desk. "Knock, knock!" Maggie said.

"Maggie!" the woman said. She leapt from her chair and rushed around the desk to draw Maggie into a hug. "It's so good to see you, honey! How have you been?"

Molly Williams was the department secretary and Maggie's supervisor when she worked as a graduate assistant in the office during her graduate work. "I've been doing well. My shop is thriving! I expanded it last year! Have you had lunch yet? I was hoping to take you to lunch," Maggie answered.

"I haven't! And I'd love to go. I have so much to tell you! Let me just grab my purse!"

"Any special place you'd prefer? It's been so long since I've been here," Maggie mentioned as Molly retrieved her purse.

"There's a new Italian place that opened a few months ago. We could go there if you're up for it?"

"Sure! How's the food, have you tried it yet?"

"I have. I had lunch there a while back with Dr. Kensie. You remember Dr. Kensie, don't you?"

"Yes, I remember Cate," Maggie answered as they exited the office. "How is she? I should stop by and say hello to her before I leave."

"Don't bother!" Molly answered. "She's not here anymore. She moved... to SCOTLAND! Can you believe it?"

"What?" Maggie exclaimed. "For another position?"

"No, no," Molly informed her. "She inherited a castle and now she's a countess."

"Wow! Hey, I'd have moved, too!" Maggie said.

"Me too! I'm visiting her in October. Leaving on the eighteenth and staying just over a week!"

"Aww," Maggie lamented. "You'll miss the Fall Ball!"

"I will, but Lady Cate, as they call her in Scotland, is hosting a costume ball at the castle, so I get the better end of the deal."

Maggie and Molly strolled into town, continuing their conversation about Molly's trip to Scotland. Over lunch, they discussed their lives and caught up on anything that had happened since the last time they had spoken. As they walked back to campus, Maggie explained her true reason for the visit. She recounted the story of receiving the golden scarab from her uncle along with the cryptic note and phone call. She explained that he mentioned notes in the call, and she hoped to check his office for them.

Molly agreed Ollie's office was the best place to begin a search, and using her master key for the building, opened the door for Maggie. "Just make sure you lock it before you leave," Molly said. "I hope you find something to help. Keep me informed! Gosh, I hope nothing's happened to him!"

"Me too. I'll stop by before I leave and let you know if I find anything. Hey, enjoy your trip to Scotland if you leave before I finish my search!"

"Oh, trust me, I plan on it!" Molly chuckled as she disappeared down the hall.

Maggie giggled at Molly's statement. She sunk into the chair behind her uncle's desk, staring at the piles of unsorted clutter covering it. Neatness was not a trait Uncle Ollie possessed. As she assessed where to begin, a tinkling sound whispered through the air. It dawned on her after a moment the noise came from her phone, stuffed in the front pocket of her purse.

She reached down and pulled it out. The phone's display signified a call from Piper. Was there a problem at the shop? Maggie swiped the answer button. "Hello, Piper, everything okay?"

"Dude, answer your phone once in a while."

"Sorry, I've been busy. What did you need?"

"It's not what I need. Your goofy boyfriend is here, and he's pestering me about where you are. I told him I don't know what you're doing. He tried to call you like seven times and you didn't answer, so he insisted I call you." Maggie overheard Leo's voice in the background. "No way, dude, it's my phone," Piper murmured before her voice grew louder. "Listen, I will not play intermediary between you two. Just answer your damn phone." The line clicked as Piper ended the call.

"Ah!" Maggie said, staring at her phone. She noticed several missed call notifications and a few unread text messages. She hadn't checked her phone after arriving at the college or during lunch with Molly. As she swiped into her text message app, her phone rang. This call came from Leo.

She swiped to answer it. "I…" she started.

"Where the hell have you been? I have been texting and

calling you all morning and no answer. Finally, I stopped by the shop only to have Piper tell me she has no idea where you are either."

"I've been busy," Maggie snapped. "I had a few things to do, and I wasn't checking my phone."

"Really? A few things to do. And it never occurred to you to check your phone or let me know, given what happened last night at your apartment?"

"No, it didn't," Maggie stated. "Why would I have let you know? After last night, I didn't feel the need to run anything past you."

Leo sighed. "I'm sorry I said that. I overreacted, but I'm concerned about you. I was worried when I couldn't reach you this morning. I even brought a peace offering when I came to ask you to go to lunch."

Maggie sighed. "Thanks, but I went to lunch with a friend. And I'm fine. You can stop worrying."

"So, am I forgiven? I realize we've hit a bit of a rough patch, Mags, but we can work through it. Let's have dinner tonight."

"I'm not sure I'll be back in time for dinner." Maggie eyed the stacks of "notes" on the desk to sort through.

"Really? What's got you so busy, Mags? And why so secretive about it?"

Maggie clamped her mouth shut, seething. "I'm not being secretive. Just because I didn't call you after your outburst last night to clear my schedule with you doesn't mean I'm being secretive. I'm busy. What I'm busy with is my business." Maggie poked the screen to end the call before shoving the phone into her purse.

She pushed the conversation from her mind as she dug into the stacks of papers on the desk. It took her hours to sift through the clutter. Most of it was ungraded student papers. She moved on to the desk drawers. She found office supplies in each drawer. In the file cabinet, there were more student papers from previous semesters.

Maggie spent hours searching every corner of the office. She uncovered no notes tied to the golden beetle. She sighed, sinking into the desk chair. She glanced around one last time before grabbing her purse. She'd try one other place before returning to her hotel.

Maggie popped her head into Molly's office before departing, thanking her again for providing access to her uncle's office and telling her again to enjoy her trip to Scotland. Molly promised to email pictures from her trip. Maggie descended the stairs and entered the warm late afternoon air. She sauntered across campus to her car. Throwing her purse into the passenger seat, she climbed behind the wheel and fired the engine.

Maggie backed out of the parking spot and pulled onto the road, aiming her car toward Uncle Ollie's house. He lived only a few minutes from campus in a Craftsman-style house with a big front yard. Maggie always found it ironic that he had such a beautiful house since he was rarely home to enjoy it. She pulled into the driveway, parking her car near the path leading to the house.

Maggie approached the front door, knocking just in case. As expected, there was no answer. Uncle Ollie kept a key hidden under a large potted plant. She struggled to lift it but managed to tip it enough to grab the key from under it. As she did, her hand hit another object. She pulled it, too, from under the plant. It was another key with an orange marker reading 148. Shoving it into her purse, she inserted the house key into the front door.

She unlocked the door, letting it swing open as she placed the house key in her purse. When she stepped inside it took a moment for her eyes to focus in the waning light. When they did, her jaw dropped open. The house was in disarray.

Drawers were pulled out, their contents dumped. The couch cushions were sliced open and strewn about the room. The scene was almost identical to her apartment last night.

She pulled her phone from her purse and dialed 9-1-1. As she waited for the police to arrive, she texted her mother to update her on the situation. While her mother was concerned, she was too far from Aberdeen to offer any assistance. Maggie assured her she was fine and had the situation under control.

When the police arrived, Maggie explained the situation, telling them she was checking on her uncle's house while he was away. Although she felt disingenuous, Maggie did not mention the package, note or mysterious call she received.

The police spent several hours collecting evidence. Maggie waited until they were finished, locking the house after they left. She chose to keep both keys with her. She also decided not to clean up the house. The long day exhausted her, and she craved a warm bowl of soup and a cup of tea to soothe her nerves.

She tossed her purse into the passenger seat and started her car. Her mind rambled as she drove the short distance back to the Grand Hotel. Exhausted, she slogged through the front door, intent on ordering room service the moment she arrived at her room.

As she entered the lobby, she saw a figure stand from one of the seats near the fireplace. Maggie repressed the urge to roll her eyes as she recognized Leo. She was in no mood for a discussion with Leo.

"Maggie…" He approached her.

"No, Leo," Maggie interrupted. She held up her hand. "I can't do this now. I'm exhausted."

"What is going on, Mags?" He squeezed her arms. "Talk to me. Where have you been all day? Does it have anything to do with your ransacked apartment?"

Stress overcame Maggie for a moment. She sank into Leo, putting her forehead against his chest. He pulled her closer to him. "It's okay, Mags. Just tell me what's going on."

"I'm okay." She pulled herself upright. "I'm fine. There's just a lot happening."

"Come on, let's talk about it over dinner," Leo suggested.

"I'm too tired and sore. I'm planning to order room service and eat in my room. I just want to change and sit down," she muttered, stepping toward the elevator. "Come on." She glanced to Leo. "I'll fill you in while we wait for room service."

Leo nodded, following her to the elevator. Leo ordered room service while Maggie changed, donning her pajamas and a bathrobe. She shuffled into the living room in fluffy slippers, finding Leo sitting on the couch. "I ordered us a bottle of wine to help you relax," he said, patting the couch next to him. "Now what's going on, Mags?"

Maggie collapsed in a heap next to Leo. She reached for her purse, digging into it and removing the gold beetle and the note. "This came in the mail from my Uncle Ollie." Leo read the note and studied the object. "I received that Wednesday. Last night I received a call from Uncle Ollie. The call was breaking up, I could only catch a few words. He mentioned something about danger and protecting the scarab and staying safe. Anyway, he also mentioned notes about the beetle. At least I assume that's what he meant; it was the only word I caught. I went to his office and his house today to look for them."

"Did you find them?" Leo asked as she paused.

"No. But what I found was his house trashed the same way my apartment was."

"What?" Leo exclaimed. "Did you call the police?"

"Yes, I just finished with the Aberdeen police. These incidents have to be connected. My apartment is wrecked like someone was searching for something. My uncle's place is the same. And all this happens within days of me receiving this scarab."

"We don't know when your uncle's house was broken into," Leo argued.

"Oh, come on, what are the chances..." Maggie began when a knock sounded at the door.

Leo answered it, allowing the room service attendant to push the cart into the room. The attendant reviewed the items, ensured the order was correct, and retrieved a signed copy of the bill before leaving them alone.

"One tomato bisque." Leo delivered the bowl to her.

"Thanks," Maggie answered. "Like I was saying, what are the chances my apartment gets tossed the same week Uncle Ollie's does?"

"Again, we don't know it was the same week. And over this? Come on!" Leo argued. He picked up the small beetle and studied it again before digging into his meal.

"What else could it be?"

"It doesn't look THAT valuable," Leo said.

"Oh, your vast knowledge of ancient artifacts tells you that, does it?" Maggie asked between spoonfuls of soup.

"No, my common sense tells me that. Are these jewels real? Is this solid gold? Come on, Mags, you're somewhat of an antique dealer. Would you assess this as a high-value item?"

Maggie shrugged. "What other explanation can there be? Perhaps it's not valuable in terms of cost, but in some other way?"

"What way?"

"I'm not sure. That's why I tried to find Uncle Ollie's notes. Perhaps there's a clue in them about why this little guy is so important."

Leo laughed. "Little guy? Have you named it?"

Maggie shot him a wry glance. "Watch it. I still haven't forgiven you for the last few days."

"Ah, yes." Leo grabbed his wine glass with a sigh. "The real issue comes to light. Our argument. You can't still be mad? Are you still mad about the whole dinner thing?"

"It's not the 'dinner thing,'" Maggie answered. "It's the idea that you built this up over some stupid car and then when I was disappointed you laughed about it."

"Okay, first, it's not a stupid car. I was excited about that car, Maggie! And I didn't laugh about it."

"You did!" Maggie insisted. "When I told you I assumed you wanted to discuss something important about our relationship, you laughed."

"I'm sorry I laughed, but come on, Mags. We're nowhere near a place to discuss marriage. I'm not saying we won't get there, I just think we have a lot of growing up to do."

"You mean you think I have a lot of growing up to do."

"I didn't say that, you're putting words in my mouth."

"You didn't have to." Maggie dumped her empty bowl on the coffee table.

"Don't start, Maggie."

"Don't start? Don't start what? Overreacting? Anytime I disagree with you or don't see it your way, I'm overreacting. And you wonder why I didn't bother telling you anything about what I was doing today."

Leo rolled his eyes, then leaned forward and kissed Maggie's forehead. "I'm going to head out. You're tired, I'll let you get some rest."

"How magnanimous of you."

"Good night, Maggie." Leo strutted from the room.

Maggie sunk back onto the couch. Her and Leo together were like oil and water, they didn't mix. They were like a powder keg that could explode at any minute. While she didn't want to continue the conversation they were having, it frustrated her to no end when he played the "bigger person" and walked out on her.

She sighed, standing and collecting the dishes. She stacked them on the room service cart and wheeled it into the hallway. Exhausted, she stumbled through the living room into the bedroom, collapsing into bed. After a few moments, she rose, popping a few over-the-counter pain relievers for her aches. She slid back under the sheets and dropped off to sleep within seconds.

CHAPTER 4

$\mathcal{M}$aggie awoke the next morning stiff. She stretched and crawled from bed, heading straight for the pain relievers and a cup of coffee. She dreaded restoring her living room tomorrow. Her muscles ached already. But she would give her muscles a break today by working at the shop instead of her apartment.

Maggie grabbed her laptop, settling in bed with her coffee. She checked her email, finding one from Molly. Molly stated how enjoyable she found their lunch and passed along the email address for Dr. Kensie that Maggie requested. Maggie thanked her, then opened a new email. She typed *Hello from Maggie Edwards* in the subject line. In the body, Maggie typed:

> Hi Cate! I'd say I hope you are doing well but from the sounds of it, you are doing VERY well! I was on Aberdeen's campus yesterday and had lunch with Molly. She told me all about your recent developments. A Scottish Castle, wow!!!! How exciting!! And I bet Riley is LOVING his new yard!

Too bad we weren't able to get together for lunch before you moved. I would have loved to have seen you before you left and that cute pup of yours.

Please send me some pics of your new home. I'd love to see it, I bet the castle's full of beautiful antiques! I'm sure Aberdeen College misses you and all your hard work. Molly is so excited for her upcoming trip. I'm sad she is missing the Fall Ball, but it sounds like she'll have another ball to enjoy (and perhaps a better one!).

Well, I'll let you go, I'm sure you have much more fun things to do than read emails. Go enjoy that Scottish countryside!

Yours,

Maggie Edwards

After finishing her email and coffee, Maggie climbed from bed and dressed for the day. As she finished applying her lipstick, she received a message from Leo: *Good morning, babe, hope you slept well.*

Despite being mad, Maggie returned his text. This was not unusual for their relationship. They always got through it. Mad or not, life continued and eventually, Maggie would get over it.

She drove to the shop, opening it for the day. Within minutes of opening, bells announced her first weekend customer. "Good morning, welcome!" Maggie called from the back of the shop.

"It's me," Leo's voice answered her.

"Hey," Maggie greeted him, returning to the front of the store. Leo held two coffees and a bag in his hand.

"I stopped by your favorite bakery and got you one of those chocolate croissants you love and a coffee."

"Aww, thanks!" Maggie relieved him of a coffee and the bag.

"Did you sleep?"

"I did," she said, "with a little help from a pain reliever. I am not looking forward to finishing the work at my apartment tomorrow."

"Want some help?" Leo sipped his coffee as Maggie bit into her croissant.

"Mmm," she murmured. Her enjoyment of the pastry clear with the gesture. "Yes, please."

"I would have helped you the other night, too, if you weren't being so stubborn." Leo winked at her.

Maggie rolled her eyes. "Don't start. I'm still mad at you."

"You are not," Leo insisted. He leaned over the counter to steal a kiss.

"I am so," Maggie countered. She avoided his kiss.

"I'm sorry I disappointed you, Mags." Leo stared in her eyes. Maggie gave him a soft kiss. "Am I forgiven?"

"Let's say you're on probation." Maggie flashed him a coy glance.

"It's like that, huh?"

"Mm-hmm, it's like that."

"Well, I better start my community service then. Do you need any help here today? And does the pastry delivery count?"

"I'll count it since you remembered my favorite kind. And to answer your first question, yes. I want to move a few things. I could use your help with some boxes."

Leo finished his coffee. "Lead the way."

Maggie and Leo spent Saturday rearranging items in the store, packing away others and reorganizing many. They grabbed dinner at a local restaurant before Maggie returned to the hotel. Sunday was spent restoring Maggie's living room to its normal state. Her next task was to tackle cleaning her uncle's house. But Maggie did not plan on dealing with that project for several days. Her aching muscles and busy schedule with the shop prevented her from starting earlier.

When Monday arrived, Maggie dragged herself from bed. While her apartment had been restored to its normal state, she had chosen to remain at the hotel. Uneasiness still lingered within her over the incident. Perhaps in the next day or so she would return, she reflected.

Maggie started her day in the usual manner, with a cup of coffee while lounging in bed with her laptop. She began by checking her email, finding a response from Cate Kensie.

Hello Maggie–It's good to hear from you! I'm sorry we weren't able to see each other before I left. Everything happened so fast. I never realized I had relatives in Scotland, then suddenly I was inheriting a castle. Riley loves it here. He has plenty of open space to bound around.

I attached some pictures. The castle is incredible! Lots of antiques, it's like living in a museum. You'd love it! You'll have to visit us sometime; we'd love to see you.

I hope everything is going well for you and your shop is thriving (I have no doubt it is; you are an excellent businesswoman)!

Hope to hear from you again soon!
Cate

Maggie smiled at the email. It appeared Dr. Kensie was doing well. She was happy for her, if anyone deserved happiness it was Cate. She decided to answer the email later. Instead, she used her morning to try another bevy of internet searches, attempting to locate any information on the mysterious object sent to her. Again, she found nothing.

Frustrated, she hopped out of bed and dressed for the day. Despite the distance, she enjoyed a slow walk to her shop, appreciating one of the last few warm mornings before cool fall weather set in. A slow trickle of customers wandered in and out of the store during the morning hours.

During lunch, Maggie closed the shop, leaving a note that she would reopen mid afternoon. She planned a trip to the area's museum, hoping to track down some information about the item she received from Uncle Ollie.

It was a long shot but if anyone could identify the object or determine if it was valuable, it would be someone there. The museum employed several individuals whose expertise was artifacts and antiquities. The local Museum of Natural History was a mid-sized museum with several experts in various time periods and locations.

Maggie grabbed a sandwich on her way to the museum, taking a few bites as she strolled toward it. The large, tan building stood in stark contrast to the blue sky. Maggie climbed the stone steps, glancing at the massive columns supporting the stone peaks of the roof. The building was beautiful. She loved the museum ever since her Uncle Ollie had taken her here as a child. Ironic that she was returning now with a mysterious object from Uncle Ollie.

Maggie swung through the revolving door, approaching the docent. She asked to speak with Amy Nash, one of the curators in the antiquities department. Since her uncle was a frequent consultant for the museum, Maggie was well acquainted with many staff members here.

The docent picked up the phone, dialing a few numbers. She waited a moment, then spoke into the receiver. After she replaced it, she directed Maggie to the offices on the left. Maggie thanked her and strode down the hall.

She found Amy in her office, bending over a small object while she munched on her salad. Maggie knocked before stepping through the door. "Hi, Amy!" Maggie greeted her.

"Thanks for seeing me on such short notice. Sorry for not calling ahead."

"Hey, Maggie! No problem! Come in, have a seat."

"Thanks," Maggie said, sitting down across from Amy.

"What brings you by, Maggie?" Amy asked.

"I've got something I'd like you to take a peek at." Maggie opened her purse and removed the gold beetle. "My Uncle Ollie sent this to me with a rather cryptic note. Have you ever seen anything like it?"

Amy reached across the desk, accepting the object from Maggie. She studied it a moment, turning the object over in her hands. She peered closer at it before giving it an overall glance again.

"Well?" Maggie asked.

"You received this from Oliver?" Amy inquired.

"Yes, a few days ago. I haven't been able to track down much information on it."

"I'm not surprised. I've never seen one like this before. I mean, I've seen scarabs, even golden ones, but nothing with gems like this. And it appears there are markings inside the gems. I can't make them out, but they don't appear to be the result of damage or random."

"Do you imagine it's valuable?"

Amy didn't respond. She studied the object with interest.

"What is it?" Maggie asked.

"I'm not sure." Amy's eyes never left the object as she spoke. "I mean, I've never seen a scarab like this in person, but something about this reminds me of a picture I saw once."

"A picture?" Maggie questioned.

"Yes, just a minute." Amy set the object on the desk and stepped to a bookcase nearby. After a moment of perusal, she pulled a thick book from the shelf and paged through it.

When she located the correct page, she plopped the book in front of Maggie, pointing to the center of the page. "Here."

"The Golden Scarab of Cleopatra," Maggie read. She glanced at the picture. It was a sketch of Cleopatra holding a bejeweled golden scarab. Hieroglyphics decorated the page behind her. "It's not an exact match, but it looks similar. But this is just a drawing!"

"Yes." Amy sat down behind the desk again. "That's about all you'll find of it. It's never been seen by anyone other than the ancient Egyptians. Well, assuming it exists."

"Assuming it exists?" Maggie screwed up her face.

"Yes," Amy answered. "It's really something of a legend. The supposed key to finding and opening Cleopatra's tomb. Many archaeologists consider it only a legend. That there is no actual truth to the rumor, and it originated as a story to keep tomb raiders busy seeking the key rather than the tomb. Others deem it a true story. There is little information, however, about the object or its potential location. Finding any information is often painstaking."

"What do you deem is true?" Maggie inquired.

"I'm not sure to be honest," Amy responded. "The existence of an object like this makes sense to an extent, but given the fact that there is little information regarding it makes me question its existence. Someone must have kept records somewhere, right?"

"Or perhaps the lack of information points to it being real rather than fake," Maggie conjectured. "Perhaps it was a well-guarded secret with as much information concealed as possible."

"Now you sound like your uncle." Amy laughed.

"What do you mean?"

"He supposed the same thing you did. The lack of information pointed more to the existence of the object than against it. I'm not sure. Either way, I'm not sure I can be of more help to you. Oliver would be the best one to answer any further questions. He's built a repository of information on the object. I only have stories like this one to share." Amy pointed to the book.

Maggie smiled at her, not wanting to give too much away. "Thanks. Uncle Ollie is still out of the country, so I figured I'd take my chances here before he was back. This is helpful. Would you mind making a copy of this page for me?"

"Not at all," Amy agreed. "Just give me a sec." She grabbed the book and disappeared from the room. Within two minutes she returned, handing a warm paper to Maggie and placing the book back on her shelf. "Sorry, it's only black and white, my copier isn't color!"

"No problem, this is all I need. Thank you so much for your time, Amy. I really appreciate it!"

"No problem! Tell Ollie I said 'hi' next time you see him! And if you wouldn't mind, could you let me know the origin of this once you speak with him? I'd love to know where he found it!"

"Sure! Thanks again." Maggie stood and retrieved her purse, slipping the beetle inside along with the folded copy.

"Your welcome. How's your business going?"

"Good! My customer base has increased with the addition of the antiques. Stop by sometime if you have a chance. I'm sure you'd enjoy looking through our collection."

"I've been meaning to, but I always end up staying at work too late. With my master's defense around the corner, it seems all I do is work."

"Ha! I understand completely! Well, whenever you need a break, we're open! Thanks again," Maggie said. She backed from the room, making her way down the hall and back to the lobby.

She exited the museum, descending the large stone steps. The warm sun shone overhead. Maggie strolled through the parking lot, a shortcut to the nearest street. As she passed the cars, her mind turned to her conversation with Amy. She failed to notice movement to her left until it was too late.

A figure darted from between two vehicles, approaching Maggie from the rear. A scream rose from Maggie's throat as hands grabbed her. A firm hand clamped over her mouth, muffling her it. She struggled but was dragged backward toward a van and tossed inside. Maggie scrambled toward the door as it was slammed in her face.

CHAPTER 5

"*H*ELP!" she screamed as she heard another door slam shut. The engine turned over, and the van lurched backward. Maggie banged against the van's side, screaming for help. The vehicle paused for a moment before moving forward. Maggie pounded against the van's wall to no avail.

They drove for fifteen minutes. Tears streamed down Maggie's face. Wiping them away, she glanced around the interior for anything that may help her either now or when the van stopped.

She realized her purse was missing. She dropped it as she struggled to free herself, she recalled. Her phone was inside, so she couldn't call for help. The golden beetle her uncle had implored her to protect was in the bag, too.

Maggie buried her head in her hands and wept. Her head shot up as the van slowed to a stop. She scrambled to her feet, prepared for what came next. No matter what, she wouldn't go down without a fight, she resolved.

The door swung open, bright light streamed in. It blinded Maggie for a moment. She shielded her eyes against the it.

The silhouette of a man wearing a hat stood at the door. The figure climbed into the van toward Maggie.

Maggie lunged at him, lashing out to strike his face. He grasped her wrists, preventing any attack. Maggie screamed for help while struggling to free herself.

"Shh," he hissed. "I will not hurt you. Stop!"

Maggie continued to thrash, knocking his hat from his head. "Let me go!"

"Stop it, stop!" the man insisted. Maggie detected an Australian accent as he spoke. "I'm a friend of your uncle's. I'm a friend of Ollie's."

"What?" Maggie ceased her writhing for a moment.

"I'm a friend of Oliver Keene," the man said. "I won't hurt you."

"Then why did you throw me in the back of a van?" Maggie probed.

"I had to get you away from that museum fast. You were being watched. You can't show this thing about as though it's a toy." The man held up the golden scarab.

Maggie grabbed at the object. "Give that back to me."

The man handed the scarab to her. "Fine, but you must be more careful with it. It's a damn good thing I found you."

"You claim to be friends with my uncle. But you are nowhere near his age. And I have no reason to trust you," Maggie asserted.

"I am. He is like a father to me. And you don't. Here." He removed his phone from his pocket. He swiped at it, pressing various spots with his thumb. He swiveled the screen to Maggie's viewpoint. "See. We're mates, me and Ollie. Good mates." Maggie glanced at the picture. The man stood with his arm around Ollie's shoulders, both wearing genuine smiles. "Here's another." He swiped the screen to another picture. "And yet another."

Maggie studied the pictures, then the man before her.

"Okay, so you know my uncle. It still doesn't explain why you kidnapped me."

"I told you, for your own good. I'm Henry Taylor." He introduced himself, sticking his hand out toward Maggie. Maggie ignored it.

"Explain to me how kidnapping me is for my own good." He laughed. "Why are you laughing?"

"I'm sorry. But Ollie was right. You're one hard-nosed lady." Maggie narrowed her eyes. "Okay, okay. You're flashing this scarab all about. Do you imagine they tossed your apartment for fun? They'll come after you if they realize you're carrying the scarab around. You're lucky no one's grabbed it from you yet."

"How did you..." Maggie began.

"You don't realize who you're up against. I do. It's why your uncle sent me. When we parted ways, he was going deep underground, trying to hide. He told me he planned to post this to you and asked me to come and make sure you're safe."

"Well, I'm safe, as you can see, now let me go."

"You're far from safe, Maggie. You have no idea what you're up against. And the way you're showing this off to anyone who'll have a peek, tells me you're about to get yourself into serious trouble."

"I haven't been showing it off. For your information, I was trying to learn more about this thing. The note my uncle sent with it was cryptic. He called, but I couldn't make out a lot of what he said. The call was breaking up."

"He called? When?"

"A few days ago."

Henry sighed. "At least he's still alive."

"Still alive?" Maggie asked incredulously.

"Yes. As I mentioned before, these people will stop at nothing to get this scarab."

"Why is it so important?" Maggie inquired.

"Because this little scarab will unlock the greatest archae-ological discovery of the modern world."

"What? Greatest discovery of the modern world?" Maggie asked.

"Yes," Henry answered. "This little bugger is the key to finding and opening Cleopatra's tomb."

"This is the Golden Scarab of Cleopatra?" Maggie held up the beetle.

"So, your uncle has told you the story, eh?" Henry replied.

"I've heard him talk about finding Cleopatra's tomb, but not about this. The museum's curator must have heard the story from Uncle Ollie. She had a reference to it, but she said it was legend. Most people wrote it off, said it wasn't real."

"Your uncle always believed it was real. After years of searching, he found it. Then they found him."

"Who is 'they?'"

"A group of militant tomb raiders. They'd prefer to keep this quiet as I'm sure you can understand. They'd rather raid it for the billions they could make in selling the contents on the black market. Whereas your uncle would give the contents to museums around the world for everyone to enjoy."

"And you're saying these tomb raiders are the ones that tossed my apartment? And most likely Uncle Ollie's place?"

"Most likely."

"So, what do we do now?"

"You do nothing. You've done your part. Now you give this back to me and I'll try to hunt down your uncle."

"No way! If he wanted you to have it, he'd have given it to you. He sent it to me! I'll see it through."

"You don't understand…"

"I understand just fine. You're here to help me. So help me! What do we do next?"

"You really are one stubborn girl. But I admire your grit to see it through."

"I want to make sure my uncle is okay. Plus, he sent it to me. I feel responsible."

"Okay, agreed. Well, first, we need to move to the front seats. Next, we'll need to track down any notes your uncle had. Perhaps they can lead us to his next move."

Henry slid out of the van, donning his hat again. He held out his hand to assist Maggie. After they climbed into the front of the van, Maggie answered his last statement. "I tried to find some notes on this little guy already. I found nothing in Uncle Ollie's office, and his house was in shambles. When the police left, it was late. I was too drained to do anything. I haven't been back there since."

"So, we start there." Henry fired the van's engine.

"Not yet," Maggie advised. "I've got to open my shop for the afternoon."

"Open your shop? We need to move fast. Every second we waste puts your uncle's life in danger."

Maggie sighed, unsure of what to do. "Okay," she acquiesced. "We'll go straight there. I'll text my assistant and tell her to reopen when she can." Maggie grabbed her phone from her purse, retrieved earlier from the passenger seat of the van. She texted Piper about reopening the shop, being intentionally vague about her whereabouts. Within moments she received a response of "Whatever, yeah, okay."

In twenty minutes, they arrived at Oliver's house, parking in the driveway and letting themselves in through the front door.

"What a mess." Maggie sighed as they walked through the door.

"These people don't mess around."

"Is there any sense to searching here? If there was any information, I'm sure they found it."

"If it was obvious, yes. But it's possible they missed it. Did your uncle have any hiding spots that weren't obvious?"

"Not that I know of," Maggie answered. "I'm not sure, he didn't confide any hiding spots to me. But I've only been to this house a few times."

"Well, let's get started." Henry righted the couch and set a few pillows on it.

They spent the next several hours searching and restoring Ollie's house. They found nothing. They located no personal notes related to the object or anything else.

Maggie collapsed on the couch. "Well, it looks like your tomb raider friends got the info they were searching for."

"I doubt that." Henry plopped down next to her.

"Why? We found nothing. They probably have whatever notes he gathered."

"I don't imagine your uncle was foolish enough to have left them laying just anywhere. If they were here, they're hidden, well hidden."

"But where?"

"Does your uncle have a safe?"

"I didn't see one when we were cleaning up, did you?" Maggie queried.

"No. What about a safe deposit box?"

Maggie shrugged her shoulders. "I'm not sure. If he did, he didn't mention it to me."

"Do you still have the note he sent with the scarab?"

"Yes." Maggie pulled the note from her purse and handed it to Henry.

He took a moment to read it. "Damn, no information in it. I hoped there might be a clue that I could ferret out and you may have missed." Maggie sunk into the couch further. "And you're sure there was nothing in his office? Nothing hidden, no hiding spots you missed?"

"Nothing there, hidden or otherwise. I can't come up with anywhere else he could…" Maggie paused.

"What?"

She dug in her purse, pulling out a key. "This!" she exclaimed.

"What is it?"

"No idea, but I found it here under his planter out front. Maybe it's for a safe deposit box?" Maggie conjectured.

"Perhaps, but this little key with the number on it suggests a storage locker or the like."

"Oh, maybe!" Maggie exclaimed. "Wonder where the locker could be? Did you spot anything from a storage facility? A bill or a confirmation?"

"No. Just guessing here, but I'm wondering if this came from a locker at a bus station or train station."

"Hmm. There's a train station on the other side of town. We could try there."

"Doesn't hurt to try. Come on, let's go." He stood, pulling Maggie off the couch.

"Ugh," Maggie groaned, exhausted. "Okay."

Once they were in the car, Maggie directed him to the train station's location. They entered the station's lobby and located the lockers. "Which number is it?" Henry asked as they approached the bank of lockers.

"Number 148," Maggie answered, reading the number off the orange tag.

"Moment of truth," Henry said as they approached the section containing locker 148.

"The key is missing!" Maggie exclaimed. She presumed this was a sign the key she held fit this locker.

"Try the key," Henry said.

Maggie inserted it into the lock and, to her elation, it turned and the locker door swung open. "It worked!" Maggie exclaimed. She grinned at Henry.

They both glanced inside the locker. A small brown leather journal sat on top of a stack of money and a weapon. Maggie gasped at the sight of the gun. Henry reached inside, quickly pocketing the weapon and the money. He handed the journal to Maggie. "Put this in your purse, don't dally," he whispered. His eyes darted all over the room. "Let's go." He grabbed her arm as she shoved the journal into her purse. He led her straight to the car, putting her in the passenger's seat before crossing to the driver's side. He fired the engine and sped away from the train station.

"What's the rush? Where are we going?" Maggie questioned.

"Nowhere just yet," he answered. "But if anyone followed us, I'd like to be far away from there."

"Followed us?" Maggie glanced in the car's mirror. "Do you think they have?"

"I don't see anyone at the moment, but I'd rather be ahead of the game. We need a safe place to hole up, read that journal, and plan our next move."

"Hole up?"

"Yes, hole up. Somewhere safe, where they won't find us."

"I've been staying at a hotel since my apartment was broken into. We can go there."

"How long have you been there?"

"About a week." Henry shook his head. "What?"

"Too risky. If you've been there a week, they realize you're there."

"So, where then?"

"Another hotel. That may be our best option. I haven't spotted anyone tailing us."

"Okay. Just swing by my hotel and I'll pack and…"

"No, Maggie. There's no time for that."

"Oh, come on. You're exaggerating. It's not that dire, is it? I've had this thing for over a week and I'm still fine."

"You're still fine, but is Ollie?"

"But I need things! Clothes, cell phone charger."

"We'll buy anything we need along the way. Or you could give everything to me, and I'll handle it on my own. You can return to your normal life."

Maggie set her jaw. "No. I told you I'm seeing this through to the end."

"Okay, so we ditch your things, and go straight to another place. We learn what we can from the journal and plan our next move."

Maggie sighed. "I don't see the harm in stopping for a few necessities."

"Because if they are surveilling you, they'll follow us to our new location and I'd rather they didn't do that. I will not argue about this. I have more experience with these types of situations."

Maggie harrumphed. "Fine, fine. Whatever you say, mister 'I have more experience.'"

After a few moments of driving, Maggie realized they were following signs to the airport. Smart, she concluded. There would be lots of hotels near the airport. As they approached the terminal, Henry veered off the highway onto a side road. He traveled further down, turning at various spots until he finally pulled off the road.

"What are you doing?" Maggie asked.

"Renting a room," Henry said, throwing the gear selector into park and pulling on the emergency brake.

"Where?"

"Here." He removed the keys from the ignition.

Maggie glanced around. "Here?!" she asked skeptically.

"Yes, here. What's wrong with here?"

"The Roadside Motel? It looks like the Roachside Motel. It's awful! We can't stay here! There's a great Marriott over nearer to the airport. We could get a nice suite…"

"This isn't a vacation, princess. We need somewhere fast, quiet, out of the way. This is perfect."

"No, it's not perfect! It's a health code violation."

Henry was already exiting the van. "Stay there, I'll be right back."

Annoyance filled Maggie. She sighed, crossing her arms in frustration. Within moments, Henry returned, opening Maggie's door. "After you, princess."

Maggie slid out of the seat to the ground. "Stop calling me that. Just because I want a clean, respectable hotel doesn't mean I'm asking for too much."

"We're in room 7."

"We? Where is my room?"

"I rented one room."

"I don't suppose they had any suites?" Henry glanced at her before rolling his eyes. "I'll take that as a 'no.'"

Henry unlocked the room and pushed the door open, signaling for Maggie to enter before him.

"Ugh," she muttered as she entered the room.

Henry locked the door, switched on the light and drew the curtains. "You'll survive. Let's see the journal."

Maggie reached into her purse and withdrew the leather notebook. Henry reached for it. Maggie pulled it back. "Uh-uh! I want to read it too. I'm not staying in this disgusting room only for you to sideline me."

Henry held his hands up, admitting defeat. "Okay, okay. We'll go over it together." Maggie eyed the two beds, grimacing at each. Henry plopped onto the bed nearest the window, patting a spot next to him. Maggie eased onto the bed next to him. "Careful, you might actually touch the bed."

"Don't remind me." Maggie shuddered but dismissed the idea as she opened the journal. "Let's see what we have here." They opened the journal to the first page. Notes were scattered in disarray. Maggie flipped through the pages. They were all similar, notes scattered about, drawings, sketches of maps. "This will take some work to decipher."

"Ollie was never a linear thinker."

"Nor neat."

Henry laughed. Maggie handed him the book. "Given up already, have you?"

"No." Maggie dashed over to the dresser to retrieve the tablet and pen. She snatched them and returned to her spot next to Henry. "Taking notes may help us make more sense of this."

Maggie and Henry spent the next several hours pouring over the mishmash of notes and illustrations. They began by glancing through all pages before attempting to piece together the meaning of any entries. It took them over an hour to search through all the journal had to offer. Once they had a handle on the volume of information, they tried to make sense of it. After two hours, they had pieced together a small amount of information. In particular, they identified passages in the journal referring to the scarab sent to Maggie.

"Whew!" Maggie stood and stretched. "Before we go any further, I need something to eat. I am starving. I don't suppose they have room service here."

"Sorry, princess, no room service. But I'm sure there's a pizza place that delivers. You Americans all love pizza, right?"

"That's a gross overstatement. But at this point I would eat anything. I'm so hungry."

"All right, I'll order us a pie. We can jot down the notes about our little beetle friend while we wait for it."

"Don't forget the soda," Maggie called as he dialed a number from the room's phone book. "I'm not drinking anything that comes from a tap in this room."

He waved her comment away as he spoke into the

receiver to order a mushroom pizza and a two-liter of soda. He remembered to request plates, cups and napkins which surprised Maggie.

"Wow," she commented as he replaced the receiver on the phone's cradle, "plates, napkins and cups. You really know how to treat a lady."

He grinned at her. "You're not just any lady, princess. You're Ollie's niece. Wouldn't want a bad report given to him once we find him."

She smirked at him, then wrote a few additional notes on her notepad. "Making any progress?" He peered over her shoulder.

"A little," Maggie answered. "Some of these notes are just conjecture, others seem to have a reference or source. I'm sorting the notes by what is fact, what is conjecture, and what we should follow up on."

"Smart idea, Maggie."

"There are references everywhere about the Golden Scarab of Cleopatra and its importance in both locating and opening Cleopatra's tomb. Some of that has references, which, to me, indicates it's true. Some of it doesn't. But I would put this information in the "fact" column."

"I agree. For as long as I've known your uncle, he's considered all that true, and he's not one to give in to foolish nonsense. His information coincides with mine, so I'd say there is a Golden Scarab of Cleopatra and it leads to and opens her tomb. How it does that is another matter. And whether or not the beetle you received is, in fact, the Golden Scarab of Cleopatra is yet another."

"There are some notes about that, too. I haven't finished compiling them yet. Give me a few minutes." Maggie continued writing before flipping through the journal to another entry to continue her note-taking. She continued in silence until the pizza arrived. Maggie threw the pen and notebook down as Henry squeezed the pizza box onto the night table between the two beds. "Perfect timing! Mmm, that smells so good!"

He dished out two pieces onto plates while Maggie poured soda over the ice he retrieved earlier. "Here you are, princess." He handed Maggie a plate.

Without hesitation, Maggie bit into the pizza. She took several bites before Henry asked, "So, you finished your notes on the little bugger, huh? What have you learned?"

"According to my uncle's scattered notes, the beetle's gems contain tiny etchings that when projected with a strong light, he suggests sunlight, form a map. This leads one to the tomb. Then, the beetle, when combined with the Staff of Pasherienptah, opens the entrance to her tomb."

"Okay, so we'd first need to test the strong light theory to determine if what your uncle found is, in fact, the Golden Scarab of Cleopatra."

"That sounds like a good start," Maggie agreed.

"It also gives us a hint about where your uncle may be."

"It does?" Maggie questioned.

"Yes. I'd bet money he's trying to figure out a way to get the Staff of Pasherienptah."

"Get it? From where?"

"The Cairo Museum."

"What? Like he plans to steal it?"

"I would. In fact, if this beetle has a map in him, I will be heading to get the staff."

Maggie's eyes widened. "Are you kidding?" Maggie asked.

"Nope, I am not." Maggie eyed Henry, trying to decide what to make of his last comments. The two were quiet for a moment. Each mulling over the information from the journal and their next steps. "So, how long have you known my uncle?" Maggie asked after a few moments.

"About ten years. Met him in Morocco. I had gotten myself into a spot of trouble with some locals."

"You? In trouble? I can't imagine it." Maggie laughed.

"Very funny, princess. Anyway, he bailed me out then took me for a drink. He fascinated me with his tales of ancient history and the search for lore and legend."

"You weren't already in Morocco hunting for treasure?"

"No, I was a lost soul traveling the world. Trying to find my place in it. Figure out where I fit."

"And did you?" Maggie eyed him.

"I'm getting there," he said, meeting her gaze and grinning. Maggie smiled at him. "So, what's your story then, princess?"

Maggie shrugged, grabbing another piece of pizza and taking a bite. "Nothing interesting. I have a small bookstore and antique shop in the town neighboring Aberdeen. I moved here when I went to Aberdeen College, but I'm originally from just outside Philadelphia."

"Never been in trouble with a Moroccan street gang?"

Maggie laughed. "No. I can't say I ever have."

"Come on, princess. There must be more to your story! What's the most exotic place you've traveled?"

Maggie considered the question. "Most exotic? Hmm. I traveled to Egypt once with my parents and visited my uncle on one of his digs. It wasn't my favorite trip, but I was an ungrateful, unimpressed teen, so what did I know!"

"What was your favorite trip?"

"Paris," Maggie answered between bites of pizza.

"Paris? You are quite the world traveler, too! Why is it your favorite?"

"I guess because it just has this romantic feel about it. Strolling the Seine, Eiffel Tower, Louvre, there's just so much to see and life seems so different there. Slower somehow. What was your favorite place to visit?"

"Fair enough. I'd go with Egypt. There's something profound about walking in modern times amongst so many ancient relics."

"There is a lot of history there. My uncle could talk for hours just on Egypt alone!" Maggie chuckled.

"Oh, I have firsthand knowledge of that fact. But his stories are fascinating!"

Maggie nodded, chewing another bite of pizza. About to respond, her phone, vibrating in her purse, distracted her. She reached for it. "I haven't checked this in hours. I hope everything is okay at the shop. My assistant can be... difficult," she said, carefully choosing her words.

Henry nodded, biting into another slice of pizza. "Problems at the shop?" he asked as Maggie checked the incoming call.

"No." She swiped at her phone. "Hello," she answered the call.

"Mags, where the hell have you been?" Leo chastised. "I've been trying to get in touch with you for hours. I'm going crazy here wondering what happened to you."

"Sorry, it's been a crazy day." Maggie motioned to Henry to excuse herself from the room. She scrambled to the bathroom, closing the door behind her. "Something came up. I didn't have a chance to call or text."

"What would stop you from checking in?" Leo questioned.

"Checking in? I'm not your child, Leo. Anyway, it's about that golden scarab. I asked a friend at the museum about it. She didn't have much information but then I..." Maggie paused, searching for the best way to explain it. "I ran into a... friend... a friend of my uncle's. He was able to help with some information. We discovered my uncle's notes on the scarab. We've been..."

"Notes on the scarab? THAT was more important than

checking in. Maggie, I was worried sick! I couldn't get a hold of you. Piper said you texted her to open the store, and she hadn't heard from you since. And all this time you've been with your uncle's friend reading notes about that stupid bug?"

"It's not a stupid bug. This could be really important. And it's obvious how important it was to my uncle."

Leo sighed, waiting a moment before speaking again. "Okay, well, anyway, when do you plan on wrapping it up. It'd be nice to grab dinner together."

"Oh... ah..." Maggie hesitated.

"What?"

"Well, I'm not sure when we'll finish. And I've already eaten."

Silence filled the airwaves between them. "Ah, ok. Well I guess let me know when you're back at the hotel and I'll catch you tomorrow."

"Okay." Maggie preferred to end the conversation rather than give Leo more fodder to argue. "Sure. I'll text you as soon as we're finished."

"Okay," Leo retorted. Annoyance filled his voice along with restraint.

"Bye!" Maggie said, although Leo was already gone. She rolled her eyes and sighed. As usual, when Maggie's plans differed from Leo's, he was not happy. No surprise there, she ruminated as she dismissed the many notifications on her phone.

Maggie emerged from the bathroom to find Henry sprawled on the bed, still consuming pizza. "Trouble at your shop?" he asked, assuming the call was from Piper.

"Ah, no," Maggie answered. "My boyfriend, who is not happy that I didn't check in with him."

"Oh, in a bit of hot water with the old man, eh?" Henry joked.

"Par for the course," Maggie answered. She plopped onto her bed, sipping her soda before grabbing the remains of her slice of pizza to finish. "It's nothing new, I'm used to it. Our relationship is... complicated."

Henry offered a brief smile but did not push the matter further, a fact for which Maggie was grateful. "We should keep going on these notes. Learn as much as we can tonight before we check out that beetle tomorrow. With the sun setting, there's not enough strong sunlight to check the beetle for the markings your uncle suggests exist in the gems."

Maggie nodded in agreement. "Yes. There's a ton of information in here about the tomb itself. It might be useful to summarize that in case we need it."

Henry nodded. They finished their meal and together worked to outline the remaining notes from her uncle's journal. The task took several hours to complete. The midnight hour approached as they wrapped up their rigorous examination of the notebook.

Maggie stuffed the notes into the front cover of the journal as they finished. "Wait a second." Henry stopped her. "Perhaps we should keep these separate. If we lose the journal, we'll still have the notes and vice versa."

"Good idea. Maggie placed their notes into a zippered compartment in her purse. "You hang on to the journal, I'll keep the notes."

"Good plan."

Maggie stretched and yawned. "I am so ready for bed."

"We should try to get a few hours of sleep before tomorrow," Henry agreed.

Maggie slipped off her shoes, not enthused about sleeping in her clothes but refrained from grumbling about it. She crawled under the covers, reaching to turn out the light. "Oh, shoot!" she exclaimed. She hopped out of bed. "I'm supposed to text Leo. Well," she explained as she crossed the room to her purse, "I told Leo I'd text him when I got back to my hotel, but I guess this will do."

"When you got back to your hotel? You didn't tell him you were staying in another?"

"No," Maggie stated, dropping it at that. Henry raised his eyebrows for a moment but didn't answer. "I told you, it's complicated. Don't judge."

"I said nothing!" he exclaimed. "No judgement here!"

Maggie retrieved her phone and opened her text app. She typed a brief message to Leo stating she was heading to bed. It wasn't a lie, she surmised. However, she omitted the part about her bed being in another hotel.

She dropped her phone into her purse. "I will need a charger soon. My phone will be close to dead in the morning."

Henry didn't answer, which irked Maggie. She wrote it off, climbing into bed and turning the light off. "Good night," she said as darkness surrounded them.

"Good night, princess," Henry answered her.

Maggie suppressed an eye roll before she drifted off to sleep. Exhaustion from the day consumed her along with the late-night hour.

CHAPTER 6

When Maggie awoke the following morning, the room was still dark. She switched on the light, checking the time. It was a few minutes after seven. "Sorry if I woke you…" she began. She glanced at the other bed. She stopped speaking when she realized it was empty. She scanned the room, finding no one.

The bathroom door popped open and Henry strolled out. "Well, good morning, princess."

"Good morning," she answered. "I thought you left me."

"Nah. Just a quick morning shower before I head out for breakfast. Anything special you'd like?"

"A Belgian waffle with strawberries and whipped cream?" Maggie asked.

"Would you settle for one of those little egg sandwiches on a muffin?" Henry countered.

Maggie sighed, sagging her shoulders dramatically. "I suppose that will do. And coffee, please!"

"The coffee I can do. Cream and sugar?"

"Oh, yes, please. Two sugars and cream."

"All right. I will be back in a jiffy with your breakfast."

"Thanks. I'm going to hop in the shower while you're out."

Maggie grabbed her purse and headed for the bathroom, closing the door behind her. The motel's door banged shut moments later. Maggie showered and applied the limited amount of makeup from the assortment she carried in her purse. She redressed in her clothes and exited the bathroom just as Henry came through the door.

"I come bearing gifts," he announced. Several bags dangled in front of him. "Here is the coffee." He set down a drink carrier. "The breakfast sandwiches. A phone charger, a few necessities like a toothbrush, et cetera."

"Oh, yay!" Maggie grabbed the phone charger and plugged her almost dead phone in to charge. "Thank you!"

"You're welcome," he answered. He handed her a breakfast sandwich and her coffee. She sipped the coffee, then unwrapped the sandwich and took a bite.

"Up to your standards, princess?" Henry asked as he dove into his breakfast.

Maggie smiled. "They're better than I remembered."

"Better than a Belgian waffle with strawberries and whipped cream?"

"Oh, yes, a definite win. Hands down." Maggie chuckled. "So, what's the plan?"

"First thing to do is compare the scarab to the description in your uncle's notes. Determine if it matches up."

"Suppose it matches. What then?"

"Then I take it and try to find your uncle."

"And I go with you."

"No, Maggie. If it is the Golden Scarab of Cleopatra, it's far too dangerous."

Maggie ignored it, opting for a slight change of subject instead of a confrontation. "So, do you suppose it is?"

"I do. People were after your uncle for it. And judging by

your apartment being ransacked, these people realize its value. I'd bet it's not just because of the pretty gems."

"I guess we'll find out," Maggie concluded. They finished their breakfast in silence. Maggie used the time to check her cell phone for texts and emails. Judging by the time, she would open her store later than normal once they completed their homework with the beetle.

After they ate their breakfast, Maggie unhooked her phone from the charger, stuffing both the phone and charger into her purse. She stepped into the bathroom with the bag of toiletries to brush her teeth and freshen up before heading out.

When she was done, Maggie grabbed her purse and headed for the door. "Ready to check this guy out?" she asked.

"Yep," Henry answered.

Maggie stepped outside, sliding on her sunglasses. "Good thing it's a sunny day!" she exclaimed.

"Okay, hold it up to the sun, let's see what she can do," Henry prompted.

Maggie removed the scarab from her purse and held it up to the sky. She peered into the stones but couldn't detect anything. She glanced at the ground under the scarab. "Do you see anything?" she asked.

"Nothing."

Frustrated, Maggie frowned, pulling the scarab closer to her and staring at it. "I really thought that would work. I swear I saw etchings in here once before when I examined it."

"Let me take a peek." Henry held his hand out. Maggie gave him the object. He held it close to his face, studying it. "It does look like there are markings. Let me try it." Henry held the scarab toward the sun. They stared into it, searched on the ground below it, twisted and turned it at every angle, but it did no good.

"Ugh! Nothing! Perhaps Uncle Ollie was wrong, and this isn't the golden scarab of Cleopatra."

Henry was silent for a moment as he studied the beetle. He shook his head. "Ollie's never wrong. I doubt he'd make this large of a mistake. Further, I doubt anyone would have torn apart his place and yours for a meaningless artifact."

"So, what's the problem then? Why can't we see the map?"

"We must be doing something wrong," Henry concluded. "But what?"

They stood pondering the question for a moment. "Wait!" Maggie exclaimed. An idea formed in her mind. "Uncle Ollie wrote BRIGHT light. Perhaps it's not bright enough yet!"

"Hmm, that's possible. We may need to try it later in the day when the sun is stronger. Or try to magnify the sun's rays with something like a magnifying glass."

"I have one at my shop. We can try that or wait for the sun to get stronger."

Henry shook his head. "I don't like it, Maggie. Returning to your shop where someone may be watching is dangerous."

"We need somewhere to hang out for a few hours anyway if our magnifying trick doesn't work. Come on. I trust you'll protect me," Maggie stated. She strutted to the van.

"At least you have a magnifying glass there. That's one less stop to make," Henry said, giving in to her request. "But at the first hint of trouble, we're gone. Agree?"

"Agree. I don't like trouble."

Maggie directed Henry to the shop, instructing him to park around back. She opened the shop from the back door, entering and flipping the lights on. She crossed the room to the front door, unlocking it and turning the store's sign to open. A note waited for her near the cash register. She found it as she retrieved the magnifying glass she kept in the drawer there.

Did the best I could with your cryptic instructions. I'd rather not make it a habit. What is up with you, anyway? Not that I care, but I'm just curious.
  -Piper

Maggie chuckled at the note. It was clear Piper cared, even if she hated to admit it. She was more than just curious. Maggie's behavior of late had been odd. She decided to text Piper a longer explanation later.

Henry meandered through the store. "Nice shop!"

"Thanks!" Maggie said.

"Ah, the magnifying glass. Good, let's try this again. We'll go out the back. Less chance of being spotted."

"Okay!"

Once outside, they positioned the scarab in the sun's rays and used the magnifying glass to enhance the sun. After some repositioning, Maggie pointed to the ground. "Look!" she exclaimed.

"I see it!" Henry shouted.

"It's faint, but it's there. I can't make anything out though."

"Me either," Henry admitted. "Maybe if I..." His voice trailed off as he moved the magnifying glass in various positions. "Nah, no good. Sun's not bright enough yet."

"No," Maggie agreed, dropping her hands to her sides, still holding the scarab. "But we learned there is something etched in those gems."

"We did. Now we'll have to wait until the sun's brighter to find anything more."

Maggie nodded. "You can browse my shop until then! If you find an interesting book, I've got a nice armchair you can lounge in to read while you wait."

"It makes me uncomfortable staying in one place, but okay."

"Come on, try it, you might like it!"

Maggie pulled the door open, both of them laughing as they re-entered the shop. They stopped dead as they noticed they weren't alone.

"Good morning. Oh, sorry, Mags, didn't realize you had a customer already."

"Oh…" Maggie hesitated. Awkward silence filled the air and tension hung heavy.

"Ah, I'm no customer, mate. Good friend of Maggie's Uncle Ollie. Well, and of Maggie's. Henry Taylor's the name." Henry thrust his hand out for Leo to shake.

With an abundance of reluctance, Leo shook it. "Leo Hamilton, Maggie's boyfriend. Friend of Uncle Ollie's? Are you here about that bug thing he sent her?"

"Ah, the scarab, you mean?" Henry corrected.

"Right, the scarab," Leo answered, his eyes narrowing at Henry.

"That'd be the reason, mate, yep."

Leo offered a half-smile. "Well, did you give it to him, Mags? I'm sure he'd like to be on his way."

"Ah, no, nope. No need to be on any way. Ollie sent the scarab to Maggie, and she intends to keep it. Rightfully so, mate. We were just brainstorming our next move."

"I see. Maggie, may I have a word with you?" Leo asked, turning the conversation to Maggie.

"Sure," she responded.

"Alone," he added when no one moved.

"I'll just be browsing the books. Don't mind me." Henry backed away a few steps to glance over at a nearby bookcase.

Leo guided Maggie a few more steps away. "What the hell is going on here? Blink twice if you're in danger and can't talk now."

"What?" Maggie asked. "No! I don't need to blink twice! I'm fine!"

Leo glanced at Henry, who turned back toward the bookshelf as though he hadn't been watching them. "Who is this guy?"

"Henry Taylor, a friend of my uncle's. He explained it all to you. We're trying to sort through my uncle's things and determine the significance of the scarab."

"Why?"

"Because my uncle sent it to me for a reason. He may be in trouble and the scarab may be the key to finding him!"

"Says who? Him?" Leo waved his arm at Henry.

"And the cryptic note from my uncle and the strange phone call."

"Why not just give him the beetle thing and let him solve it?"

"It's MY uncle. And he sent it to ME! What is with the third degree, Leo?"

"Third degree? Maggie, your apartment was ransacked. You've been acting sketchy ever since, disappearing, no one can get a hold of you. Yesterday, you didn't even come back to open the shop after lunch. This isn't like you. I, for one, would prefer to be rid of that scarab and move on. Get back to a normal life."

Maggie was incensed by his statements. His suggestion that she forget any trouble her uncle may be in to get back to normal infuriated her. "Did you miss the part where my uncle may be in trouble? Henry says some dangerous people may be after him and I…"

"Oh, Henry says, Henry says," Leo mimicked. "How long have you known Henry Taylor?"

Maggie hesitated. "I met him yesterday."

"You met him yesterday and already his word is gospel."

"He's known my uncle for years!" Maggie countered.

"Did he tell you that? You have no reason to trust this guy, Mags. You don't even know him! You are so naïve. Use common sense!"

Maggie resented the accusation that she failed to use sense. "I trust him. And I have to help my uncle!"

"And nothing I say matters, does it? Like always."

"That's not fair!" Maggie exclaimed.

"Everything all right over here?" Henry approached the arguing couple.

Leo shook his head. "Butt out, 'mate.'" Leo shoved Henry away.

"Watch yourself, friend," Henry countered. He grasped hold of Leo's arm.

"I am not your friend, and neither is she," Leo retorted.

"Enough!" Maggie shouted. "Stop it!"

"I think you'd better leave," Henry said, dropping Leo's arm.

"I'd better leave? Really? That's rich coming from a man Maggie's known for… what, twenty-four hours?"

Maggie sighed. "Leo…" she began.

"No, no, Mags. This is ridiculous! Are you kidding me? Do you want me to leave?"

Maggie grimaced. "No, but…"

"But?" Leo questioned. "But what?"

"If you're going to act like this, it might be best if you do."

"Are you serious?" Leo asked. "Maggie… please tell me you aren't picking someone you barely know over me."

"I wouldn't say barely know," Henry chimed in. "We did spend last night together."

Maggie closed her eyes, biting her lower lip and staring at the floor when she opened them. Leo's eyes widened. "Tell me he's not telling the truth," Leo demanded.

"It's not what you're assuming," Maggie began.

"Stop, don't. I don't want to hear anymore." Leo stormed toward the front door.

"Leo, wait! We didn't..." Maggie called after him. She raced toward him as he slammed the door behind him, disappearing down the street.

Maggie's shoulders sagged as she skidded to a halt.

"Good riddance," Henry called after him.

Irritated, Maggie spun to face him. "Why did you do that?"

"What?"

"You know very well what! You made last night sound like it was romantic when it most certainly was not."

"I didn't insinuate that. I said we spent the night together, which we most certainly did, princess. You shouldn't be mad at me! You should be mad at him."

"Mad at him?" Maggie shouted. "He didn't make misleading statements. You did!"

"No, he just assumed the worst of you." Maggie scowled at Henry. "Oh, come on, Maggie, the guy's a jerk."

"Now you're the one assuming the worst."

"Are you going to pretend you didn't tell me it was complicated between you? I can understand why. The guy's a pushy jerk."

Maggie shook her head. "I should text him and try to explain." She rushed to her phone, retrieving it and sending a long message describing the circumstances by which she and Henry "spent the night together." She sent it then paced the floor, checking her phone every other second for a response. Henry sighed. He approached her, interrupting her pacing. "Don't," she said, trying to side-step away from him.

"I'm sorry," he admitted. "I didn't mean to upset you. But it's best he's not here anyway. The fewer people involved, the better. We don't want Leo becoming a target."

Maggie opened her mouth to answer when her phone

chimed. She ignored the comment, opening the text instead. A response from Leo awaited her: *I don't want to hear your excuses... you were with him all night and you didn't tell me when I called? Then you picked him over me! That's everything I need to know.*

Maggie answered him: *No, it's not everything you need to know... but I didn't tell you because I realized how you'd react! Nothing happened!!! You know me, or you should!*

She sent the text and waited for the response, resuming her pacing. Within a few moments, a response arrived: *You expect me to believe that after you lied?*

Frustrated, Maggie typed back: *I didn't lie! Yes, I withheld some stuff, but I planned to tell you when we were together.*

Maggie tossed the phone onto the counter, sinking onto the stool behind the register. She spotted Henry lounging in the armchair near the bookshelf. He gave her a weak smile before returning his gaze to the book in his hand. Maggie sunk her head into her hands, awaiting a response.

When her phone chimed again, Maggie grabbed it. She found a text from Leo: *Of course you did... easy to say after the fact.*

Frustration filled her. She responded and spent the next twenty minutes arguing with Leo. It became clear the bickering was leading nowhere. After several messages, Maggie typed: *You always say I'm ridiculous, but this time it's you! I told you what happened and you won't listen... you always assume the worst of me even after I explained... you're something else!*

Leo responded in minutes: *I'm not the one who spent the night with someone else*

Maggie's patience, already wearing thin, ran out. He had no concern for her life or her safety. She responded: *If that's the way you feel, perhaps we should end our relationship because you don't trust me and I'm tired of explaining and saying I'm sorry.*

A response arrived in seconds: *Fine.*

Maggie slammed the phone down, frustration overcoming her. Tears rolled down her cheeks, both from anger and sadness. She wiped at them, hanging her head for a moment to collect herself. She squeezed her eyes shut.

An arm wrapped around her shoulders. Startled, her eyes shot open. "Don't cry, princess. He's a bloody fool for walking out on you."

Maggie wiped away a few more tears. "You don't have to be nice to me just because I'm crying."

"I'm not. I'm being honest. And in my opinion, he's a bloody fool for leaving you. I realize how I made it appear, but you explained it to him, and he still assumes the worst of you. That's his bloody problem. You're better off without him if you ask me."

"I didn't ask you, but thanks," Maggie said. She wiped the last tear from her cheek and fished a tissue from her purse.

"There we are," Henry said as she dried her eyes and blew her nose. "Good as new! I hate to see a pretty girl cry!"

Maggie smiled at him. She shoved her phone into her purse. "Let's retry that 'bug' and see if we can make progress."

"There's the spirit! Grab the magnifying glass and the bug and let's go!" Henry exclaimed.

Maggie grinned at him, grabbing the scarab and magnifying glass from their resting spots atop her counter. Together, they exited through the rear of the shop into the back parking lot.

"Sun's much brighter now. We may have some luck!" Henry said.

Maggie held the scarab up toward the sky. Henry positioned the magnifying glass between the sun and the scarab, directing the rays onto the gems. They glanced at the ground.

"There it is," Henry cried. He pointed at the ground.

"Yes!" Maggie exclaimed. "It's so clear now. Look at the

detail in it. It's amazing!" They stared at the multicolored map created by light and shadow on the pavement. "Do you recognize anything on it?"

"Not off hand. It could be anywhere, we'd have to reference a map," Henry said. He reached for the beetle. "Give me the scarab and grab your phone. We'll take a picture to examine and compare to a map."

"Good idea," Maggie said. She handed the beetle to Henry and dashed into the store. She grabbed her purse and hurried to the back. As she stepped into the bright sunshine, she heard Henry shout. "MAGGIE! Get back inside! Lock the doors!"

Maggie's eyes grew wide as her attention focused on the scene unfolding in the parking lot. Henry struggled with a man, each of them grasping at a gun. The man attempted to aim it at Henry while Henry struggled to keep it pointed high in the air. "Run, Maggie, go!" he shouted again.

CHAPTER 7

*B*efore Maggie realized what she was doing, her feet were moving. She ran, but not inside her shop. She sprinted toward the ensuing fight. A bullet fired in the air as the two men struggled, but Maggie continued barreling toward them. The loud bang of the gunshot rung in Maggie's ears. As she approached the fray, she swung her purse with both arms, knocking the assailant on the head.

It wasn't enough to knock him unconscious, but it gave Henry an advantage to aim the gun away from causing any harm.

Maggie swung again, hitting the attacker in the head a second time. The second hit was enough to disorient him. Henry used the opportunity to finish the fight with a head butt, knocking the attacker unconscious.

Maggie stumbled back a step as his body slid to the pavement. Henry, breathing hard with the effort from the fight, tucked the gun in his waistband. "Thanks for the assist," he breathed. "We need to go before he wakes up or any of his friends arrive."

Shock set in as the reality of the situation ingrained itself into Maggie's mind. "He's not…" she began, unable to finish her question.

"No, but he'll wake up with a killer headache," Henry answered. "Come on." He took Maggie's arm, guiding her to the van. "We need to go."

"The scarab…" Maggie mumbled.

"I have it," Henry assured her.

Maggie nodded but didn't respond. She climbed into the passenger seat, securing her seatbelt as if on autopilot. Henry shut her door, scrambling to the driver's side and firing the engine the moment he was inside. He threw the gear shift into reverse, backing up a short distance before switching to drive and speeding out of the lot.

"We need a place to lay low while we figure out our next move," Henry asserted. Maggie didn't respond, shock still apparent on her face. Henry glanced to her. He reached over, taking her hand in his. His voice softened. "Maggie, hey, Maggie," he said. He shook her arm. "Look at me."

Maggie gawked at him. "You're okay. I need you to breathe and push what happened to the back of your mind, okay?"

"O-okay," Maggie answered. Her voice trembled as she spoke.

"You're okay, we're okay. Focus on that, focus on me. We'll find somewhere to stay out of sight until we can figure out our next move. Don't worry. I'll keep you safe."

This elicited a nervous chuckle out of Maggie. "M-more like I'll keep YOU safe," she mumbled.

Henry howled with laughter. "Good come back, princess."

Maggie offered him a wry smile, emerging from her shock induced stupor. "I just… I'm shocked is all. You said there was danger, but I didn't fully grasp it until it was there, staring us right in the face."

"And it had a gun!" Henry added.

"Yes," Maggie said, returning her gaze to the road ahead of them.

"Hey, don't go funny on me again, princess. Put it out of your mind," Henry said. He squeezed her hand.

Maggie squeezed his hand in return, nodding. "I'm okay. But now I'm very concerned for my uncle."

"Old Ollie is pretty scrappy. He can take care of himself well. He'll be all right until we can get to him," Henry reassured her.

Maggie nodded. "So, where are we going?" she asked.

"Right now, as far away from here as we can. I'd like to put as much distance between us and the town of Rosemont as possible."

Maggie glanced back through the side mirror. "I'm all for that." They drove in silence for a few moments before Maggie exclaimed, "Shoot!"

"What is it?"

"I didn't lock my shop! It's open with no one there!" She pulled her phone out of her purse to send a text to Piper: *Had to leave unexpectedly. Something came up. Shop is unlocked, please get there ASAP. SORRY! Will explain later!*

Piper returned her text in a few moments: *Dude... you're becoming a real pain! I expect a fat bonus for this. :P*

The message earned a chuckle from Maggie. "Oh, Piper," she murmured at the phone before agreeing to Piper's terms and stowing the phone in her purse.

"Got it covered?" Henry asked.

"Yes, but Piper expects a nice bonus for it."

"If we find Cleopatra's tomb, you'll be able to give her one," Henry joked.

"Right now, we need to focus on finding Uncle Ollie."

"We will," Henry promised.

They drove for an hour, heading east toward the neighboring state. Signs posted along the highway announced food and gas stations at the upcoming exit. Henry veered off the highway, following the signs toward civilization.

"Stopping for gas?" Maggie asked.

"In a way," Henry answered. "There's a shopping center ahead. It'd be a good idea if we stopped and bought a change of clothes and something to eat."

Maggie agreed. Henry eased the van into a parking spot near the back of the lot. They entered the store and made a few selections on new clothes. Both opted for jeans, pullover t-shirts and a light jacket. Maggie also purchased a weekend bag to hold pajamas, an additional change of clothes for each of them, and toiletries.

They purchased everything, then used the restrooms of the store to change. After, they walked across the parking lot to a fast-food restaurant.

"How far away are you planning on going before we stop?" Maggie inquired. "Do you need to fuel up?"

"That depends," Henry answered.

"On what?" Maggie asked.

"How much gas our next car has in its tank."

"What?" Maggie questioned, confused.

"We should ditch the van. The license plate is too easy to track. We are not sure how well-connected our enemy is. Even if they aren't well-connected, they could report it stolen and have every law enforcement agency searching for it."

"So, what? Rent a car?"

"No. You need a credit card for that. That's too easy to track."

"What are you suggesting?" Maggie asked. Henry issued a knowing glance at her. "No. No, you can't mean... are you saying... you want to..." Maggie lowered her voice to a whisper, leaning toward him. "Steal a car."

He leaned toward her, closing the gap between them and whispered, "Yeah."

"No!" Maggie said, leaning away from him but keeping her voice low. "We can't do that. I'm not a criminal."

"I didn't say you'd steal it," he explained.

Maggie shook her head at him. "We can't..."

"I can and I will," Henry said. He balled his burger wrapper and stuffed it in the empty fry container. "I promised I'd keep you safe, and this is the best way to do it. Now you wait here. I'll honk twice when you should come out."

"But..." Maggie began as he stood from the table. "Henry!" she called as he stalked away, tossing his garbage in the trash can near the door. He spun as he pushed through the exit door, winking at Maggie before he disappeared.

Maggie glanced around the dining area. Everyone continued eating as though nothing important was happening. Maggie's stomach performed backflips while she cleaned up after her meal, tossing her trash in the garbage can before settling into another seat near the window.

Her leg bounced up and down as she stared out the window, biting her lower lip. Within a few minutes, a car pulled alongside the curb near the door. The horn sounded twice. Maggie leapt from her seat, racing outside and to the passenger door. She slid into the passenger's seat and fastened her seatbelt with a shaky hand. She breathed a deep sigh as the car rolled away from the restaurant.

"I can't believe I'm in a stolen car," she said as they pulled onto the highway. "Won't someone report this stolen, too?"

"Most likely, but I tried to pick one that wouldn't be missed for several hours at least."

"How do you know that?"

"Took it from the employee parking section of that store. They're probably not changing shifts for a few hours, so we'll have a head start." Maggie shook her head with a sigh and stared out the passenger window. "What?"

"I can't believe you stole someone's car. Someone will get off their shift only to find out someone stole their car. What a nightmare for them."

"It couldn't be avoided. And consider the upside."

"Upside?" Maggie questioned.

"Yeah. I picked blue just for you, princess. I figured it was your favorite color."

"Oh," Maggie groaned. "Well that sure makes it better." Maggie rolled her eyes.

"Well, there is always the other upside: we've less chance of being caught by our good friends. The gun-toting ones," Henry pointed out.

Maggie nodded in agreement. "Okay, THAT is a valid point." Henry glanced at her, grinning.

They drove for several hours, crossing the border into the neighboring state to the east. As the sun set behind them, Maggie wriggled in her seat, uncomfortable from the several hours in the car. Henry glanced over. "Stiff?"

"A little, yeah," Maggie admitted.

"We'll stop in a bit, once it gets dark," Henry promised.

The sun sunk lower in the sky and as the darkness grew, Henry exited the highway. They followed signs toward lodging. Henry selected a hotel near the highway but hidden off the main drag. He eased the car into a parking space around the back of the hotel. "Does this one pass muster, princess?" Henry asked as he killed the engine.

"It's quite a step up from the last dump you took me to," Maggie admitted. She glanced up at the mid-sized hotel.

"And you reckoned I didn't know how to treat a lady!" Henry joked. He climbed from the car and leaned in before shutting the door. "Be right back."

Maggie shook her head, opening her door and jumping

from the car. "No way are you leaving me alone after this afternoon. I'm going with you."

Henry nodded. "After you, princess," he stated. He bowed to her.

They walked around the hotel and entered the lobby. Henry skipped the unmanned front desk, grabbing Maggie's hand and leading her down the hall. "What are you doing?" she asked. He wound through the halls until they arrived in a back hallway of rooms. Henry approached an exterior door. Maggie spotted their stolen car just outside. Henry noted the number of the room nearest the exterior door.

"Now we're ready to check in," he stated.

They exited through the nearby exterior door and made their way back to the lobby, this time approaching the front desk. Henry rang the call bell on the counter. A woman emerged from a back room. Henry requested a room for the night.

"Just one night, sir?" the clerk asked.

"Yes. Oh, is room 134 available? It's the room we stayed in last time. Great stay!" He winked at the clerk.

She smirked, glancing between Henry and Maggie. Maggie offered a demure smile as Henry wrapped his arm around her. "We do have that room available, sir. I'll just need a form of ID and a credit card."

"Sure," Henry said. He opened his wallet and slid two cards across the marble desk.

"Thank you." The clerk clacked keys at the computer, swiped the credit card, glanced at the ID card, then slid them back across the desk. "Here are your cards back, Mr. Farlow. And here is your room key, Room 134, as requested. I assume you can find your way there?"

"Oh, we can," Henry said. "Thank you." He placed the cards in his wallet and shoved the wallet and hotel key card into his pocket.

They disappeared down the hall toward room 134. "Wait here, I'll grab our stuff," Henry said, pushing through the exterior door near the room.

Maggie watched him as he grabbed their weekend bag from the backseat. She pushed the door open for him to reenter the hotel. They disappeared into room 134.

"Didn't want to ask for the room next to the noisy ice maker?" Maggie teased.

"Nah, not loud enough. This is just perfect, next to a highly used exit door. Plenty of noise."

Maggie giggled. "I call first in the bathroom!" she shouted. She grabbed the weekend bag and disappeared through the door. Once inside, she called, "Hey, how about ordering some food! I'm starved!"

"Right away, princess!"

Maggie began her routine for the evening, removing her makeup and changing clothes. She emerged from the bathroom, pulling her hair into a topknot.

"Here are your choices, princess," Henry said, perusing an open menu book. "Pizza, onion soup, burger, grilled cheese."

"That's it?"

"Sorry, it's a 'limited menu' at this time of night," Henry answered.

"Uh," Maggie said, sinking onto the bed.

"Does it help to know the grilled cheese comes with chips and a pickle?"

"It does." Maggie chuckled. "Sold. I'll take the grilled cheese."

"Done." Henry picked up the receiver of the room's phone. He jabbed at the keypad, then placed the order. Maggie dug her phone and charger from her purse.

She plopped on the bed, plugging the charger into the plug behind the nightstand. With her phone charging, she checked her messages and emails. She had a message waiting from Piper stating she had gotten to the shop; everything was fine, and she would stay until close.

Maggie appreciated how flexible Piper was, given her recent unusual activity. She grimaced at the phone, realizing this was her only text message. Despite her frustration, she hoped to receive at least one message from Leo.

"What's that poor phone done to deserve that frown?" Henry asked. He collapsed onto the bed across from her.

"Nothing," she answered. "I'm texting Piper to see how things are going."

"No texts from Leo, eh?"

"No and that's fine by me," Maggie lied.

Henry studied her, trying to determine how genuine her response was. After a moment, he said, "I'm going to make a few calls to arrange our next move."

"Sure," Maggie answered, already typing a message to Piper. She asked how it was going, apologizing again for the short notice and last-minute request.

While she waited for a response, Maggie retrieved her notes from her purse and performed an internet search on the Staff of Pasherienptah. Her search revealed a few pictures of the staff along with information about how and where it was discovered. Maggie read a few different sites regarding the staff. She then searched for information on the whereabouts of the staff, recalling Henry stating it was in the Cairo Museum.

As she searched for information, it surprised her to find the staff contained two parts. One was a scepter like piece and the other formed the bottom of the staff. Jewels and carved hieroglyphs covered both pieces of the golden staff. The scepter piece was in the Cairo Museum, just as Henry relayed to her. However, the staff's bottom was located in The British Museum in London.

Maggie jotted down the location of the two pieces as a

text arrived from Piper. She clicked to read it as Henry entered the room. "No food yet?"

"Not yet," Maggie responded. "Hey, I found some interesting information about the Staff of Pasherienptah. Only part of it is in the Cairo Museum. The other piece is in London."

"London, eh? I thought both pieces were in Cairo."

Maggie pulled up the webpage to show him. "The Cairo Museum loaned the bottom piece as part of a traveling exhibition to The British Museum in London last spring. It'll be there for two years."

Henry rolled his eyes. "I've got to make another phone call." He excused himself from the room. Maggie focused her attention on the phone, opening her text app to read Piper's message: *It's fine, but I'm getting tired of being your social secretary... try letting people know where you are next time.*

Maggie wrinkled her brow, hope filling her. Leo must have stopped in to talk. Finding her gone, he probably was too angry to text her. Maggie texted Piper: *Sorry, it's been crazy, lots of unexpected things... did Leo stop by again?*

She waited for a response, drumming her fingers on the bed. Her phone chimed, and she snatched it off the bed, swiping it open. She read the message, the crinkle deepening in her brow: *No... two foreign guys... heavy accent... asked for you, said it was urgent. No idea what they wanted. I told them I had no idea where you were... they weren't pleased with the answer, but they finally left.*

Maggie's heart skipped a beat. They must be connected to the tomb raiders, part of the group that had attacked her and Henry earlier. So, they returned hoping for another chance to take the scarab from Maggie or worse. Maggie swallowed hard, concern for Piper filling her. She texted back: *Piper... close the store and go home, text me when you're there. Don't reopen it for a few days. Take a vacation, catch up on schoolwork.*

Just put a sign that says we are closed for one week due to a family emergency.

Maggie jumped off the bed, pacing around as Henry reentered the room. "Worried about your grilled cheese, princess?"

"No," Maggie answered. She continued to pace. "Piper texted me. A few of our foreign friends came by asking for me. I'm worried about her. I told her to close the shop and stay away for a few days."

"Sounds like a good idea. Better safe than sorry, although I suspect they'll catch on soon that you're long gone."

Maggie nodded as her phone chimed another text alert. She read the message from Piper: *Say what? First it's all race over and man the shop and now it's close it for a week and go home? Are you sick or something?*

Maggie texted back: *No, I'm not sick. I've gotten myself involved in something that might bring a lot of trouble, and I don't want you dragged into it. Please, Piper, just listen and close the shop.*

A knock sounded at the door. Henry answered it, relieving the server of a tray of food and signing the receipt. "Dinner is served," he announced. He set the tray on the desk near the door.

Maggie stared at her phone. "I've got to finish this with Piper first," she mumbled.

"Suit yourself. I am starving," Henry said. He removed the lid from one of the plates and consumed a chip.

Maggie's phone chimed, and she opened her text message thread with Piper: *Closing now, just posted a sign... Maggie, are you okay? Do you need help? Should I call the police?*

Maggie smiled with relief at the message. Piper should soon be safe. She also smiled at the kindness. While Piper often hassled her and acted nonchalant, deep down she cared about Maggie's well-being. Maggie typed back: *I'm okay... I'm safe and with someone who can help me... PLEASE text when you are home so I know you're okay too.*

Within seconds, she received a text back: *Yeah, yeah, ok mom... leaving now*

Maggie chuckled at the message, relaxing a bit. She set the phone down, plugging it in to charge again. "Now I can eat," she said. She issued a sigh of relief.

"Got it all taken care of?" Maggie nodded in response. "Come on then, before your dinner gets cold." Henry removed the lid from the second plate, handing the plate to Maggie.

She took a few bites then said, "Is it just me or is this the best grilled cheese you've ever eaten?"

"It's just you," Henry said.

Maggie stuck her tongue out at him in response, then continued eating. After a few moments, she asked, "So, your phone calls about our next move..." Her voice trailed off.

"Yeah?" Henry prompted.

"Ah... what is our next move?"

"At first it was go to Cairo, but after our brief discussion about your discovery, we'll be making a pit stop in London first."

Maggie stopped eating, shock filling her face as she stared at Henry. "Go to Cairo?!" she exclaimed.

"Yeah, go to Cairo, princess. It's the next logical step. We have the scarab, we have the map. We need the staff. Then we can put everything together and find the tomb."

"Wait, wait, wait, wait, wait," Maggie protested. She shook her head. "We need the staff to open the tomb but we can't get the staff. It's in a museum, well, actually, two museums. We can't just ask to borrow it."

"I wasn't planning on asking," Henry said.

"I was afraid you would say that. We can't steal a priceless artifact from a museum though."

"It's the only way to find your uncle and keep him safe. Listen, don't worry about that part. I'll do the stealing bit."

"You'll do no such thing!"

"Maggie," Henry chided, "we don't have a choice. Do you imagine we'll find your uncle safe and sound lounging under an umbrella somewhere? And we'll explain to the people after him and us that, while we have the scarab, we've no intention of giving it to them or using it to find Cleopatra's tomb?"

Maggie was silent for a moment, considering everything. "You're right. I just... cannot believe I'm contemplating stealing something from a museum."

"You're not, I am. You can wait somewhere safe."

Maggie's phone chimed before she could answer. She checked the display, finding a message from Piper. She swiped her phone open to read the message. *Made it home safe and sound. Stop worrying and take care of yourself!*

Maggie typed back, thanking her for sending a message and telling her she was glad she was safe. As she set her phone down, Henry's rang. Henry grabbed it from his pocket, answering it. He spoke a few words, made a few affirmations, then thanked the person on the other end. He ended the call and turned to Maggie. "We leave tomorrow, airstrip near Columbus at 10 a.m."

Maggie placed her plate on the tray, glancing at Henry. "Going to London?"

"Yeah, London." Henry tapped around on his phone. "It's about a three-hour drive from where we are. We should leave by at least six."

Maggie nodded. She checked the time. "I should get to bed. I need my beauty rest if I'm getting up early!"

"Before you run off to bed, we should try to get a picture of that map generated from the scarab," Henry suggested.

"So much for my beauty rest. And how can we? It's dark out!"

"You don't need beauty rest, princess. We need a bright light. Your uncle suggested sunlight, but perhaps we can rig up something with a lamp. It'd be nice to have a picture of that map to study."

Maggie considered it for a minute. "We'll need to take the lamp shade off, direct the light right through the scarab. But this carpet has a pattern, it'll be impossible to see any detail. We should project it onto plain backdrop, like a towel or a sheet."

"Good idea. We'll spread a towel on the floor first." Maggie retrieved a towel from the bathroom while Henry discarded their room service tray outside the door. She spread the towel on the floor between the beds. Henry removed the lampshade from the desk lamp. Maggie grabbed the beetle and the magnifying glass. She held the scarab high above the towel. Henry pointed the beam of light at the scarab. He used the magnifying glass to intensify the beams.

"It's working!" Maggie exclaimed as the colorful map appeared on the towel.

"Grab your phone and snap a few pictures," Henry instructed.

Maggie retrieved her phone from the night table. She repositioned the scarab in the light's beam. The map's detail formed on the towel below. Maggie swiped her phone open, selecting her camera application. Careful to hold the scarab steady, she snapped pictures from as many angles as she could manage.

"Have a peek at them, make sure they are okay," Maggie said. Henry lowered the lamp.

He glanced through them. "Good job, these will do nicely," Henry responded. He tapped at Maggie's phone. "I sent them to my phone so I can study them too." He returned the phone to Maggie.

"All right! Now we can get some sleep."

Maggie picked the towel up off the floor, returning it to the bathroom. Henry restored the lamp's shade. He placed the scarab in Maggie's purse. Maggie emerged from the bathroom and set the alarm for 5 a.m. Henry promised to grab breakfast at a drive-thru window once they were on the road. Maggie climbed under the covers, switching off the light.

CHAPTER 8

$\mathcal{S}$he settled into bed, closing her eyes and attempting to sleep. After a moment, she popped them open. Light streamed from across the room. She frowned at Henry. "Are you going to study that for long?" Maggie asked. Henry stared at a picture of the map on his phone.

"Perhaps," Henry answered. He zoomed in and out on the picture.

"Put the phone down and go to sleep," Maggie urged. She shut her eyes again, popping them open within minutes. "Will you please put that away? I can't sleep with that light blinding me."

"Close your eyes, it won't blind you," Henry suggested.

"I can't, even with my eyes closed I see it."

Henry sighed, clicking his phone off. "Fine, fine. Happy now, princess?"

Maggie settled back on her pillow. "Very." At first, Maggie found it difficult to sleep even without the bright light. She tossed and turned, a bundle of nerves about the upcoming trip. A few times she lifted her head, staring at the other bed. Henry lay still, unmoving. Each time she collapsed back into her own bed rather than disturb his presumed slumber.

She stared at the ceiling, turned to stare at the wall, rolled to stare at the other bed in an endless cycle. After almost two hours, Maggie's eyes grew heavy, and she felt drowsy. Her eyes closed, and she drifted off to sleep.

A loud ringing sounded in Maggie's dream. She glanced around, wondering where the noise originated. Her eyes snapped open as the sound pulled her from her sleep. It took her a moment to realize the noise came from her phone. Becoming fully cognizant, she grabbed the phone from the charger, staring at it. The phone's screen showed Leo was the caller.

Henry stirred as the noise continued. Maggie swiped the phone to answer. "Leo?" she whispered. She climbed from the bed and hurried to the bathroom.

"Mags... hey, did I wake you?"

"Yes, it's the middle of the night!" Maggie said. She sat down, teetering on the edge of the tub.

"Sorry, Mags," he mumbled. "But I had to know."

"Know what?" Maggie questioned.

"Why?"

"Why what? Leo, what are you talking about?"

"How long have you been seeing him? Has it been a while? Does he make more money? Do you love him? What is it about him that made you do this to us?" he slurred.

"Are you drunk?" Maggie questioned.

"Just answer," Leo insisted. With each word he spoke, it became clearer and clearer he had been drinking.

"You're drunk. But to answer your question, Henry and I are NOT together. I told you that already. He's my uncle's friend. I barely know him. We just met!"

Henry stumbled through the bathroom door. "Who is it?" he mumbled.

Maggie attempted to answer when Leo interrupted on the other end of the line. "Wait, are you with him right now?"

"No, yes. It's not what you assume," Maggie answered.

"Ugh, hang up and go back to bed, Maggie. We've got a long day ahead of us tomorrow," Henry droned as he staggered back to his own bed.

"Are you kidding me?" Leo continued.

"I told you, it's not what you assume. But you are determined to think the worst of me, so you keep thinking it while you go sleep it off." Maggie poked at the phone to end the call, frustrated. She sat for another moment, letting her frustration pass before she plodded back to bed. She crawled in, putting her phone on the charger.

"What did the idiot want?" Henry asked.

"He was drunk, just babbling nonsense," Maggie answered.

Henry grunted a response, turning over to go back to sleep. Maggie laid awake for a bit longer before drifting off.

An hour later, the phone rang again. Maggie rolled over to grab it. "You've got to be kidding me."

"Don't answer it," Henry murmured.

Maggie swiped it open without looking at the display. "What, Leo?"

"Maggie?" Ollie's voice answered her.

"Uncle Ollie?!" she exclaimed. Maggie sat straight up in bed. Henry also jolted awake, bolting upright.

"It's Ollie?" he asked. "Give me the phone."

"Stop," Maggie replied. She pushed his hand away as she toggled the phone onto speaker. "Uncle Ollie, you're on speaker phone. Henry is here, too."

"Oh, Maggie," he murmured again. Static crackled on the line.

"Uncle Ollie? Are you okay? Where are you?"

"You must find the tomb," Ollie cried.

"We're trying, but…" Maggie began.

"Maggie, please find it! Please…" Ollie started before there was a scuffle.

"Ms. Edwards," a deep voice with a thick foreign accent said, "get the staff pieces and bring the scarab to Egypt if you want to see your uncle alive again."

"No! Don't give it to them, Maggie, find the tomb!" Ollie shouted in the background before a loud thump and cry sounded.

"If you want to keep your uncle alive, do as we instruct," the voice threatened before the line went dead.

"Uncle Ollie?" Maggie shouted.

Henry grabbed the phone. "Ollie? OLLIE?" he yelled. "Damn it! He's gone."

"Who was that with him?" Maggie asked, dismayed.

"Our friends," Henry confirmed.

"That's what I was afraid of," Maggie answered. "They said… they said…" She found herself unable to finish the statement.

Henry grabbed Maggie by the shoulders. "Maggie, we'll find him."

"What if we don't?" she asked. She gazed at Henry as tears filled her eyes.

"We will. I promise. And I keep my promises," Henry assured her.

Maggie leapt from her seat on the bed, pacing the floor. "He sounded terrible. Do you imagine he's hurt?"

"Maggie," Henry began. He stopped her from pacing. "Stop." He sat her on the bed. "Focus. We will find him. Ollie's my friend, too. I won't let anything happen to him."

"It doesn't sound like you have any choice in the matter!" Maggie exclaimed.

Henry grabbed hold of her shoulders again, staring square in her eyes. "Maggie, I need you to trust me. The best thing we can do right now is focus on our next task: to get the staff piece from The British Museum. Okay?"

"But…" Maggie started to protest.

"No buts, Maggie. If you dwell on that phone call, you won't be focused on what needs done. We can't lose focus. Now, I promised you, I need you to promise me." Maggie pondered for a moment. "Maggie? Promise?"

"I promise," she relented.

"What are we focused on?" Henry prodded.

"Getting the staff from the British Museum."

"Good. And to do that, we need sleep."

"Ugh, I'll never sleep now," Maggie groaned.

"Try," Henry insisted. "Lie back. Get under the covers." Henry pulled the covers over her as she settled into the pillow.

"Okay," she sighed. "But I'll just lay awake because as soon as I close my eyes, my mind will drift to that phone call." Tears fell from her eyes.

"Hey," Henry chided, "you promised." Maggie wiped them away, nodding. Henry grasped her hand. "I'll wait until you fall asleep. Every time you think of that call, squeeze my hand and remember I promised you we will find Ollie."

Maggie gave him a slight smile. She nodded. "Okay," she agreed as she closed her eyes. She squeezed his hand tight.

* * *

The alarm woke her the following morning, screaming in her ear. She picked up her head, taking a sharp breath. "Oh, you're kidding me," she muttered.

"Rise and shine, princess. We've got a long day ahead of us," Henry said. He emerged from the bathroom still drying his hair with a towel.

Maggie sat up, teetering on the edge of the bed, forcing

herself awake. She sunk her head into her hands before taking a deep breath and forcing herself to stand. She lumbered into the bathroom, shutting the door behind her. As she waited for the water to reach a comfortable temperature in the shower, she glanced in the mirror. The two unexpected wake-up calls in the middle of the night left her exhausted, and it showed. She frowned at herself before disrobing and stepping into the shower.

The call from Uncle Ollie still disturbed her. But Henry assured her they would find him. He seemed so sure, so confident. She drew on his confidence to bolster her own. She firmed her resolve as she climbed into the shower.

She let the hot water flow over her and the steam soothe her. After the shower, she was more awake and calmer. Wrapping a towel around her, she wiped the steam from the mirror and dried her hair and applied her make-up. She dressed in her spare set of clothes, tossing the others back into the weekend bag. "Good enough," she said to herself as she did one last check in the mirror.

She zipped the weekend bag and dragged it into the bedroom as she emerged from the bathroom. "Please say we can stop for coffee early," she entreated.

"Good morning to you, too," Henry answered.

Maggie gathered her phone and charger, stuffing it into her purse. "Good morning," she said with a chuckle. "Sorry, I'm not a morning person. I never get up this early. Also, the phone calls in the middle of the night just as I fell asleep didn't help."

"And we won't worry about the second phone call, right?"

"Right," she answered. She nodded her head. "Focused."

"Good. So, about the other call, did you make up with the poor bloke?" Henry asked. He shouldered the weekend bag as they prepared to leave the room.

"Does it matter? And 'poor bloke?' I thought 'idiot' was your choice of words for him?" Maggie asked. She opened the door and stepped into the hallway. They walked to the front desk, checked out, and backtracked to the door nearest their car.

"He is an idiot, but it's still a shame for him if he lost a beautiful girl like you."

Maggie slid into the passenger seat, buckling in for the drive. Henry tossed the weekend bag in the backseat before sliding into the driver's seat. He fired the engine and pulled out of the parking space. Within minutes they were on the highway after a brief stop at a nearby drive-thru for breakfast sandwiches and coffees.

"I didn't make up with him," Maggie answered after a few sips of coffee.

"No?"

"No. He was drunk. Kept insisting on me explaining what it was about you I found so irresistible."

"I hope you were honest."

"I was. I tried again to explain there was nothing between us. But he was too drunk to listen. I just hung up on him." Maggie shrugged. She took another sip of her coffee.

"You mean you didn't tell him it was my tantalizing good looks and alluring accent?"

"No, I left that part out, sorry," Maggie said, glancing at him with a smile. They drove for a few more miles before Maggie spoke again. "Where are we getting our flight again?"

"Just outside of Columbus," Henry answered.

"Columbus International? Which airline?" Maggie asked.

"Eh," Henry hedged, hesitant to answer, "private airstrip, private flight."

"Oh!" Maggie answered. This was promising, she reflected. A private plane was perfect for a relaxing flight to London. She could catch up on her rest. Contented with the idea, she turned her attention to the passing scenery as the sun brightened the skies. There wasn't much to see, mostly flat farmlands, but it still helped pass the time as they approached Columbus. It also helped soothe her mind and stop her from dwelling on the reason behind this trip.

Before reaching the city, Henry veered off on another highway, heading south. They drove for half an hour before he exited the highway, navigating to the airstrip. He eased the car into a parking spot outside a small building. Maggie glanced around as she unbuckled her seatbelt, unsure they were at the correct location.

Henry climbed out of the car, retrieving the bag from the backseat. Maggie stood, stretching. She grabbed her purse, slinging it over her shoulder as Henry shouldered the luggage.

"Ready?" he asked.

"Yeah," Maggie said. "Where's our plane?"

"Just over there," Henry said. He gestured in a vague manner toward a group of planes.

Confusion showed on Maggie's face, but she followed him into the small building. A man sat behind a desk. Henry approached him.

"G'day, mate," he greeted him. "I'm Henry Taylor, good friend of Patrick Brown. He's made arrangements for us to travel to New York."

"Hello," the man answered. "Yes, he left a note about that. Said you could pay him back later. Plane's on the tarmac right outside, can't miss it."

Maggie smiled at the man as they walked toward the exit door leading to the tarmac. They stepped into the bright sunshine. Maggie shielded her eyes, searching the tarmac for the plane.

"Didn't he say the plane was right outside? Where is it?" Maggie asked. She turned to stare at Henry.

"Right there," Henry said. He pointed to the plane dead ahead of them.

"Where?"

"The big one, right there, dead ahead, twelve o'clock."

Maggie stopped walking, shock on her face. "Are you kidding?" she asked. Maggie sincerely hoped he was.

"No," he stated. Henry stopped to wait for her.

Maggie shook her head. "No, no, no! That can't be our plane. That's not… no."

Henry sighed, waiting as Maggie stared at him.

"Tell me that's not our plane," she said. When he didn't answer she continued. "That's not… it's a cargo plane!"

"Yeah, it's a cargo plane."

"We can't fly in that! Are there even seats?"

"Sorry, princess, but we can fly in that. And we are flying in that." Maggie groaned. She crossed her arms, frowning at the plane. "Are you finished? We should board prior to take off."

"Why don't you load me through the cargo bay?" Maggie retorted as she stalked toward the plane.

"Don't tempt me," Henry said. Maggie shot him a glance. They climbed aboard and Henry greeted the pilot. He and the copilot were just starting the engines and doing their pre-flight checks. They spoke a few unintelligible words to each other; the drone of the engines made it impossible for Maggie to make out their conversation. The pilot motioned around the cargo bay, shook Henry's hand and clapped him on the back before returning to his tasks.

"Are there assigned seats, or will any crate do?" Maggie asked as Henry approached her.

"I arranged a crate by the window for you." Henry winked at her. Maggie rolled her eyes at him but chuckled despite herself. "Come on, it won't be that bad. It's only just over an hour."

They settled on the floor, leaning against one of the crates. Within moments, the drone of the engines rose to a fever pitch. The plane lurched and lumbered down the runway. Seconds later, the plane's front lifted and a moment later, the back wheels stopped clacking on the pavement. The plane climbed for a few minutes before leveling off.

Maggie shifted around. The floor was hard as was the crate she rested against. At least it was only a little over an hour, she figured.

"Not comfy?" Henry shouted over the drone of the engines.

Maggie sighed. "That's putting it mildly," Maggie admitted. "Good thing it's a short flight."

"Here," Henry said, wadding up his jacket and pushing it next to her. "Sit on this."

"Oh, you don't have to, it's okay."

"Please, princess. I insist," Henry said. "Although I'm shocked you're uncomfortable in these luxurious conditions."

"Me, too," Maggie said. She slid the jacket under her. It cushioned the floor enough to make sitting bearable. "I'm not sure I've ever experienced this level of luxury before."

Henry grinned at her. The flight was bumpier than a commercial flight, although Maggie figured it may have been from their seating arrangements. As they began to descend, approaching New York, Maggie said, "I hope our flight to London isn't on a cargo plane."

"No, I sprung for real seats on the next plane," Henry assured her.

"Wow, big spender," Maggie teased, grinning.

"Nothing but the best, princess," Henry said as they touched down. As the plane rolled to a stop, Maggie stood, stretching. Henry retrieved his jacket. "Thanks," Maggie said. She nodded to the clothing item.

"No problem, princess," Henry answered her.

They disembarked from the plane. "So, what's the plan?" Maggie asked as they strolled into the sunshine.

"We've got a few hours before our flight," Henry said. "We should get something to eat. Perhaps study the pictures we took of the map. We can do some research on the staff piece in London, too."

"I don't suppose there's a cab around," Maggie said. She glanced around the barren airstrip.

"Don't worry, I got that covered." Henry clicked off his phone.

"Let me guess, we're planning to ride into the city on the back of a chicken truck," Maggie postulated.

"Hilarious, princess. But no," Henry answered. He motioned to a small car pulling up on the opposite side of the gate. The horn sounded as the driver jumped from behind the wheel, waving.

"Mr. Henry!" the man called, "I am here!"

"There's our ride," Henry said. He waved to the man. They strolled to the car. "Viraj!" Henry greeted him, wrapping him in an embrace.

"Henry, my friend. It is delightful to see you," Viraj said. His voice was heavy with an Indian accent.

"Ah, it's been too long, mate. How are things? How does your wife like the city?"

"She is loving it. And you? You are married now? Your wife is so very beautiful." He grinned, signaling to Maggie.

"Oh, no," Maggie corrected. She laughed and waved her hand at him. "No, no. I am not his wife."

"No, Viraj, she is not my wife. Please meet the beautiful Maggie Edwards. You remember Ollie Keene? This is his niece."

"Ah, Dr. Keene's niece. A pleasure to meet you," Viraj said. He extended his hand to shake Maggie's. He turned to Henry.

"Where can I take you? I have cleared my afternoon. Shall I show you the city?"

"Maybe later, Viraj. Right now, we need a good lunch."

"Oh, I know just the place. Please." He motioned to the car.

Maggie slid into the backseat while Henry joined Viraj in the front. They drove toward the city. The buildings closed in around them as they entered the city. Maggie stared out of the window. She hadn't traveled to New York in a while. The last time she visited, she enjoyed the city a great deal. She didn't expect this trip to provide the same level of amusement.

Viraj wound around the streets. He drove down an alley and parked the car in the rear of a building. "Please, my friends, I hope you will enjoy this restaurant!" he said. He motioned to the building as they exited the car.

"I'm sure we will, Viraj," Henry assured him. Maggie wasn't as certain, but she wasn't a picky eater so she was sure she could find something on the menu.

"The restaurant is owned by a good friend of mine," Viraj told them as they entered through the kitchen door. "Authentic Indian cuisine! Just like home!"

They entered the hot kitchen. Cooks worked at various stations preparing food. Viraj sought out a specific man, overseeing the preparation of a dish unknown to Maggie. "Fariq!" Viraj said. He greeted the man with an embrace. They spoke in a language Maggie didn't understand but assumed was an Indian dialect.

After a few moments, Viraj motioned to Henry and Maggie. "Please meet my good friends Henry and Maggie," he said. Henry greeted the man in his native dialect while Maggie stuck with an American "hi." "I have brought them for your authentic Indian cuisine, best in the city!"

"Welcome," Fariq greeted them. "Come to the dining room. I will prepare a special dish for you."

He seated them in the rear of the restaurant. Henry and Viraj made conversation for a few moments before Viraj asked more about Maggie. In less than fifteen minutes, Fariq arrived carrying a tray laden with several dishes. He set out various things on the table.

Viraj waited, allowing his guests to serve themselves first. Maggie followed Henry's lead. He was well-versed in Indian customs. Within moments, Maggie was gulping water, the food proving spicier than she was accustomed to.

Henry and Viraj chuckled at her as she choked out the words "too spicy." Despite being spicier than she expected, Maggie enjoyed the meal. When they finished, Maggie and Henry thanked Fariq for the hospitality. Viraj embraced Fariq again, promising to visit him again soon.

As they strolled down the alley to the car, Viraj asked Henry where he'd like to go next. Henry requested a library or internet café where they could do some quiet research. Their flight was scheduled to depart at 6 p.m., giving them a few solid hours to research their next steps.

They spent their time researching the staff and its where-abouts in the London museum. They also noted as much as they could about the location of the second piece in Cairo. Henry made a few phone calls to prepare for the trips ahead of them.

As late afternoon approached, Viraj dropped them off at the air terminal, wishing them luck on their journey. Henry guided Maggie to the ticket counter to pick up their pre-arranged tickets. They kept their bag as a carryon. A security guard met them at the ticket counter, taking them through a back hall to their gate. Maggie found it strange. It was apparent Henry had major connections.

CHAPTER 9

*O*nce boarded, Henry suggested Maggie try to sleep. They would arrive in London in the early morning, and Henry wanted to visit the museum as soon as possible to plan how he would retrieve the staff piece.

Maggie nodded and once their flight was airborne, she settled in her seat to attempt to sleep. Henry gave her the window seat, taking the aisle for himself. She turned to lean against the wall, staring out of the window before closing her eyes. She fidgeted, trying to get comfortable. She turned toward Henry, squirming in her seat again.

Despite it not being a cargo plane, the small seat did not provide much more comfort. "Not comfortable?" Henry asked.

"No plane seat is comfortable," Maggie responded.

"Come on! I spring for a seat and you're still uncomfortable?" Maggie reached up to adjust the air flow, rubbing her arms against the chill. "Cold?"

"A little," Maggie said.

"Here," Henry said, offering his jacket. He draped it over her shoulders.

"Thank you," she answered, snuggling into the jacket. "I've used this jacket more than you have," she joked.

"Good thing I bought it," he answered.

Despite the early evening hour, Maggie was sleepy. Her lack of rest the night before caught up to her. She yawned, pulling the jacket a little higher and drawing her knees higher toward her chest. She drifted off to sleep under the warm cover.

Maggie awoke with a start as the plane dipped and swayed in the sky. She glanced around, getting her bearings. The memory of her situation flooded back to her. Henry detected Maggie was awake. "Just a little turbulence," Henry whispered.

Maggie glanced up at him, realizing she was laying on his shoulder. "Sorry," she said. She pushed herself up to sitting.

"No worries," he answered. He smiled at her. "You were sleeping so peacefully, I didn't want to wake you."

"What time is it? Are we almost there?" Maggie asked.

"Sorry, princess. We're only about halfway there."

"Ugh," Maggie moaned.

"Go back to sleep, I'll wake you when we're close."

Maggie nodded as the turbulence settled. She squirmed in her seat, trying to get comfortable again.

"Come on," Henry said, extending his arm to her.

"Thanks, but no," she declined. "I'm okay."

"Oh, come on, princess. Don't be shy. You know you're not comfortable."

Maggie considered it for a moment. She could get several more hours of sleep before they landed. "Okay," she agreed, "but don't get the wrong idea."

"Never, princess. I'm only a pillow, nothing else implied." Maggie laid her head against Henry's shoulder, settling in and closing her eyes. She fell asleep in minutes.

A few hours later, a gentle rocking woke Maggie. She

opened her eyes, glancing around, reminded again she was on a flight to London. "We're almost there," Henry said.

Maggie pushed herself to sitting, yawning and stretching as much as the confined quarters allowed.

"What time is it?" Maggie asked.

"Just before six, London time," Henry informed her. "Did you sleep well?"

"As well as can be expected on a flight," Maggie quipped, then added, "I had the best blanket and most luxurious pillow though." She winked at him, folding his jacket and returning it to him.

"Luxurious? Not rough around the edges?" Henry joked back.

Soon the flight attendants were readying the cabin for landing, and within fifteen minutes they were on the ground. They climbed to their feet and Henry retrieved their bag from the overhead compartment. As they deplaned, Maggie whispered to Henry, "Uh, I never thought about this before. Everything happened so fast. I don't have my passport. The guard in New York never asked for my ID!"

"Yeah, I doubted you carried it in your purse. You won't need it." Maggie knit her brow, staring at him. "Just trust me. Besides, I don't want your passport showing up on the grid right now. It's too easy to track."

They made their way through the airport, heading to immigration and customs. A sinking feeling grew in Maggie's stomach with every step. How could she not worry about her passport? You couldn't just walk into another country with no passport.

"Mind if I stop in the ladies' room?" Maggie asked as they passed the facilities.

"Not at all," Henry said. "I'll wait here."

Maggie stepped into the short line to use the facilities. The image in the mirror reflected her hours-long flight across the Atlantic. She took a few moments to freshen up before rejoining Henry in the corridor.

They proceeded toward the customs queue. Nervous agitation filled Maggie. Her hands were shaking as they approached the agent. "Passports?" the blonde woman said in a crisp British accent.

Henry slid two passports to the women. "Here you are. How are you today?"

"Fine, thank you, sir. What is the nature of your business in London, Mr. Harvey?" she asked, opening the passports and holding them up as she eyed Henry and Maggie.

"Second honeymoon," he answered. He put his arm around Maggie's shoulders. "Our first was in Paris and I promised the missus in five years we'd take another trip to Europe. Here we are!"

The woman smiled at the two of them, scanned the passports, checked her computer screen and then passed the passports back to Henry. "Enjoy your stay," she said. She smiled at them both.

"Thank you!" Henry said. He pocketed the passports and took Maggie by the hand to lead her away.

As they walked from the desk, Maggie whispered, "How did you do that? Where did you get that other passport? It's not mine!"

"No, it's Tamara Harvey's. She's married to Thomas Harvey. He's a nice bloke, perfect husband, some might say," Henry said. He grinned at her.

"Does she look that much like me?" Maggie questioned.

Henry stopped and flashed Maggie the passport. "She looks identical to you, Maggie."

Maggie was speechless. The passport photo was the same as her own passport, but nothing else matched. "How did you..." Maggie began.

"A tale for another time. Now, come on," he replied. He

grabbed her hand. "We have a few things to do before we visit the museum."

Henry hailed a cab, asking the driver to drop them off at a storage facility. When they arrived, Henry hopped out of the car, pulling Maggie with him. He paid the driver before they entered and wound through the hallways to a specific locker. Henry pulled a key from his pocket, unlocking the storage space. He rolled up the door, pulling Maggie inside before shutting it.

He turned on an overhead light, illuminating the room. Maggie gasped. There were several items in the room: money, guns, equipment of various natures. Henry grabbed a handgun, bullets, cash and a few other items.

Alarmed, Maggie realized how little she knew about Henry and his background. His tricks never ceased to amaze her. But who could pull things like this off? Who could have a new passport made with her picture? Who had a storage locker full of cash and weapons? Maggie suddenly wanted to be anywhere but here. She realized she may have made a grave miscalculation in agreeing to join Henry.

She recalled their initial meeting. Being tossed in the back of a van didn't qualify as agreement in Maggie's book. She then found herself in a foreign country after being shot at. Whom had she gotten herself involved with? Perhaps the gunfight hadn't even been about the scarab Uncle Ollie sent to her. Even if it was, perhaps the man after Henry was trying to protect her, not harm her. Henry could have faked the pictures he showed her considering he did create a fake passport with her picture on it. How hard could it be to photoshop a few pictures of him with Ollie to fool Maggie into trusting him? Ollie never spoke to Henry while on the phone, despite Maggie informing him Henry was with her. Odd, Maggie pondered, wouldn't he have acknowledged his good friend? Perhaps Henry wasn't on Ollie's side, but the opposite one.

Panic filled Maggie. The realization that she'd given this little thought dawned on her. She glanced around the locker. Could she open the door and make it out before he caught her? She doubted it. She'd have to make her getaway at another time.

As she turned her gaze to the center of the room, she found Henry standing right in front of her. She jumped, startled to find him so near. "You okay?" he asked her.

"Yeah," she stated. She bit her lower lip, her eyes wide.

"Not losing focus, are you?" Maggie shook her head. Henry raised an eyebrow at her but didn't pursue it further. "Okay, let's go. We'll check into a hotel and dump the bag before we go to the museum."

She smiled and nodded, swallowing hard. They exited the facility and began walking down the street. Maggie glanced around, trying to surmise the safest place to run. Not familiar with the area, she was loath to attempt an escape at the moment, afraid she'd end up in worse trouble than she was in now.

Within minutes, Henry guided her up steps into a hotel. He spoke with the desk clerk, requesting a room for three nights. A haze clouded Maggie's mind. The conversation between Henry and the desk clerk sounded miles away.

Her senses returned somewhat when Henry tugged on her arm, pulling her toward a bank of elevators. He pressed the call button, and an elevator slid open. They stepped inside, with Henry pressing the button for the fourth floor. A wave of nausea passed over Maggie as the elevator whisked them upwards.

Dazed, she followed Henry out of the elevator and to their room. They entered and Henry set their bag down on the luggage rack. Maggie hovered near the door, agitation consuming her.

"We've got some time before the museum opens," Henry said. He glanced at his watch. "Want to freshen up a little? Maybe take a nap?"

Maggie smiled at him without answering at first. After a moment, she replied, "You know, I think I'll just go downstairs and see if there's a breakfast shop or something close and..."

"We can grab some food on our way to the museum. I'd rather not leave you alone and you shouldn't be wandering around London yourself."

"I'll be fine," Maggie said. She pulled the door open and backed out.

"Maggie..." Henry started as Maggie broke into a run down the hall. She heard him curse as he tore out of the door after her. He caught up with her as she reached the elevator bank, pressing the button frantically, hoping for one of the elevators to open in time.

She had no such luck. No elevator doors whooshed open to provide her sanctuary at the last moment. She moved away as Henry approached her, searching for an exit. "Stay away," she warned.

"Maggie?" he questioned. "What's wrong?"

"Just stay away," she warned again.

Her eyes darted around the hall, searching for refuge. As she searched, Henry lunged toward her, grasping her arm and pulling her toward him. She opened her mouth to shout for help, but his arm clamped over it first, muffling any sound emanating from it.

He dragged her down the hall toward their room. Maggie was no match for Henry's strength and within a minute, he pulled her through the door. He released her as he closed and locked the door, positioning himself between her and it.

"Maggie, calm down. What's wrong? What's frightened you?" he asked. He inched toward her.

She backed a step away. "Oh, Maggie, I thought we were past this?"

"I don't even know who you are," Maggie replied in a shaky voice. "You grabbed me and threw me in the back of a van. You are familiar with guns, it appears. You somehow got a fake passport with my picture. And you have a storage locker full of money and weapons. Who does that? Who are you?"

"I can explain," Henry said. "Calm down." Maggie glanced at him; uneasiness written across her face. "I'm friends with Ollie, remember I showed you the pictures?"

"You could have faked those! You faked a passport!" Maggie cried. "And why didn't Ollie acknowledge you on the phone call?"

"Okay, okay, I get where you're coming from, but I can prove it."

"So, prove it," Maggie demanded.

"How about if we sit down…"

"Prove it!" Maggie shouted.

"All right, fair enough," Henry said. He shook his head at her. "I can prove I know your uncle. When we were in Morocco together, we had some time to kill. He told me a story about his niece when she was a little girl. She was an adventurous little girl who thought she could fly. One day as she swung on the swing set in her backyard, she pumped until the swing flew high in the sky. When the swing was at its highest, she leapt off, convinced she'd sail above the ground. Unfortunately for the little girl, she couldn't fly and ended up sprawled on the ground. She had skinned knees and bruised elbows and even had to get stitches where she cut herself on a stray branch she landed on. His niece has a scar from it on her left forearm. He remembers her showing him the scar and telling him her experiment to fly failed. But he told her she didn't fail, she succeeded..."

"Because she had the courage to test her theory," they finished together.

"Yes, and then he warned her not to test any more theories about flying," Henry added.

Maggie sunk onto the bed. It appeared Henry was a friend of her uncle's. Few people were familiar with the story of the tiny scar on her left forearm. Henry stepped over and sat next to her, putting his arm around her.

"I'm sorry," she said. She felt foolish.

"It's okay, Maggie. You're tired. It's been a rough couple of days. Why don't you take a quick nap, I'll wake you when it's time to go?"

Maggie smiled up at him. "I'm okay," she assured him.

"No, you're exhausted. And it's making you paranoid."

"Sorry," she said again.

"You should be. Distrusting a wonderful bloke like me," Henry said, grinning at her.

Maggie shook her head at him. She relaxed onto the bed, closing her eyes and yawning. "Still..." She stifled a second yawn. "Who has that many guns in a storage locker?" she asked before drifting off to sleep.

Two hours later, Maggie awoke. She stretched before sitting up in bed. Henry lounged in a chair, his feet propped on the bed.

"Good morning, princess," he said as she stretched again.

"Good morning," she answered. "What time is it?"

"About ten thirty," he responded.

"What? Why didn't you wake me? We wanted to be at the museum when it opened!" Maggie said, leaping off the bed and finger combing her hair into a ponytail.

"Ah, thirty minutes won't kill us. You looked so peaceful there. And you needed the sleep."

"I would have been fine," Maggie insisted.

"Well, now you'll be better than fine," Henry said. He stood from the chair and stretched.

"Give me ten minutes," Maggie said. She grabbed a few items from their shared luggage and disappeared into the bathroom. She emerged fifteen minutes later, tossing everything back into the bag and grabbing her purse. "Okay, ready."

Henry checked his watch. "You said ten minutes."

Maggie rolled her eyes at him. "Come on," she said. She grabbed his arm and pulled him. "I hope that promise of breakfast is still good. I'm starving!"

"Yes, it's still good," Henry assured her.

They stopped at a local café for a quick meal before taking a cab to the museum. They climbed the stone steps and entered the building, grabbing a museum map at the entrance. They navigated through the halls, finding the exhibits on loan from the Cairo Museum. They found the partial Staff of Pasherienptah. It sat inside a glass case, resting on a velvet-covered box. Hieroglyphics covered the golden staff.

"There it is," Maggie said. She bent closer to take a better look. "It's beautiful. The craftsmanship, how intricate the carvings are. Wow!"

"Yeah," Henry said. He glanced around the room. "Doesn't look too difficult. There's only one camera with an angle on it and a lock."

"Is that all you can think about?" Maggie questioned as she returned to standing.

"You can appreciate the craftsmanship when you've got it in your own little hands," Henry assured her. "Now, we need a picture of the staff and its case. Stand by the case and wave, try to look like a typical tourist."

Maggie shook her head at him but stood by the case. She

smiled and waved, posing for the picture. Henry shooed her a tad to her left, then snapped a few pictures. They made their way around the room, taking various pictures with other exhibits.

"Did you get enough for your scrap book?" Maggie inquired as they moved to the next room in the museum.

"I got the room from every angle, yeah. Now we need to check the other security to enter the museum."

They spent several hours perusing the rest of the museum. While Maggie spent most of her time appreciating the artifacts and museum items, Henry concentrated on mentally mapping exits, entrances, security guards, badges for swipe entries into restricted areas and more security related items.

Around 3 p.m., Maggie requested they eat an early dinner once Henry had completed his mental stock of the museum. Henry grabbed another map of the museum on their way out. They found a quiet café and settled into a corner table in the rear.

Once the waitress had taken their order, Henry pulled the additional map from his jacket pocket and marked several items on it.

"What's your plan?" Maggie asked.

"Get in, grab it, get out."

Maggie wrinkled her nose at him. "Funny. How do you propose we 'get in?' Let's start there."

"The less you know, the better."

"Well, what am I supposed to do? Wait at the hotel? What if something goes wrong?" Maggie questioned.

Henry sighed. "As much as I'd like you to wait safely at the hotel, it's a bad idea to leave you there alone."

"Yes, in case something goes wrong. I may be able to help."

"No, because you're a sitting duck there. If someone

tracks us, you'll never stand a chance. So, you'll have to go with me when I do it."

"When you pull the job, you mean?" Maggie asked. She raised her eyebrows at him.

"Don't say that. People only say that in movies," Henry informed her as the waitress served their meal.

"So, what's the plan?" Maggie asked again after the waitress left.

"Let's start with 'grab it,'" Henry said, "that's the easy part. The lock on the case shouldn't be a big problem, we drill it out, open the case, take the staff, easy peasy."

"Did you just say 'easy peasy?'" Maggie asked. She giggled.

Henry gave her a look. "I didn't see any pressure sensors. I should be able to take the staff without worrying about an alarm being triggered. So that part is simple."

"Okay, now how do we get in? And then how do we get out?"

"That's the tricky part. We need to achieve that without setting off an alarm. And without having a guard spot us in person or on the cameras. There is one camera that has a view of the display case."

"Oh, I've got it, we snip the wires on the camera!"

"No. The camera's not reachable. No snipping wires. Besides, that would trigger a response from the guard. He'd investigate to see why the camera is out. I have a friend who can help with the camera. Leave that to me."

"You have a friend for everything," Maggie said. She took another bite of her pasta dish. "Do you have a friend that can get us in and out?"

"Perhaps, but we'll need one of those ID badges everyone had on today."

"How do you propose we get one of those?"

"We'll have to take another trip to the museum tomorrow and try to grab one."

"Maybe we can just ask nicely?" Maggie joked.

"I'll leave that method to you to try, princess."

"Eh, on second thought, let's go with your plan to snag one," Maggie answered.

They finished their meal. Henry suggested they do some shopping and stop by the storage locker for a few supplies. At first, the prospect of London shopping thrilled Maggie until Henry informed her they only needed to buy something darker for their daring museum theft than the bright pink t-shirt Maggie had picked. Maggie was less than thrilled to only be buying a black t-shirt, hoodie and yoga pants.

After their shopping trip, they made their way back to the storage locker to gather a few items Henry felt they needed for the mission. Henry informed her as they left, they had one more stop to make. They took a cab to an apartment building across town. Henry asked the cab driver to pull around the corner before getting out. He paid the driver, and they meandered to the front entrance of the apartment building. Henry's head was on a constant swivel, eyeing every person on the street.

They entered the building, taking the elevator to the fifth floor. Henry produced a key, unlocking one of the doors halfway down the hallway from the elevator bank. He pushed inside, closing and bolting the door. The small flat contained little furniture. Maggie glanced around as Henry opened a lockbox he pulled from a desk drawer.

Despite the meager décor, Maggie spotted a picture frame on the desk. Maggie strolled to the desk, picking up the frame. Pictured in the photograph was her Uncle Ollie. He gave the camera a thumbs up. Next to him stood Henry, his arm around Ollie's shoulders.

Maggie glanced to Henry. "And that one's not photo-shopped, princess," he said as he noted her stare. Henry shuffled through a few papers inside the box, pocketing one before locking and placing the box into the drawer. "Okay, princess, let's go."

They ended up back at the hotel in the early evening. Maggie collapsed on the bed despite the early hour. "I'm bushed!" she exclaimed.

"Get a good night's sleep. It'll be a long day tomorrow."

"Every day with you is a long day." Maggie sighed.

"I need to make a few phone calls before you turn in for the night."

"I'm going to take a shower before bed," Maggie said. She grabbed her things from the weekend bag and disappeared into the bathroom. She emerged about forty-five minutes later, ready for bed.

"I hope you left some hot water for the rest of the hotel." Henry laughed. "I'll take the chair, just toss a pillow over for me," he said, referencing the single bed situation.

"That won't make for a very comfortable night's sleep," Maggie noted. "I don't mind sharing. I'll use this pillow as a buffer, so I don't creep onto your side of the bed." She stuffed a pillow under the covers separating the two sides.

"How generous of you. Thanks for the pillow divider. I'll bet you like to sprawl, princess." Henry disappeared into the bathroom, emerging a few minutes later. He chose the side of the bed closest to the door in case anyone should try to enter. While the idea of someone accosting them in their sleep unsettled Maggie, she fell asleep within minutes of her head hitting the pillow.

CHAPTER 10

The jangling of Maggie's phone interrupted their sleep. Maggie startled awake, fumbling to reach for the phone on the night table. She checked the display with squinted eyes. Noting the caller, she swiped it off, choosing not to answer the call.

"Who is it?" Henry mumbled.

"Leo," she replied.

Within seconds, the phone chirped with a voicemail notice. Maggie sighed, rolling over to go back to sleep. Moments later, the phone rang again. Maggie swiped at it again, sending the caller straight to voicemail. Seconds later, the phone rang for a third time. "Are you kidding me?" Maggie asked. She reached for the phone.

"Shut that damn thing off," Henry complained.

Maggie glanced at the screen. Leo's name showed on the display again. She rolled her eyes as she answered it. "Why are you calling me?" she asked. She crept from the bed and into the bathroom.

"Maggie?! Are you okay? Where are you?"

"I'm fine. But's it's the middle of the night, I'm trying to sleep."

"Middle of the night? Where are you?"

"What does it matter? Stop calling me!" Maggie said. She was about to hang up when Leo stopped her.

"Wait, Maggie, wait, wait. I called to apologize. Actually, I stopped by the shop to apologize and I saw the note that you were temporarily closed. I went to your place, I asked at the hotel and couldn't find you. I texted Piper to ask what was going on and she told me you were in some kind of trouble. But that was all she knew. And she hadn't heard from you in days. Maggie, what the hell is going on?"

Maggie sighed. "I'm fine. I'm in London. I told you before if you would have listened. I'm trying to find my uncle. Someone is after him because of this scarab he sent me. I need to find him."

"Maggie, you shouldn't be there alone! This is dangerous. Why didn't you contact the authorities?"

"I'm not alone…" Maggie began as Henry trudged into the bathroom.

"Is it Leo again?" he asked.

"Yes, it's Leo, go back to bed," Maggie answered him. Henry rolled his eyes, stalking from the room.

Leo overheard the exchange and launched into a tirade. "Is that the guy you were with in your shop? HE'S the one you're with? Maggie, this is a terrible idea. You need to call the police. Stop running around the globe trying to do this on your own."

"Leo, I appreciate your concern, but I'm fine. I'm in good hands. I'll keep in contact via text."

"I thought you said that package came from Jordan, why are you in London?"

"We're following up on a few things," Maggie fibbed. "The

scarab is connected with a staff in the British Museum. It used to be in Cairo, but part of it is on loan here. We were doing a little research before going on to Cairo, where Henry supposes my uncle is now."

"Henry thinks so, huh? Henry supposes?"

"Leo, we're not going to have this argument again. I've explained myself a hundred times already. You continue to believe the worst of me no matter what I say. I'm finished with this conversation. Now I'm tired and I want to go back to sleep."

"But, Maggie…" Leo started.

"Don't call again tonight," Maggie said. She ended the call. She shuffled back to bed, turning her phone off before placing it on the charger.

"That bloke's becoming a real pain in the arse," Henry said. His forearm was flung over his eyes.

"He was worried about me. That's why he called," Maggie said, her comment intending to defend Leo while she settled back under the covers.

"He cared enough to call after he hasn't heard from you for days! We should give the chap a medal!"

"Oh, stop it and go to sleep," Maggie said though she was unable to hold in a snicker.

"I'm trying. I hope you turned the phone off this time. In case Romeo gets any bright ideas about calling again."

"Yes, yes, I turned it off. Now be quiet and go to sleep!" Maggie said. She turned over and squeezed her eyes shut. It took her almost thirty minutes to fall asleep, but once she did, she slept for the rest of the night.

* * *

Maggie slept well into the morning, waking just before 8:30 a.m. "Good morning, you slept well," Henry noted. He handed her a cup of coffee as she sat up and stretched.

"Thanks," she said. "I did. I was exhausted!"

"When you've finished that, we've got another exciting day ahead of us." Maggie pushed herself up to get out of bed. "No rush, we're meeting my colleague around ten thirty at the museum," Henry said, waving her back to bed.

Maggie didn't complain. She was happy to drink her coffee from the comfort of her bed. "Colleague? Is that what they're calling them these days?" she joked. She finished her coffee after asking about Henry's sleep and their plans for after they had the staff in their possession.

Henry planned to return to the hotel and take an early morning flight to Cairo, where he hoped to find Maggie's uncle. "Shouldn't we change hotels or something?" Maggie shouted as she applied her makeup in the bathroom mirror.

"It'll only be a few hours," Henry assured her. "We should be fine here. Plus, this is far enough from the museum they may not check it when they realize the staff is missing."

Maggie nodded in agreement as she gathered her clothes from the bag, disappearing into the bathroom to change.

"Okay," she said. She emerged into the room. "Let's get it started, I guess."

They exited the hotel, hailing a cab to the museum. As they entered the museum, Henry took another map, practicing his act as a tourist. "Let's go visit our favorite artifact," he said to Maggie. They wound through the museum to where the staff was displayed. Henry and Maggie approached the case. A few people milled around it, moving off as they approached. One gentleman remained on the opposite side of the viewing case. Henry circled the case, sidling next to him as he stared at the staff.

"This is it, huh?" the man standing next to Henry asked.

"The one and only. Well, part of it," Henry answered.

"Security doesn't look terrible. Only one camera on this guy," the man answered. His eyes never moved from the case.

"We'll need that taken care of and a security badge made so we can enter the museum without setting off an alarm," Henry said.

"Yeah, I saw the badges. No problem on that front. I just need access to one for about fifteen minutes. You need eyes up top during?"

"I'll get you one. Yeah, would help to have eyes in the sky."

"I'll be in the restroom off the main entrance, fourth stall. Give me thirty minutes to set up and get into the system, then I can clone the badge you give me."

Henry nodded at him and the man walked away. Maggie's gaze followed him until Henry pulled her away. "Stop staring at him," Henry said. He dragged her to another exhibit. "We need to get one of those security badges, preferably a guard's."

Maggie glanced around at the employees. "How do you propose we do that? They're attached to their shirts or around their necks on lanyards!"

"I don't suppose you could distract one of them for a few moments?"

"How am I supposed to do that?" Maggie asked.

"You're a pretty girl, Maggie. Feign needing some assistance. Bat your eyelashes, squeeze out a tear, be a damsel in distress. Here, give me your purse, tell him you lost it."

"Wha..." Maggie began as Henry pulled her purse from her arm and stalked away. Before he disappeared from the room, he nodded to her. Maggie stood unmoving for a few moments. She blinked a few times, glancing around, wondering if this was happening. Her palms were sweaty, and her legs felt like jelly. She swallowed hard before preparing herself to approach the guard. She took a few deep breaths, then hurried toward him.

"Excuse me," she said breathlessly. "Excuse me, can you help me?" She didn't wait for an answer before launching into her request. "I lost my purse. I can't find it anywhere. I retraced my steps, but I don't see it. Is there a lost and found? Or something? Oh, it has everything in it, my passport, my wallet, my phone, half of my make-up for the trip. If I can't find it... I have to find it," she stated, shaking her head as if dismissing the first option.

"All right, miss, calm down. We can file a report and I'll radio the other guards to see if it's in lost and found. Come with me," the guard said, motioning for her to follow him.

Maggie's hands shook as she followed the guard. "Thank you," she mumbled as he led her through the main lobby toward a door marked STAFF ONLY. As they crossed toward it, Maggie heard her name being called. She expected Henry's voice and accent, but the voice wasn't Henry's. "Maggie! Maggie!" Leo waved from near the entrance. He rushed over toward them.

"Leo?" Maggie murmured, more to herself than anyone.

"Oh, Maggie, it's good to see you in the flesh. I've been so worried."

"What are you doing here?" Maggie asked.

Leo's arrival threw Maggie a curveball she didn't expect. She wasn't sure how to proceed.

"I got on the first plane I could. I..." Leo began.

"I lost my purse," Maggie blurted out, cutting him off. "Sorry. I asked the officer for help. I need to deal with this first."

"But, Maggie..." Leo started again.

"I really need to find my purse," Maggie interrupted. "It has everything in it. My passport and credit cards and... and... phone, just everything. I need..."

Another voice interrupted Maggie's babbling. "I found your purse, love," Henry said. He handed the purse to Maggie. "And I see we've picked up a stray along the way. How dare you follow us here?" Henry shouted. "What the hell do you think you're doing here? Come to steal my wife? You sorry excuse for a man!"

"Sir, sir, you need to calm it down or you'll be made to leave," the officer said. He held his hand between Henry and Leo.

"Oh, I'll calm it down all right. Right after I take this arse-hole down," Henry said. He reached for Leo. Leo leaned away from him while the officer placed his body between the two men, holding Henry back.

"Sir, I said that is enough. I'll have to ask you to leave."

Henry held up his arms. "Sorry, I'm sorry. My anger got the best of me. My apologies, mate. I promise I won't cause any more trouble. I will finish enjoying the exhibits with my wife." He placed his arm around Maggie. "Sorry for the outburst."

"All right. No harm done, but if it happens again, I will personally escort you off the premises."

"Won't happen again," Henry said. He smiled at the guard. "You have my word."

The guard glanced between the two men, then to Maggie. "I'm glad your husband found your purse. Enjoy the museum." He issued another glance between them, then stalked off, taking a post in the lobby and keeping his eye trained on the three of them.

Henry turned to Maggie as he left. "I need to drop something off with our friend. See if you can get rid of the third wheel." He nodded to Leo and disappeared into the men's room.

"Maggie! What the hell is going on here?"

"It's difficult to explain," Maggie answered.

"Try," Leo insisted.

"Well…" Maggie began before Henry rejoined them.

"No luck, huh?" he asked. He circled his arm around Maggie's waist. "Let's move this conversation out of the guard's view."

They moved to another exhibition room. "You were saying?" Leo asked Maggie as they stopped, pretending to look at a statue.

"She wasn't," Henry said.

"I asked HER," Leo snapped. He spun to face Henry.

"Look, mate, let's not have another go. We're a little busy. She can explain everything to you as soon as we leave, but right now, we've got a little something going on."

"Maggie?" Leo asked. He glanced around Henry to Maggie.

Maggie shrugged. "It would be a lot easier to talk once we're at the hotel."

"Unreal! Okay, fine, fine. So, now what? Are we still enjoying the museum exhibits or what?"

"Go outside and wait for me on the steps," Maggie suggested to Leo.

"Go outside and wait for you on the steps? Go outside and wait for you…" Leo shook his head, his voice trailing off. "Okay, fine! Whatever!" Leo said. He shrugged and waved his arms in the air as he strolled away from them.

"Now he's really becoming a pain in the arse," Henry said as he left. "What the hell is he doing here? How did he find us?"

Maggie made a face. "I might have told him where we were when we talked last night," she admitted.

Henry rolled his eyes, shaking his head. "Maggie! You've got to be more careful!" he scolded. "Never mind. Charlie should be done by now. Let's finish up here and get back to the hotel. Wait for me here."

Henry disappeared, leaving Maggie to wander around pretending to peruse the exhibits. When he returned, he handed the guard's badge to her. "Here, return this to the guard. Tell him it fell in your purse during the scuffle."

"Why do I always have to do the hard stuff?" Maggie complained. She snatched the badge from him.

Maggie and Henry navigated back to the lobby, finding the guard in the location where they left him. Maggie sauntered to him, leaving Henry waiting near the entrance. "Excuse me?" Maggie said. She batted her eyelashes.

"Yes?" the guard asked. "Haven't lost your purse again, have you?"

"No," Maggie said. She laughed a little too much at his joke. "I've got it right here! But I found this inside. I think it might be yours? It must have fallen into my purse during the scene courtesy of my husband." Maggie handed the badge to him. He accepted it, his brow wrinkling. "I'm sorry for that. My husband has a bit of a temper and my ex hasn't accepted that I married someone else." Maggie smiled at him, batting her eyelashes.

"Well, it isn't any wonder with that pretty face," the guard answered. "Thanks, I'd be in big trouble if I lost this." He waved the badge at her before clipping it to his shirt.

"You're welcome. Thank you for being so understanding." Maggie flirted, glancing up at him. "We'll be out of your hair now. Have a nice day."

"Enjoy your day, miss," the guard said.

Maggie crossed the lobby, rejoining Henry. He waved to the guard as they disappeared through the front doors. "We're all set for tonight. For now, we'll return to the hotel, eat and get a little rest."

They descended the steps, finding Leo sitting halfway down them. "Oh, the happy couple," Leo said as they approached.

"Save it until we're back at the hotel, mate," Henry warned.

They hailed a cab and piled into it, heading back to Maggie and Henry's hotel. None of them exchanged a word during the cab ride. Maggie sat in between the two men, uncomfortable the entire ride. One could cut the tension in the cab with a knife.

They arrived at the hotel and Henry paid the cab driver. "I suggest we have room service so we can keep any discussions private."

"Okay," Maggie agreed.

They took the elevator to the fourth floor, navigating to their room with Leo trailing behind. They entered the room and Maggie made her way to the room service menu. Leo glanced around the room, noting one bed. "Now, can you tell me what's going on?"

Henry ignored him. "What looks good, princess?" he asked Maggie.

"Ah, the walnut-cranberry salad sounds excellent. Maybe with a bowl of their clam chowder?"

"I'll try the burger, thanks," Henry said.

"Hello?" Leo shouted. "Anyone care to tell me what's going on here? I expect some answers now that we can talk."

"Do you mind if we order something to eat? I'm starving!" Maggie said. "Do you want anything?"

"Burger with a side of answers?" Leo asked.

Maggie rolled her eyes and placed the room service order. When she finished, Leo said, "Great, now maybe you'll stop avoiding the question and explain to me what the hell is going on."

Maggie glanced to Henry. "Don't look at me, princess. This discussion is between the two of you," he said. He lounged on the bed.

"I explained it to you already. We're trying to find my

uncle. The scarab he sent me is related to a museum piece here in London and we were doing some... research before going on to Cairo to continue the search for Uncle Ollie."

"Yes, you told me that. Perhaps you can explain that little scene at the museum. Your 'lost purse' that this guy retrieved and his outburst about you being his wife."

"Ah..." Maggie paused. "Perhaps you'd like to explain what you're even doing here?" she retorted after a moment. "Showing up at the museum? How? Why?"

"I came because I'm worried. Piper made it sound like you were in real trouble, and our phone call last night didn't ease my mind at all. Maggie, you just met this guy and you're traipsing all over the world with him. What is going on here?!?"

"I told you, I'm fine."

"I'd like to hear how you found us at the museum. You omitted that part when answering, mate," Henry chimed in.

"Can we talk somewhere in private, Maggie?" Leo requested.

"She doesn't leave this room alone," Henry argued.

"She wouldn't be alone, she'd be with me," Leo retorted.

"Same difference," Henry suggested.

"Stop, both of you!" Maggie exclaimed. "I'd like to hear the answer to his question and whatever you have to say you can say in front of Henry."

Leo glanced at the ceiling, hands on his hips, annoyed. "This is unbelievable. Fine. Maggie told me last night you were researching there. When we hung up, I went to the airport, booked the first flight out to London and took a cab straight there. I planned to wait until you showed up."

"Why?" Maggie asked. "I told you I was fine. And I thought we agreed to end things."

Leo sighed. "Aw, Mags, we always say that and we never mean it. We just... we say it because we're angry, but I care about you. You say there's nothing romantic between the two of you. Even if that's not true, I don't care. I'm here to fight for you, Maggie. The minute Piper told me you were in trouble, all I could think of was being here to protect you."

"Oh, boy, it's getting deep," Henry commented.

"Thank you, that's enough from the peanut gallery," Maggie chided.

"That's why I wanted to speak in private. It's between us like you said before, MATE, so stay out of it," Leo grumbled.

Maggie sighed. "Thanks, Leo. I appreciate what you've said and you coming here, but it's best if you go home. I don't want you involved in this. It could be dangerous."

"I don't care, Mags," Leo said. He knelt in front of her as she sat on the bed and took her hands in his. "If you're in trouble, I want to be there for you." Maggie glanced to Henry. He shrugged his shoulders at her. "Maggie, please. Stop asking for his approval and do what's in your heart."

Maggie gazed at Leo. She considered his request. After a moment, she responded, "I don't want to be responsible for you getting hurt, Leo."

"Getting hurt how, Mags? What is going on? What happened? Are you in that much danger?"

Maggie sighed. "The scarab my uncle sent me; we think it's the Golden Scarab of Cleopatra. It contains a map and when paired with the Staff of Pasherienptah, it can open Cleopatra's tomb."

"And this is a big deal?" Leo asked.

"No, mate, it's only Cleopatra's tomb, one of the last great archeological mysteries of the world. But it's no big deal," Henry answered.

Maggie shot Henry a glance. "Yes, it's a big deal. A big enough deal that people are willing to kill for it."

"What?" Leo exclaimed.

"After you left us at the shop that day, someone attacked

us while we were checking the scarab for a map. Tomb raiders, according to Henry. The man had a gun, he could have killed us. I'm afraid the same may happen with my uncle, if it hasn't already. We received a call last night telling us to get the staff pieces if we wanted to see Uncle Ollie alive again. Half of that staff was on loan to the British Museum. The other half is in Cairo. We came here to get it before we go to Cairo and try to find Uncle Ollie."

"Get it? As in ask to borrow it? I don't understand, Mags."

"In a way," Maggie said, dancing around her answer.

"In a way?" Leo questioned.

"We're here to steal it, mate," Henry answered for her.

"Right," Maggie confirmed. "I can't ask you to become involved, Leo. It's too dangerous between the people after us and the methods we are forced to use to retrieve this staff and find my uncle. I just can't ask you to stay."

"Are you listening to yourself, Maggie?" Leo asked. "What has this guy told you? What spell does he have on you? You aren't acting like yourself! You're STEALING something. For what, to find some buried treasure?"

"Haven't you been paying attention? It's not buried treasure, mate. It's Ollie's life. We need those staff pieces to find the tomb and save Ollie. We need to use any leverage we can to bargain for Ollie's life, whether it be the staff pieces or the tomb's location."

Leo mulled everything over for a moment before responding. "Well, I'm not leaving," he answered. "I'm here for you, Mags, and I'm not leaving."

"But…" Maggie began.

"No, no buts, Mags, I'm not going. We're in this together," he insisted. He took her hand and squeezed it.

"This is all very touching," Henry said, "but you're a liability. I don't care what you do, stay or leave, mate, but don't get in our way."

"Would it hurt if he tagged along?" Maggie asked. "An extra set of eyes may help. Although I guess it would be harder for three of us to sneak around than two of us."

"He's not going to the museum with us tonight," Henry stated. "He can stay here if he insists, but that's it."

Maggie's brow furrowed. "But you said it was too dangerous to stay here alone."

"I said it was too dangerous for you to stay here alone."

"What's the difference?" Maggie asked.

"I care about what happens to you, I couldn't give a fig what happens to him." Maggie stared at him, concern on her face. "Oh, princess, he'll be fine here. They've seen you, if they find you, well, never mind. They don't know Romeo, if they find him here, they'll assume they got the wrong room." Maggie sighed, still not responding. "Maggie, we can't take him with us. He'll be fine here, I promise."

"Perhaps I should stay with him," Maggie postulated.

"No. It's safer for you with me. They'll recognize you if they find you here. They won't recognize him. You stay with me. He waits here. Safest option for everyone. Trust me, Maggie," Henry said. He put his hands on Maggie's shoulders.

Maggie gazed into his eyes. After a moment, she nodded. "Okay. I trust you."

"I don't. I'm not on board with this," Leo added.

"No one asked you," Henry sniped as a knock sounded at the door. Henry pushed between Maggie and Leo to open the door for their room service. They ate in relative silence, the tension still thick. Afterwards, Henry suggested they take a quick nap. They were scheduled to meet Henry's associate, Charlie, at 10 p.m. They'd likely not get much sleep, if any, before their morning flight.

Maggie agreed, snuggling under the covers. Henry took his spot from the previous night, still separated by the pillow wall. Before he closed his eyes, he informed Leo he was the lookout since he likely had a fair amount of sleep in the last few days, unlike them. Leo grumbled but took up his post on the chair, allowing Henry and Maggie to sleep for a few hours.

CHAPTER 11

*H*enry woke first, just before eight thirty, and opted for a shower before their mission later. Maggie awoke twenty minutes later. She stretched and climbed out of bed, asking where Henry was. Leo rolled his eyes, pointing at the bathroom door. She was about to discuss the situation with Leo further when Henry emerged from the bathroom.

"You're up," Henry said. He still dried his hair with a towel. "Good. You should get ready. We'll leave in about an hour."

Maggie nodded, grabbing her new clothes and disappearing into the bathroom to shower and change. As she pulled on her yoga pants, Maggie glanced into the mirror. The reality of what she would soon attempt stared back at her. She wasn't sure how she felt about it. She hardly knew which way was up. She sunk onto the edge of the tub, dropping her head into her hands. Tears formed in her eyes as she considered the gravity of the situation she faced.

A knock sounded at the door, pulling her from her musings. "Maggie," Henry called. "You almost ready?"

"Yes, I'm almost ready," she called back. She glanced upwards, blinking a few times until the tears receded. She pulled on her shirt and donned her hoodie. She checked her makeup in the mirror before she opened the door.

"Ready?" he asked as she stepped out.

"Yeah," she answered. Her voice cracked.

Leo approached her. "Mags, be careful." He wrapped her in his arms, pulling her close to him and kissing her on the top of the head.

She glanced up at him, wrapping her arms around his waist and kissed him. "I will," she promised. "See you soon."

Henry shouldered a bag of equipment while Maggie stuffed her phone into her pocket. They left Leo in the room, heading to the elevators. "You okay?" Henry asked as they entered the waiting elevator to descend to the ground floor.

Maggie was quiet for a moment, her mind distracted. "Huh? Yeah, I'm okay. You promise Leo will be okay here?"

Henry gave her a brief smile. He wrapped his arm around her shoulders. "He will be okay. And so will we. Piece of cake, okay?" She nodded, her arms crossed tightly against her chest as she tried to steel her nerves. "Maggie, look at me." Maggie gazed into his eyes. "Trust me. We'll be fine."

She offered him a small smile. "Okay," she said. Her tone was more resolute this time. "I trust you."

"Good," Henry said. He took her hand and gave it a squeeze as the elevator ground to a stop. "Come on, princess. Time to retrieve the first piece of the puzzle and get one step closer to finding Ollie."

Maggie followed him from the elevator and through the front door. A white van was parked across and down the street. Henry approached it and the side door slid open. Charlie was inside with an array of computer and technical equipment.

"Ready?" he asked as they climbed into the van.

"Yep," Henry answered. "We good?" he asked as Charlie handed him an earpiece.

"All good," Charlie answered. "Looks like two night guards. They don't spend a lot of time walking around. They play cards most of the time. Should be easy. Wanna give that a test for me?"

"Test test," Henry said as he placed the earpiece.

"Loud and clear," Charlie answered. "Let's get this show on the road."

"Stay here with Charlie," Henry said. He jumped out of the van and closed the door. Moments later, the van's front door slammed shut, and the engine fired. The van lurched forward as they made their way toward the museum.

Charlie eyed Maggie sideways while he clacked on his keyboard. Maggie smiled at him. He gave her half a smile, cleared his throat and continued to bang around on the keyboard.

"Known Henry long?" he asked as the van crept to a stop.

"No, I..." Maggie began as the door slid open again.

Henry reached inside, grabbing a few items from the bag he brought and placing them into his dark cargo pants. "Stay here, Maggie. I'll be back in a jiffy." He winked at her. "Charlie, you know the drill. Anything happens you bail and make sure you take her somewhere safe."

"Wait, what?" Maggie asked. Henry's new orders shocked her. "No!" she protested.

"Yep." Charlie answered. "You're clear on the side entrance. Key code 9999. Fifteen seconds before that door registers as open to the guards, stay to the left of the hallway when you enter. I've got the door on a video loop now and will loop video on the staff piece in two minutes."

Henry slid the door shut despite Maggie's protestations. Charlie handed her a headset. "Here, chicky, you can listen to your boyfriend."

"He's not my boyfriend," Maggie said. She slid the head-phones on. "And what did he mean, take me somewhere safe if anything happens?"

"He means if he gets caught. Really? You're not his girlfriend?"

"No, I'm not."

Charlie appeared surprised by the admission. "Never knew Henry to bring a chick on a job. Not his girlfriend, huh? You looking?" He raised his eyebrows at her a few times, grinning.

"No, I am not. My boyfriend is waiting for me at the hotel."

"Too bad. We'd have made a good pair, you and I," Charlie said.

Maggie rolled her eyes at him as Henry's voice crackled into her headphones. "Wouldn't try it, mate," Henry warned. "Reached the side door, inputting key code now." Within seconds, Maggie overheard noise then Henry's voice again. "I'm in."

"Key card worked like a charm, did it?"

"It did." Henry whispered.

Charlie glanced to Maggie again, raising his eyebrows up and down at her. "You're clear on the cameras as long as you stay to the left. The tricky spot is at the entrance to the next gallery room. You'll make a quick zigzag there before you continue down the hall."

"Got it," Henry whispered. Maggie monitored the screens. Charlie could spot Henry on the cameras, but the feeds the guards monitored were oblivious to Henry's presence. Maggie and Charlie could see both the real feed and the feed being streamed to the guard station.

Maggie clenched her sweaty palms together. Her heart was in her throat as she observed Henry creep through the museum. It was painstaking to watch, and Maggie imagined it was more painstaking to live through. After twenty minutes of careful movement, Henry arrived in the room the staff piece was housed in.

"You're all clear, mate," Charlie told him.

Henry snuck toward the case holding the staff piece. He fiddled with the lock. "Damn, they locked it," he joked through the earpiece. He removed a small drill and placed it near the lock. The drill sprung to life.

"Careful, mate. Those decibels are a little too high. Slower." The whir of the drill toned down as Henry slowed its spinning to lessen the noise. "Better," Charlie said.

"Will take forever at this rate," Henry whispered.

"You got time. Guards haven't moved since we got here." Charlie popped open a bag of chips and a soda. "Chip?" he asked. He shoved the bag at Maggie.

"No thanks," she said.

"Soda?"

"No. How can you eat at a time like this?"

"He's a pro, princess," Henry whispered to her.

"I didn't realize you could hear me," Maggie said.

"I can hear you, princess."

"Good. Don't get caught. I'm not going anywhere with this guy, safe or not."

"I'll try my best," Henry whispered. "Halfway through this lock."

"Uh, might want to hurry it up, mate. We've got movement. Looks like one of the guards is going to make his rounds."

Henry cursed under his breath. "I can't go much faster without him hearing it if he's leaving the guard station. Keep an eye on him."

"Will do," Charlie promised. He chomped on another chip.

Maggie and Charlie followed the guard on the security

cameras. He moseyed through the back hallway, emerging from the STAFF ONLY door into the lobby. He crossed the lobby, glancing around, heading toward the gallery Henry was working in.

"He's heading straight for him!" Maggie exclaimed. "He'll walk through the first gallery, then into the room Henry's in!"

"She's right, mate." Charlie confirmed. "Can you leave it until he's passed through?"

"No way, the lock'll give it away." The drill continued to whir.

"Do something!" Maggie entreated Charlie.

"There's nothing I can do!" he insisted.

"Ugh," Maggie said, pulling the headphones off and sliding the van door open. She heard Charlie calling after her, but she ignored him. She ran around the building to the door that entered the lobby.

Maggie pounded on the door, shouting. She continued pounding until the door opened. The guard peered outside. "What in the bloody hell do you think you're doing, miss?" he said.

"Ah," Maggie paused. She was unprepared for the question despite having achieved her goal. "I need help! There's a man… out here who is having a heart attack. I forgot my phone. Can you call for an ambulance?" The man hesitated. "Please! I need your help!" Maggie grabbed onto the guard, tugging on his shirt dramatically.

The guard radioed to his coworker. "Yeah, mate, I've got a hysterical woman out here claims a guy's having a heart attack. Can you call for an ambulance?"

They waited a moment until the guard's voice crackled over the walkie talkie. "10-4. Calling now. Get her name and information for a report."

The guard removed a small notebook and pencil from his pocket. "Can I get your name, address and phone number?"

"What?" Maggie stalled. She glanced around. "Uh, sure, but then I better go check on that man. It's Susan Smythe, that's S-M-Y-T-H-E. I don't live here, I'm just on vacation, but my cell phone number is 640-555-7642. Now I've got to get back to check on him, thank you!"

Maggie ran down the steps and away from the building. A horn sounded from around the building's side. Maggie hurried toward it. She rounded the corner, spotting the van. Henry stood outside it, the door open. She rushed toward him as he approached her.

"What the hell were you thinking, Maggie?" Henry asked.

"That you were about to get caught!"

"Ah! We'll argue about it later, get in the van, we've got to get out of here."

Maggie climbed into the back of the van as Henry slid the door shut. Within seconds, they were moving, pulling away from the museum. When the van stopped and the door opened, Maggie was surprised to see they weren't at the hotel.

Charlie had been packing up much of his stuff during the short ride. Henry retrieved his bag. "Where are we?" Maggie asked.

"Parking garage. We walk from here."

Maggie hopped out of the van, followed by Charlie, pulling on his backpack stuffed with his gear. They wiped down the van inside and out. They closed and locked the van and exited the parking garage on foot. "Is he coming with us?" Maggie asked.

"I am. Try not to get too excited, chicky," Charlie said. He raised his eyebrows at her.

"Did you get the staff?" Maggie asked Henry.

"I did," Henry answered. He stopped walking, turning to

Maggie. "You shouldn't have done what you did, Maggie. It was foolish and impulsive, and you could have gotten hurt!"

"If I hadn't, you wouldn't have gotten that staff! You would have gotten caught!" Henry shook his head as Maggie continued. "You should be thanking me, not scolding me."

Henry sighed. "Thank you, but next time don't put yourself at risk, Maggie."

"But…" Maggie attempted to argue.

Henry cut her off. "But nothing," he said. He grabbed Maggie's arm and pulled her down the sidewalk as he resumed walking. "I just don't want anything to happen to you."

"I'm a big girl, I can take care of myself," Maggie retorted.

"Maybe so, but if it's all the same, I'd prefer to take care of you while we're together."

Charlie witnessed the exchange with great interest. "I'd like to take care of you, too." He winked at her.

Maggie rolled her eyes, drawing closer to Henry as she walked. They reached the hotel in fifteen minutes, going straight to their room. As they entered, Leo leapt from the chair. "Maggie! Thank God!" Maggie rushed to him, embracing him.

Henry threw the bag onto the floor, pulling his jacket off. "Got about two hours before we head out," he stated.

Leo eyed Charlie. "Who's this?" he asked.

"A friend," Henry answered.

"Name's Charlie Rivers," Charlie said. He stuck his hand out to shake Leo's. Leo nodded, shaking his hand without responding.

Henry pulled the staff from the bag. Maggie pulled away from Leo, rushing to his side.

"Is this it? Can I have a peek?" she asked. He handed it to her. "Wow, it's heavy! It's really something!" She turned to Leo. "Leo, come look!"

Leo didn't budge. "Yeah, it's great," he called.

"On to Cairo!" Maggie exclaimed. She handed it back to Henry, who stowed it in their weekend bag amongst their clothes. He condensed the other materials he carried into the bag as well.

"Yeah," Henry answered. He zipped the bag and stalked to the bed. He plopped onto the bed, fiddling with his phone. Maggie glanced at him. Was he still angry about her stunt at the museum?

Leo interrupted her musing. "Hey, Mags, you hungry?" he asked. "I bought some snacks while you were out down at the sundries shop. Got your favorite. Pretzels and peanut butter cups!"

"Oh! Yes, please!" Maggie said. She snatched the food from his hand.

"Anyone else want any?" Maggie asked.

"I'll take one," Leo answered. He reached into the bag of pretzels. No one else responded.

The remaining time crawled by as they waited to depart. Maggie struggled to stay awake despite the nap. Her adrenaline surge at the museum drained her. After an eternity of waiting, the time arrived to leave the hotel.

Henry shouldered their bag and checked out at the front desk as everyone else waited outside. When Henry rejoined them, a cab pulled up. They piled in with Charlie, Maggie and Leo in the backseat and Henry taking the passenger seat. The driver took them to the air strip. As they climbed from the cab, Maggie groaned.

"Oh, no. Not another cargo plane," she moaned.

"Yes, princess, another cargo plane," Henry answered.

CHAPTER 12

*T*hey met the pilot on the way to the plane. Henry spoke with him, apologizing for the change in plans that led to their group being four rather than three. The pilot didn't mind and told them to take a seat anywhere in the cargo hold.

"Get prepared for the most uncomfortable plane ride of your life," Maggie warned Leo as they climbed aboard.

Leo crinkled his brow at her. They settled on the floor, leaning against the cargo for support. Charlie dug in his backpack, removing headphones and his cell phone. He jabbed at the display before propping it in his lap to watch.

Within ten minutes, the engines screamed, and the plane made its way down the runway. "Wanna put your head down and try to sleep?" Leo asked Maggie.

"Thanks," she said. She rested her head against his shoulder as he wrapped his arm around her. She closed her eyes, trying to fall asleep. Despite her exhaustion, she found herself unable to sleep.

After forty-five minutes, she glanced up at Leo. His head rested against the crate behind them, lolling as the plane moved. He had fallen asleep a few moments after the plane had taken off.

Maggie lifted his arm, sliding out from under it. Henry sat a few feet away, eyes closed, head resting against a crate.

Maggie crawled over to him. "Are you awake?" she asked. Her voice just above the roar of the engines.

"Yes, princess, I am awake," Henry answered. He opened his eyes a slit. "What's the matter? Is the lug's arm too heavy on you?"

Maggie laughed. "No. I couldn't sleep."

"Something bothering you, princess?"

"Is everything okay? You've been kind of quiet ever since the museum. You're not still mad at me, are you? I was only trying to help."

Henry smiled at her. "I was never mad at you, Maggie. I hate that you endangered yourself. But I sure am glad you did, princess. You're one brave lady." Maggie returned his smile. "How could you imagine I was mad at you?"

"You yelled at me. And you were kind of cool back at the hotel."

"You're exaggerating! I didn't yell at you!" Henry exclaimed.

"You kind of did," Maggie argued.

"Believe me, princess, if I ever yell at you, you'll know it. Now, try to get some sleep."

Maggie nodded, sliding next to him to lean against the crate. "Something else wrong?" he asked as she leaned her head back.

"We're getting closer to finding Uncle Ollie..." Maggie began.

"Yeah, we are. And that bothers you?"

"What if he's not okay? What if we can't find him? That man that called didn't sound nice."

Henry glanced to her, then put his arm around her shoulders. "He's okay, Maggie. Ollie's smart and a fighter. He's scrappy. He can hold his own against them until we get to him. We'll find the tomb, the danger will disappear, the entire world will know." Maggie swallowed hard, allowing herself to lean into Henry. She nodded, holding back tears as her mind continued to dwell on the possibility Uncle Ollie wasn't okay. A few tears fell onto her cheeks and she wiped them away. "Come on now," Henry cooed, "don't cry. We'll find him, Maggie. I promise."

Maggie nodded again, wiping her face and smiling at Henry. "Okay, as long as you promise," she quipped.

"I do and it's a promise I plan to keep," Henry assured her. He squeezed her shoulders.

Maggie leaned against him, letting her head rest on his shoulder. "He's lucky to have a friend like you," she said. She grabbed Henry's hand and squeezed it.

"And he's lucky to have a niece like you." They sat for a few moments, comforting each other. "Now stop fretting and try to get some rest," Henry answered after a time. He received no response. "Maggie?" he asked. He glanced down at her. He smiled as he realized she was fast asleep. He leaned his head against the crate and closed his eyes.

Maggie awoke a few hours later as the plane's wheels jarred against the ground. She blinked a few times, glancing around. "Good morning, princess," Henry said as she picked her head up.

"Good morning," she mumbled. "Did we land?"

"Yep," he answered.

Maggie took a deep breath, stretching a little. She sat up, glancing around again. Charlie was stowing his phone and headset. Leo awoke and stretched, confusion crossing his face as he realized Maggie was missing. He glanced around, spotting her next to Henry. He scowled at the scene. Maggie shimmied to him. "Good morning," she said. "I couldn't fall asleep last night, and you were out, so I figured I'd pass the time talking to Henry."

"I'm glad he was there for you," Leo pouted.

Maggie smiled at him, trying to smooth over any hard feelings. The plane crept to a stop and the pilot's door popped open. Everyone stood and climbed off the plane.

"Whew!" Maggie exclaimed. She doffed her hoodie and tied it around her waist. "It's hot out here already!"

"Welcome to Cairo," Henry said. He placed his hat on his head.

"Thanks, Indiana Jones," Leo said. He grabbed Maggie's hand as they followed Henry off the tarmac.

They passed through a small building and into a parking lot. Henry approached a utility van, feeling under the front wheel well. He retrieved a key and key fob.

"Shotgun," Charlie called as Henry unlocked the doors.

Maggie sighed, sliding open the back door and climbing in.

"Couldn't even spring for seats, cheapskate," Leo complained as they climbed in to sit on the floor.

"I hope we find Uncle Ollie soon," Maggie voiced. "I'm worried about him."

"I'm sure he's fine, Mags," Leo assured her. Maggie smiled at him. Funny, she mused, Leo's assurances did less to assuage her worry than Henry's.

The van lurched backward before pulling forward and beginning its winding course around roads unseen by Maggie and Leo. Maggie rested her head against the side of the van. Exhaustion was taking its toll, but nervous energy kept her awake.

They drove for about twenty minutes before the van came to a stop. The engine shut off and Maggie heard the front doors opening. Within seconds, the side door slid open. Bright sunshine streamed into the van. Maggie squinted against it as she accepted Henry's hand to climb out.

"This isn't the museum," Maggie said. She stared up at the apartment building in front of her.

"No, it's the last place I saw Ollie before we went to Jordan."

"Here?" Maggie asked.

"Yes, he has an apartment here. Come on," Henry said. He led them into the apartment building. They climbed the stairs to the third floor and followed Henry down the hall. He stopped at the end, feeling around on top of the door jamb. Grabbing a key, he unlocked the door then shoved the key into his pocket. "I always told Ollie it was a bad idea to leave a key out, but he insisted."

"Good thing he did," Maggie said. "For both him and us."

"He really is terrible at remembering things like his keys, isn't he?" Henry chuckled.

"He is," Maggie agreed.

They entered the warm apartment. Henry flicked a switch on the wall, illuminating the space. It was small with a combined living room, dining and kitchen space in one room and a doorway leading to the bedroom and bathroom. Henry stepped into the other room, returning within seconds.

"What?" Maggie asked. She fanned herself with a takeout menu she found on the counter.

"Nothing. I hoped we'd luck out and Ollie had escaped and returned here."

"So, that was your big plan, huh?" Leo questioned. "Search for Ollie right here at home."

Henry ignored him. "Next stop is the museum. We'll grab something to eat first and then head over there and check out what we're working with for the second piece of the staff."

"Perhaps we'll find information on Uncle Ollie's whereabouts there," Maggie said. "Or anyone who has been paying special attention to the staff."

"Charlie, I'll leave it to you to inventory what it will take to get our hands on that staff."

"So, you're planning to steal yet another priceless object from a museum. Remind me again how this helps find Maggie's uncle."

"Because Ollie's captors want the staff pieces and the scarab. They want to find Cleopatra's tomb. Once we at least have the pieces, they'll come for them. And us. That's the only chance we have to determine where Ollie is."

Leo approached Henry. "And how are we sure you're not just searching for this tomb for your own fame and glory?" he asked.

"Maggie has good reason to trust me. I will not waste my time explaining it to you. If she trusts me, you should, too."

"Maggie is sometimes too trusting for her own good," Leo informed him.

"So, you are saying you don't trust her judgment. Then again, I guess that's obvious considering you didn't believe anything she told you when we first met."

"I didn't trust or believe YOU," Leo countered.

"You didn't believe in her either, mate," Henry retorted. "Left her in tears and took off as I recall it. Don't worry, mate. I comforted her. I dried her tears."

"You son-of-a..." Leo began as Maggie sprang between them.

"Stop! Enough!" Maggie shouted. "That's enough from both of you. Henry is our best shot to find Uncle Ollie. We have no reason not to trust him."

"Except the part that he's a thief," Leo muttered.

"Leo, I have already asked you to leave so if you stay, it's your choice, but you don't get a say in any of this," Maggie informed him.

Henry smirked at Leo behind Maggie. Frustrated, Leo grimaced but did not respond.

"With that settled, let's get going," Henry suggested. "We'll walk to a café, then take a cab to the museum."

They exited the apartment with Henry leading the way. As they made their way down the stairs, Charlie sidled next to Maggie.

"Say, chicky, if all that testosterone-laden hostility is getting boring for you, you and I could always steal away for some one-on-one time." He jiggled his eyebrows at her in his usual manner. Maggie rolled her eyes at him, grabbing Leo's hand and hurrying to walk ahead of Charlie. "Something I said?" Charlie called after her.

The bright sun broiled overhead as they navigated to the café. They were seated under a ceiling fan. The wooden fan's efforts did little to cool them as temperatures soared. They shared their meal in relative silence. Between Maggie's exhaustion, Leo and Henry's mutual hatred for each other and Charlie's awkward nature, small talk was nonexistent. Beyond nourishment, lunch provided no distraction for any of them.

Maggie was glad when the meal ended, except that meant they went back into the heat to get to the museum. Henry hailed a cab, directing the driver to the Cairo Museum. Henry paid the cab driver, and they approached the stone building. Entering, they paid the museum fees, grabbed a map of the museum and began their tour.

Maggie commented the trip would have been fun had her missing uncle not been the reason for the visit. She enjoyed the museum and all its contents, despite the dire circumstances surrounding them. As they wound through the museum, they found the second piece of the Staff of Pasherienptah. It lay in a glass case surrounded by other objects from a similar era.

"There it is," Maggie stated. She stared at it through the glass.

"Yep," Henry answered. He glanced around. "The last piece we need to put this puzzle together."

"So, what's the plan?" Maggie asked.

"That'll take a bit of working out," Henry answered. "Come on. We have more surveilling to do." Maggie nodded, and they spent another hour and a half exploring the museum. Afterwards, they grouped together in a quiet corner.

"Well?" Henry asked as they gathered.

"Not good, mate," Charlie answered. "Multiple cameras on that case, no electronic locks to open exterior doors."

"So, we brute force the exterior. You'll have to cover all the cameras."

"It's messy and those doors are alarmed. I can handle the cameras, but can you make it through a door and to the display without setting off an alarm or alerting someone?"

"I will have to damn well try. I've got the map here. Can you cover the alarm signal? We can mark the exteriors and determine which might be best to open."

"It's possible, I have to see when I get into their system."

"Better get to work then."

"Gonna take a good amount of lead time to pull this off," Charlie admitted.

"This doesn't sound good," Maggie mumbled to Leo.

"You mean Crocodile Dundee can't pull it off?"

Maggie grimaced at him. "Oh, stop."

"Yeah, no one asked your opinion, mate," Henry said. "Let's go back to Ollie's. We've got a lot of planning to do."

They crossed the room, heading for the museum exit. As they navigated through the crowds of people, a voice called, "Maggie? Maggie Edwards?"

Maggie spun around, searching for the source of the

voice. A blonde woman, her hair pulled into a loose bun, carrying a notebook and pen, an ID badge hanging around her neck stood staring at them.

"Emma?" Maggie answered. A smile lit up her face. "Oh my gosh!"

The two women approached each other, embracing. "I can't believe we're meeting in the Cairo Museum of all places!" the woman exclaimed.

"Right?" Maggie answered. "Who would have expected this!"

"So, are you here on vacation?" Emma asked.

"Not exactly. I'm here..." She hesitated. "Helping my uncle with some research. What about you?"

Emma held up her badge. "Working! They offered me a position as an assistant curator, and I couldn't pass it up."

"No wonder! This museum is great!"

"It is! I love it. I'm so happy I took the position. How long are you in town for?"

"I'm not sure. But we should catch up if you have some time between working!" Maggie said, an idea forming in her head.

"I'd love to! Dinner? I've got about an hour left. We could meet at the café down the street?"

"Perfect," Maggie agreed.

"Great! I'll go finish up and meet you there in an hour," Emma said. She grinned at Maggie.

"See you there!" Maggie said. She waved as Emma disappeared through a STAFF ONLY door.

"What was that all about?" Henry inquired as Maggie rejoined them.

"An old college friend. We are sorority sisters. We're going to catch up over dinner in an hour," Maggie announced.

"Catch up over dinner?" Henry asked, following up with, "Maggie, you shouldn't be alone."

"I'll stay with her," Leo said, putting his arm around her.

"No," Maggie disagreed, "girls only. You go with Henry and Charlie."

"Are you kidding?" Leo asked.

"I am not. Please just go with them."

"Nope, no way," Henry disagreed, shaking his head.

"Yes," Maggie argued. "I'm not a child, I'll be okay."

"Maggie, are you crazy? You do realize what we're dealing with here, don't you?"

"I'm going. I'll be fine. You can walk me there and I'll take a cab straight home."

"You'll go straight to the restaurant and then take a cab to Ollie's?" Henry confirmed.

"Yes, text me the address." Henry sent her the address via text message. They agreed they would stay with her until she left for the restaurant. It gave them another opportunity to inspect the museum.

As the hour waned, they parted ways, the men dropping Maggie at the front of the restaurant where she planned to meet Emma and hailing a cab to return to Ollie's apartment.

Maggie entered the café, requesting a table for two. After she was seated, she perused the menu then used it to fan herself as she waited for Emma. She glanced around, still finding it hard to comprehend her current situation. She had a momentary panic that staying here alone may have been foolish. She didn't have long to consider it before Emma entered the café, searching for Maggie. Maggie waved, calling Emma's attention to their table. Emma returned the wave, mentioning to the hostess she found her friend.

Emma approached the table, sitting down next to Maggie. Maggie pulled her in for another hug. "I'm so glad we could do this!" Maggie said.

"Me, too!" Emma agreed.

They ordered cocktails and dinner. Maggie asked Emma about her life after Aberdeen College, learning Emma completed her graduate studies in Boston and worked in a museum there before taking the position with the Cairo Museum. They chatted about Maggie's shop and her life following college. Afterwards, Maggie steered the conversation back to Emma's current job.

After the waitress served their meals and they refreshed their cocktails, Maggie commented, "The museum is beautiful. I enjoyed it this afternoon." Emma agreed. "So, do you work any night shifts? Is it spooky?" She chuckled.

"Oh, I have pulled some late ones, yes. At first it's a little unsettling, but you get used to it."

"I'll bet there's a certain beauty about it," Maggie agreed.

"Mmm, there is," Emma responded. "Speaking of beauty, weren't you with a few guys at the museum?"

Maggie laughed. "I was, yes."

Emma raised her eyebrow at Maggie. "Family? Friends? Boyfriend?"

"One is my boyfriend, the other two are friends. Just showing us around," Maggie said.

"I see," Emma said. She gave Maggie a sly grin. "So, which one is the boyfriend? Tall, dark and handsome? Tall, blonde and handsome? Or the other one? Whom I'm sure is a wonderful, wonderful man," Emma added.

Maggie laughed at her reference to Charlie. "Tall, blonde and handsome," Maggie lied, referring to Henry.

"Mmm. I could get used to that face," Emma asserted.

"Me too," Maggie giggled, waving the waitress over to order another round of cocktails. They ordered a dessert, continuing to chat. Afterward, they ordered one final drink.

"Aw, this has been so great, Maggie," Emma said as they neared the end of their drinks.

"It has been great to catch up."

"I suppose I shouldn't keep you and let you get back to that hunky boyfriend of yours."

Maggie laughed. "Hey," she started, pausing, "I wonder…"

"Yeah?"

"No, never mind, it's too much to ask," Maggie said, waving her hand in the air.

"What is it?"

"No, it's asking too much," Maggie stalled.

"Oh, come on, we're Alpha Alpha Kappa sisters! Just ask!"

"Well, I wanted to surprise Henry. Do something romantic, you know?"

Emma nodded. "I don't blame you. I'd want to do something romantic for him if he was my boyfriend, too." She winked at Maggie.

"He loves this ancient Egypt stuff. Ancient artifacts and all that stuff. I mean, LOVES it. He and my uncle are great friends, and they talk about this stuff all the time. He's just fascinated by it. Anyway, he'd love to spend more time in the museum. I was wondering if maybe… Aw, I feel terrible asking this but would you be able to let us walk around a little after the museum closes?"

"Hmm," Emma hesitated.

"It's a big ask, I know and I don't expect anything, so if you can't do it, that's fine, no hard feelings. But it'd be so romantic."

"Eh, I mean, I really shouldn't," Emma started.

"Aw, it's no problem. Like I said, it was a big ask and I totally understand if you can't do it. It's fine, don't worry about it."

"Well, you didn't let me finish. I really shouldn't but I will for my Alpha Alpha Kappa sister! Anything for love."

Maggie smiled, throwing her arms around Emma. "Oh, thank you, thank you! I can't tell you what this means to me!

And what it will mean to Henry! He'll be thrilled! I can't wait to see the look on his face when I tell him."

"Oh, I'll bet," Emma said. "I'm sure he'll REALLY appreciate you after this." Emma winked at her.

"Would tomorrow night work?" Maggie asked.

"Good for me. Only one who'll miss me is my cat. I'll let you in the employees' entrance on the side around 8 p.m."

"Aww, and I'm sure he'll miss you! Eight's great! We'll see you then! Oh, thanks so much, I'll make it up to you. I will. I promise!"

"Perhaps you could introduce me to tall, dark and handsome? Assuming he's single?" Emma asked.

Maggie hedged, "I'll find out for you." She winked at Emma. "He's Henry's friend, not mine," she lied.

"Well after my favor, if he's single, Henry should introduce us."

Maggie laughed. "He'd probably be happy to do that!"

"Good, tell him he owes me one while he's gazing into those big, brown eyes of yours over the mummies!"

"I'm sure that'll be the first thing that springs to mind at that moment," Maggie replied. "Anyway, I better get back before tall, blonde and handsome misses me too much."

"Can't have that!" Emma said, raising her hand to call the waitress for the check.

Maggie pulled her credit card from her purse.

"Let me just figure out half," Emma said. She pulled her phone from her purse.

"No, I won't hear it! My treat!"

"No way, my city, my treat!"

"MY treat," Maggie insisted. She put her credit card on the bill and waved to the waitress. "Call it partial payment for the favor."

"Okay, but this doesn't discount my favor. I don't want to

be introduced to the other guy. Again, who I'm sure is a very, very nice man."

Maggie laughed as the waitress took their check. "No, this is just a down payment. Believe me, I'll make it more than worth your while!"

Emma nodded as the waitress returned. Maggie signed the restaurant's copy, stuffed her card in her purse, and stood. The women exchanged goodbyes outside, hugging one last time before parting ways. Maggie hailed a cab, giving the cab driver Ollie's address. As the cab navigated to the apartment building, Maggie checked her phone for messages. She found one waiting from Henry: *Haven't heard from you in a bit, just checking in.*

Maggie smiled at the message, texting back that she was on her way to the apartment now. Before she reached the apartment building, Henry texted to tell her he'd left the door unlocked for her. As they arrived, Maggie paid for the cab, hopping out and climbing the stairs to the third floor. She continued down the hall to the end and let herself into the apartment.

Inside, she found Henry and Charlie arguing over options to enter the museum. Leo lounged on the couch, scrolling social media sites on his phone.

"... can't use C-4, you'll blow a hole into the whole bloody side of the building and call so much attention it won't matter what you're trying to steal," Charlie said.

"We don't have another option, do we?" Henry countered. "We've got no way in there. I can't pick the lock. We're stuck using brute force."

Charlie sighed, flinging his arms in the air. Maggie approached the table they leaned over. Annotated maps of the museum and notes were spread across it. "I have a way," Maggie announced.

Charlie glanced at her, unconvinced. "Welcome back, I'm

glad you're home, here, back, whatever," Henry greeted her. "What's your idea?"

"I'm almost afraid to hear it," Charlie mumbled.

"Well, I used my dinner with Emma to ask for a favor. I asked her if she could let us in for a private night tour of the museum. I told her my boyfriend was into this stuff and it'd be romantic for us to spend some alone time in the museum. And she agreed!" Maggie exclaimed. "I feel awful using her like that, but my uncle's life is on the line."

Charlie crinkled his brow. "So, she's just going to let you in?"

"Tomorrow night at eight!" Maggie said. Giddy excitement filled her.

He scratched his head. "You just... asked her?" Henry asked.

"Well, I mean, I played it up a bit. How important it was and how much it would mean. And we are sorority sisters, that helped."

"Well..." Henry paused. "Ah, I guess that's our in then. Do you think you can handle drilling a lock?" he asked, turning to Leo.

"Oh!" Maggie replied. "Oh, no. I didn't... I... I assumed you'd be going," she said to Henry. "So, I told her YOU were my boyfriend." Leo groaned, rolling his eyes, unimpressed by the twist of events. "I mean, I just assumed that would work best."

Henry smirked. "Right, you did good, Maggie. Well, this makes it a lot easier. I am capable of drilling the lock."

"Okay, so we have our in," Charlie said. "But now, how do we shield you from the cameras while you abscond with the precious cargo?"

"Can't you just do whatever you did in London?" Maggie asked.

"No, that won't work. The guards will know you're there. So, it wouldn't work if you just disappeared."

"Perhaps they'll think we left?" Maggie suggested.

"Unlikely and even if they did, they'll likely go checking and then what?" Charlie asked.

They stood in silence for a few moments, pondering the predicament. "Maybe there's a blind spot or something we can use. I'll check the cameras tomorrow morning when the museum opens. See if I can spot anything we can use where you could 'disappear' for a bit while I mask you on the other cameras."

"Good idea, we'll hope for the best and try to think of alternatives in case," Henry agreed.

Maggie nodded, proud of her contribution to the plan. She wandered over to the couch, plopping on it next to Leo. "How are you holding up?" she asked.

Leo didn't glance up from his phone. "I've been better. I've got a splitting headache from listening to those two argue about explosives for an hour."

Maggie yawned. "Perhaps we should try to get some sleep," she said. "Those cocktails are hitting me hard."

"Good idea," Henry chimed in. "I figured you could have the bed," he said to Maggie.

Maggie smiled at him. "Thanks. I will take you up on that. We can switch in a few hours…"

"Don't worry about it, princess. We'll manage," Henry said. He smiled at her.

"You don't want to build a pillow wall and share with her?" Leo asked.

Maggie rolled her eyes. "I'm heading to bed. See you in the morning."

"Sleep well," Henry said.

"If you get cold or want some company just yell for me, chicky," Charlie added.

"Don't hold your breath," Maggie answered. She disappeared through the doorway into the bedroom.

Maggie found the weekend bag in the room, changed clothes and prepared for bed. Maggie eyed the lumpy bed, determining at a glance comfort was not a virtue it possessed. Still, it would provide the most comfortable option.

Maggie stretched out on top of it. The heat from the day continued to make the apartment stuffy. She laid on her back, fanning herself. Sleep would not come to her. She didn't understand why. The events of the past several days and the intermittent sleep schedule should have exhausted her.

She rolled onto her side, staring out of the window. The city lights glittered through the glass. Perhaps it was the incredulousness of the situation that kept her awake. Perhaps it was the tension among the group.

Maggie glanced over her shoulder toward the living room. A light still shined from there. No sound came from the room. Maggie wondered if they fell asleep with the light on or if someone was still awake. She returned her gaze to the window, spending a few more moments contemplating her circumstances while admiring the city's lights.

After fifteen minutes, restlessness overcame her, and she rose from bed. The light was still on in the living room. She peeked through the door. Sprawled across most of the couch, Leo slept, his arms across his chest. Charlie curled on the remaining portion of the couch; his head propped on the arm. Henry sat at the dining table, cleaning a pistol while he continued to look over the notes.

Maggie shook her head at the scene. She plodded bare foot into the room, taking a seat at the table. "Aren't you supposed to be sleeping?" Henry asked. He glanced at Maggie.

"Aren't you?" Maggie countered.

Henry chuckled at her. "Just finishing up a few things."

Maggie glanced at the couch. "Tight quarters out here, huh?"

Henry nodded. "Yeah. Lover boy likes his space."

Maggie shook her head at Leo. "Want me to build a pillow wall?" she asked.

Henry chuckled again. "Thanks for the offer, princess, but I'll be just fine. You stretch out on that bed and get some sleep."

"You sure?" Maggie asked. "I don't mind."

"I am sure, Maggie. I don't want to cause any more strife between you and your beau. There's already enough tension."

Maggie smiled at him. "All right. I'm going back to try to get some sleep. See you in the morning."

"See you in the morning, princess."

Maggie sauntered to the bedroom. Before she stretched out to try to sleep, she grabbed a pillow. Returning to the living room she tossed the pillow onto the chair near Henry. "Least I can do is give you a pillow."

Henry nodded at her. "Thanks, princess. I appreciate that."

Maggie smiled, disappearing into the bedroom. She crawled into bed, laying on her side, choosing to face the living room door. The light went off within minutes. The room darkened around her. Maggie took a deep breath, closing her eyes. She drifted off to sleep.

CHAPTER 13

*M*aggie startled awake, gasping for breath. In her panic, she failed to recognize where she was. She fumbled, searching for the light. In the process, she knocked the alarm clock off the night table.

The lights flicked on overhead, blinding her. She shielded her eyes, glancing around as her heart returned to normal speed. "Maggie? Are you all right? What is it?" Henry asked. He rushed to the bed.

"Oh, ah," she paused, her eyes still adjusting to the light. "Nothing. Bad dream."

"I heard you scream. You sure you're okay?"

"Yeah," Maggie said. Her breathing and pulse began to settle. "Yeah, I'm okay. It was just a bad dream. When I woke up, I was disoriented, forgot where I was."

"With all that's happened, that's understandable."

"What time is it? Oh, I knocked the clock over," Maggie mumbled. She glanced at the clock strewn on the floor.

"I'll get it. Relax, Maggie," Henry said. He leaned over, gathering the clock from the floor and setting it on the night table. "There. It's four thirty."

Maggie nodded. "Sorry for waking you."

"It's fine. Do you think you can go back to sleep?"

Maggie took a deep breath. She nodded. "Yeah, yeah. I should be able to sleep. Sorry."

"All right. Lay back. You sure you're okay?" Henry asked.

Maggie nodded, smiling at him. "I'm sure, thanks."

"No worries. You know where I am if you need me." Henry switched off the light, leaving Maggie to sleep. Maggie settled into the bed, adjusting her pillow. Despite her breathing and heart rate returning to normal, Maggie remained unsettled by the dream. She reminded herself she was safe and wasn't alone. Leo, Charlie, and Henry were feet away from her. The idea comforted her enough to fall asleep.

Maggie slept well into the morning, awaking after nine. The sun already lit the city from high overhead, scorching the air. Maggie sat up, perching on the edge of the bed. She trudged to the living room and kitchen in search of coffee. Leo still slept on the couch.

"Good morning, princess," Henry said as she approached the kitchen. He handed her a mug of coffee. "Two sugars and cream just the way you like it."

"Thank you," she said, sinking into a chair at the table and sipping the coffee.

"And how do you like your eggs, princess?"

"Mm," she said, taking another sip of coffee, "you're cooking?"

"I am. Now, what's your request? Over easy, scrambled, omelet?"

"Scrambled," Maggie requested.

"Coming right up," Henry said. "Did you sleep okay after your nightmare?"

"I did, thanks."

"Nightmare?" Charlie asked. "Why didn't you call for me,

chicky. I'd have comforted you." He wiggled his eyebrows at her.

"That may have given me another nightmare," Maggie pronounced.

"Ouch," Henry chuckled. "Here we are." Henry placed a plate of eggs and toast in front of her.

"Wow, real food!" Maggie exclaimed. "I'm excited!" She picked up her fork to dig in as Leo slogged across the room, crumpling into a chair next to her. "Good morning, sleepyhead."

"What's so good about it?" Leo complained. "Ugh, my neck is stiff." He rolled his neck around, wincing in pain. "Is there coffee?"

"In the pot," Charlie said. He pointed to the appliance on the counter.

Leo stood and poured a cup. "Is scrambled all you make?" he asked Henry. "I'm not a fan."

"There's toast, mate," Henry answered.

Leo grabbed a slice as Henry dished another two plates of scrambled eggs for Charlie and himself. He and Leo sat down at the table. "These are delicious!" Maggie said. "Thank you!"

"You're welcome, princess."

They finished their breakfast and cleaned up. Maggie offered to wash the dishes since Henry cooked. Charlie set up his laptop. The museum would open in minutes and he wanted to view the angles of the cameras. Despite having a way to enter and exit the museum, they did not have a plan to procure the staff piece.

Henry assisted in the drying of the dishes. Maggie twisted Leo's arm to put them away. "How are we looking there?" Henry asked Charlie when they finished.

"Here are the cameras that cover the case," Charlie said. He pointed out several images on the display.

Henry settled in a chair next to Charlie. "Got a few of them." Maggie leaned over his shoulder.

"Yep," Charlie answered. "All different angles. There's no way we can cover what you're doing."

"No," Henry agreed. "One of the cameras will pick it up no matter what we do."

"Can't hide you in plain sight, so we'll need you two to 'disappear' somewhere. The question is where. Is there a spot where we can park you two for a bit where they won't be any the wiser that it's a recording? And what would you two be doing there for the approximate fifteen minutes you'll need?"

Maggie's phone chimed as they considered Charlie's questions. "It's a text from Emma," Maggie announced. "We're in. She's got us covered for our private date from eight to ten. She hopes that's enough time for us."

"Plenty of time," Henry said.

"Shouldn't we perhaps report Ollie's disappearance to the police here instead of all of this?" Leo questioned. "Let them sort it out."

"That's a great idea, if you never want to see Ollie alive again," Henry retorted.

Maggie gasped. She swallowed hard at the stark reality of the situation that faced them and her uncle. She fled the room, tears falling to her cheeks.

"Maggie! Maggie, wait!" Henry called after her.

"Good job, jerk," Leo said, following Maggie from the room.

Maggie collapsed on the bed, sobbing. She tried to remain optimistic, but hearing the harsh truth from Henry crushed her. Leo entered the room. "Don't cry, Mags," he told her as he leaned against the door jamb.

Maggie uncovered her face, wiping at her tears. "Sorry, it just upset me to hear that. To realize things are that serious.

To suppose Uncle Ollie is…" She broke down in tears again, unable to finish the sentence.

Leo perched on the edge of the bed, putting his arm around her. "Maggie, shh, come on. The guy's a total ass. He's just being a jerk."

"What he said was true. Uncle Ollie could very well be in a lot of trouble… or worse," she cried. Leo hugged her tighter, unsure of what to say to calm her.

Henry appeared in the doorway. He knocked on the door jamb. "Maggie?" he probed.

"Haven't you done enough damage?" Leo asked.

"It's okay," Maggie answered. She wiped her tears away. "I'm okay."

"It's okay not to be okay, Maggie," Henry said. He stooped in front of her and took her hands in his. "But I'm sorry I upset you with what I said. I didn't mean to come off so callous."

"Thank you, Dr. Phil. We don't need any more of your brand of help," Leo argued.

"You only told the truth," Maggie said. Her tears still flowed down her cheeks.

"No, I'm sorry. We can't go to the police, that is true, but I lashed out and spoke out of turn. Only because I was aggravated with Leo's ignorance."

"So, you were a jerk because I have a different opinion than you," Leo pointed out.

"That's the long and short of it," Henry answered. His eyes didn't leave Maggie.

Maggie glanced at him, sniffling. "Do you think Uncle Ollie is okay?"

Henry nodded. "I do. I think even if he's in trouble, he's alive because he's the best resource in the world on this stuff. So as long as no one has located Cleopatra's tomb, the odds are good he's still alive. They need him to get into it."

Maggie nodded, her bottom lip trembling. Henry retrieved a tissue from the bathroom, returning with it for Maggie. "Here, princess. No more tears, promise?"

Maggie dried her eyes, sniffling. She nodded, taking a deep breath. "I promise."

Leo, his arm still around her shoulders, pulled her closer. "That's better," he said. He kissed her on the forehead.

Maggie smiled at Henry, then turned to Leo and nodded. "Thanks," she said.

"Hey, I've got something in here if you are done playing white knights with the damsel in distress," Charlie shouted from the other room.

"Ready?" Henry asked.

Maggie nodded again. The group returned to the living room, joining Charlie at the table.

"What do you have?" Henry asked Charlie.

"This," Charlie pointed to the screen.

"Okay? What is it and how does it help us?" Henry inquired.

"Keep watching," Charlie suggested. As they watched the camera feed, a few people passed by. Then a woman passed through, heading toward the top of the screen. "There!" he said, pointing.

"Ah-ha," Henry said.

"Ah-ha what?" Leo asked.

"She almost disappeared." Maggie answered. "You can only see the bottom of her leg and she's not anywhere on any of the other cameras."

"One hundred points for the smart chicky," Charlie said. "There's a blind spot. Likely no exhibits there, so you could 'disappear' there for a bit. We could create a loop where it appears as though you're standing there, we'd see the lower portion of your legs and feet."

Henry compared the camera location to the map. "It's about two meters from the restrooms."

"Disappear into the bathroom for fifteen minutes?" Charlie asked.

Henry weighed the option.

"What if they suppose whoever disappears into the bathroom is sick? And they send help?" Maggie questioned.

"She's got a point," Henry said.

"So, what else would you be doing against a wall two meters from the restroom for fifteen minutes?" Charlie asked.

Henry pursed his lips, considering the question.

"Kissing," Maggie answered.

"What?" Leo asked, incredulous.

"I mean not actually kissing, you'll just see our legs but that's what they'll assume we're doing. We're supposed to be on a romantic date alone in the museum. Why wouldn't we take a few minutes to kiss?"

"Right, you two are making out against the wall," Charlie said. He nodded. "I'd buy it."

"Yes. I mean, we'll kiss on camera, back toward the wall and let you create a tape to loop that shows us still standing there. Then we'll circle back to the staff which isn't far from here and steal it and be on our way. In fact, we can put the cameras back to normal and show us walking out," Maggie outlined.

"This is the stupidest plan ever," Leo cried.

"Hey!" Maggie exclaimed. "It's not!"

Henry agreed. "It's ingenious, Maggie. It plays right into what they'll already be expecting."

Maggie grinned, proud of her accomplishment.

"If you are uncomfortable with any part of this plan, mate, I'll step in for you. I have the talent to pull it off," Charlie offered.

"I'll be just fine, thanks, mate," Henry answered.

Charlie shook his head. "If you get cold feet, just say the word." He returned to watching the screen.

"Okay, given the new plan, I should step in for Henry," Leo argued. Maggie gave a hearty chuckle. "What? It'll be easier to pull off for you if you're with me."

"You wouldn't even know how to start the drill," Maggie answered, still laughing.

Leo grabbed the drill from the coffee table. He pressed a button, raising his eyebrows at them. He frowned when nothing happened.

Henry relieved him of the drill. "That reverses the drill, mate," he said.

"Well, I'm sure if you tell me which button turns it on, I could turn it on," Leo countered.

Maggie continued to laugh at the scene. "Oh, Leo, just leave it. You wouldn't know what to do with it once you started it either. Just leave Henry do it before we're in more trouble than we are right now."

"So glad you'd rather kiss him than me," Leo complained.

"Oh, stop being a baby. It's just a quick kiss for the cameras. It's fake, it's nothing."

Leo raised his hands to signal surrender. "Fine, fine, whatever."

"Well, with that settled, we've got a good bit of time to kill," Henry said. "We should prepare for our next move. Once we have all three pieces, we need to decipher how they can lead us to the tomb."

"I saw a laptop in Uncle Ollie's bedroom," Maggie said. "We can do some research with that. And I'll go over his notebook to see if there are any references to finding it."

They spent the next several hours tracking down any references they could find to Cleopatra's tomb. A good bit of information existed, much of it contradictory. They parsed through the various theories and tried to cross-reference them with Ollie's notes. They considered the pictures they had of the supposed map from the golden scarab.

"Is any of this making any sense to you?" Maggie queried after hours of researching.

"No," Henry admitted, "we've narrowed it down to this thing could be anywhere."

"What about the map? Do you recognize it as anywhere in particular?"

"Nope," Henry answered. "Part of it seems familiar but the other parts don't correspond to anything when I try to match them to a map."

"Ugh," Maggie squealed. "This is so frustrating!" She tossed the notebook she was using onto the table, slumping in her chair.

"Somebody's 'hangry,'" Leo said.

"I am not 'hangry,'" Maggie snapped.

"Yes, you are. You're always frustrated and crabby when you're hungry," Leo said.

Henry checked his watch. "It's probably a good idea to get something to eat. We have three hours before we leave for the museum."

"I saw a takeout menu in the kitchen yesterday. Do you suppose they deliver?" Maggie asked, scurrying to the kitchen to get it. "Ah, they do!"

She read it over, sharing it with Charlie and Henry. She handed it to Charlie to continue to peruse after she made her selection. With everyone's selections made, Henry placed the order.

They made quick work of eating when the food arrived. Everyone was famished. When they finished eating, they had about thirty minutes before leaving to meet Emma at the museum. They prepared for the trip. Maggie changed clothes. She shifted items around in her purse, making room for the drill. Henry joked the drill didn't add much weight to the rest of the items.

Nervous butterflies filled Maggie's stomach as they proceeded down the stairs to the van. They would use a similar approach to the heist in London. Charlie would stay in the van, communicating with Henry via an earpiece. He would provide technical assistance from afar while Henry and Maggie were on site.

They piled into the van. Henry drove to a spot near enough to the museum to provide a quick exit, but far enough not to be suspicious. They left Leo and Charlie at the van after checking that the communication lines worked.

Maggie and Henry strolled to the museum. They were a few minutes early, so they took their time. As they approached the building, Henry asked, "Are you sure you want to do this? Last chance to back out."

"What? Back out? You can't get in without me!" Maggie answered.

"We'll go back to the drawing board and find another option. But that's fine. If you're not comfortable with this, we'll find another way. No questions asked, no problem."

"I'm fine," Maggie answered. Despite her weak knees and racing pulse, she was determined to see this through. "Now, let's go before we're late. We wouldn't want to miss our romantic date!"

"I've been looking forward to it all day." Henry laughed.

Henry took her hand, leading her to the side door where Emma informed them to meet her. He knocked on the door when they arrived. The door popped open.

"Hi!" Maggie said.

Emma grinned at her. "Hi! Come in!" Maggie and Henry entered. Maggie introduced Emma to Henry.

"It's a pleasure to meet you," Emma said, shaking his hand.

"Maggie is a very lucky girl. Well, you two, I've got you two hours. I told the guards you'd be here working on a special project and you'd let yourself out the same door. The door has a sensor on it, so it'll register you leaving. No need to notify them."

"Great. Aw, thanks so much for this," Maggie said. She hugged Emma. "We really appreciate it."

Henry chimed in, "Yeah, you've no idea how excited I was when she told me. I just love this museum and ancient Egyptology."

"You're welcome," Emma said. "Oh, and don't forget my other favor!" Emma whispered, winking at Maggie.

"I wouldn't dream of it. Like I said, I'll make it worth your while!"

"Okay, well I'm heading out for the night! Enjoy!"

They watched Emma disappear through the door they used to enter.

"Well, I suppose we should start our romantic tour," Henry suggested.

"I suppose so," Maggie said. Henry took her hand as they strolled hand-in-hand around the museum, pretending to inspect exhibits.

"So, what's this favor Emma mentioned?" Henry asked as they strolled around.

"Oh," Maggie laughed. "She asked to be introduced to Leo if he's single."

Henry winced. "Too bad he's not."

"Yeah, I'll feel bad breaking that to her. Especially given our ulterior motive."

"She'll likely be in a lot of hot water."

"I realize that. They'll probably fire her," Maggie lamented. "But I couldn't let Uncle Ollie down. We didn't have another way. I hope Uncle Ollie will hire her to work on Cleopatra's tomb. Assuming we find it... and him."

Maggie stared at the floor, upset washing over her. "What a mess this is."

Henry pulled her into a hug. "Hey, I realize you're upset about your friend. We will find Ollie and we'll make everything right with Emma."

Maggie leaned into him. "I sure hope so," she murmured.

"We will, I promise. And I never break my promises," Henry answered. He cupped Maggie's face in his hands. "Okay?"

"Okay," she nodded. "And I'm sure this scene is quite in line with what they are expecting." Maggie flicked her eyes to the ceiling.

Henry smiled at her. Maggie gazed into his eyes for a moment longer than she should have. "Ah, perhaps we should move on," she suggested after a moment.

"Right," Henry agreed.

They wandered to a few more exhibits. "So, Emma's a nice girl. After all this, perhaps I could introduce her to you. After the dust settles and she realizes Leo is my boyfriend, not you."

Henry smiled at her. "Nah, princess. She's not my type."

"Oh? Not your type, huh?" Maggie laughed. "What's your type?"

"Pretty brunette, big, sparkling brown eyes, happy-go-lucky personality, adventurous, quick-thinking," Henry answered, stopping near the spot where they planned to enact their disappearing act.

Maggie brushed off the comment, deciding he wasn't alluding to her despite the description fitting her. She smiled at him, nervousness overcoming her. She shook it off. She was acting ridiculous. The kiss meant nothing. It was just a show for the cameras to get them into position hidden against the wall. It gave them a reason to be there for a bit while Charlie masked them on the other cameras.

"Well," Maggie said. She glanced around. "I guess it's showtime."

"Kiss her, mate," Maggie overheard from Henry's earpiece as he leaned toward her. Maggie snickered as Henry rolled his eyes. "Note every detail so you can share it with me later."

"Ignore him," Henry whispered.

Maggie nodded. She leaned into Henry, closing her eyes as their lips brushed together.

"YES!" Charlie shouted in Henry's ear. "Go for it, mate. Kiss her real good."

"I can't..." Maggie said. She pulled back, holding in a laugh. "I'm sorry." She composed herself. "Okay, okay." She took a deep breath. "Ready, let's do this."

Henry nodded. "Next stop: the wall!"

He leaned in to kiss her again. He and Maggie backed toward the wall, their lips locked. Henry's earpiece crackled. "Okay, mate. Just stand still for about fifteen seconds and I'll grab the clip to loop."

"Sounds good, mate. Just give us the all clear when we're good to move."

"Yep. Don't stop kissing her on my account though, mate. I'll give a holler when we're ready." There was a noise Maggie couldn't distinguish. "Scratch that, mate. The boyfriend is not happy. Do not continue kissing the girl. Repeat, do not continue kissing the girl."

Maggie glanced up at Henry. They were in close quarters against the wall. "Shouldn't be much longer," Henry said. He brushed a lock of hair away from her face. Maggie nodded.

"And we're good on the recording. Hold tight while I loop it on their feed." They held their position as silence filled the air before the radio crackled back to life. "And... we're good on all feeds."

"Got it," Henry said, "we're heading back to the staff piece now." He pulled Maggie from the wall, directing her back to the staff piece. "We're here." He held his hand out as Maggie removed the drill from her purse. "Starting the lock now."

Henry began drilling the lock. Maggie paced in a tight square near the display case. "Relax, Maggie," Henry cautioned.

"Sorry," she said, grinding her pacing to a halt. "I'm nervous. Can't you go any faster?"

"Patience, princess. Any faster and we might break the bit or call too much attention to us." Maggie stood with her arms wrapped around her waist. She tapped her foot on the floor, a nervous tic. "Almost there."

"Thank God," Maggie said.

"And we're through." Maggie relieved him of the drill, stowing it back in her purse. Henry opened the case, removing the staff piece from the case. Maggie removed her sweatshirt, wrapping the staff in it. "We're good, ready for extraction," Henry said to Charlie.

They returned to their spot against the wall. Henry pressed close to Maggie. She heard Charlie through the earpiece. "Removing the loop in five, four, three, two and you're live again."

"Copy," Henry answered. They spent another moment there before Henry backed away. He stood for a moment while Maggie fiddled with the staff wrapped in her hoodie. After a moment, she stepped into view of the camera, holding her jacket as though she had just removed it. "Ready?" Henry asked, smiling at her.

"More than ready," she answered. Her legs felt like jelly as she stepped toward him.

"Straight to the door. You okay?"

"Yeah," she said breathlessly. "Can't wait until we're out of here and safe in the van."

Henry put his arm around her to steady her. "We're fine, Maggie. Just a few more steps. Relax."

They approached the exit. Henry pushed the crash bar to open the door. He guided Maggie through the door, stepping through after her.

As they exited into the night air, a shout came from across the street where they parked the van. "Maggie, Henry, run!" Charlie shouted as a masked man shoved him back in the van.

Henry grabbed Maggie's arm, pulling her around the building. As they rounded the corner, they ran into two more masked men. "Maggie, go, run!" Henry shouted to her.

CHAPTER 14

"*M*aggie! Run!" Henry instructed again.

Maggie stood dumbstruck for a moment, reluctant to flee into the night alone. "What? No!" Maggie said.

"Maggie, go!" Henry insisted. "They can't get all the pieces!"

Maggie's mind whirled. She remembered leaving one of the staff pieces in the van. She carried the other, and the scarab was still in her purse. Wide-eyed, she turned and fled around the corner away from the two assailants.

One of the men shouted in a language she didn't understand. She refused to glance back, running as fast as her legs could carry her. A scuffle sounded behind her. She continued to run. The footsteps following her ceased. Maggie continued running. Tears streamed down her face, but she didn't let up.

Maggie headed to the café where she met Emma. Before arriving, she slowed her pace, wiping her face. When she arrived, she asked to be seated inside away from the view of the street.

She ordered a ginger ale, explaining to the server she was waiting for a friend. With a shaky hand, she texted Emma: *Need your help... urgent... meet at café*

Her leg bobbed up and down as she waited for a response. Within minutes, Emma answered: *On my way... what happened?!?!*

Maggie answered: *Long story... but I need help desperately... please hurry*

Maggie's ginger ale arrived. She sipped at it as she fidgeted in her seat. Fifteen minutes passed before Emma arrived. To Maggie, it seemed time had stopped. When she saw Emma arrive at the door, she almost leapt across the table and bolted to the door to hug her.

Emma navigated to the table. "Maggie," she said as she sat down at the table, "what's wrong? What happened? Don't take this the wrong way, but you look terrible!" Maggie held back tears. "What is it? Is it Henry? Did something happen on your date?"

Maggie nodded. "Something happened all right. Oh, Emma, what I'm about to tell you will make you hate me. But you must understand, I had no choice in this."

"Oh, it can't be that bad, Maggie! What is it?"

Maggie swallowed hard before continuing. "My Uncle Ollie is in some trouble. He found a scarab he believes contains a map to Cleopatra's tomb. This scarab, when combined with the Staff of Pasherienptah, can also open her tomb. When he found it, a few less than admirable people wanted it. He sent it to me. That's how I became involved in all of this."

"All of what, Maggie?"

"Henry is a friend of Uncle Ollie's. We needed to secure the staff pieces to help find Uncle Ollie. So..." Maggie paused. "So, we stole the staff piece from the British Museum. And then we came here and we..." Maggie paused again. Tears escaped her eyes. "We stole the other piece earlier."

Emma's eyes were wide. "I know, I'm sorry. I'm sorry I used you, but we had no choice, Emma! Anyway, when we left, two of our friends were being kidnapped. Henry told me to run, and I did. I don't even know what happened to him. Oh…" Maggie sunk her head in her hands, sobbing. "Emma…" Maggie sobbed, grabbing Emma's hand. "I realize I've betrayed you and you owe me nothing but… I have nothing. I don't know where to go! I'm not familiar with this city. I have nowhere to turn. I'm alone here, my uncle is missing and now the person who was helping me is likely gone too, along with his associate and my real boyfriend, Leo."

Emma rubbed Maggie's shoulder. "Oh, Maggie," Emma said, "I'm shocked to hear about your uncle. And the rest of it, how terrifying. I'll help any way I can."

"Thank you," Maggie said. She pulled Emma into a hug. "And I am so sorry for the position we put you in. I… I'll speak with your boss when this is over. I'll have Uncle Ollie speak with him, too. I'll fix things, I promise."

Emma stopped her. "Maggie, Maggie, Maggie, let's not worry about that right now. Your life is in danger! We need to go to the police!"

"NO!" Maggie stated. "No, Henry said if we tell the police, we'll never find Uncle Ollie alive."

"And you trust him?"

"I do," Maggie said. She nodded. "Oh, I'm sick over this. Everyone is gone. Just gone." Shock set in as Maggie realized how alone she was.

"It's okay, it's okay. Let's get you out of here. We'll go back to my place and figure out a plan."

Maggie nodded. They paid their tab and Maggie gathered her things. Emma paused as Maggie scooped up her jacket with great care . "Wait… Is that… do you have…"

"The staff, yeah. I have it and the scarab. We need to be careful and make sure we're not followed. If we are, I don't know what we'll do. But with any luck we won't be."

"I... I just can't..." Emma began. "Sorry, this is very exciting for me! That staff is amazing!"

"Well, I only have one piece."

"It's still exciting."

They exited the café. Maggie's head swiveled, craning to see every dark corner as they hastened to Emma's apartment. Maggie was unaware of anyone following them, so they entered the apartment building after circling the block twice to be sure.

Maggie collapsed on Emma's couch after they entered. Exhaustion overcame her. The adrenaline she used to run from their assailants was waning. Emma retrieved a glass of water for Maggie. "Can I have a peek at the staff and scarab?"

Maggie nodded her head. "Sure. Perhaps you'll have an idea about what to do next, once you examine it." Maggie unwrapped the staff from her jacket. Emma's eyes went wide. With care, she picked it up, turning it over, studying every angle. "Here's the scarab." Maggie pulled the beetle from her purse.

As she did, she spotted her notification light blinking on her phone. She handed the scarab to Emma and removed her phone. Maggie toggled on the display as Emma studied the two objects. A text message awaited her. Tears sprang to her eyes. The message was from Henry's number: *You okay? Text when you get this.*

Maggie's thumbs flew across the virtual keyboard, sending a response: *I'm okay... where are you?????*

"These are amazing!" Emma said. "Oh, I'm sorry. I don't mean to sound so enthusiastic given your circumstances."

"It's okay," Maggie said. "Henry texted me. I just

answered. I'm just waiting to hear from him. At least he's okay!"

Emma opened her mouth to answer, but Maggie's ringing phone interrupted her. Henry's number appeared on the screen. Maggie's hand shook as she swiped to answer.

"Henry?" she asked.

"Maggie! Oh, thank God. Are you okay?" Henry asked.

"Yes, I am, I am. Are you okay?"

"I'm fine. Where are you? You didn't go back to Ollie's, did you?"

"No, no I didn't."

"Good, okay, good. We can't go back there. Where are you?"

"I'm with Emma. I'm at her place. She knows everything. Can you come here?"

"Yes, what's her address?"

Maggie handed the phone to Emma, asking her to provide Henry with her address. Emma did so, ending the call when she finished. Maggie hopped from the couch, pacing the floor, awaiting Henry's arrival. She bit her lower lip, stalking back and forth in front of the couch.

Within ten minutes a knock sounded on the door. Maggie raced to it, using the peephole to ensure it was Henry. She pulled the door open, throwing her arms around him. "Thank God," Maggie blurted. "Are you okay? Oh no! Your face! Henry!" Maggie cupped his face in her hands. He was bruised with a gash above his left eye and a split lip. He also sustained other injuries to his face and hands.

"I'm fine, princess," he said. He gave her a lopsided smile.

Maggie gave a worried glance. "Come in," she ordered, pulling him through the door. She locked it behind them. "Emma, do you have a first aid kit?"

Henry turned to Emma. "Really I'm fine. But thanks for helping Maggie," Henry said.

"No problem. She's one of my best friends from college. And, yes, I have a first aid kit."

"We're very sorry about misleading you," Henry apologized.

Emma shook her head. "No need to explain, Maggie already did. I understand why you did what you did. Let me get the first aid kit for you." Emma returned in a moment with her first aid supplies.

"I can do this," Emma began.

"No, I've got it, thanks," Maggie said. She grabbed the supplies from Emma. "You keep working on the staff and scarab," Maggie told her. "Sit here, let me take care of these," Maggie said to Henry.

"Really, I'm fine, Maggie."

"Sit there and let me take care of these, I said," Maggie insisted.

"I'd like to do a bit of research on a few things," Emma stated. "I'll be in the next room."

"Okay, thanks," Maggie answered. Maggie wet a cotton ball with antiseptic. She dabbed it lightly on the cut over Henry's eye. He winced as she patted it. "Sorry," she whispered. She bandaged the cut and moved on to treating his other wounds. She used the antiseptic on the larger cut on his lip, garnering another flinch from him.

He grabbed her hand, holding it. He gazed in her eyes. Maggie met his gaze. "Maggie, I..." Henry began.

Maggie broke eye contact. "When I ran, I..." Maggie interrupted him. A tear fell down her cheek.

"Maggie, it's okay. We'll find Leo and Ollie."

Maggie swallowed hard. "I'm just glad you're okay," Maggie cried. She threw her arms around Henry's neck. "I thought I'd never see you again!"

Henry was caught off guard. "Oh," he exclaimed. He wrapped her in his arms. "I'm fine, princess. I'm just fine.

Don't cry." Maggie released him, sniffling. "You know how I hate to see you cry." He cupped her face in his hands, wiping her tears away with his thumbs. Maggie grasped his hand in hers. She glanced at him. He gazed in her eyes.

Emma walked into the room. "Hey, do you..." Emma began. "Oops, I'm sorry, I'm interrupting."

"Ah, no," Maggie said as they scooted apart. Maggie began cleaning up the first aid supplies. "No, it's fine. We were just finishing up. What is it?"

"Oh, ah," Emma answered. Her voice sounded a bit flustered. "Did you ever discover if this scarab does, in fact, contain a map?"

"We did," Maggie said. "I've got pictures. Just a second, I'll send them to your phone." Maggie grabbed her phone and tapped a few times. "There we go."

"We didn't recognize this as anywhere in particular," Henry chimed in.

"Oh! This might help, too. I've got my uncle's notebook. We put together a set of notes to help us, but this might make more sense to you." Maggie pulled her notes from her purse and handed them to Emma.

"Ah! Thank you! I'll study these and see what I can figure out." She turned toward her bedroom. Before she left, she said, "Oh! Can I get you anything? Water, something to eat?"

"No, no, we're fine," Maggie assured her. "I'm pretty exhausted. If you don't mind, I'll just put my feet up and close my eyes for a moment."

"Not at all," Emma replied. "I'll get you a blanket and pillow."

"Aw, thanks, Emma."

Within a minute, Emma returned and unfurled a blanket for Maggie and handed her and Henry pillows. "You may not need the blanket, but I always like to have one to sleep."

"Thank you!" Maggie said. She threw it over her and

shoved the pillow behind her head.

"Okay, have a good nap." Emma switched off the light and exited the room.

Maggie settled back on the pillow. It was warm enough to not need the blanket, but Maggie still clung to it. She stared at the ceiling, lit by the lights outside the window. She glanced to Henry. She rolled on her side, facing him. "Are you awake?" she whispered.

"Yes," he answered, "it's only been a few seconds. Even I can't fall asleep that fast, princess."

"I felt so tired before, but the moment I closed my eyes, I couldn't sleep."

Henry's eyes opened to slits. He slid his eyes sideways to glance at her. "There's a shocker," he said. He rolled on his side to face her. "What's wrong, princess?"

Maggie took a deep breath. "We'll find them, right?" Maggie asked.

Henry took her hands in his. "We'll find them. I promise. We'll find Charlie and Leo and Ollie."

Maggie squeezed his hands. "Thank you." She paused a moment, still holding tight to his hands. "And you... you... they're okay, right? Do you think they're okay?"

Henry pushed a lock of hair from her face. "Yes. They won't hurt them. They need them."

"Need them?" Maggie asked.

"Ollie has the best knowledge of anyone about how to put the pieces of the puzzle together to find Cleopatra's tomb."

"And Charlie and Leo?"

"They'll be fine, too, princess. We still have two of the pieces they need to enter Cleopatra's tomb. If they want them, they'll keep everyone alive to get them."

"To bargain with?"

"Right."

"So, we'll be forced to give them everything to get them

back alive. But how can we trust them?"

"No, princess, we will be smarter than them. We won't give them anything until we are sure everyone is safe and back with us. And if we can avoid giving them anything, we will."

"But how…" Maggie began.

"Shh, Maggie. You're getting yourself worked up over things we can't control."

"But that's why I'm worked up! We have no control over this," Maggie cried. She pulled her hands away from his and flailed them in the air before slamming them at her sides.

Henry grabbed hold of her shoulders, turning her to face him again. "Maggie, you're tired and you're scared. And you have every reason to be scared, but we'll find them, and we'll get them back. Just focus on that, otherwise you'll drive yourself crazy."

Maggie glanced at him. "You mean I'll drive you crazy." She sighed.

"No, I mean you'll drive YOURSELF crazy. You aren't driving me crazy. You need some rest. You'll feel better, stronger, more ready to face this with some rest. Give Emma some time to work."

Maggie opened her mouth to protest, then closed it. She shook her head, then acquiesced within a moment. "Okay, I'll try to rest but I'm sure I won't. Too many thoughts keep racing through my mind. I just can't…" Maggie babbled.

"Maggie, Maggie, Maggie," Henry interrupted. "Shh. Put it out of your mind. Concentrate on something else, anything else. What's exciting for you after we find Ollie?"

"Um, what?" Maggie asked, the question surprising her.

"Tell me about something you're looking forward to when you get back home."

"Uh, I hadn't even considered it."

"Well, start considering it. Life will go back to normal.

What's exciting after this?"

"Uh... the Fall Ball," Maggie answered.

"The Fall Ball. Okay. What is the Fall Ball?" Henry asked. Maggie took a deep breath. Henry slipped his arm around her, pulling her toward him. Maggie nestled closer to him, pulling the blanket over her despite the warm weather.

"Ah, it's a big charity event we do every year in our town in late October. It's a great event, lots of music, dancing. They do raffles and a Chinese auction. It's fun and they do a red carpet and everything. And everyone gets dressed up, it's the event of the season, people plan their attire for months!"

"All dressed up, huh? I bet you love that!"

"I do, how did you guess?" Maggie laughed.

"Just a lucky guess! Now, I suppose you already have a dress? Been planning it for months?"

Maggie giggled. "Yes, I have a dress."

"And what's it like?"

"I suspect you don't care what it's like," Maggie said. She yawned.

"Humor me."

"Okay, I won't turn down talking about fashion. It's a beautiful auburn color, just like the leaves in the fall. Perfect match for the season."

"I'd expect nothing less from you, princess. What else?"

"It's one-shoulder, cinched around the waist with a full skirt. Nice and flowy when I walk. Or dance! Oh! And it has a ruffle along the one shoulder, it's a really pretty detail."

"I understand nothing you've just told me, but please continue."

"Um, well, it's a flowy chiffon fabric. And, oh, guess what? You'll never believe this!"

"I'll bet not!"

"I found shoes that match!"

"No! You're joking!"

"I'm not!" Maggie assured him. "They are black strappy sandals with one strap in the SAME color as my dress. It wraps around and up as an ankle strap. Now, I know what you're thinking…"

"Somehow I doubt that," Henry murmured.

"Shh, you're thinking: sandals? In October? But it'll not only be warm enough where we live, but they're very strappy so they're more like a shoe than a summer sandal."

"Ah, a very important distinction," Henry agreed as Maggie's head dropped onto his shoulder.

"Yes, yes, it is," she confirmed, yawning. "Very important."

"And are these flats or heels?"

"Heels! Are you kidding? I'm not a grandma. Flats, ha!"

"Okay, I'm learning. Flats are for grandmas. Although flats or heels I doubt anyone would mistake you for a grandma."

Maggie giggled again and yawned. "I sure hope not!"

"Going with Leo?"

"Ah, I assume so. We never talked about it. And now we can't…"

"No," Henry chided, "don't dwell on that. Go back to the outfit. Jewelry? How are you planning to wear your hair?"

"Oh, I'm planning to curl it a little and sweep it to one side with a big jeweled hair clip. And some dangly earrings."

"You'll be beautiful, Maggie."

"Aw, thanks," Maggie said. She smiled. "I can't wait." She closed her eyes, picturing her dress, her shoes, her entrance on the red carpet. Within seconds, she was fast asleep. Maggie slept for several hours. She dreamt of the event. Pictures snapped as she was escorted down the red carpet, her dress flowing as she danced, wrapping her arms around her date's neck. She leaned back to gaze into his eyes before kissing him. Her eyes met Henry's, and she tipped forward to kiss him.

CHAPTER 15

She awoke with a start. She had been attending the Fall Ball with Henry, not Leo. Her subconscious mind was playing tricks on her. It melded her conversation with Henry before falling asleep with their kiss earlier.

Henry roused next to her, his eyes slits. "What is it? Something wrong?" Henry mumbled.

"Huh? Nothing."

He sighed, closing his eyes again. "What time is it?"

Maggie checked her phone. "Almost six."

Henry opened his eyes and stretched. "I'll get up and see if Emma discovered anything in her research."

Maggie nodded. "I'll check on her." Maggie stretched and rose from the couch, stretching again. She followed the path Emma had last taken before they had fallen asleep. She found Emma in the bedroom, asleep. Emma was sprawled on her desk, notes underneath her. Her laptop was open but blank, long since in sleep mode. She clutched the golden scarab in her left hand, a pen in her right.

Maggie smiled at her sleeping form. It was a good time for her to use the bathroom to wash before waking Emma.

She emerged from the bathroom, hair still wet. As she stepped into Emma's bedroom, Emma awoke, bolting upright in her chair.

"Good morning," Maggie said.

"Ugh, good morning," Emma answered.

"Bet you've got a stiff neck."

"Ugh, yes," Emma agreed. "And all for nothing."

"Nothing?" Maggie asked.

"Yep, for nothing. I studied it most of the night and couldn't make sense of the notes. Ollie must be much smarter than me, I feel so stupid."

"Aw, give it a break. You've only looked at it for a few hours and you were tired! Uncle Ollie's studied this for a lifetime!"

"I'm going to shower, try to get this stiff neck loosened if you don't mind."

"Not at all! Do you have a hair dryer I could borrow?"

"Yep, I'll get it for you, just a sec!" Emma disappeared in the bathroom and returned with the hair dryer.

"Thanks!" Maggie plugged it in and dried her hair near the desk where Emma's notes were sprawled. She studied the documents. Her uncle had amassed a large amount of information about Cleopatra's tomb. His notes must contain a clue. What were they missing? A sinking feeling grew in the pit of Maggie's stomach. Neither she nor Henry had luck figuring this out, and Emma had made no headway either. What if they couldn't solve the puzzle?

Maggie shook her head. No, they had to solve it. Maggie finished drying her hair, unplugged the hair dryer and wrapped the cord around the handle, laying the hair dryer on Emma's bed. She returned to the living room, digging her makeup out of her purse. Using her compact mirror, she applied a little makeup. Henry was cooking breakfast.

"So, Emma didn't make much headway," Maggie told him as she applied her mascara.

Henry scrambled a few eggs. "No? We need to come up with a plan," he replied.

"What do you suggest?" Maggie asked. She brushed on a little beige eyeshadow.

"After breakfast," Henry insisted. "Come eat."

"Just a second," Maggie said. She put her final touches on her makeup. She checked the overall result in the compact.

Emma appeared in the living room. "Wow! You cook, too? It smells great. Is there enough for me to join?"

"Absolutely. Hope you like scrambled eggs."

"I love 'em!" Emma answered. She sat down at the breakfast bar as Henry served her a plate. Emma grabbed a fork, digging in.

"Maggie, come on," Henry said. He set another full plate out. "You look great. Now, come eat."

Maggie closed her mirror. "Okay, okay, coming!" She climbed onto the bar stool next to Emma.

"Mmm," Emma murmured. "You make one good breakfast!"

Henry leaned against the counter, eating his eggs. "Thank you!"

"Just so I'm clear," Emma said between bites, "Leo is your real boyfriend not Henry, right?"

"Uh, yeah, that's right," Maggie answered. She pushed her food around on her plate. "So, you didn't find anything in your review of Uncle Ollie's notes?" she added to change the subject.

"Not really. He's got a lot of things about the tomb itself, but not a lot about the location beyond rumor and innuendo. I hoped the pictures you sent of the map would help, but I didn't get very far with that either."

"We couldn't make head or tail out of it either," Maggie admitted.

"Perhaps I could ask around at work?" Emma inquired.

"You're going to work?" Maggie asked. She nearly choked on her food in shock.

"Well, yeah!" Emma answered. "I mean, it will seem suspicious if I don't show up. I may get fired, but if I don't show up for work, I will be fired."

"Good point. Well, I hope you don't get fired."

"So, should I ask around work?"

"I'd caution you about that, Emma. If they don't suspect you are involved already, it might seem suspicious if you make mention of the staff after the incident. Plus, I don't know who may be involved in this. I don't want you landing in hot water with these tomb raiders," Henry cautioned.

"Oh, didn't consider that. Either scenario, actually. Thank you so much," Emma said. She smiled at him. She batted her eyelashes as she handed her plate to him. Maggie pouted at the scene, annoyed. She wasn't sure why it bothered her, but it did. "Well, I guess I better finish getting ready for work."

Maggie slid off her stool, joining Henry on the other side of the counter. "I'll wash these," Maggie offered.

"I'll dry them," Henry added.

"Thanks." Maggie smiled at him. She filled the sink with hot, soapy water and began washing dishes. She rinsed and handed them to Henry to dry. "Any thoughts on a plan?" she asked.

Before Henry could answer, Emma appeared in the room. "Well, how do I look? Do I get the stamp of approval?" Emma twirled around in her outfit.

Maggie opened her mouth to answer before realizing Emma directed the question to Henry, not her. Maggie swallowed hard, returning to her dish washing.

"Good enough for government work, as they say!" Henry laughed.

Emma gave a nervous giggle. "Well, wish me luck! Fingers crossed I don't get fired!"

"Good luck!" Maggie yelled over her shoulder.

"I'll text you!" Emma called as she left the apartment.

Maggie took her frustration out on the dishes, slamming them into the dish drainer for Henry to dry.

"Yikes! What did that poor dish do to you, princess?"

Maggie finished the last dish, spinning around and grabbing a towel to dry her hands. "Nothing. Just more tired than I realized, I guess."

"Didn't sleep well on the couch?"

"Should we stay here? Perhaps we should leave a note and get out of here. Leave Emma out of this as much as possible." Henry smirked at her. "What?"

Henry shook his head. "Nothing. You're right, we should involve her as little as possible." Maggie smiled to herself, nodding. "But we may need her. Neither of us has any leads on how to move forward."

Maggie sighed. "Well, she didn't have any leads either!" Maggie contended. "She was more concerned about how her outfit looked," she muttered, crossing her arms. Henry continued to smirk at her. "What? Why are you giving me that look?"

"No reason. Listen, you're upset. Why don't you sit down and put your feet up and rest a bit? I've got a few calls to make, then we can talk about a plan." He guided Maggie to the couch, sitting her down. He propped her feet on the coffee table. "There you are, nice and comfy. Want your blankie?"

"No, I'm fine," she answered. She gave him a demure smile.

"All right," Henry said. "I'll be right back. My turn for the shower and to make a few calls." He turned toward the bedroom.

"Henry?" Maggie said.

Henry turned back toward her. "Yeah?" he answered.

"Thanks," she said. She settled back onto the couch with a smile.

"You're welcome, princess," Henry said. He grinned at her. He disappeared into the bedroom, pulling his shirt off as he went.

Maggie laid her head back on the pillow, sighing. "What is wrong with you, Maggie?" she whispered to herself. Was she stressed from the entire situation? Why was she so short with everyone? It must be stress, she assured herself. Lack of sleep was taking its toll. Worry for her uncle, Leo, and even Charlie disturbed her, causing her to act out. She'd never been this touchy before.

She rolled onto her side, glancing at the empty pillow next to her. She recalled their conversation last night. Henry had taken her mind off her stress and lulled her into a calm, easy state that allowed her to fall asleep. She smiled at the memory, reaching out to touch his pillow.

Her mind turned to the current situation. They had found no traces of Uncle Ollie since arriving in Egypt. Now, Leo and Charlie were gone, forcibly taken right in front of her eyes. Tears formed in her eyes as she pictured their panicked faces the last time she had seen them. Alive, her mind added, the last time she had seen them alive.

Tears rolled down her cheeks as she dwelled on the last statement. She recalled her last dinner with Leo at her favorite restaurant. The silly argument they had over his intentions seemed so petty at this moment. She recalled how angry she had been, how she stalked out of the restaurant. Maggie bit her lower lip as more tears spilled onto her cheeks. It seemed like the incident was so long ago, like it was ancient history.

Ancient history, something about that statement rung in Maggie's head. "That's it!" Maggie exclaimed. She leapt from the couch, grabbing her phone and hurrying into Emma's bedroom. She raced to the desk where the laptop still sat open with its black screen. Maggie rubbed a finger on the touchpad, bringing the laptop to life. The screen showed a map of Egypt. Maggie toggled her phone's display on, pulling up the picture of the scarab's map.

Maggie navigated to the search bar, requesting a map of ancient Egypt rather than modern-day Egypt. She didn't expect them to look noticeably different, but she figured the subtle differences between how the maps were drawn might provide the correct context for the scarab's map. Maggie compared the shadow map on her phone to the cities listed on the ancient map. A smile spread across her face. She smacked her hand on the desk in celebration.

"Gotcha!" she shouted.

"Oh, Maggie!" Henry shouted. "I didn't realize you were in here."

"Sorry, but I..." Maggie said as she turned to face him. "Oh! Sorry! I didn't realize you were... half-dressed." She spun to face the computer as Henry buttoned his jeans and pulled on a shirt.

"Aren't you supposed to be resting?"

"Yeah, I was just doing a little research on an angle that popped in my head while I was trying to rest."

"And what idea was that?" Henry asked. He leaned over her shoulder to peer at the computer screen.

"Oh!" Maggie jumped as she realized he was standing behind her. "Well..." She cleared her throat. "Everything was rolling around in my mind and I was dwelling on stuff and whatever.

Anyway, I was reflecting on the last date Leo and I were on and it felt like it was a million years ago. Like it was ancient history. And it just hit me! All the maps we've studied were modern-day maps. We needed to look at a map of ancient Egypt."

"But the country hasn't changed THAT much, right?"

"Well, the layout of the major cities is different. See?" Maggie pointed to the screen. She positioned both maps side-by-side.

"Ah, I see what you mean, yes."

"And compare it to the picture we took of the scarab's map." Maggie held it up next to the laptop. "It's almost an exact match!"

"Pretty damn close, yeah."

Maggie smiled at him. "We'll just need to follow the path marked, based off these landmarks!"

Henry returned her smile. "Maggie, you are a genius!" he said. He squeezed her shoulders and kissed the top of her head. "Excellent job! Brains must run in your family!"

Maggie beamed. "So, what's our plan?"

"We've got two of the pieces to open the tomb. The third, unfortunately, isn't in our possession any longer."

"Perhaps we can get away without it," Maggie suggested.

"I'm not sure, but the logical next step is to head to the tomb. I've got some calls to make. I will make our arrangements to travel." He picked up his cell phone, giving Maggie a rub across her shoulders and another kiss on her head.

Maggie turned back to the desk, finding a pen and gathering her notes. She jotted down several notes, comparing the scarab's map with the ancient map. Maggie glanced around the room, hoping Emma had a printer. Not seeing one, she took a picture of both maps on her cell phone.

Maggie spent a few minutes ordering the notes from her uncle's journal. Given the circumstances, she also photographed each page of her notes. As she studied them, her phone chimed. The notification showed a text message from Emma. Maggie opened the app and read Emma's message: *Place is buzzing with police... so far no one's said anything to me... will keep you updated.*

Maggie typed back: *Good... hope you're not in any trouble... keep us informed!*

She finished snapping pictures of the notes. Guilt coursed through Maggie as she recalled her poor behavior this morning when her friend showed interest in Henry. She had landed Emma in a world of trouble, used her, lied to her, and then became jealous when she showed interest in a single man. Maggie reasoned her jealousy sprung from an irrational fear of not finding Ollie and Leo. Perhaps she assumed any distraction of Henry's attention meant they were less likely to find everyone. Yes, that must be it, she decided.

Maggie received another text from Emma, diverting her thoughts: *Talked to the guards... played dumb... they said the robbery must have happened after the two of you left... said they had eyes on you two the whole time so they know it didn't happen then! Fingers crossed we're in the clear!*

Maggie texted back: *Great news! Keep us posted... working on next steps now... will keep you posted.*

Emma responded: *Don't do anything without me... I've got my eye on that fake boyfriend of yours!*

Maggie read the message and clicked her phone shut, shoving the irritation to the back of her mind. She reminded herself she only experienced these emotions because of the stress she was under. Perhaps it was Emma's light-hearted preoccupation with scoring a boyfriend, despite the circumstances. However, to be fair, Emma hadn't lived through the past two weeks as Maggie had. She had only just become involved; it was easy for the seriousness of the situation to escape her. Maggie returned to studying the notes.

Henry returned a moment later. "I got a picture of the

maps and I jotted down some notes of what we found. How did the calls go?"

"Good, we should be able to head south this afternoon and be ready to head into the desert tomorrow or the day after if everything comes together."

"Do you suppose we'll find everyone before then? Get that third piece back?"

Henry sighed. "No, I doubt it. But we WILL find them, Maggie."

Maggie nodded. "I trust you. But the plan is to locate the tomb, correct?"

"Right. My hope is we'll find them along the way."

"But they don't have the map. How could they find it?"

"As bad as this sounds, I hope they'll find us." Maggie swallowed hard as the realization hit her. Their last encounter still terrified her. "This time it'll be on our terms, Maggie," Henry added to reassure her.

She nodded. "Right. Okay. Well, I guess we should get ready to go. Oh, we don't have any of our stuff."

"We will need a few things. We should do your favorite thing, princess: shop."

"Funny. Except shopping with you is far from fun." Maggie stood from the desk, making her way to the living room. She collected her phone and purse.

"I'll make it up to you one day."

"Oh, shopping spree where I get to buy more than yoga pants and t-shirts?"

Henry nodded. "I'll even let you buy heels instead of sneakers."

"You've got a deal. Oh, can I ditch the drill from my purse?"

"Do you mind keeping it?"

"It's heavy. Aren't we coming back here? We could pick it up then," Maggie suggested.

"I'd rather we didn't return here, so get everything now."

"Oh, umm, okay. Sure, give me a second to get everything in here."

"I'll carry your purse for you, princess," Henry said. He winked at her.

"Thanks," Maggie answered. "Should I text Emma?"

"What for?" Henry asked. He collected his jacket from the chair.

"She wanted to go with us. She'll want to know we're leaving this afternoon."

"Leave her a note. She'll get it when she gets back. She's not going with us. I assume since she's not back, she didn't get fired."

"She didn't. She said security was sure it happened after we departed because they had eyes on us the whole time."

"Guess Charlie's trickery worked."

"Guess so," Maggie answered. She grabbed a notepad she found near Emma's refrigerator and a pen. "She'll be so disappointed when she gets this note."

"Had a burning desire to travel into the desert, did she?" Henry joked.

"Had a burning desire to get to know you better is more like it," Maggie cracked. "Plus, I'm sure finding Cleopatra's tomb didn't hurt her interest."

"Hmm, well, it wouldn't matter on the first point if she went or not."

"No?" Maggie asked while finishing the note to Emma.

"No, I already told you. She's not my type. Finished?" he asked as Maggie tore the top sheet from the notepad.

"Yep," Maggie answered. She secured the note to the fridge with a magnet.

"Let's go," Henry said. He grabbed her purse.

"That bag really clashes with your outfit." Maggie laughed.

Henry chuckled as they exited the apartment. As they shopped for suitable clothing, two rucksacks and a few other items, Henry informed Maggie of their travel plan. They would travel south on the train to Luxor, meet Henry's contact and prepare to travel into the desert in search of the tomb.

They stopped at a café for an early lunch before their train departed. Maggie checked her phone after they ordered. She found two text messages waiting from Emma. The first read: *One of the exterior cameras caught two masked men running away from the museum... they are the presumed robbers... was shortly after you and Henry exited, they figure they used your exit to enter, grab the staff and leave when the guards weren't watching the screen.*

The second message read: *Hope everything is okay... haven't heard from you*

Maggie relayed the messages to Henry. "I'm worried," Maggie said.

"About what?" Henry asked after taking a sip of his water.

"Emma. What if they track this to us or think we were involved? What if the tomb robbers come after her?"

"It'd take them a few steps to work out you two are acquainted. I hope by then their attention is focused in southern Egypt."

"What if it's not? Henry, I can't be responsible for another person disappearing or worse!"

Henry considered her statement for a moment. "It's a risk to take her, too. We can't guarantee she'll be any safer with us than she will be here. In fact, she may be at more risk with us than here."

"No, she's more at risk here alone. With us, at least she has us, well, you to protect her from harm."

"All right, all right. If it makes you feel better, we'll take her. Text her, tell her she has one hour to meet us at the train station if she wants to go."

Maggie nodded, smiling at him. She grabbed her phone and texted the message to Emma. "Thank you," she said when she finished. She grabbed Henry's hand and gave it a squeeze.

"You're welcome, princess." He squeezed her hand, leaning forward toward her.

Maggie's phone chimed, and she pulled her hand away to check her messages. Emma had a rambling message to her: *OMG! Okay, I'll tell them I'm sick and need to go home... hopefully that'll work... also will explain me being absent for a few days... I need to pack... Just an hour? Gosh, I hope I make it!*

Maggie answered, telling her to be as quick as possible and pack a few light items in a backpack as they would be traveling into the desert. Within ten minutes, Emma answered, saying she was home and rushing to pack a few items before going straight to the train station.

Maggie and Henry finished their lunch with no other messages from Emma. After eating, they walked to the train station. Henry purchased three tickets for their journey south. Maggie texted Emma to tell her they arrived at the station and to arrange a meeting spot. They waited for about ten minutes before Emma arrived, spotting them across the open hall. She carried a backpack and had changed from her work outfit to shorts, a tank top, and a blouse.

"Whew, glad I made it," Emma said as she approached them.

"Me too," Maggie said. She hugged Emma. "And I'm so glad you're not in any trouble at work! Sorry for the short notice, everything happened so fast!"

"No problem, thanks for including me," Emma said. She smiled at Henry.

"You should understand the danger here," Henry advised her. "This isn't a pleasure trip."

"No, no, I understand. The desert is a dangerous place," Emma replied.

"The desert is the least of our worries. The tomb raiders are the real threat. If you want to bail, stay here where it's less likely you'll run into them, you need to decide now."

"Right, of course," Emma nodded. "I understand, but I want to go."

Henry nodded his head. "All right," he agreed. "Then let's go. Train leaves in ten minutes."

"I'm glad you came," Maggie confided to Emma as they walked to the platform. "I worried about you staying here, about someone connecting us. I guess you're in danger either way though."

Emma eyed Henry. "Better to be with friends," she said.

Maggie nodded her head in agreement as they stood on the platform waiting for their train. Within minutes, the train whooshed into the station, squealing to a halt in front of them. "Come on," Henry directed.

"Please tell me we're not riding in the baggage car," Maggie joked.

"How d'you know?" he joked back. "No, no. This time I think you'll be happy, princess." They boarded the train, and Henry led them to their seats.

"First class? You're kidding?" Maggie exclaimed.

"You must be rubbing off on me," Henry said. "This is us." Henry motioned toward two seats. "And yours is there," he said, pointing to a single seat across the aisle.

"Oh, right," Emma said. She slid her backpack off and stepped into the seat across the aisle.

"You have a nice window seat," Henry told Emma.

"Thanks," Emma answered. She glanced out the window.

"And you, princess, can also have the window," Henry said

to Maggie. "There're some great views as we leave the city. You'll enjoy it."

"Thanks," Maggie answered. She slid into the window seat. She glanced out of the window. "When will we arrive?"

"About ten thirty."

"Ten thirty?! Boy, am I glad you sprung for first class," Maggie said.

"I almost got you a seat in the baggage car, but I figured ten hours might be too long to lean against a box."

"You figured right," Maggie agreed.

"He's joking about sitting in the cargo space, right?" Emma joined in the conversation.

Maggie leaned over Henry. "Unfortunately, not," she said. "Big spender over here has had me on not one but TWO cargo planes on this trip alone."

"You're kidding," Emma said. She glanced between the two of them.

"I'm not," Maggie answered. "And I've got the sore butt to prove it!"

"Ah, you loved it, princess! Didn't you say you found it exciting?"

"I didn't! Must have been the last girl you dragged into an adventure who expressed that sentiment." Maggie laughed.

"Oh, you're one of those, huh? A rogue! Always dragging women into adventures with you?" Emma asked.

Henry laughed. "Me? No, never. Maggie's the first girl who's gotten dragged into an adventure with me. Although she did the dragging, I promise," Henry answered. "And as for you," he announced, turning to Maggie, "nothing but the best this time, princess."

Maggie leaned back, slouching a bit in her seat as the train pulled out of the station.

CHAPTER 16

*T*he city faded away and after a brief stop in Giza; the scenery gave way to green fields dotted with mud-brick houses. The train followed the Nile Valley to Upper Egypt.

By late-afternoon, Maggie began fidgeting in her seat. Emma pulled a sweater over her blouse. The train was cooler than expected. Maggie dug her hoodie from her knapsack and shimmied into it. "I'm cold, too," she called to Emma.

Emma pulled a jacket from her bag, draping it over her legs. Maggie wrapped her arms around herself, rubbing them. "Still cold, princess?" Henry asked.

"Yeah, it's freezing in here!" Henry grabbed his jacket, offering it to Maggie. "Thanks," she answered, accepting it and draping it over her legs.

Within an hour, a dinner meal was served. They ate and discussed the change in scenery. When they were finished, Maggie checked Henry's watch. "Ugh, it's still forever until we get there!"

"Yep. Perfect time for a nap," Henry suggested.

Maggie yawned. "I guess," she agreed. Her full stomach

and lack of sleep made her tired. She stretched in her seat and squirmed to get comfortable. Henry pulled his hat over his eyes, slouching in his seat. Emma glanced at them before nestling into her seat for a nap, too.

A jolt awoke Maggie as the train lumbered over the tracks. Her eyes opened to slits. She glanced around, noting Emma was also awake across the aisle. "What was that?" she murmured.

"Mmm, nothing, princess, just the bumpy train," Henry answered. His eyes never opened. "Go back to sleep." He looped his arm around her shoulders, drawing Maggie closer to him.

"Mm-kay," Maggie mumbled. She laid her head on his shoulder. Within moments, she was asleep. Henry leaned his head on hers, exhaling deeply as he relaxed back into sleep. Emma wriggled in her seat, pushing her backpack against the side of the train to prop her head up.

Maggie and Henry slept for most of the rest of the trip. Henry awoke about thirty minutes before they reached Luxor. He glanced at Maggie, who still slept snuggled against him. Emma smiled at him as he glanced toward her.

"Couldn't sleep?" he asked her.

"No. Not since the bump that woke everyone. I just couldn't get comfortable."

"That's too bad. Looks like Maggie's still sleeping."

"Yeah, she looks nice and comfy there."

"She does, doesn't she? Sleeping like an angel," Henry said. "I'll wake her in a few minutes. Have you been to Luxor before?"

"Once when I first arrived here. Then work got busy. I never made it back. It's exciting to come back. How about you?"

"Oh, sure, I've been here loads of times," Henry answered.

"So, you're from Australia?" Emma asked.

"Yep, accent gave me away, did it?"

"Sort of, yeah," Emma giggled. "It's cute." She gave him a coy smile.

Henry stared straight ahead, avoiding eye contact with Emma. "Thanks," he answered. Emma opened her mouth to say something, but Henry beat her to it. "I should wake Maggie," he said, cutting off her next statement.

"Oh, right," Emma agreed.

"Maggie, Maggie," Henry cooed as he rubbed her shoulder, pulling her from her slumber.

"Hmm?" she asked groggily. "What?"

"We're almost there. Time to wake up."

"Mmm, okay," she said. Maggie opened her eyes without moving. She smiled at Emma across the aisle.

"Good morning," Emma said.

Maggie yawned. "Good morning," she answered. "Did you sleep?"

"Not since the bump heard 'round the train," Emma admitted.

"Aw," Maggie said, stretching and sitting up. "That stinks. I slept."

"I noticed," Emma said. "You looked quite comfy."

"Oh, I was," Maggie answered. "You should have used your backpack to prop you up."

"Oh, I tried. It was too lumpy," Emma said. She poked at the bag.

"Same trouble here," Maggie giggled. She poked at Henry.

"Oh, lumpy, am I? We'll see who lets you sleep on them next time," Henry joked. He poked back at her. Maggie folded Henry's jacket, handing it back to him while dodging his pokes.

"I'm next in line for that pillow if she doesn't want it," Emma joked. Her comment provided an awkward end to the conversation.

A few minutes later, Maggie asked about the plan when they arrived in Luxor. Henry informed the ladies they would meet a contact of his who would provide them with a place to stay for the night. Depending on the supplies his contact collected, they may be able to leave tomorrow in search of the tomb.

The train ground to a halt, its brakes screeching. They gathered their things, exiting from the train to the platform. Henry glanced up and down, slinging his bag over his shoulder. "Come on," he urged. He grabbed Maggie by the hand. Maggie grabbed Emma's arm, leading her along with them.

Henry led them from the platforms to the lobby. They waded through other passengers and locals clamoring to take them to a hotel or offer them a room. As they crossed the lobby, Maggie kept a tight hold on both Henry and Emma. Henry approached a tattooed man with dark hair and dark eyes.

He smiled as they approached. "Henry, my friend," he said, his Egyptian accent apparent. "You made it."

"Tarik, good to see you, mate."

"What a lucky man, you did not tell me your traveling companions were so lovely."

"Oh, thank you!" Maggie answered. She grinned at Tarik.

"Ah, this is Maggie," Henry said. He put his arm around Maggie's shoulders. "And this is Emma." He pointed to Emma. Emma waved.

"Maggie! You are the niece of Dr. Keene, correct?"

"I am, yes!"

"A pleasure to meet you. I was sorry to hear about Ollie's troubles. But we will find him. You are no doubt tired from your journey?" he asked. He motioned for them to follow him out of the station.

"We caught some sleep on the train, but I'm sure the girls would like a bed and more than a nap."

"I have a place. My car is just here." He pointed toward a line of cars. They climbed into Tarik's car. Henry took the front seat with Tarik driving, leaving Emma and Maggie in the back seat.

"How are we looking for tomorrow?"

"Looking good. I have a couple of things to arrange. I expect to have everything prepared by tomorrow evening."

"Great. We can leave the day after. I need to make myself visible, see if I can pick up a tail."

"I've already laid the groundwork. If they have ears in the city, they should realize you're coming."

"Your place is safe until we're ready to move?"

"Very. But I must tell you, Henry, the land you spoke of… there is nothing there. I checked maps, ancient and modern, satellite images, all of it, I found nothing."

"The scarab tells a different story," Henry answered.

"We shall see, my friend."

"Indeed, we shall," Henry agreed.

Despite the late hour, traffic still congested the narrow streets. After twenty minutes, they made it to Tarik's building. The group climbed the stairs to the third floor and followed Tarik down the hall to the flat. It was small but suitable for their needs. Tarik pointed out a doorway leading to the bedroom. Henry suggested Emma and Maggie try to get some more sleep, stating he would take the couch and leave them to share the bed.

Emma and Maggie headed to the bedroom, finding a double bed in the middle of the room. Maggie stretched out on the side nearest the door while Emma curled up next to her. "Reminds me of the sorority days," Emma said.

"Yeah," Maggie agree. She smiled at Emma. "Except we usually fell asleep giggling about the boys we met at a party instead of due to exhaustion from a ten-hour train trip after we robbed a museum."

"Ha, yeah," Emma admitted.

Maggie rolled on her side, facing Emma. "Perhaps we can recreate at least some of our sorority days to relax us into sleep."

"Did I miss a party?"

"No, but what about Tarik?"

"What about him?" Emma asked.

"He's kind of cute," Maggie answered.

"Eh," Emma hedged.

"You don't agree?" Maggie asked.

"I didn't pay that much attention, I guess," Emma said. She rolled onto her back to stare at the ceiling.

"Come on! Where were you looking? Those dark eyes, so soulful and dreamy!"

"Mmm, I guess I was too busy staring into those dreamy blue eyes of our Australian friend! And what were you doing checking out those dark eyes when you've got tall, dark and dreamy already?"

"A girl can look, can't she?"

Emma considered her statement before swinging back to face Maggie. "I guess so. So, what's tall, dark and dreamy like?"

"Leo? Oh, he's... he's fun! He lives life large, and he's always ready for fun."

"Well, he sounds... fun," Emma said. She laughed. Maggie laughed with her.

"So, tell me, what's the skinny on Henry? I want to learn everything!"

"Umm," Maggie hesitated. She rolled onto her back to stare at the ceiling as Emma had moments ago. "I don't know much. He's friends with Uncle Ollie. I guess Uncle Ollie sent him to make sure nothing happened to me after he sent me the scarab. I don't know him that well."

"He seems protective of you," Emma probed.

"Probably because he's friends with Uncle Ollie."

"Right. So what's he like? I bet he's sweet."

"I'm not sure," Maggie answered. She faked a yawn. "Oh, I'm getting sleepy, you?"

"Not really. Well, what's he like then?" Emma pressed.

"You didn't sleep that much on the train. I'm surprised you're not tired!"

"Well, I didn't have a hunky guy holding me tight. I may have slept better if I had."

"I'm sorry your seat wasn't that comfortable. Anyway, uh, should we try to get some sleep?"

"Right after you tell me what Henry's really like. He seems so sweet."

Maggie sighed, preferring not to continue the conversation but realizing Emma's insistence made that impossible. "Uh, it's all been such a whirlwind, but I guess he is, yeah. He's understanding and calming. I guess he's used to this kind of stuff. He was very understanding when I tried to run away from him."

"You ran AWAY from him? Girl, I'd be running toward him for sure!"

"Yes! It was all very confusing at first. I mean..." Maggie rolled onto her side to face Emma before continuing. "One minute I'm at the museum in Rosemont. I walk out and next thing I'm being thrown in the back of a van and driven somewhere. Turns out it was Henry who 'kidnapped' me. Then Henry tells me this whole story about Uncle Ollie sending him and I trusted him. And things just spiraled from there. Someone attacked us and shot at us, then we flew to London and he takes me to this locker full of weapons, passports and equipment. I panicked!"

"And you ran away?"

"Not right then, but later I did. At the hotel in London, I told him I was going to get something to eat and took off."

"Did you go back? How'd he find you?"

"He realized as soon as I went for the door, I didn't get very far before he caught up to me and dragged me back to the hotel room."

"Dragged? Wow, did you fight?"

"Yes, dragged. Kicking and screaming! Well, muffled screaming."

Emma seemed engrossed in the story. "And then what?" she prodded.

"He told me the story about how I got the scar on my arm and I realized he must know Uncle Ollie. He was very nice about it. Very sweet."

"Aww, I bet!"

Maggie yawned again. "Anyway, that's about all the information I have. Time for bed!"

"Okay, okay. I'll let you off the hook. I'll take pleasure in finding out more firsthand." Emma winked and giggled.

Maggie gave her a fake laugh before she rolled over to face away from her, closing her eyes and pretending to go to sleep. The bed jiggled as Emma rolled over to find a more comfortable spot. Within moments, Maggie heard rhythmic breathing indicative of someone asleep.

She opened her eyes, glancing around the darkened room. Craning her neck, she glanced at Emma, asleep with her back toward Maggie. The events she discussed with her earlier flooded through her mind. This experience had been unbelievable. Uncle Ollie, Leo and Charlie were all missing, held against their will. Upset overcame her and tears formed in her eyes. She shook her head, refusing to cry. She took several deep breaths, blinking her tears away.

After a few moments, she gave up on sleep. She stood and tiptoed from the bedroom to the living room. Maggie leaned against the doorway, peering into the room. She did not spot

Tarik, only Henry, sitting on the couch, his feet propped on the coffee table.

Maggie wanted to race over to the couch and sit near Henry. She wanted to feel close to someone who would tell her everything would be okay. Her upset grew instead of diminishing. She glanced back toward the bed. There was no sense in returning to the bed, she wouldn't be able to sleep.

An armchair sat near the couch. Maggie snuck to the chair, easing into it. "Can't sleep, princess?" Henry asked as she stretched back into the chair.

She jumped a mile. "Will you stop doing that?"

"I will when you stop sneaking up on me," Henry answered.

"I wasn't sneaking up on you."

"You're supposed to be sleeping, not slinking around the living room."

"I'm not slinking. Anyway, I couldn't sleep."

Henry patted the couch next to him. Maggie crawled over from the chair. "Dwelling on everything again, princess?"

Maggie leaned her side against the back of the couch, facing Henry. "No, I'm not dwelling on stuff. But…"

"But you keep reliving everything that's happened and reminding yourself Ollie, Leo and Charlie are missing."

Maggie nodded. "Sorry. I keep trying not to, but…" Her voice broke off.

"But you can't stop yourself."

"Yes." Maggie slouched, disappointed in herself. Tears formed in her eyes and she fought to hold them back.

Henry smiled at her. He reached out, pulling her close to him. "It's okay, princess." Silence hung in the air between them. "Maggie, it's okay to ruminate on everything, but you have to take a deep breath and realize everything will be okay." Maggie nodded, unable to speak. Tears rolled down her cheeks. She clung to him as she sobbed. "Maggie, don't cry. I hate to see you cry."

"Sorry," she cried.

"Don't apologize, Maggie. Did you forget that I promised everything would be okay?"

"No," Maggie whimpered.

"So, you don't trust me?"

"I do trust you," Maggie contended. She wiped her eyes as tears continued to spill over.

"Really?"

"Yes, really," Maggie sniffled.

"Doesn't seem that way."

"That's not fair," Maggie protested.

"It is fair. You can't say you trust me and then worry yourself sick and cry yourself to sleep."

"But…"

"No buts, princess. If you trust me, then let's lose the tears and work on getting some sleep."

Maggie wiped at her tears. "Geez, you're tough." She sniffled.

"Yeah, I'm a terrible meanie." Maggie laughed. "And I expect you to listen! No excuses!"

Maggie laughed again. "Aye, aye, sir!" Maggie saluted him.

"Now, time for some sleep."

"Can I stay here with you? At least for a little?"

"Of course, you can, princess." He motioned for her to settle next to him. Maggie smiled at him, sniffling a bit as she relaxed next to him. Henry looped his arm around her. "You okay?"

"Yeah," she sniffled.

"You sure?"

"Yeah, I'm sure," she said, gazing up at him. "Thanks."

"You're welcome. Now, as much as I love peering into

those beautiful brown eyes, I'd like to see them closed because you're sleeping."

"Okay, okay," Maggie said. She closed her eyes and let her head loll onto Henry's shoulder and within moments she was asleep. Henry covered her with his jacket. He settled next to her, pulling his hat over his eyes.

CHAPTER 17

Maggie awoke the next morning sprawled on the couch. Henry's jacket still covered her. She pushed herself up to sitting. Henry and Tarik sipped coffee and discussed plans at a small table near the kitchenette. Maggie yawned, running a hand through her hair. She stretched. "Is that coffee?" she asked.

"It is, princess," Henry said. He retrieved a mug and poured a cup for Maggie. Maggie plodded from the couch to the table, collapsing into a chair next to Henry.

"Thanks." She sipped at the coffee. "What time is it?"

"A little after ten," Henry answered.

"Wow, I haven't slept this late in years!" Maggie marveled. She returned to sipping her coffee.

"So, we're set, other than the... special requests?" Henry asked.

"All set. Special request will be ready by 4 p.m. today. I'll pick it up myself," Tarik confirmed.

"Great. You want some breakfast, princess?"

"If you're offering, I'm accepting," Maggie said.

"Breakfast? How long have I known you, Henry? You've never made me breakfast," Tarik said with a loud laugh.

"You're not as pretty as she is, Tarik," Henry answered.

Henry scrambled eggs while Maggie made toast. Emma wandered in as they were dishing up the eggs. "Good timing," Maggie said.

"No one woke me, sorry."

"No problem, Emma," Henry said. "Best you girls get sleep while you can. We'll have a rough couple of nights coming up starting tomorrow."

"Ugh," Maggie groaned. "Why do you always have bad news?"

"I love keeping it exciting for you, princess," Henry answered. He passed her a plate of eggs.

They ate breakfast, making light conversation. It was almost noon when they finished eating and cleaning up after their meal.

"So, what now?" Maggie asked.

"We need to prepare for the journey into the desert," Tarik answered.

"Right," Henry agreed. "We'll leave tomorrow morning. And in the interim, we have another job to do," he said, glancing to Maggie.

"Is it something I won't like?"

"Probably not," Henry admitted.

"I'm afraid to ask," Maggie said.

"We're going out on the town."

"Oh!" Maggie exclaimed. "Well, that doesn't sound so bad!"

"Like a trip to a bar?" Emma questioned.

"At least one, yep," Henry confirmed.

"Sounds like fun!" Emma said. "One last carefree night out before the tedium of desert travel, huh?"

"Not quite," Henry challenged. "We need to make sure

someone sees us in Luxor. We need those bad guys to get here and bring our friends with them."

"So, you want us to get caught?" Maggie asked.

"No, not get caught, get spotted," Henry asserted. "We just want to let them know we're here, so they'll follow. We need to be careful we aren't caught. We've still got to make it to that tomb. It's where we'll stand the best chance of bargaining."

Maggie nodded.

"Bad guys or not, I could use a night out!" Emma said.

"No, you'll stay here," Henry asserted.

"Oh, I figured…" Emma began.

"Will she be safe here?" Maggie asked.

"Yes, I'll be here," Tarik assured Maggie.

"So, how about it, princess? You up for a mission?"

"Uh, I guess so. As long as you promise we don't get caught."

"Oh, I promise, princess, I promise. And you know I'm serious about my promises."

"If you don't feel comfortable, Maggie, I'd be happy to go in your place," Emma offered.

"No," Henry countered immediately, "they need to see her face."

"Looks like you're stuck," Emma said to Maggie. She shrugged.

"Oh, well, it should be easy enough, I guess," Maggie answered.

* * *

They spent the afternoon preparing for the trip the next morning. Discovering sleeping bags and tents amongst their gear unsettled Maggie.

"Oh, come on, princess. You've never camped?" Henry asked.

"No, I have never camped. I don't understand why that's so hard to believe!"

"How have you never camped? Who doesn't camp? Not even as a kid? Or in your backyard?"

"Ah, no? We went on other vacations, not camping. And no, we never camped. Not even in the backyard."

"Other vacations? What sort of parents did you have?"

"Rich ones," Emma answered for Maggie. "Their vacations were to ritzy places like South Beach, Vail, the Caribbean, Europe."

Maggie scoffed. "That's not accurate!" Maggie stated.

"What? Come on! It is!" Emma argued. "I, on the other hand, have camped quite a bit," Emma told Henry, rolling a sleeping bag like a pro and attaching it to her knapsack.

"It's not! My parents didn't find camping... fun."

"How is it not fun?" Henry asked.

"Same question!" Emma exclaimed.

Maggie struggled with her sleeping bag, smashing it into a ball and trying to attach it to her backpack. As she fiddled with the strap to attach it, the sleeping bag unraveled. "Ugh, I guess this is how," Maggie answered. She flung her hands in the air.

"Give it here, princess," Henry offered. He moved toward her.

"Oh, I've got it, I've got it," Emma said. She leaned over to roll Maggie's sleeping bag and attach it to her backpack.

"Great, thank you," Maggie said. "Can't wait to build the tent!"

"I've still not gotten an answer to my question, princess."

"What question?" Maggie asked, sighing with a disgusted look on her face.

"How is camping not fun?"

Maggie rolled her eyes. "Okay, you answer this: how is it fun?" She motioned to the sleeping bag and backpack.

"The stars in the sky, the fresh air, the calls of wildlife, the crackling sounds of a fire, the simplicity of nature," Henry answered.

"I was planning to say the same," Emma nodded. "We camped a lot when I was growing up. I have tons of fond memories of telling scary stories around the campfire, roasting marshmallows and hanging out with my family."

Maggie shrugged. "We just never did it. It seems dirty and uncomfortable. I mean, it's your vacation, you should be comfortable! Not... grimy and covered in poison ivy and bug bites." Maggie grimaced.

Henry howled with laughter. "I've never once been covered in poison ivy on my camping trip."

"Me either." Emma laughed, shaking her head.

"Fine, fine," Maggie answered. Annoyance filled her. "I don't see what's so wrong with having a non-camping vacation. Just because I didn't camp doesn't mean I didn't have fun on my vacations with my family."

"Okay, okay, nobody's knocking your vacations, princess."

"No, but," Emma continued, "most people have slept in a tent at some point. You never did, even with your friends in your backyard. It's kind of weird."

"It's not weird!" Maggie insisted. "I don't find it weird."

"No sleeping bag sleepovers, princess?"

"Nope," Emma answered for her. "Her room was perfect for sleepovers, complete with her princess canopy bed and separate princess playroom."

Maggie rolled her eyes. "I liked my princess room!"

"So, my princess had a princess room?"

"I did, yes," Maggie answered. "And I liked it. I liked it a lot better than I liked sleeping outside with the bugs."

"Uh-huh. I'll pack some extra bug spray just for you, princess."

"Thank you. And I'd appreciate it if you carried it, not me. I have to walk with this thing!" Maggie complained, holding up the backpack to show how unwieldy it was.

"Aww," Henry began as Tarik entered.

"Everything is ready," Tarik announced.

"Oh, good, so excited," Maggie groused. She stalked from the room.

"Oops, I think she's mad at us," Emma giggled.

"Yeah, we were a little hard on her," Henry said. "I'll go check on her." Henry climbed to his feet. "I think we've got everything ready here, too, Tarik."

"I can check on her," Emma offered. "Don't worry, we teased her plenty of times at Alpha Alpha Kappa, she's used to it!"

Emma disappeared into the bedroom. Within a few moments, Maggie emerged. "Okay, I'm ready to be spotted!" she said. She grabbed her purse and struck a pose as she flicked her hair.

"Okay, I guess we should be on our way," Henry said. "We'll grab some dinner and make sure we're seen a few places, then be back."

"Should we all be going together? I mean, we need to eat, too!" Emma said.

"Never fear, I've got us dinner!" Tarik announced. He held up two takeout bags.

"Great," Emma mumbled.

"Mmm, is this the good place?" Henry asked. He opened the bag and sniffed the food.

"You know it, my friend," Tarik answered.

"Aww, come on! We're going to miss it?" Henry whined.

"Next time, my friend, next time."

"You promise?" Henry asked.

"I promise," Tarik said, grinning at him.

"All right," Henry said. "Ready, then?" He glanced at Maggie.

She nodded. "Ready," she said. She slung her purse over her shoulder and stalked to the door. "Have fun!" she called to Tarik and Emma.

Tarik tossed a set of keys to Henry who caught them mid-air. He followed Maggie to the door. The two disappeared into the hallway. They took a few steps toward the stairs when Maggie stopped. "Forget something?" Henry asked.

"You trust Tarik, right? Like with your life?" she asked.

"Yes, why?"

"We're leaving Emma with him. I just... want to be sure she's safe."

Henry smiled at her, tucking a lock of hair behind her ear. "I trust that man with my life and Emma's. She's fine. And she may even enjoy his company. He's a nice guy!"

"Ha! I told her that last night. She wasn't having any of it," Maggie answered, approaching the stairs.

"You told her he's a nice guy?" Henry asked.

"No. I told her he's cute."

"You think he's cute?" Henry asked as they neared the bottom of the stairway.

"Yeah! He's cute! He has beautiful eyes."

"Beautiful eyes, huh? Uh-huh," Henry murmured. He opened the passenger door to Tarik's car for Maggie to enter. Henry climbed into the driver's side. He fired the engine and pulled from the spot.

Their first stop was a restaurant. Henry ordered for them both. As they ate, Henry said, "Princess, about our conversation earlier, I was only teasing about the camping."

"It's okay. Honestly, I just don't see the fun in it. And I

don't see why everyone has such a big problem with having a nice, relaxing, five-star vacation. It's not a crime!"

"No, it's not. I'm sure they're lovely."

"They are," Maggie assured him.

"So, am I forgiven?" Henry asked.

"Yes, you are forgiven. Don't worry about it, most of my friends get on my case about my cushy vacations. I mean, when I'm going on vacation I want to be pampered, not doing chores or being rustic."

"I wanted to say something at Tarik's but Emma insisted she go after you," Henry admitted.

Maggie nodded, realizing why Emma suggested she speak with her rather than Henry. "You said something now, that's what counts," Maggie assured him. She squeezed his hand.

Henry smiled at her, changing the subject to ask if Maggie was enjoying her meal. They made light conversation as they finished their meal. As they waited for their check, Henry told Maggie they needed to make another stop. They paid their bill and left. Henry drove them to another locale, a night club.

Maggie marveled at Henry in a night club, teasing him about it as they entered. "Funny, princess," Henry said. "Except this is a hot spot for our good friends to have a presence."

"They have good taste," Maggie said. She eyed the club's decor. Music blasted as they approached the bar. Henry led them to seats at the center, ordering a bourbon and allowing Maggie to select her cocktail.

"So, are they here? Can you tell?" Maggie inquired after a few sips.

"If they're not, I hope they will be soon. Someone'll tip them off. We just have to wait."

"Won't it be obvious to them we're flaunting our presence here? Wouldn't they expect us to stay hidden?"

"Good assessment, princess. You're one smart cookie!"

"Okay, so… why are we here then? Isn't this obvious that it's a ploy?"

"We do have travel arrangements to make."

"But Tarik did that," Maggie noted.

"But they don't realize that. Someone will meet us. It'll appear to them to be a legitimate business deal, some loose end we're tying up before we leave."

"Won't they just follow us back to Tarik's?"

"I hope not," Henry said, laughing and finishing his drink. He waved to the bartender and requested another for both of them.

"So, if they don't, how can they follow us to the tomb?"

"They'll realize where we're leaving from. With their connections, they'll be able to determine roughly where we're heading. We just need to be careful to stay a step ahead of them. Now, try to relax and enjoy your drink."

Maggie and Henry spent the two hours sipping drinks and chatting. Despite the circumstances, Maggie's nerves eased. Perhaps it was the alcohol or the rhythmic music or the normalcy of chatting over drinks, but whichever the case, Maggie felt a great sense of relief.

After two hours, Henry texted someone on his phone. "Are they here?" Maggie asked. Henry nodded. "Where?"

"Back, corner booth. Two men, two women." Henry grabbed her as she turned. "No, don't look."

"Sorry," she whispered, leaning toward Henry. "Now what?"

"Just waiting on our friend to appear."

"Oh, for the 'transaction?'" Maggie asked. Henry nodded.

The tension crept back into Maggie's shoulders. Unease rattled through her as she glanced toward the corner booth. Maggie took a gulp of her drink. She crossed her arms, drumming her fingers against her forearm. The music now seemed too loud. She wanted to shut it out. She exhaled a shaky breath, noting Henry's unchanged attitude during the situation. How was he so calm, she wondered?

"I'm going to go crazy if your person doesn't get here soon," she huffed.

"Just a few more minutes," Henry assured her. Maggie nodded, swallowing hard. Henry patted her leg. "Relax, princess. They won't come after us in a crowded bar." Maggie clutched his hand for reassurance.

Within a few minutes, a man sidled up to Henry. He ordered a drink, then turned, leaning his back against the bar. Henry slid his drink toward the man along with some cash. The man turned back, facing the bar, picked up the drink and swiped the cash. He reached into his pocket and removed something small, laying it on the bar along with a few bills. The man disappeared into the crowd. Henry swiped the object, tossed a few bills on the bar and picked up his hat.

Securing it on his head, he stood. "Time to go, princess."

Maggie stood, unsure her legs would hold her. Henry guided her to the exit and to the car. "Did they follow us?" Maggie asked when they were in the car.

"Probably," Henry admitted.

Maggie glanced around, searching for their tail. "Well, now what?" she asked.

"Put your seatbelt on, princess," Henry answered.

"Okay," Maggie answered, securing her seat belt.

Henry eased the car out of their spot into traffic. He monitored the road behind them often. "Well?" Maggie asked after a few moments.

"Three cars back, silver BMW."

Maggie turned back, searching for the car. "How do you know?"

Henry made a turn at the next street. The silver car

followed. Henry made another turn a few streets up, again followed by the silver car. After a third turn, Maggie was convinced.

Maggie's eyes were wide. "What do we do?" she asked.

"Hold on, princess," Henry advised.

CHAPTER 18

"*H*old on?" Maggie inquired. "What? Why?"

The road opened wider and Henry shot into the left lane, gunning the engine. The silver car lurched behind them, speeding to catch them. Henry wove through traffic, dodging cars as he sped through the town.

Their car closed on a car in front of them. Maggie squeezed her eyes closed, bracing herself against the dash, and she pushed her foot against the floor as though she could brake the car. She opened her eyes as Henry veered into oncoming traffic. Headlights shined in their eyes and a horn sounded as he swerved back into their lane.

"Oh!" Maggie cried out.

"Easy, princess. We're fine," Henry assured her as he gunned it, swinging into the lane for oncoming traffic again. This time no oncoming car approached. They sped down the street approaching the traffic heading their way. Maggie expected them to swing back into the correct lane of travel after passing the car they were following. Henry did not.

The car picked up speed, continuing in the wrong lane.

Traffic sped toward them, the lights becoming blinding as they approached.

"Ah," Maggie began as they continued driving toward oncoming traffic. Horns sounded and lights flashed, but Henry continued. "Henry..." Maggie gasped. "Henry!" she said again. She braced her hand against the roof of the car. "HENRY!" she screamed. She squeezed her eyes shut as she braced for the inevitable impact of a head-on collision.

A horn blasted, flying past them, as the car swung back into their lane. Headlights no longer pierced her eyelids. She opened her eyes, glancing at Henry, surprised she was alive. Henry's focus remained on the road ahead of them. He glanced into the rearview mirror.

"Please tell me we lost them," Maggie puffed.

"Sorry, princess. Not yet."

The car picked up speed, weaving through traffic. They approached a signal at lightning speed. The light changed from green to red. "Oh!" Maggie pointed toward the signal. "It's red, red, RED!" she shouted as Henry skidded through the light, pulling the emergency brake as he turned the wheel to skid them to the left, making a hard turn. Their quick turn on red caused an accident as two cars swerved to miss them, crashing into each other.

Maggie groaned, leaning her head against the headrest. "Are they still following us?" Henry asked. Maggie glanced in the side mirror, then turned to survey behind them. Her eyes darted around. "Well?"

"Umm, I'm not sure," Maggie hedged.

"Focus, Maggie, are they there or not?"

Maggie swallowed hard, taking a deep breath. She focused her energy on methodically checking the cars behind them.

Maggie steeled her nerves. "Ah, yes, yes, they're still there," she answered.

"How far?"

"Ah, I don't..." Maggie hesitated.

"How far, Maggie?"

"Four car lengths, give or take."

Henry nodded, swerving to the right onto another street. The car followed. "They're still there," Maggie announced.

Henry urged the car faster, tromping on the accelerator. They approached the car in front of them like a bullet shot from a pistol. "Oh!" Maggie cried out again as the car vaulted onto the sidewalk. People screamed, dodging out of the way, leaping into doorways or pressing against the buildings. The car plowed through tables at street cafes, tossing them aside.

Henry pulled back into the line of traffic as they approached another intersection. He sped through the cross-roads. A cacophony of horns sounded behind them. Maggie glanced back. "They're still coming," she announced.

They approached another intersection where the road widened. Henry inched to the curb, speeding into the cross-roads. As they entered it, he turned the wheel hard, pulling the emergency brake again. The car spun one-hundred and eighty degrees. They faced the direction they had been driving as two cars skidded to a halt to miss them. Henry wasted no time in stepping on the accelerator. The car shot in the direction they had come.

"Keep your head down," he urged Maggie. Maggie slouched in her seat, still bracing herself against the roof. Maggie heard tires squealing as the silver car attempted to change directions to follow them. She risked a glance back, spotting traffic snarled as the silver car fought to find a path to follow them.

"Ugh," Maggie groaned. "They're through and coming up fast."

"How far?"

"Ten cars and closing," Maggie reported.

Henry made a hard left, racing down another street with limited cars scattered about. He skidded to a halt halfway down, throwing the gear shift into reverse. He slammed his foot onto the gas pedal and the car lurched backward.

He threaded it into a small, dark alley almost hidden between two buildings. The car screeched to a halt and Henry killed the engine, dousing the lights. "Stay down," he urged. He pulled Maggie down. Maggie stayed low, straining to peer above the dash. Within seconds, a silver BMW sped past their hiding spot.

"Was that them? Do you think they'll circle back?" Maggie whispered.

"That was them. Just a second," Henry cautioned.

Within ten seconds, two more silver BMWs sped past them.

"Now we're good," Henry said. He sat up.

"There were three of them?"

"Yep," Henry answered. He pulled the keys from the ignition. "Come on." He opened his door, exiting the car into the alleyway. Maggie unbuckled her seat belt and pushed her door open. She stood on shaky legs, shutting the door and leaning against the car. Henry approached her. "You okay?" he asked.

The experience was catching up with her. "Uh," Maggie said in a shaky breath. "Yeah, yeah."

"Take a breath, princess. We're okay," Henry said. He stroked her hair.

Maggie turned to face him. She nodded, her hands shaking. "I just need a second to catch my breath."

Henry pulled her to him, embracing her. "You're okay, Maggie." Maggie wrapped her arms around him, grateful to be alive.

After a moment, Maggie stepped back, exhaling. "I'm okay, I'm good."

"You sure?"

"I'm sure," she said. She smiled at him and grabbed his hand.

"You okay to walk?"

"Yeah," Maggie answered.

"Good, 'cause we walk from here," Henry said.

"Okay." Maggie nodded as Henry pulled her toward the back of the alley. "Kind of a welcome change from the driving."

Henry laughed, putting his arm around her. "You did good, Maggie. You did real good."

"Thanks." Maggie grinned at him. After a moment, she added, "Your driving could have used some improvement."

"Oh, it could, could it?" He laughed as he pulled her into another side street. "I'll keep that in mind for our next car chase."

"I hope there isn't another," Maggie admitted.

They wound through the city streets on foot. It took them over thirty minutes to navigate to Tarik's apartment. As they approached the building, Henry slowed, surveying the area.

"What is it?" Maggie asked. She glanced around, not spotting anything.

"Just being cautious," Henry answered.

"They couldn't have followed us here, could they?"

"I doubt it, but better safe than sorry." They crossed the street away from the building, coming to a stop across from it. Maggie gazed up at the building. She and Henry made conversation to pass the time. After twenty minutes, Henry was satisfied, and they crossed the street and entered the building.

They climbed the stairs. The time walking had calmed Maggie's nerves. As they returned to the apartment, Henry had her laughing at some of their latest experiences.

"Stop, stop," Maggie giggled as they reached the landing for the third floor.

"Oh, admit it, you're loving this!"

"I am so not! I am not loving wondering if I'm going to die at any second!"

"This was your most exciting first date."

"First date? This wasn't a date."

"It was kind of like a date," Henry countered. "We went to dinner, then out for drinks and a romantic walk home."

Maggie continued laughing. "Oh, no, no, no. If this was an actual first date, you'd have to do much better!"

"Much better? Do tell!" Henry said as they reached the apartment door.

"You couldn't handle a first date with me," Maggie said. She pushed through the door.

"No?" Henry asked.

Tarik sat on the couch alone.

"Hey, Henry, Maggie, everything go okay?" he asked as they entered.

"Perfect," Henry answered. He dangled the key for Tarik, who swiped it from him.

"Still in one piece?" Tarik asked.

"Not a scratch on her, friend." Henry assured him.

"Is Emma asleep already?" Maggie asked.

"Uh, I'm not sure. She wasn't feeling well after we ate. I knocked a few times, but there was no answer. Perhaps she fell asleep," Tarik answered.

"Oh, I'll check on her," Maggie said.

Henry nodded. "You should get some sleep before tomorrow, too," he said.

Maggie agreed. "Okay, good night! Thank you for not getting me killed tonight!"

"You're very welcome, princess." Henry winked at her.

Maggie disappeared into the bedroom. She found the bed

empty. Maggie set her purse on the nightstand and meandered to the bathroom. She knocked on the half-closed door. "Emma?" she called. She pushed the door open, peering in. "Emma?" she asked again. She glanced around the room, finding Emma collapsed on the floor next to the toilet. "Emma!" she shouted, racing toward her limp form. Emma lifted her head, moaning. "What happened?"

"I feel awful," she whimpered. "Something in that food Tarik brought didn't agree with me."

"Aw," Maggie said. She stroked Emma's hair.

"I have vomited more times than I can count," Emma groaned.

"You poor thing. Can you walk? You should get to bed and rest."

Emma nodded. "I just stayed here in case I had to throw up again."

Maggie helped Emma to her feet, keeping her arm around her as they walked back to the bedroom. She guided Emma to the bed, getting her under the covers. Emma curled in a ball, closing her eyes. "Need anything?" Maggie asked her.

"Sleep. And no more 'authentic Egyptian food,'" Emma lamented.

Maggie snickered. She stroked Emma's hair. Emma moaned again, her face scrunching in pain. "I'm gonna be sick again," Emma whimpered.

"Take a deep breath, do you think it'll pass?"

"Uh-uh, nope." Emma shook her head, grimacing as she swallowed hard.

"Okay, let's get you into the bathroom," Maggie answered. She pulled Emma up to sitting and helped her to stand. With Emma clinging to her, Maggie dragged her to the bathroom. She held her hair as Emma retched again. Maggie retrieved a washcloth, wetting it and using it on Emma's forehead and neck. "Any better?"

"I hope so," Emma answered.

"Let's get you back to bed." Maggie lifted her from the floor where she knelt and half-carried her back to the bed. She snuggled her under the covers, using the washcloth on her forehead again.

Emma whimpered again. "Shh," Maggie soothed, "go to sleep." Maggie grasped Emma's hand. Within a few minutes, Emma's hand relaxed and her breathing became rhythmic.

Maggie stood and adjusted the covers around Emma. She returned the washcloth to the bathroom, hanging it on the towel rack to dry. Exhaustion hit her like a brick as she glanced in the bathroom mirror. "Ugh," she whined to herself as she turned the water on to wash her face. After washing, she slogged to the bedroom, collapsing on the bed.

Within seconds of her head hitting the pillow, Maggie drifted off to sleep. A moan startled her awake. "Huh? What?" Maggie asked.

"Mmm," Emma moaned. "Sick." She tossed the covers off. Maggie leapt from bed, tugging Emma out of bed and to the bathroom. She held her hair back as she vomited again. Afterwards, Maggie helped her back to bed, climbing in after Emma settled.

She fell asleep in seconds again. After an hour of sleep, Emma woke her again for another trip to the bathroom. "Ugh," Emma cried as they made their way back to the bed. "I hope that's it."

"Any better?" Maggie asked as she settled her under the covers.

"A little," Emma admitted, "I just want to sleep now."

Maggie tucked her in then circled the bed, climbing in under the covers. She relaxed back into her pillow, glancing at the clock. It read 2:30 a.m. She'd have a few hours of solid sleep before they had to be up to travel. She planned to enjoy her last night in a bed. She breathed a deep, full breath. Within minutes, she was asleep.

* * *

Maggie startled awake. "Emma?" she asked. She was still half asleep.

"Maggie," a voice whispered. Her body shook all over. "Maggie, wake up."

"Henry?" she inquired.

"Wake up, we need to leave," Henry urged.

"What?" Maggie said, confused. She glanced at the clock. It read 5:13 a.m. "Why? It's only five."

"Come on. Get up, get your shoes on. We need to go."

Henry pulled her up to sitting, pushing her shoes onto her feet. "Okay," Maggie replied. She yawned. "I've just got to put my makeup on."

"No time for makeup, princess. We've got to go."

Maggie was confused. "What?" Maggie asked.

"Emma, wake up," Henry said. He shoved Emma's form in the bed.

"Henry," Maggie said, "she's been up all night, sick. Leave her sleep."

"Maggie, we have to go NOW."

"You're scaring me," Maggie stated.

"Good. Now tie your shoes. Emma, get up." Henry shoved at her again.

Maggie tied her shoes as Emma groaned. "What?" she asked.

"Get up, we've got to go," Henry told her.

"Ugh, I'm so tired," Emma answered.

"She's exhausted. Is it imperative that we leave this early?" Maggie asked.

"Maggie, they've found us. We need to go now."

"What?" Maggie exclaimed. She leapt from the bed.

"Emma, get up," Henry insisted. He tugged on her arm. He turned to Maggie. "We have to make a run for it. Straight out and down the steps, around the corner to Tarik's rental car. Red Toyota parked around the corner. Got it?"

"Okay," Maggie said. She nodded. "But Emma's been sick all night, she'll never make it. She's exhausted."

Tarik appeared in the door. "Henry, we must leave NOW. Are the girls ready?"

"I'll need your help with Emma. She's been sick, she'll never be able to run."

"I'll carry her, but it'll slow me down," Tarik said.

"Take Emma and Maggie out the back. I'll draw them off at the front. Get to the car, I'll meet you there."

"What?" Maggie asked. "No, we shouldn't split up."

Tarik scooped Emma up.

"I'll be fine, princess. Follow Tarik."

Maggie grabbed her purse, running a hand through her hair. Her brain felt frazzled. Panic coursed through her. Tarik raced from the room, Emma in his arms. Henry pulled Maggie toward the door. Her legs were like lead and her stomach churned.

They raced across the living room. Maggie rushed in front of Tarik, opening the door for him. He skirted through it, darting left after exiting. Maggie followed him with Henry behind her. She spotted movement to the right out of the corner of her eye. She took a step to the left when Henry pulled her back. "Run, Tarik!" he shouted. He shoved Maggie against the wall, covering her with his body. He pulled a gun from his waistband, firing twice. The noise was deafening. Maggie's ears rung from the sound.

The figure down the hall ducked behind the railing. Henry pulled Maggie down lower, firing again. Time seemed to stand still. The opponent fired from his position behind the railing. Henry fired again, and the figure slumped to the floor. "Come on," he said, grabbing Maggie's hand.

Maggie stood, allowing Henry to pull her along. They approached the stairs where another assailant approached, rounding from the landing below to the stairs just below them. Henry fired, dropping him on the landing.

Maggie swallowed hard as they passed the first body. Henry pulled her close. Maggie's eyes slid toward the body. "Don't look," Henry advised. "Focus, right here, focus on me." Maggie focused on Henry's face. "We're going straight down to the bottom, okay? You keep your eyes on me, got it? We need to get out of here before the police come." Maggie nodded.

Henry looped his arm around her waist, guiding her down the steps. They made it to the second floor before another man approached. Henry whisked Maggie behind him as he shot the man. They hurried down the last set of stairs to the building's lobby. Two men approached. Henry shot both, killing one and wounding the other. "Tell your boss we expect our friends to be joining us when they follow us next time," he said, kicking the man's gun away from him. He tugged Maggie's arm, rushing her to the door. Before leaving, he glanced outside, gun at the ready. A car raced from the left, drawing his attention. "Come on," he said, He tugged Maggie with him.

The red car screeched to a halt right outside the door. The passenger door and rear passenger doors flung open and Tarik shouted, "Get in!" They raced to the car. Henry shoved Maggie toward the open back door, diving into the passenger seat. Maggie pulled the door shut as Tarik sped off. Sirens rung out in the morning air.

Tarik glanced in the mirror. "Don't see a tail," he said.

Henry glanced behind them, searching the streets. "Me either. We're clear."

Maggie reached out to take Emma's hand. "Are you okay?" she asked her.

"If I wasn't sick already, I would be now," Emma groaned. Maggie squeezed her hand.

Henry shifted in his seat to face Maggie. He reached back, pushing a lock of hair from her face. "Are YOU okay, Maggie?" Maggie nodded. "Yeah? You sure?" he asked.

Maggie nodded again, biting her lower lip. "Yeah, I'm okay." She smiled at him, reaching for his hand. She squeezed it to reassure him.

Tarik glanced at them. "My friend isn't scheduled to meet us until ten on the city outskirts. We need to contact him, see if he can move it up." He held his phone up toward Henry. Henry grabbed it, swiping it open and poking around. He pressed the phone to his ear, speaking a few words after a moment. He pulled the phone away from his head, poking the screen and handing it back to Tarik.

"We're good, he'll meet us at eight."

"Perfect," Tarik answered. "Got some time to kill."

"Yeah," Henry answered. "May be a good idea to grab some breakfast. The ladies need nutrition."

"What? Restaurant? Might not be safe," Tarik questioned.

"No, mate, takeaway. We'll eat in the car."

"Good idea."

Henry turned to face Maggie. "Ladies, any special requests for breakfast?" he asked.

"Caffeine," Maggie groaned.

"I'll make sure you get a coffee, princess," Henry said. He grinned at her.

"Eggs would be great for Emma," Maggie added. "She had a rough night. She needs some protein."

"You got it, princess," Henry answered.

"I know just the place," Tarik answered. He navigated the city streets, pulling over in front of a local restaurant. "Just a minute. I'll leave it running in case you need to make a quick getaway." Tarik disappeared into the restaurant for a few minutes, returning with a bag of food and a carrier of drinks.

"My stomach is turning at the sight of him carrying a bag of food," Emma complained, dropping her head to the seat behind her.

"Let's hope it's better than last night's," Maggie answered. She patted Emma's hand. Tarik entered the car, handing the bag to Henry. He pulled away from the curb, navigating to a bridge to cross the Nile, heading west away from the city.

Maggie leaned forward, pulling a coffee from the carrier. "Coffee, coffee, coffee," she muttered. She sipped at it. "There's cream and sugar in the bag," Tarik announced.

"I honestly don't care as long as it's coffee, but thanks," Maggie said. She grabbed the cream and sugars Henry handed back to her. She added them to her cup, stirred it and replaced the lid, sipping at it again.

"Breakfast sandwiches, ladies," Henry said. He handed two wrapped packages back to them.

"Thanks," Maggie said. She balanced the coffee on the seat between her legs and grabbed the sandwiches. She handed one to Emma, who held her hand up in protest. "You need to eat, Emma." Maggie unwrapped her sandwich, taking a bite. "Mmm, it's very good. Come on, try some." She waved the package under Emma's face.

Emma snatched it from her. "Fine, only to stop you from waving it in my face," she groaned.

"It'll make you feel better," Maggie promised. Emma took a tentative bite. "Well?"

"It's fine," Emma answered.

They finished their breakfast as the city receded behind them. As the buildings disappeared, Tarik pulled to the side of the road. He checked his watch. "Still about forty-five minutes to wait."

Maggie balled her and Emma's sandwich wrappers up, shoving them into her empty coffee cup and tossing them into the empty to-go bag. Tarik and Henry climbed from the car, stretching. Emma propped her door open, slouching in her seat. Maggie swung her door open, turning so her legs rested on the ground. She grabbed her purse, retrieving her compact mirror and a few makeup items.

"Makeup, princess? We're just going into the desert," Henry said.

"So?" Maggie asked.

Henry chuckled at her as she swiped on her mascara. "Ugh," Emma groaned.

"Sick?" Maggie asked her.

"Not physically," Emma answered. "You're such a diva with the makeup though."

"It's just part of my routine. It makes me feel better, like things are normal," Maggie replied. She brushed on a bit of eyeshadow.

"Can I talk to you when you're finished primping, princess?" Henry asked.

"You can talk to me while I'm primping," she answered. She snapped her eyeshadow case closed.

"In private, if you wouldn't mind," he whispered.

"Okay," Maggie muttered to herself. She checked her eye makeup in the mirror. Satisfied, she slicked on lip gloss. After a final check, she clicked the mirror closed and returned all her tools to her purse. Slinging her purse over her arm, she stood, smoothing her clothes after having slept in them.

Henry leaned against the trunk of the car, staring into the desert. Tarik stalked around on his phone. Maggie approached Henry. "What's up?" Maggie asked.

"We need to discuss Emma," Henry stated.

"Seems like she's feeling better," Maggie began. "Perhaps the food helped."

"She can't go with us," Henry said.

Maggie's jaw dropped open in shock. "What? Why not?" Maggie asked.

"She was sick all night. The desert is a harsh and unforgiving environment. She can't go into the desert weak and recovering. She needs to stay here and take care of herself."

Maggie shook her head, struggling to answer. "So... so what? We just dump her on the side of the road here and leave?"

"No, of course not, Maggie," Henry said. He stood to face her.

"Well, what then, Henry? Give her the keys and let her drive herself home?"

"No. Let her stay with Sefu. She'll be much better off."

Maggie's jaw dropped again. "Are you serious? Just leave her with some friend of Tarik's?"

"Oh, come on, Maggie. He's not some stranger off the street. Tarik trusts him, so by extension I trust him."

Maggie scoffed, incredulous. "You don't even know this guy and you want to leave her with him?" she said, her voice rising in pitch.

"Maggie, please calm down..." Henry started.

"Calm down? CALM DOWN?! Yes, that sounds like a wonderful idea! I can calm down, we can leave Emma here with a stranger and then I can wonder when you'll ditch me because I'm inconvenient," Maggie exclaimed, flailing her arms.

"No, Maggie, that won't happen. If you remember, I didn't want her coming along to begin with."

"Oh, I remember, yes. I also remember you shoved me in the back of a van when we first met. Your first solution to a problem is usually illegal, and I just witnessed you kill a bunch of people." Maggie stalked a few steps away. "Oh my God, oh my God. I just witnessed you kill a bunch of people," she repeated.

"Maggie, Maggie," Henry soothed, approaching her. "Stop dwelling on it."

"Stop dwelling on it?" Maggie asked. She pulled away from him. "I think I need to start dwelling on it! I mean, who or what am I involved with?"

"Maggie, these are not nice people. They weren't coming to talk. They were coming for the scarab and the staff piece. Anyone who got in their way they wouldn't have hesitated to have hurt or worse." Maggie crossed her arms, staring at the ground. "Come on, Maggie," Henry said. He approached her and grabbed her arms. "I'm not a cold-blooded killer. I did what I had to do."

Maggie covered her face. "I just can't get those images out of my head," Maggie cried.

Henry wrapped her in his arms. "It's hard, I realize that. But Maggie, you must put it out of your mind, okay? I'm sorry you had to witness that. But I'd never let anyone hurt you."

After a moment, Maggie pulled away, nodding. "You did it because you had to," Maggie repeated. Maggie hugged him again. "Thank you for keeping me safe. This is the reason Emma needs to come with us."

Henry pulled away from her. "Maggie, no. She's in more danger going with us than if she stays here."

Heat entered Maggie's voice again. "I don't agree," she answered.

"Noted. But I'm in charge. So, it's my call."

"Says who?" Maggie demanded.

"Says me. I'm the one with the experience."

"Oh, says you? Because you have the experience? It's not like your decisions are above reproach, Henry!"

"I never said they were, but my decisions have kept us alive so far, so we'll continue following them."

"No!" Maggie objected. "You don't get to have a monopoly on the decisions because so far we're still alive!"

"This isn't up for a discussion," Henry announced.

"No, it's not. Emma comes with us," Maggie stated.

"No, she does not. Maggie, let's not argue about this, please?" Maggie crossed her arms, staring at Henry, a pout on her face. "Pout all you want, I'm not changing my mind."

Maggie raised her eyebrows at him. "Fine, then I won't go either."

"No, I'm not letting you out of my sight."

"Either we both go or neither of us go."

"Maggie…"

She stormed away with Henry following her.

"Maggie! Maggie, don't you walk away from me. We're not finished!"

"Oh, we're finished," Maggie assured him. She collapsed into the car's backseat.

"No, we're not. Maggie…"

"You're a jerk," she shouted at him. She slammed the door shut.

"Whoa, what was that about?" Emma asked.

"Nothing," Maggie huffed. She crossed her arms and set her face in a scowl.

CHAPTER 19

hey sat in silence for the remaining minutes before Sefu arrived. Maggie spotted the truck approaching, bringing the traditional dust cloud with it. The truck dragged a closed trailer behind it. Henry and Tarik approached the truck as the driver slid out. A second man emerged from the passenger's side of the truck. They all greeted each other, exchanging handshakes.

Sefu motioned to the trailer. They conversed for several more minutes. Sefu shook their hands again and strode to the back of the trailer, opening it. Maggie opened her door and climbed from the car. Emma followed suit, climbing out on the opposite side.

Tarik opened the trunk, revealing their backpacks and gear. Henry approached Maggie. "Sefu will take care of Emma, no problem. Have you told her?"

"Nope. Hope he's a nice guy because I'll be staying with him, too."

"Damn it, Maggie. Stop acting like a child. Get your stuff ready, because you're going with us. Emma is staying here."

"You handle telling Emma. It's your idea."

"Fine. I will," Henry answered. He stalked past her and toward Emma. He turned back before reaching Emma. "And you'll go with me." Maggie followed him to the driver's side of the car, crossing her arms and waiting for the show.

"Emma?" Henry called.

"Yeah?" she answered.

"Uh…" He paused, glancing to Maggie. "Emma, you had a rough night, the desert is extremely harsh, it's best that you stay back and not go with us. Sefu will make sure you're safe and we'll catch you when we get back."

"What? No!" Emma argued.

"Yes," Henry countered. "This is for the best. You'll thank me for it later."

"I'm fine, really. I'll be fine! I've done this before. I understand how challenging the desert can be. It's fine. I can do it. I won't be a burden, Henry. I promise! I'm tougher than I look!"

"This isn't a discussion, Emma. You'll be staying here."

"Like hell I will," Emma declared. She pulled her backpack from the trunk and slung it onto her back. "I'm going."

"Emma…" Henry began.

"I'm going," Emma restated.

"All right, I can't stop you, but I'd advise against it. But if you insist, the decision is on you."

"Fine," Emma answered. She crossed her arms defiantly.

Henry reached into the trunk, grabbing his own pack before stalking away from the car.

"That went well," Maggie commented as he passed her. Maggie reached into the trunk, pulling her backpack out and slinging it onto her back.

"I'm fine. I feel fine," Emma sniped at Maggie. "So, thanks for the fake concern but I'm going."

Maggie's brow wrinkled in confusion. "What?" she asked.

"Your so-called concern for me. It won't stop me from going."

Maggie made a face at Emma. "Okay? I'm not the one who wanted you to stay here!"

"Oh, really? That's not the argument you and Henry were having earlier?"

"Yes, it is the argument we were having earlier. Henry didn't want you to go, and I argued you should go."

"Oh, right. I'm sure," Emma answered. She rolled her eyes at Maggie.

"Are you not listening? I'm the one who wanted you to go. I argued for you to go and Henry insisted you stay. So, get over yourself and stop attacking the one friend you have here!" Maggie clicked the waist strap securing her backpack before storming away.

She stopped dead as she witnessed Sefu unloading the trailer. She staggered to Henry, staring at the sight at the back of the trailer. "Are those..." Maggie began, unable to finish.

"Camels," Henry confirmed. "Yeah."

Maggie stared at him, incredulous. "For what?"

"How did you think we planned to cross the desert, princess?"

"Car? Like an SUV. With special sand tires, maybe." Henry chuckled. "Don't laugh at me! I'm not riding on that thing."

"Oh, come on, princess. Come meet her." Henry grabbed her hand, pulling her toward the camels. "Maggie, meet your ride."

Maggie grimaced. "She smells." Henry smirked at her. "She does! But she's kind of cute." Maggie put her hand out toward the camel to pet it. The animal unleashed a high-pitched bleat, pulling away from her. "I take it back, you're a jerk just like he is!"

"Oh, Maggie..." Henry began when Emma interrupted

him.

"Which one is mine?" she asked.

"Uh, this one." Henry pointed to one Sefu was unloading from the trailer.

"Great! I haven't been on a camel in a few years, I'm so excited to ride one again!" Emma approached her camel, rubbing its neck. Maggie scowled at the scene. She reached out to her camel again, earning herself another screech from the animal. Maggie huffed at the camel.

"You gotta do it like this, princess," Henry instructed. He approached the camel and caressed its neck.

"Oh, good, she loves you. You keep her," Maggie pouted.

"Come here," Henry said.

"No, she hates me. I'll walk."

"Oh, come here," Henry said. He grabbed her hand and pulled her closer to the animal, placing her hand on its neck. "See? She likes you."

Maggie rubbed the camel's neck. With no reproach from the camel, she smiled at the animal. "Hi," she cooed to it. The animal reared back, sneezing in her face. Maggie scowled at it. "We're going to have a rough time of it, aren't we?" she asked the camel.

"Must be allergic to your perfume," Emma chimed in.

Maggie rolled her eyes. "This trip is going to be fabulous," Maggie muttered.

Tarik approached them, handing his keys to the man with Sefu. He spoke with the two men in a language Maggie didn't understand. After a moment, they shook hands and Sefu climbed into the truck. The other man headed to Tarik's car.

"Okay, we are all set," Tarik said. "Let's mount up and head out! We can make good progress today." Tarik urged the camels to sitting. Emma mounted her camel with ease, swaying as it stood.

Maggie pouted at her camel. "Come on, Maggie," Henry

encouraged her. "Jump on."

"I'll walk the first leg."

"Haha, come on, Maggie, she will not bite you! Here, I will help you," Tarik offered.

"Oh," Maggie cooed. "Thank you. What a sweetheart you are!"

Henry shook his head at her as Tarik took her hand. He informed her to place her foot in the stirrup and swing her leg over to mount the camel as quickly as she could. He helped her place her foot in the stirrup and steadied her as she swung her leg over. "Now, lean back as she starts to stand, then forward to balance, okay?"

"Okay," Maggie replied. She grinned at Tarik. The camel stood under her. She struggled a bit to hang on, but managed to stay upright as the camel stood.

"Great job!" Tarik declared. He gave her a thumbs up.

"We did it!" Maggie said to her camel. She patted her neck. The camel groaned at her. "Listen, honey, it wasn't my best experience either, okay?"

The men mounted their camels. They set off, heading southwest. Maggie found the movement of the camel awkward and she struggled to adjust to its gait. Tarik called back to her after an hour to ask how she was doing. She smiled and waved, shouting sarcastically, "Oh, great, just wonderful!" to him.

The heat of the desert pierced through her. Despite it being October, the temperatures were above normal. Maggie preferred riding to walking in the heat, even if it was uncomfortable.

They took a break around noon to eat and allow the camels to rest. The desert already surrounded them despite only traveling a few hours. "How are you enjoying your ride, Maggie?" Tarik asked as they sipped water from their canteens.

"It's better than walking," Maggie admitted.

"I told you! Very brave of you climbing on her. You did well for your first time. Now you will be a pro!"

"Thanks." Maggie laughed. "You're being too kind calling me a pro, but I may end up liking this old girl before the end of this trip!" Maggie patted the camel on the neck, earning a bleat from the animal.

"She likes you, too. I can tell," Tarik informed Maggie.

They ate a light lunch. Emma led the conversation, chatting about her previous experience in the desert. She detailed how her last trip left her with a desire to return one day.

As they prepared to set off for the afternoon leg, Henry approached Maggie. "Need help with the camel?" he asked.

Maggie slicked on lip gloss before she adjusted her kerchief to protect her face as they traveled. "Mmm, doubt it. I'm an expert now," Maggie answered.

"Uh-huh. Well, I'm sure Tarik can help you if you still need help."

"I'm sure he could. He's quite a gentleman."

"So, you're still mad at me, huh?" Henry asked.

Maggie turned to face him. "Should I not be?"

"No," he replied, grinning, "you should not be."

"Then, I guess I won't be. Since we always follow your decisions." She strode away toward her camel.

Henry rolled his eyes, following her. "Maggie," he called after her, "come on. Okay, okay, listen, I'm sorry. Now can we put our disagreement behind us?"

"We have, you decreed it," Maggie said. She petted her camel's neck.

"That's very funny, princess, very funny. But I'm being serious. I am sorry. I don't like it when you're mad at me." Despite her snide comments, she allowed Henry to assist her to climb into the saddle. The camel stood. "Going to make me suffer, are you?"

"I should," Maggie admitted, "but I won't."

"Truce?"

"Truce." She laughed, grinning at him. "You're lucky I like you."

"I agree," Henry replied.

They spent the afternoon traveling another fifteen miles into the desert. It was slow going, but the scenery amazed Maggie. They had long since left civilization behind, traveling into what appeared like an alien landscape to her. Sand stretched as far as the eye could see. The desert rose and fell in sand dunes of varying heights. The solitude was both startling yet somehow relaxing.

Maggie found herself lulled into quiet reflection as they traveled. As the sun lowered in the sky, she considered the events that led to their current circumstances. The episode this morning at Tarik's apartment popped into her mind. The incident still disconcerted her, but not because she didn't trust Henry. His quick actions to protect her and the others were methodical, almost surgical. He was unruffled by the situation. Who reacted with such cool confidence while being shot at? Who was Henry Taylor?

She recalled Henry speaking to one of the assailants. He instructed the man to inform his boss to bring their friends when they followed them. Friends, Maggie mused. Those friends included her uncle and her boyfriend. Would she ever see them again, she wondered?

Anxiety weighed on her. Combined with her exhaustion, the upset of the situation threatened to overcome her. When they stopped to set up camp for the night, she was glad for the break and the upcoming chance to rest.

Henry and Tarik pulled the tents from their gear. Emma pitched in to help set up one tent, selecting to work on the tent Henry worked to build. Tarik worked on his own. Maggie approached Tarik to help. "Need some help?"

"Sure," he said. He smiled at her.

Maggie stood staring at the parts scattered in the sand. "Umm…" She hesitated. "Yeah, okay, I have no idea what I'm doing."

Tarik laughed. "You never camped?"

"No, I have never camped. Everyone asks me that. Why is it so hard to believe that I never camped?"

Tarik nodded. "I believe it," he answered. He laughed loudly and pointed to a piece near her right foot. "Hand me that piece right there," he said. Maggie grabbed it, handing it off. "Okay, now hold this steady for me," he said. He placed a rod in her hand as he built another part.

Emma and Henry had their tent built in short order. They approached Maggie and Tarik to help finish the second tent. "Here, let me do that," Emma said. She snatched the pole from Maggie's grasp.

"Perfect, you two finish the tent," Henry said. He pointed to Maggie. "And you can help me start a fire."

Emma and Tarik finished the tent as Henry, with a minuscule amount of assistance from Maggie, started the fire. Together, they cooked a small meal and ate as the sun set and darkness covered them.

As the stars appeared in the sky, they discussed a plan for the night. Henry offered to take first watch. Before anyone else could speak, Emma expressed her desire to join him. Tarik voiced that he would relieve Henry at 1 a.m. Maggie offered to join him to pull her weight. With that settled, Maggie said goodnight.

She climbed into her tent, unrolling her sleeping bag. She slid in, stretching out inside. She fidgeted around, trying to get comfortable. The realization that she laid in a tent in the Egyptian desert struck her. She hoped she could sleep. Despite the exhaustion and limited sleep the night before, she laid awake staring at the tent's roof.

The sound of her tent unzipping sent her bolting upright to sitting. "Comfy, princess?" Henry asked, poking his head into the tent.

"Comfy would be a stretch, but I'm okay, yeah."

"Your first night in a tent," Henry noted. He grinned at her.

"Yep," she answered. "What a thrill!"

Henry chuckled. "Need anything?"

"Nope, just some sleep."

Henry smiled at her. "Okay, I'll leave you to it. If you need anything, I'm just a holler away."

Maggie returned his smile. "Okay, thanks."

"Good night, princess."

"Good night." Henry paused a moment before ducking out of the tent and zipping it shut. Maggie sat for a few more moments before she laid back. She laid awake for fifteen minutes, her mind jumping from one thing to another. While she was tempted to get up, she stayed in her sleeping bag. After a while, she dozed off.

* * *

The sound of her tent flap unzipping woke Maggie. It seemed as though she had been asleep for mere minutes. "What now?" she asked.

"Your turn," Emma announced. She crawled into the tent and rolled out her sleeping bag. Maggie nodded, sighing and yawning as she crawled from her sleeping bag. "Have fun!" Emma exclaimed as she snuggled into her sleeping bag and closed her eyes.

Maggie grumbled as she crawled from the tent. Tarik lounged near the fire. Maggie stretched in a few directions before she joined him. "Good morning, Maggie," he greeted her as she plopped down near the fire.

"I'm not sure I would categorize this as good but..." Maggie groaned. She yawned again.

Tarik laughed, poking at the fire to reignite a few logs. "If you fall asleep, I will be okay," he assured her. "If you want to go to your tent, it's okay."

"Thanks, that's very nice of you," Maggie said. "But, no, I'll be okay."

"You are a stubborn woman, Maggie, huh?"

"Very," Maggie admitted.

"Admirable trait."

Maggie reflected on his statement for a moment. "I think you're the first person ever to tell me that."

"Really?" Tarik questioned.

"Yes. Most people find it aggravating," Maggie admitted.

"Ah, but you stick to your convictions, you don't back down. Very admirable."

"I'll remember that next time someone tells me it's annoying."

"And who has told you this?"

"Lots of people. Uh, the latest is my boyfriend, Leo," Maggie replied.

"He does not find your tenacity admirable?"

Maggie laughed. "In a word, no."

"He finds it annoying?"

"Oh, yes. And he tells me all the time."

"Ah, well, perhaps Leo is not very wise to realize what an outstanding character you have."

Maggie smiled at him. "I'll remember to tell him that, too."

"Please tell him I said so."

Maggie smirked. "I will do that."

"Why do you remain with him if he does not appreciate you?"

"He does, in his own way," Maggie answered.

"It doesn't sound like it."

"He doesn't appreciate my stubbornness, no. But... he loves me in his own way. And I love him."

"He loves you but doesn't appreciate all your qualities. Never remain with someone who doesn't know your worth, Maggie. It is beneath you."

Maggie considered the statement. Perhaps he was on to something, Maggie mused. They spent the rest of the night making intermittent conversation. When they weren't talking, Maggie laid on her back enjoying the stars. She'd never seen so many. They polluted the cloudless sky, it seemed.

An unexpected coolness in the night air drove Maggie to search out another hoodie to wrap around her shoulders. She didn't expect the desert to be so cold at night given the roasting temperatures during the day.

At long last, hints of light brightened the eastern sky. The sun would rise soon. Maggie welcomed the sight. Despite Tarik's pleasant company, Maggie itched to get moving. They now seemed so close to their goal, yet still so far.

As the first ray's lit the sky, Tarik rose to feed the camels and prepare their breakfast. Maggie offered to help with the camel feeding. After a brief set of instructions from Tarik, she found the task easy.

"Wow! Look at you," Henry said as he emerged from his tent. "It seems like you are actually enjoying that!"

"It's not so bad," Maggie answered, feeding her camel some oats. "Did you sleep?"

"I did," Henry answered. "Did you get any sleep before your shift?"

"Yes, although not enough," Maggie said.

"Didn't Tarik let you sleep anymore? I might have to let him have it."

Maggie laughed. "He said I could, but I didn't. He's such a sweetheart."

"Yes, you've told me." Henry paused for a moment. "Maggie, how well do you know Emma?"

She shrugged. "Umm," Maggie replied, "we were sorority sisters in college. We spent a lot of time together then. We weren't best friends. She seemed to be jealous if she perceived you had an easier life. She was on an academic scholarship, and she had to work hard for everything. So, she was always a little intense. We lost touch after grad school. I haven't talked a lot to her in recent years. Why?"

Henry shook his head. "No reason, just curious."

"Breakfast is almost ready," Tarik shouted to them.

"Thanks, mate," Henry answered.

"Just curious? I don't buy that," Maggie said. She dusted her hands off for breakfast.

"Ah…" Henry began choosing not to finish his sentence when Emma appeared.

She crawled from the tent. "Good morning," she said. "Why didn't anyone wake me?"

"We were just about to," Tarik answered. "Breakfast is almost ready!"

Emma stood, stretching and pulling her hair into a low ponytail. Maggie retrieved her purse, slicking on a little mascara before breakfast. They ate breakfast, packed the sleeping bags and tents, and were on their way for their second day in the desert.

Quiet solitude filled the morning hours. Maggie would have found it relaxing if a major crisis was not hanging over their heads. As they stopped for lunch, Maggie asked how close they were to their destination.

Henry pointed it out on his map along with their approximate location. They appeared to be less than halfway to the location marked by the scarab.

Maggie scowled. "That's it?" she asked.

"'Fraid so, princess," Henry answered.

"Trip wearing on you?" Emma taunted.

"No," Maggie claimed. "I just figured we were further."

"The desert can be tedious," Emma snarked, using a sarcastic, know-it-all voice.

"I'm finding it calming," Maggie retorted.

"Calming?" Emma repeated. She laughed derisively.

"Yes, calming," Maggie reiterated. She stalked away to end the conversation.

After their lunch, they continued their journey through the late afternoon. They stopped their journey at the same time as they did the previous day. The group ate dinner and pitched their tents for the night.

"First watch, again?" Emma asked Henry.

"Ah, I figured we'd change it up tonight…" Henry began.

"Second watch, then?" Emma interrupted.

"Yeah, second watch for you."

"For us, you mean," Emma corrected.

"No, for you and Tarik. Maggie and I will take first watch."

"Oh…" Emma began.

"That sounds great! Conversations won't get stale this way," Maggie chimed in. She gave Emma a huge grin.

"Sounds great," Emma mumbled. Though she sounded less than convinced. "Guess I'll head to bed then." Emma rolled her eyes.

"Oh, just a sec, let me lay out my sleeping bag so I don't have to do it later."

"By all means," Emma groused. She motioned for Maggie to precede her into the tent.

After a few minutes, Maggie emerged. "All set. Well, have a great sleep. I'll wake you when it's your turn."

"Great," Emma groaned. She climbed into the tent.

Tarik was already in his tent. Maggie approached the fire where Henry sat. She plopped down next to him. "Hope I'm as good company as you had last night," she said. She winked at him.

"I have a feeling you'll be better company," he said. He grinned at her.

"It's beautiful," Maggie said. She motioned to the painted sky in the west. Hues of red, purple and blue streaked the sky where the sun slipped below the horizon.

"It is," Henry agreed. He stared at Maggie.

"I can't wait to watch the stars again tonight," Maggie said.

"The stars?" Henry asked.

"Yes. I've never seen so many! There seems to be more stars here than I've ever seen at home!"

"You weren't lying when you said you found it calming here, were you?"

"No, I wasn't. I realize Emma assumed I was being disingenuous, but I wasn't."

"You continue to surprise me, Maggie Edwards."

Maggie smiled at him, settling next to him to enjoy the last moments of light. As the sky darkened and the stars began to appear, Maggie reclined to have a better view. Henry laid next to her. The stillness of the desert night provided a perfect venue as the stars filled the sky.

"Do you always stargaze, princess?"

"No. I mean, I've looked at them before. But I've never paid tons of attention. I guess I just never took the time to appreciate them."

"Do you know the constellations?"

"No," Maggie answered.

Henry spent the next few hours pointing out constellations in the sky. "It seems like you've spent a lot of time stargazing," Maggie said.

"I've camped before, remember?" Henry joked. "It's one of

the things my father did with me when I was little before he passed away."

"How old were you?"

"Twelve," Henry answered.

"I'm sorry," Maggie said.

"It's all right, princess," Henry answered. "It's been a long time. It's not that raw anymore."

"Still, that's hard to lose a parent that young."

"Probably why I took to your uncle. He's rather like a father to me."

"That's nice," Maggie said. "I bet Uncle Ollie considers you the son he never had. What about your mom? Do you see her much with all your traveling, camping and stargazing?"

"My mom passed away when I was nineteen."

"Oh, I'm really sorry," Maggie uttered.

"It's fine, Maggie."

"So, after your mom died, is that when you traveled?"

"Yep. I left right after her funeral. Bounced around from place to place. Met your uncle when I was twenty-two and he got me on a better path than I was on."

"You?! On a questionable path? You don't say!"

"You should take your comedy routine on the road, princess. You're hilarious."

"My humor is my best quality," Maggie joked.

"You've got a lot of good qualities, Maggie," Henry said. He stared at her.

Maggie smiled at him, suddenly feeling awkward. As a distraction, she reached for her hoodie, pulling it over her. "Cold, princess?"

"A little," she whispered. A shiver shook her body.

"Come here," Henry said. He wrapped his arm around her, pulling her toward him.

Maggie bolted up to sitting. "You know, I'm okay," Maggie

announced. "I'm…"

Henry sat up next to her. "Maggie…" he hesitated. He gazed into her eyes. Maggie met his gaze. He traced the line of her jaw before leaning in to kiss her. Maggie returned his kiss before pushing away from him.

"Henry, we shouldn't… Not now."

"Maggie, there's something I need to tell you."

"Henry, I…"

"No, Maggie, please." Henry cupped her face in his hands. "Since we met, I have…"

"Good morning," Tarik called as he emerged from his tent. Maggie pulled away from him, fiddling with her sweatshirt.

"Good morning." Henry sighed.

Tarik approached the fire. "Ready for some rest, my friends?" he asked.

"Yep!" Maggie exclaimed. "Boy, am I tired. I'll just wake Emma." Maggie climbed to her feet, dusting the sand from herself.

Henry stood, grabbing Maggie's hand. "Maggie," Henry said, "can we finish our conversation first?"

"I'm just so tired. Can we save this for another time?" Maggie hedged as she inched away.

"Maggie, please…" Henry implored.

"Now's not the time. Let's just table it, Henry, please?"

Henry hesitated a moment, searching for an answer. He nodded. "Okay, okay, sure. Another time."

"Thanks," Maggie said. She hesitated a moment, not letting go of his hand. "Good night," she muttered after a breath.

"Good night, Maggie."

"Perfect timing, mate" she overhead Henry mumble as she walked away.

"Oops," Tarik answered, "sorry, my friend."

CHAPTER 20

*M*aggie hurried toward the tent. She unzipped it and crawled in. Emma slept curled in her sleeping bag. Maggie poked at her. It took her three tries to wake Emma. "What?" Emma protested.

"Your turn," Maggie announced as she climbed into her sleeping bag. "Have fun!" Maggie took pleasure in echoing Emma's sentiments of the previous night.

Emma sat for a few more moments then crawled from the tent, zipping it shut with a huff. Maggie slid into her sleeping bag, laying back. She squeezed her eyes shut, trying to force herself to sleep. Instead of falling asleep, she stared at the roof of the tent. She tossed and turned, trying to get comfortable. Comfort, however, was not the problem.

Maggie's mind whirled, replaying the evening with Henry over and over. She wasn't positive of what he planned to say, but she had her suspicions. If she was correct, it created a dilemma. What would she answer to him? She was with Leo. That was a fact. Wasn't it? Yet she wasn't sure she could deny the emotions that grew for Henry. She sat up, staring at the tent flap. She wanted to seek out Henry, tell him she wanted to finish their conversation, tell him she felt the same way.

Maggie shook her head. She wasn't even sure that's what Henry wanted to tell her. Besides, she and Leo were in love. Weren't they? They were well-suited. Both of them desired the same things in life: successful careers and all the perks accompanying them. Leo realized how difficult she was, and he stayed with her, more or less. They had their ups and downs. They had their on-again, off-again relationship, but they always found their way back to each other. That meant something, didn't it? She couldn't throw that away for a dalliance, a flirtation that would likely end in ruins.

She stared for another moment at the exit, convincing herself to stay put. She reached for the zipper. She rolled the zipper pull between her fingers. Her mind replayed the highlights of her evening: the magical starlit sky, the easy flow of their conversation, the effortlessness of their laughter, how perfect his embrace felt, how exhilarating their kiss was. That perfect embrace panicked her. The comfort she found in his arms had the same effect. She hadn't expected to experience the level of emotion she felt in that moment. It frightened her. It was too easy to fall into this fantasy. She dropped the zipper pull, collapsing back to laying. "Don't do anything stupid, Maggie," she whispered to herself. She had something solid with Leo. Their relationship might not have been as effortless as being with Henry, but it was safe, familiar. Safe, familiar, she focused on those words. Maggie fell asleep chanting them over and over in her head.

Maggie awoke the next morning as light filtered through the tent's material. She stretched, sitting for a few moments, gathering her thoughts. She grabbed her purse, digging out her makeup and applying it before climbing from the tent.

"Good morning, Maggie! Did you sleep well?" Tarik asked as she emerged from the tent.

"I did, thank you."

"We should get close today! Only one more night in the desert before we reach the area marked by the scarab. Then the real work begins," he stated. He grinned at her. "Come, eat some breakfast." Henry stood near the camels, staring at the horizon. "Henry, breakfast is ready, my friend!" Henry did not respond. "Henry!" Tarik called again.

"He's grumpy this morning," Emma added. "I already asked him to come over, he said he wasn't hungry. Guess his evening didn't go so well." Emma shot a glance to Maggie.

"I'll take him something," Maggie said. She grabbed two plates of food.

"See if you can get him to join us," Emma suggested. "Tarik and I are growing bored with each other. The conversation is getting stale."

Maggie held back rolling her eyes but couldn't hold back the giggle that escaped when Tarik said, "Stale? We barely talked. You slept most of the time."

Gathering the breakfast for two, Maggie approached Henry. Maggie sidled up to him. "Good morning," she said.

His eyes never left the horizon as he spoke. "Morning," he answered.

"Breakfast?" she asked. She offered a plate to him.

He took the plate without a word.

"How did you sleep?" Maggie inquired.

"We are going to make small talk?"

Maggie sighed. "Okay, about last night…" she hesitated.

"Maggie…" he began.

"Wait," Maggie interrupted him. "I want to finish this conversation, I do. But I'd prefer to do it… well, not here."

"What's the difference, Maggie?"

"Privacy, for one," Maggie said. She motioned toward their audience.

Henry glanced at them. Both Tarik and Emma looked

away as though they hadn't been watching them. "I see your point."

"Thank you," Maggie answered. She considered the conversation on hold.

"But Maggie, I don't want to avoid discussing what happened last night. It meant something to me."

Maggie considered his statement for a moment. "It meant something to me, too, but my life is upside down right now. I can't think."

"What is there to think about?"

"If you can't answer that, you haven't been paying attention."

"Leo?"

"For one thing," Maggie answered.

"What else? Because if that kiss meant to you what it did to me there isn't much to think about."

Maggie didn't answer.

"Maggie…" Henry began again.

"Henry, please," Maggie said. She stepped away. "We should get going." Maggie took another step away, then turned back. She grabbed his hand, squeezing it. "We'll finish this, I promise."

He smiled at her, keeping hold of her hand. "Okay. Let's get going then." They returned to their campsite, cleaning their dishes and packing the rest of their gear.

They set off for another long day, traveling deeper into the desert. The ride gave Maggie far too much solitude. It allowed her mind to delve into the situation with Henry far more than she would have preferred. By lunch, she imagined she may go crazy from analyzing the situation from every possible angle. Never one to overthink a situation, the constant analyzing was unfamiliar to Maggie. What was coming over her, she wondered? Was it because of her feelings for Henry? Was it because she was in love?

Their lunch was less tense than their breakfast. The solitary desert ride seemed to have improved Henry's mood. He was far less pensive and serious than this morning. Maggie spent her afternoon wondering what enhanced his mood.

They stopped in the late afternoon again, setting up camp and preparing dinner.

"Only a few more hours from here," Tarik announced as they sat down to eat.

"What do you suppose we'll find there?" Maggie asked.

"Desert," Tarik replied. Maggie frowned. "Were you hoping for something different?"

"A giant pyramid with a flashing sign that says 'Cleo's place,'" Maggie joked.

Tarik laughed heartily. "I doubt we'll be so lucky. But if the scarab says it's there, we must find it," Tarik answered.

"A girl can dream," Maggie said. "You think it's there, don't you?"

"It's there, princess. We just have to be smart enough to find it," Henry added.

"With my training, I hope to be of some help in that area," Emma piped in.

They finished their dinner as the sun set in the western sky. "Well, looks like it's me and you on first watch tonight, Henry!" Emma exclaimed after dinner. "In the interest of keeping conversations fresh."

"If you don't mind, I'll switch to first watch tonight," Tarik said, "So, if you're on first watch, Emma, you're stuck with me. Perhaps this time you'll stay awake for a conversation."

"Oh, I could switch..." Emma began.

"That sounds fine," Henry said. "Maggie and I will get some sleep and see you at one!"

"Maggie, if you prefer first watch, I'd be happy to switch," Emma entreated of Maggie.

"Uh," Maggie began.

"She doesn't," Henry answered for her. He grasped her arm and guided her toward the tents.

"Ah, good night!" Maggie called as Henry led her away.

"Good night, princess," Henry said as they arrived at her tent.

"Good night," Maggie answered. She climbed into her tent.

She readied herself for bed, hoping she could sleep, then curled up in her sleeping bag. Weary from deliberating all day, Maggie's mind was too exhausted to concentrate on anything but sleep. Within moments, she dozed off into a sound sleep for the night.

Emma rousted her from her sleep at 1 a.m., grumbling an unceremonious "Get up, your turn" before climbing into her own sleeping bag. Maggie yawned and stretched before crawling from her sleeping bag and into the night air. She zipped the tent shut, pulling on her hoodie as she stood.

Maggie approached Henry, who sat near the fire. "Good morning, princess," he greeted her.

Maggie yawned again. "Good morning."

He patted the sand next to him. Maggie collapsed in a heap. "Still sleepy?" he asked.

"I am NOT a morning person. Especially not a one-in-the-morning person."

"You don't say," Henry joked.

Maggie flopped backward, laying on her back. She closed her eyes for a moment. She took a few deep breaths before opening her eyes. Sighing, she glanced to Henry. "How are you so awake?"

"I'm used to little sleep."

"No one should be used to this, ugh," Maggie replied.

"Why don't you close your eyes for a little?" Henry said.

"No, I'll be fine. I just need a few minutes." She sat up,

drawing her knees to her chest and propping her head on her knees. "Why aren't there coffee shops in the desert?"

Henry laughed. "Aw, princess. Let me make you some coffee."

Maggie smiled at him. "I won't say no."

Henry retrieved a mug and prepared a pot of coffee. He poured a steaming mug, handing it to Maggie. "Mmm, thank you," Maggie said. She took a deep inhale of the coffee then sipped at it.

When she was halfway through her mug, Henry asked, "Better?"

"Much, thank you! You are a life saver."

"I must admit, I had ulterior motives."

"What were they? Not wanting to deal with a grumpy me for six hours?"

"I'd deal with a grumpy you for any length of time."

"Be careful what you wish for," Maggie cautioned him.

"Speaking of what I'm wishing for, perhaps we should finish our conversation from the other night."

Maggie opted for a joke in an attempt to avoid the subject. "Is this the real reason you made me coffee?"

Henry called her on her typical strategy for dealing with problems. "Maggie, stop avoiding the subject," he said.

Maggie tried to dodge the subject again. "I thought we agreed to postpone this discussion," Maggie replied.

"Until we were alone, if I recall," Henry answered.

"Being alone was only one of the reasons we postponed."

"Only one of the reasons YOU postponed. I was happy to discuss it yesterday morning or the night before," Henry replied.

"And I promised you we would discuss it, but there's kind of a lot going on right now."

Henry checked his watch. "There's not much going on at 2 a.m. in the middle of the desert."

"You're impossible," Maggie grumbled at him.

"Maggie…" Henry said. He cupped her face in his hands.

"Henry…" Maggie interrupted him, pushing his hands away. "I'm serious. With Leo kidnapped, this feels like a betrayal. I'm not used to this. I can't even think right now! All my mind can process is Uncle Ollie, Leo, finding this tomb."

"Do you love him?" Henry asked.

Maggie pondered it a moment. It was a question she'd asked herself over and over since their kiss the night before. "We've been together for a long time," she settled on as an answer.

"That doesn't answer the question."

"He understands me."

Henry abandoned his previous line of questioning. "So, our kiss meant nothing to you?" he prodded.

"I didn't say that."

"Then what are you saying, Maggie?"

"Nothing. I don't know. It's too early for this conversation and there's too much going on for my brain to process this." Maggie leapt to her feet, stalking away from Henry. She could not face this conversation. The truth was Maggie had no clue what she felt anymore. Her feelings for Henry grew stronger by the day, yet her history with Leo seemed safe.

Henry followed her. "Maggie, wait," he said. He reached for her arm.

"Please, don't," she answered. She pulled away, not trusting herself with him.

"Maggie," he said. Henry reached for her again. "Stop."

Maggie held back tears. "I can't. Not now."

"It's okay," Henry told her. He pulled her closer to him. "It's okay, Maggie."

"I'm sorry," she said. She allowed him to wrap her in his arms. "I'm sorry I don't have a better answer for you."

"Maggie, it's fine. We'll talk when you're ready."

Maggie remained in his embrace a few moments longer. She glanced up at him after a breath. "Thank you," she whispered.

Henry smiled at her. "Well, I don't want to make you cry. You know how I hate it when you cry."

Maggie chuckled. "Yes, I do."

He gazed at her a moment longer before he suggested, "Let's go back over by the fire before you get cold."

"Okay," Maggie agreed. He took her hand, leading her toward the fire. They settled near it. Relief coursed through Maggie. With the prospect of the conversation on hold, she had time to contemplate her feelings. Her tension melted. The easy ambiance between them returned.

Henry gazed upward. "Your stars are out, princess," he said.

Maggie followed his gaze. "They are."

"Let's see how much you paid attention when I pointed out those constellations last night," Henry teased, laying back.

Maggie laid back nex to him. "Oh, I didn't realize there would be a test." Maggie giggled.

They spent the remaining hours discussing constellations, navigation by the stars, and more. About an hour before the sunrise, Maggie dozed off. Henry covered her with his jacket, letting her catch a quick nap before the sun rose.

Tarik emerged from his tent as the first rays of light brightened the eastern sky. "Good morning!" he called as Henry signaled for him to lower his voice.

"She's asleep," Henry whispered.

"You're having as much luck as I am at keeping your watch buddy awake," Tarik joked. "I hope your night went well."

"Went just fine, mate, just fine." Tarik gave Henry a sly

smile. "I'll wake Emma, then feed the camels if you want to start breakfast. I'll wake Maggie as soon as I finish with the camels."

Henry roused Emma from her tent before moving to the task of feeding their camels. Emma stretched, approaching the fire and plopping down. She glanced at Maggie's sleeping form, nestled under Henry's jacket. "Need any help?" she shouted over to Henry.

The noise startled Maggie awake. Maggie glanced around. She sat up. "Did I fall asleep?" she asked.

"Good morning. Yes, you were having a little nap," Tarik said.

Maggie yawned. "Oh, oops. What a good watchdog I am, huh?" she joked. Tarik chuckled with her.

Maggie climbed to her feet, heading toward Henry. She wrapped herself in his jacket. "Good morning," she said. "Need help?"

He handed her the bag of oats and she fed her camel while he finished with the others. "Ready for breakfast, princess?" he asked when they finished.

They rejoined Emma and Tarik for breakfast. "We should make it to the spot marked by the scarab by lunch time," Tarik estimated. Maggie ate her breakfast and completed her normal routine of makeup.

"You are obsessed with that makeup," Emma noted.

"When we find Cleopatra's tomb today, I want to look my best," Maggie joked. "The selfies we take will be famous. Seriously though, I told you, it makes things feel normal for me. It's my routine, it's calming!"

After packing their gear, the foursome set off for the morning journey on camelback. Tension built with each passing moment as Maggie wondered what they might find when they reached the spot marked by the scarab. Tarik mentioned nothing being there on satellite images. Maggie hoped that was not the case. Not only would it be disappointing after all their efforts, but it also meant they were at a dead end finding her uncle, Leo and Charlie.

As Leo entered her mind, her focus turned toward her other dilemma. Her conversation with Henry played over and over in her mind. He asked her if she loved Leo. Until now, she assumed she had. Why hadn't she admitted that to Henry? Why couldn't she say those words out loud?

A shout from Tarik interrupted her musing. Before they left, he had programmed a GPS system with the coordinates corresponding to the location given by the scarab. The system showed they were approaching the location and would arrive in the next few minutes.

Maggie searched the horizon, finding nothing but sand and sky. Disappointment filled her. She wasn't sure what she expected to find there, although a part of her had hoped it would be a giant pyramid with a flashing neon sign.

Within minutes, Henry dismounted from his camel. Everyone followed suit. "GPS says we're here," he said as everyone grouped around. Henry marked the spot with a tent pole.

Maggie glanced around. "No neon sign," she lamented.

"No neon sign, sorry," Tarik said.

"Aw, shucks," Maggie said. "So, now what?"

"Spread out. Make a quick search around and see what we find," Henry suggested.

"Good idea, my friend," Tarik agreed. "We will each search in an area around the coordinates. I will go north, you go south. Maggie, go east and Emma, go west."

"Okay," Maggie answered as they each faced their assigned direction. "Wait, what are we looking for?"

"Anything, princess," Henry said.

They spread out from the coordinates and searched for any sign of an ancient tomb. After forty-five minutes,

Maggie shouted to the rest of them. "How long are we planning on doing this?" She kicked the sand around near her.

"Until we find something," Emma suggested.

Maggie rolled her eyes, her shoulders drooping as she returned to her search.

Henry waved her back over to the marked spot. She collapsed in a heap. "It's so hot. Why is it so hot?" she complained.

"'Cause it's the desert," Emma suggested. She approached them from her quadrant. Maggie rolled her eyes. "We need to keep searching."

"This is getting us nowhere. Plus, I'm hungry!"

"One of the greatest archaeological finds of our time could be right under our feet and you're worried about your lunch," Emma snarked. "We need to keep going."

"No, Maggie's right," Henry said. The comment earned him a frustrated sigh from Emma. "This is getting us nowhere. If there was anything obvious, we'd have found it."

"Plus, we could all use a break and some food," Tarik agreed. "It is well after the lunch hour."

"Of course," Emma acquiesced, "let's do what Maggie suggested."

The snide remark did not slip past Maggie. She'd noticed several from Emma of late, and they were grating on her last nerve. Perhaps the heat or lack of sleep shortened Emma's temper.

As they set up for lunch, Maggie pulled her notes from her uncle's journal out of her purse. She plopped cross-legged next to Henry. "Perhaps these will help." She handed a few pages to Henry. "Check those pages for any mention of the location. Or what to do to find the tomb entrance."

"Good idea, princess." Maggie worked her way through half of the pages by the time lunch was ready. Tarik handed her a plate, and she set the notes aside while she ate.

"Did you find anything on your pages?" she asked Henry.

"No. Most of mine referred to things specific to the tomb itself, not locating it. What about you?"

"Nothing," Maggie shrugged. "I've got a few pages left to go through, but..." she stopped mid-sentence.

"But what, princess?" Henry asked.

"Wait, wait," Maggie exclaimed as a realization struck her. "Just a second." She pawed through the notes. "I could swear I saw..." She scanned the pages. "Yes! Here!"

"The scarab provides a map and when combined with the staff can open the tomb."

"Okay, so?" Emma asked. "If we find the entrance, we'll know to combine them to open the tomb."

"Yes, the scarab provided the location, but no details on how to locate the entrance. But the staff had tons of those pictures on it, those drawings..."

"Hieroglyphs?" Emma snarked.

"Yes, hieroglyphs. They didn't spend all that time putting those on the staff just for fun. Perhaps they give us instructions to find the entrance."

Tarik retrieved the staff piece from their belongings. "We only have one piece."

"Yes, but I have pictures of the other one," Maggie said, retrieving her phone and pulling up the pictures. She handed it to Emma. "With any luck, we can piece it together enough to find the entrance."

Henry grinned at her. "Smart thinking, princess," Henry said. He kissed the top of her head as he wrapped his arm around her shoulders.

Maggie smiled at him. "Thanks, I hope it works. Emma, can you read it?" she asked. Tarik handed the staff piece to Emma.

Emma studied it. "Yes. I mean, it might take me some

time, but I can translate it. At least I can provide a rough translation."

Maggie dug a pen and some blank paper from her purse. "Here, will this help?"

"Thanks," Emma answered. Emma studied the staff and Maggie returned to her notes from her uncle.

After thirty minutes, Maggie asked, "Any luck?"

Emma sat for a moment, silent. "Emma?" Maggie asked again.

"No. No luck."

"It doesn't say anything about locating the entrance?" Maggie asked.

Emma shook her head. "No. I don't know. I can't read this."

"What?" Maggie asked. "Isn't this what you do? I mean some of what you do?"

"Yes, but with a textbook next to me and the internet and half a dozen other resources. I'm not fluent in ancient Egyptian hieroglyphs. I spent my time cataloging stuff. I can't read this."

"Emma, you're the only one of us who can make any sense of that. You have to try," Maggie answered.

"I CAN'T," Emma stressed.

"Yes, Emma, you can!" Maggie answered. "You can do this."

Emma nodded, swallowing hard and taking another look at the staff piece. Within minutes, she tossed it to the side. "It's no use. I can't do it."

Maggie crawled over to her and handed her the staff piece again. "Emma," Maggie said, "yes, you can. Just do the bits you remember, and we'll try to piece it together. You have to remember what some of these pictures mean. Like this owl-looking one or the eye or the one that looks like a zipper."

"It's not a zipper," Emma answered. She snatched the staff back.

"Yes, you realize it's not a zipper, now remember what it is and write it down. If you don't remember one, skip it and we'll try to guess what it is later."

Emma ran her fingers through her hair, readjusted her ponytail and nodded. She took a deep breath. Studying the staff again, she picked up the pen and paper and began making notes.

After an hour of work, Emma spoke. "Okay, I don't have everything. I probably won't get everything, but I have some of it translated."

"And?" Maggie asked.

"It's hard to tell. It does appear to be directions for finding the entrance to the tomb."

"Yay!" Maggie exclaimed. "What does it say? Does it say which dune its under?"

"Not exactly. And what I've translated doesn't make much sense. Granted, I'm missing a good portion of this. But what I did decipher doesn't fit with anything. Of course, I could have done it wrong, this may be completely wrong."

"Just tell us what you have, and we'll go from there," Henry advised.

Emma grabbed her notes. "All right," Emma said. "It seems to provide a set of directions based on the scarab's coordinates. It gives the number of cubits, palms or digits to walk forward or backward in reference to a few things. But that's where this falls apart. Your zipper is a symbol for water. There's no water here. And the other bad news is I've only got a partial translation for some of this because I'm missing the hieroglyphs from the other staff piece."

"Cubits?" Maggie asked.

"Yes, a cubit was a unit of measurement in ancient Egypt," Emma answered.

"Where have I seen that word before? I swear I just came across that word!" Maggie pondered aloud. She stared into space, trying to remember.

"In the research you did to figure out the scarab map reference?" Henry suggested.

"No, no that's not it," Maggie answered.

"Well, anyway, we're at a standstill. This doesn't help us," Emma said. She threw her hands in the air.

"Wait, wait, I remember. It's somewhere in these notes. Give me those papers," she instructed Henry. She reached for his stack. She spent a moment searching through the sheets. "Here!" she exclaimed. "Here it is! I wonder if these notes are Uncle Ollie's translation of the staff."

A slight smile crossed Henry's face and Emma's face brightened. "If he translated it..." Emma began.

"We can match it up with these notes and have the entire set of instructions!" Maggie exclaimed. "I never made the connection before. These translations aren't labeled in Uncle Ollie's journal. I didn't realize what they meant until now!"

"Bring those over here, we'll compare to these," Emma said. They spent half an hour comparing notes, filling in gaps and organizing the translation.

"Okay, we have it," Maggie said when they finished.

"Yes, what water does this refer to?"

"I'm not sure, but at least you didn't do it wrong. See, I told you you could do it!" Maggie told Emma.

"Could the water refer to the Nile?" Henry asked.

"In one case, yes. But in another, the direction is wrong. It instructs us to walk to the southwest. The Nile is in the east."

"The Toshka Lakes are southwest of here," Tarik informed them.

"Oh," Emma responded. "Oh! Then perhaps this is correct!"

"There's one way to find out," Maggie said, climbing to her feet. "Let's try it."

Over the course of the next hour, they tried following the directions written on the staff. After a few false starts, they moved into a position they believed was correct.

"According to the translation, it should be here," Emma said. "Unless we made another mistake."

"Think positive," Maggie urged.

"If the tomb is here, it's buried," Tarik surmised.

Maggie kicked the sand around with her foot. They all glanced around for any signs of a buried tomb. "It's no use," Emma said after a few minutes, "there's nothing here."

"Should we try again? Maybe we did something wrong," Maggie suggested.

"Ugh, I'm exhausted, I need a break," Emma said.

"Let's take a breather," Tarik suggested.

"The sun'll be going down soon, we'll be at a standstill for the night," Henry noted.

"Ugh, this is so frustrating!" Maggie said, stomping her foot on the ground. "Ouch!" she shouted.

"What happened, princess? You okay?" Henry asked.

"Yes, I'm fine but I didn't expect the sand to be so hard. It's like I stomped on a stone."

"A stone?" Henry asked.

"Yes. You don't imagine..." Maggie began. They both leaned to the ground, sweeping away the sand with their hands.

"Anything?" Tarik asked, joining them.

"Oh, yes, mate!" Henry exclaimed. "There's something here. Oh, Maggie, great work!"

Emma joined them and they spent the next several minutes brushing sand away from the large stone. "Look!" Maggie exclaimed. "A scarab symbol carved into the stone!"

"Yes, it is! This must be it!" Tarik exclaimed. "I will

retrieve some tools, we will make better progress clearing this than with our hands."

Tarik raced toward their gear. "We did it!" Maggie exclaimed. She rested on her haunches.

Henry kissed her on the top the head. "We did, princess. Well done," Henry said.

Tarik returned with shovels, brushes and other tools to help them unearth the stone hidden under the desert sands. Working together, they found the edges of the stone and uncovered the entire massive stone.

As the light waned and the skies darkened, they admired their unearthed handiwork. A raised hole sat in the middle of the stone near the scarab carving. "Now for the next problem. We don't have the entire staff. And it's likely we need it to trigger whatever mechanism is down this hole," Emma said.

"Don't worry," a voice said behind them, "we'll take it from here."

Maggie glanced behind her, noticing Tarik's gaze and raised hands. She realized the reason for his raised arms in short order. Three men approached with weapons drawn against them. Maggie raised her arms as did Henry and Emma.

CHAPTER 21

"*T*hank you for leading us to the tomb. You did all the hard work for us," the leader of the group barked. "We'll take that from you." He motioned to the staff Tarik carried. Tarik tossed it over. "And the scarab."

Maggie carried it in her pocket. She turned to Henry for guidance. Henry nodded. "Give it to him, princess."

Maggie removed it from her pocket and tossed it toward them. "Stand aside," the man said. He waved his gun toward the right. "Bring the professor."

One of his men trotted back toward a caravan of camels and people. He grabbed one of the men, dragging him toward their location. As they approached, Maggie recognized the man. "Uncle Ollie!" Maggie said. She rushed toward him.

"Get back where I told you," the lead man yelled. He grabbed for Maggie's arm.

She slipped away from him as Henry lunged at him. "Don't touch her," he shouted before the second man struck him.

"Tie them up," the man ordered his associate.

Maggie raced to Ollie, throwing her arms around his neck. "Uncle Ollie! You're all right!"

"Oh, Maggie! Yes, I'm fine, just fine," Ollie answered. He wrapped her in a hug. "I'm sorry I got you involved in this."

"It's fine, Uncle Ollie. I'm okay. Have you seen Leo? Was he with you?"

"Yes, Maggie. He's fine. He's with us," Ollie answered. He motioned toward the caravan.

"As touching as this little reunion is, we have work to complete, professor," the leader retorted.

"Let my niece go first," Ollie said. He pushed Maggie behind him.

"And me," Emma chimed in. She tugged at her restraints. "You promised."

Maggie's jaw dropped. "Emma? You? You betrayed us?"

"Oh, don't judge me, Maggie. I did what I had to do."

"Yes, I promised once we found the tomb, I would let you and your friends go. But," the man corrected, "we haven't found it yet. Now, professor, if you wouldn't mind." He motioned to the staff pieces strewn in the sand.

Ollie moved toward the pieces, picking them up from the ground. Maggie followed him. He held the bottom piece of the staff and instructed Maggie to fit the top piece onto the bottom by sliding it then twisting it to lock them together. "Now for the scarab," Ollie said, relieving their adversary of the object. "It fits right at the top in the holder," Ollie explained, ever the teacher.

Maggie slid the scarab into the holder at the top of the staff. "Good. And now," Ollie said, striding to the stone in the ground, "we slide the staff into the hole." Ollie slid the staff in, meeting with some resistance. He twisted and turned it, pushing it further and further into the crevice.

As he continued to struggle, Maggie assisted, placing

more pressure on the staff to fit it into the millennia-old mechanism. "Ugh," Maggie groaned. "How much further."

"If my research is correct, only the scarab should be visible."

"You're kidding," Maggie said. She stopped from pushing on the object. She stared at the length of the staff, most of it still visible.

"We'll know if I'm wrong if the tomb opens before we get the entire thing sunk. Until then, we keep pushing."

Maggie rolled her eyes. She motioned to their assailants. "Do you think perhaps one of you could help?" she asked.

The commander signaled another man to assist. The third man approached Maggie, zip tie in hand for her wrists. "Get away! Don't touch me!" Maggie insisted. She ducked away from him.

"Don't make this harder than it needs to be, Ms. Edwards," the man said.

"I'm not making anything hard. Why don't you help them instead of worrying about me? What am I going to do? Wrestle you all to the ground? Flee from the middle of the desert?"

Henry chuckled at her response. The man glanced to his boss. "Just help the professor get that staff into the mechanism," he instructed. Maggie raised an eyebrow at him, crossing her arms. The man shoved the zip ties into his pocket, stalking away to join the others on the stone.

Maggie retreated to where Henry and the others waited. "Good going, princess," Henry whispered to her.

"Are you okay?" she asked him.

"I'm fine. There's a knife in my pocket," he whispered. He slid his eyes to the pocket. "If you'd be a doll and retrieve it for me, I'd be forever grateful."

Maggie glanced to his pocket, then to the man still holding

the gun on them. He was preoccupied with the progress on the staff. Maggie shoved her hand into Henry's pocket and retrieved the knife. She slid it into her own pocket as the man glanced back toward them. Maggie pretended to be monitoring the progress on the staff. It inched further and further into the hole.

She waited for a suitable moment to slip the knife back to Henry. She glanced to Henry, then to the man holding the gun. His gaze wasn't on them. She pulled the knife from her pocket, opening it. She slipped it to Henry as she stepped in front of him. "Is it possible to get a drink?" she asked. "I'm so thirsty."

"No, it's not possible," the man began. Henry pushed past her, lunging at the man and knocking him over. They fell to the ground, wrestling around. Henry grasped the arm holding the gun, knocking it against the ground until the gun fell from his grasp. The man reached for it, but Maggie raced toward them, kicking the gun away from his reach.

One of the men helping with the staff hurried toward them. Henry elbowed the man on the ground, diving for the gun. He picked it up, pointing it at the man on the ground.

"I wouldn't do that if I were you, Taylor," another man barked. He held Maggie around her neck, his gun leveled at her head. "Shoot him and I shoot her." Maggie tugged at his arm around her neck.

Henry tossed the gun away, raising his arms. "Logan," he shouted to the third man. "Tie Taylor up again. And this time, relieve him of any weapons he may still be carrying."

The man on the ground stood, dusting himself off. "Clever ruse," he said. "That earned you a new accessory, Ms. Edwards." He approached her, zip tying her wrists together.

"Ouch!" she protested.

"Now, get over there with the others," he instructed her. He shoved her toward Tarik and Emma.

"Sorry," Maggie whispered as she approached Henry.

"It's fine, princess. Are you okay?"

She nodded.

"Now, if we're finished with the theatrics, let's press on, shall we?" The man motioned to his colleagues to resume their work. Before they continued, Ollie yelled over to check on Maggie. She motioned she was okay. Along with the other men, he resumed their task. "Careful, careful," he cautioned. They shoved at the staff, rocking it back and forth.

"You're stalling," one of them complained.

"I'm not. If we break this staff, there will be no way to open the tomb's entrance. We must be careful," Ollie warned.

The man glanced to the leader. "Listen to the professor," he answered.

"Thank you," Ollie said.

"But be warned, professor, if this is a stall tactic, you'll regret it."

Ollie ignored the comment, returning to inching the staff into the hole. It took them over an hour to ease the staff into the hole. "Just about there," Ollie announced. "careful, careful. Just a bit more."

The last inch of the staff disappeared into the hole. "Nothing happened," one of the men protested.

"The scarab's not lined up with the carving," Ollie pointed out. "We need to twist it." Ollie grunted with effort as he rotated the staff in the hole. As the orientation of the scarab lined up with the carving, an enormous boom sounded and the ground shook. Maggie struggled to stay on her feet as the ground shuddered and a loud whirring sounded.

The sand shifted, and the dune fell away near the stone. The men leapt back, retreating from the shifting sands. Ollie backed a step away, staring at the scene unfolding. Once the movement settled, a gaping hole next to the stone slab yawned at them.

"Gentlemen," Ollie announced, "welcome to Cleopatra's tomb."

Maggie peered into the gaping hole. Blackness stared back.

"All right," the lead man said. "Let's not waste time. After you, professor."

"Just a moment," Ollie cautioned. "We must move with caution. They built these tombs with booby traps and secret mechanisms designed to keep trespassers out. This tomb was no exception. My notes outlined everything I found on the subject."

"Logan," the man shouted, "retrieve Professor Keene's notebook."

"I don't have my notebook," Ollie admitted. "Without it, this will be slow going."

"Where is it?" the man asked.

"We had it," Maggie piped in.

"Wonderful! Logan, retrieve Professor Keene's notebook from Ms. Edwards' possession," the man answered. Ollie's face shown with hope.

"But we lost it running from you people," Maggie admitted. Everyone heaved a sigh.

The man approached Maggie. "Then why did you mention it?" he questioned. Henry stepped in front of Maggie.

"But I have my notes from your notebook."

The man blinked at Maggie. "Well, let's get them," he barked at her.

Maggie held her hands up. "If you could just remove this," Maggie said.

"After your last stunt, that's not going to happen. Logan, escort Ms. Edwards to wherever she needs to go to retrieve these notes."

The man named Logan stepped forward, grasping

Maggie's arm and guiding her toward their gear. Maggie pulled away from his grip after a few steps. They walked toward their campsite. Maggie pointed to her purse, telling Logan the notes were inside.

"Oh, wait, wait," she said. "Could you first grab my lip gloss. It's in the little front pocket."

The man stared at her a moment.

"What's the problem?" the leader shouted at them.

"Sir, she's asking for her lip gloss."

"It's not a big request," Maggie shouted.

"Get the notes and get back here!" the leader yelled.

"Yes, sir!"

"So, it's a no on the lip gloss?" Maggie hedged as she processed the situation in her mind.

"Where are the notes?"

"Front pocket. Right by the lip gloss if you can manage to grab both," Maggie said.

Logan reached inside, retrieving the notes. "Let's go," he said. He pointed back to the tomb entrance.

They returned to the group. Ollie reached for the notes, leafing through them. "What was really in the pocket?" Tarik whispered to Maggie.

"Lip gloss. My lips are really dry. It must be this desert air. Also, trying to buy us some time while I think."

Tarik gave her an odd glance and Emma rolled her eyes.

The lead man grew impatient. "Well?" he demanded.

"Ah," Ollie hesitated, "I'm not sure these are complete, but they contain a fair amount of the information."

"Excellent. Then we proceed. Logan, Mason, bring flashlights and whatever else the good professor may need."

Ollie gave them a list of a few other archaeological tools he wanted to have for their trip inside. Logan and Mason gathered the materials requested, meeting back at the tomb's entrance.

"All right, professor, it's your show."

"Uh, sir," Logan said, "perhaps we should send them in with him." He pointed toward Maggie, Henry, Emma and Tarik.

"Why would we do that?" the leader retorted.

"Because of the traps and curses and stuff. I mean, if someone's going to die, let it be them."

"Hey!" Maggie exclaimed.

"Fair point," the leader said, "all right, you four, let's move. Oh, Logan, why not have their other friends join us, too." Logan ran back toward their caravan, speaking with the men there. They dragged two people forward with them as they returned.

"Leo!" Maggie exclaimed as they approached. Leo appeared fine, although he did not answer Maggie's shout.

"And me, chicky!" Charlie chimed in from behind him. "I know you've been worried."

"All right, listen up," the boss shouted. "We are going into the tomb. You all," he said, pointing to Maggie and her friends, "are our shields. You will go first. Professor Keene, if you miss anything, their lives will be on the line. If you step out of line, if there is any funny business…" He glanced at Maggie. "We will not hesitate to end your life." He loaded a bullet into the chamber of his gun. Now," he said, "let's move out."

"Can you at least cut these off?" Maggie asked. She waved her hands in the air.

"No, I cannot," he answered. "Move!"

"It would be helpful to have an assistant," Ollie mentioned. "Maggie wrote these notes, so she is most familiar with them. Could you remove her restraints?"

Without a word, the man swung his knife open, slicing the zip tie from her wrist.

"What about me? You said you'd…" Emma began.

"Enough!" the man yelled. "No one else is getting any special treatment. Move!"

Maggie moved toward Ollie. "Thanks," she said to him.

He nodded to her. "Stay close to me, Maggie. These tombs are full of secrets, some of them deadly."

"Okay," Maggie agreed.

Logan passed flashlights to Maggie and Ollie. Each of the tomb raider team turned on the flashlights mounted to their guns. With their lights on, Ollie led the way with Maggie by his side. The tomb raiders herded the rest of the group in behind them.

The smooth stone floor sloped deep into the earth. "Careful," Ollie cautioned a few steps in. He held his hand up to stop their progress.

"What is it, Uncle Ollie?" Maggie asked.

He knelt near the sloped floor. "Here," he said, pointing, "see these tiles?" He used a brush to carefully remove sand to expose the tile set in the floor. "These are triggers for something. Stand back." Kneeling behind the tile, he depressed it. An arrow shot from the wall, glancing off the far wall.

"Wow!" Maggie exclaimed.

"Likely poison dipped," Ollie said. "Don't touch it."

Maggie nodded as Ollie informed the group to be careful of their step. They agreed to follow single file behind Ollie to lessen the chances of triggering one of the arrow tiles. It was slow-going and tedious. The tile placement became more numerous and erratic as they traveled further into the tomb.

After a nerve-wracking twenty minutes, they reached the bottom of the sloped floor. A long hallway stretched in front of them. Their flashlights did little to pierce the blackness. They could not view the end of the corridor.

Ollie positioned his light on the nearby walls. Carved pictures and hieroglyphs filled them. A channel filled with liquid ran along the corridor on both sides. Ollie dipped a finger into the liquid, rubbing it with his thumb. He sniffed it.

"What is it?" Maggie asked.

"Fuel," Ollie answered. "Anyone have a match or a lighter?"

One of the tomb raider team passed a lighter to Ollie. Ollie opened it, setting it aflame and bending the flame toward the channel. Flames burst to life, racing down the hallway.

"Wow!" Maggie exclaimed. "This is incredible!"

"These hieroglyphs," Ollie said. "Amazing! The information we will gain from these will be incredible."

"We don't care about the information," the boss said. "Keep moving."

Ollie sighed. "There's nothing in my notes or my memory about this corridor. We must proceed with extreme caution. There's nothing I am aware of to watch for."

Maggie nodded. "What's at the end?" Maggie asked as they began inching down the hall.

"We should find a chamber and passageways to different chambers from it. The other chambers contain what our friends are after."

"Treasure," Maggie concluded.

"Maggie, if you get the opportunity to leave, take it. These men are not to be trifled with."

"I'm not leaving you!" Maggie argued.

"Maggie, I'll be fine. If you have the chance, you take it and you go!"

Maggie sighed. "We'll cross that bridge if we come to it. For now, let's worry about staying alive."

"Good idea," Ollie agreed.

Maggie glanced at the walls as they continued down the hall. The craftsmanship was amazing. Massive stone slabs with intricate carvings decorated the space. Maggie marveled at the sight. Despite the immediate threat to her life, she appreciated the staggering moment. They were privileged to experience this. Maggie reached out to touch the wall next to her. She ran her hand along the stone, letting her fingertips discover the carvings. She pushed against the wall where a stone piece protruded. The piece gave way, retracting into the wall.

CHAPTER 22

"*A*hhhh," Maggie began before they heard a shout at the back of the group.

"Move!" another shout came. Maggie glanced back, screaming at what she witnessed. The floor seemed to ripple. Each massive stone slab comprising the floor flipped over before settling back to the ground. Ollie grabbed her arm, and they ran toward the end of the corridor. Everyone followed, gathering in the massive chamber as the floor near them heaved. The final stone tile of the corridor flipped over, revealing a dark abyss underneath. It snapped shut, settling with a loud clap.

"Is everyone all right?" Ollie asked. Maggie searched the group. She and Ollie had reached the end of the corridor first. She spotted Henry, breathing a sigh of relief. She glanced around him, finding Leo, Emma and Charlie. It seemed her friends had made it through alive.

"Hudson's gone," someone reported.

The leader of the group swore under his breath. He leveled his weapon at Ollie. "What did I tell you about being careful, professor?"

"It was my fault," Maggie confessed. She jumped in front of Oliver. "I touched the wall by accident, and it triggered something. I'm sorry, I didn't mean to."

"Keep your hands to yourself from now on, Ms. Edwards. Now, professor, let's continue."

Ollie nodded. "Several chambers should branch off from this antechamber. We'll systematically go through them. My notes suggest there are still a few triggers we must be careful of, so we'll continue to proceed with caution."

Each wall of the massive, unadorned room contained a doorway hewn into the stone. Ollie opted to begin at the left wall. The group waited in the main chamber as Ollie and Maggie checked the door for traps, then entered each chamber. Mason and Logan accompanied them.

The first door did not contain any apparent booby traps. Still, Logan forced Maggie through the doorway first to be safe. She made it through unscathed, followed by Ollie, then their two guards.

"Oh, wow!" Maggie exclaimed as she viewed the contents of the room lit by the fire that spread through the channel connecting to the outer room.

In the middle of the room sat a massive wooden river boat. Its enormous scale dwarfed Maggie and her companions. Workers had assembled the boat inside the chamber. It filled the space.

"Incredible, isn't it? A ship for Cleopatra to use in the afterlife," Ollie commented.

"Amazing! It's huge!" Maggie marveled.

"But worthless, let's move on," Logan griped.

Dismayed at not being permitted to study the sight further, they left the room behind. Re-entering the chamber, they joined the others.

"Well?" the leader asked.

"A stupid boat," Logan answered.

"Made of gold?" the leader inquired.

"No. Wood. Worthless," Logan responded.

Ollie crossed the antechamber to the right wall. "Let's try this one next," he suggested.

As they crossed, Maggie glanced to Henry, who waited nearby. "If you see an opportunity to run, princess, take it," he advised her as she passed him.

She nodded, following Ollie to the door. They checked the doorway, searching every inch and the area around it for any triggers. Finding none, they proceeded through the door. This time Ollie insisted he go first. Flames also lit this room. Inside sat three mummies and multiple canopic jars. "Is this the old broad herself?" Logan asked.

"Certainly not," Ollie informed him. "She'd never be buried this close to the tomb entrance, nor with such little pomp and circumstance. These are servants who wait to attend her in the afterlife."

"Were they dead when she died?" Maggie inquired.

"Probably not. They surrendered their lives upon her death and were embalmed and placed in her tomb."

"Wow, that's dedication," Maggie noted.

"I'll say," Logan agreed.

"There is nothing of monetary value here," Ollie assessed. "Let's move on."

They exited the chamber, rejoining the others in the main room. "Nothing yet," Logan reported.

"Professor, you had better not be stalling," the leader warned.

"I am not. We must check each room. We have no idea the layout of the tomb. What you seek could be anywhere," Ollie assured him.

They proceeded to the final doorway, across from the entrance to the tomb. "Last one," Maggie breathed. They checked the doorway and surrounding area for triggers.

Again, they found none. Ollie lifted his foot to step forward when Maggie grabbed him, pulling him back. As she dragged him back, his foot caught a small protruding stone near the doorway. Two massive axes swung from openings appearing in the side walls before retracting into the wall.

"Whew!" Ollie exclaimed. He wiped a bead of sweat from his brow. "That was too close. Thank you, Maggie. How did you realize?"

"Your notes had a drawing of it. I remembered just as you were about to enter."

"How can we enter?" Logan asked.

"Step over the threshold, do not touch the protrusions there," Ollie informed him.

Ollie hopped over, landing on the opposite side in another hallway. Maggie followed next, then the two guards. The floor on the opposite side sloped downward.

Moving with caution, they inched their way down deeper into the tomb. "This is amazing," Maggie marveled. "How did they build all this?" She gazed at the intricately carved walls.

"Aliens," Ollie joked.

After they descended the length of the corridor, they reached a landing. Ollie tested it, stepping on it with one foot and tapping. Nothing triggered, so Ollie stepped onto the landing with both feet. Nothing happened.

"Seems to be clear," Maggie said.

"Wait!" Ollie cautioned her. He held his hand up. "Just a moment." He moved to the wall. He shined his flashlight's light on a small stone flush against the wall. He positioned his finger flat on the floor against the stone. "Okay, Maggie only step on."

Maggie stepped onto the landing. "Just as I figured," Ollie said.

"What is it?" Maggie inquired, leaning over Ollie's shoulder.

"When I stepped onto the landing, it felt as though the landing shifted down. When you stepped on, it shifted again. It's gradually exposing this tile. When this tile becomes exposed entirely, it will trigger a trap." Ollie shined the light around. "There!" he exclaimed. He shined the light above them. Massive stones hung above their head, held back by a stone lattice. "My guess is that stone lattice will retract if we put too much weight on this plate."

"So, we should limit the number of people standing on it at any time," Maggie concluded.

"Not quite," Ollie corrected. "You may be correct, Maggie, however, I'm not taking a chance. It may be that once a certain number of people step on it, it triggers."

"You figure it doesn't reset after we step off?" Maggie asked.

"That's my concern. I'm not positive, and I don't want to take the chance."

"What do you propose?"

"We wedge this stone into place. And limit the number of people stepping on it at one time," Ollie answered.

"How can we wedge it?" Maggie pondered aloud.

"Floor jacks," Logan answered. "We have floor jacks in case of a collapse. We could wedge it between the walls to keep it in place."

"Great idea," Ollie answered. "Mind retrieving one?"

"Fine," Logan answered. "But I take her with me." He motioned to Maggie with his gun.

Maggie rolled her eyes. "Fine, come on," Maggie answered, stepping back into the angled corridor. They retreated to the main chamber above.

"What now?" the leader asked.

"Need a floor jack," Logan answered.

"What for?" the man responded.

"Disable a trap."

"Marshall," the leader hollered, "grab one of the floor jacks from the gear and take it back to the professor with Logan."

The man nodded, shouldering his weapon and digging through their gear for one of the floor jacks they'd brought. They rushed down the corridor. After a few minutes, they had the jack extended to reach between the two walls. Marshall continued to crank it until it held tight against the tile.

Ollie was satisfied with the solution. "Good," he said. "Maggie first. Step over the jack and then we'll move off the plate into the next chamber."

"No," Logan insisted. "I'll go with you. Maggie will come next with Mason. Then, Marshall, you come last."

"Fine," Ollie conceded. "Careful." Logan stepped over the floor jack onto the platform. "Now, into the chamber."

They stepped through the doorway. "Come on, Maggie," Ollie shouted. "Bring the lighter!"

Maggie and Mason stepped onto the platform and through the doorway. Marshall followed behind them. They grouped inside the doorway. They stood in a small alcove. Stone walls surrounded them on all sides except the direction they had come from.

"It's a dead end!" Logan cried.

"I doubt that," Ollie answered.

"How do you figure, old man?" Logan pressed, banging against the walls with the butt of his gun. "It's solid stone."

"We're missing something," Ollie mumbled. He referenced his notes. "Nothing."

"We're missing something all right," Logan rumbled. "Treasure."

"Uncle Ollie's right," Maggie argued. "Why build this corridor if it leads nowhere. We're missing something. Look around, see if you find anything."

"Fine," Logan sighed. They spent the next several minutes studying the walls.

"Here!" Maggie shouted, blowing dust off a dial on the right wall. Using the brush he carried, Ollie dusted it off.

"Appears to be an ancient combination lock," he mentioned.

"What's the combination?" Logan asked.

"I'm not sure," Ollie answered. Logan huffed, dropping his head back in frustration.

Maggie stared at the lock. Ollie noticed her stare. "What is it, Maggie?" he asked.

"These symbols are so familiar to me."

Ollie leafed through his notes again. "They aren't in my notes," he answered.

"No," Maggie admitted. "No, I saw them... where? Where?" She paced in a small square before it hit her. "Up there!" she exclaimed. "There's a carving showing a woman standing by a wall with a dial and some symbols."

"Careful," Ollie cautioned as they retraced their steps up the corridor. "Two at a time only!"

Maggie led the group halfway up the corridor. She shined her light on the carving she referenced. "There!"

"Great work, Maggie!" Ollie said.

"It shows all the symbols on that dial, how does this help us?" Logan asked.

"Some of them are outlined in gold," Maggie pointed out. "I bet those are the ones we use."

"Yes," Ollie agreed. "Notice the gold tracing around the symbols range from thin to thick. I'd bet that shows the order."

"Does it matter which way we turn to the symbols?" Maggie asked.

Ollie studied the diagram. "Alternating, turn right first. Notice her hand and these arrows."

"We have it! Shall we try?" Maggie asked.

"Yes," Logan insisted, "let's go." They retraced their steps to the anteroom. "You'd better be right," Logan threatened.

Ollie grasped the dial, turning it to the right. It didn't budge. "What's wrong?" Logan asked.

Ollie tried to turn it again. "It's stuck," he grunted.

"Wait, wait," Maggie said. "Let me try." She grasped the dial, pulling it toward her then turning it to the right. It moved with ease. She input the combination detailed in the diagram. Ollie confirmed each symbol as she input it. "Last one," Maggie breathed.

She twisted the dial to point to the last symbol. She landed on the final symbol.

"Nothing happened," Logan said. "You did it wrong."

"Wait," Maggie answered. She pushed the dial back into the wall. As she did, a mechanism clanked and whirred. The stone panel across from the entrance slid open. Maggie hopped with excitement.

Before entering, they checked the doorway for any traps. Finding none, Ollie stepped into the chamber. Maggie followed him, then the guards. Their flashlights did little to keep the darkness in the cavernous space at bay. Mason opened the lighter, passing it to Ollie. Ollie lit the lighter and used it to light the fuel-laden channel encompassing this chamber. As the flames ripped through the channel, lighting the room, everyone gasped.

Maggie's eyes widened. Ollie's jaw dropped. Shouts emerged from the other men. All manner of riches filled the chamber. Gold, silver and precious gems in various forms such as coins, jewelry and statues. Their guards clapped each other on the backs, congratulating themselves on a job well done.

"We'll be rich," Logan said to the other two.

"Damn right, we will be," Mason answered.

"What are we waiting for, boys? Let's inform Ben and start hauling this out," Logan suggested.

"There's likely more to the chamber," Ollie interjected.

"You keep examining the place, old man. I'm going to start filling a duffel with anything I can carry," Marshall said.

"Mason, you wait here with the professor. We'll go inform Ben. You," he motioned to Maggie with his gun, "move."

"Wait," Ollie said. "I'm coming, too."

"Suit yourself, professor," Logan shrugged. "Let's go."

"Remember, two at a time," Ollie reminded them.

They exited the chamber, two by two, with Marshall bringing up the rear. They rushed up the hallway and into the large chamber where everyone else waited.

Logan raced into the chamber. "Well?" Ben demanded.

"We hit the motherlode, boss. Gold, jewels, the whole nine." His voice was giddy with enthusiasm.

"Haha!" Ben shouted as a holler went up through his men. "We did it, boys!"

"Let's set up a system and start hauling," Logan said.

"Just a moment," Emma interrupted. "You got what you wanted. Now let us go. That was the deal."

Ben laughed at her. "We're holding the guns; we make the rules. Although, I'm feeling magnanimous, so fine. A deal's a deal. Cut her loose. One less thing to deal with while we collect our payday." One of his team cut the zip ties on her wrist. "You're free to go."

"The deal was my friends, too," Emma reminded him.

"Fine," Ben answered. "Free Mr. Hamilton. He and Ms. Edwards are free to go. The others stay."

"What about the rest of them?" Maggie demanded.

Ollie approached her. "Go, Maggie," he said. "I can't pass up a discovery like this. I'm staying."

"I'm not leaving you behind!" Maggie insisted.

"Maggie, go," Ollie insisted. "I will be fine. They still need me."

"Uncle Ollie..." Maggie began.

"No, Maggie. You'll go and that's final. Alert anyone you can once you're back to civilization," he said, lowering his voice to a whisper for the last statement.

"It may be too late then," Maggie argued.

"Maggie, this is not up for discussion! Now go!"

"Now or never, Ms. Edwards," Ben warned.

Maggie glanced to all of them, tears forming in her eyes. "I can't..." she began. She glanced at Henry.

"Go, princess," Henry told her.

"That's two votes for you to go," Ollie told her.

Maggie approached Henry. "Henry, I..." she began.

"Don't say anything, princess," he said to her. He kissed her forehead. "For what it's worth, I don't regret that kiss. And I wanted to tell you..."

"No, don't," Maggie interrupted. She put her hand against his lips. "Don't say it. Tell me the next time you see me." A tear fell to her cheeks.

"Deal," Henry answered. "Don't cry, princess. You know how I hate that."

Maggie sniffled, wiping her tear away. She nodded. "I know." She sniffled again, stepping away from him.

"I don't regret anything either, chicky," Charlie said. He approached her. "And if you want one last kiss, I wouldn't object."

Maggie shook her head at him. "Now, Ms. Edwards," Ben insisted. She glanced back at Henry. "Let's go! Take them out and let them go. Give them their camels and make sure they're gone before you return."

Two men led them at gunpoint out of the tomb. Frustration and distress filled Maggie with each step. She glanced back several times. How could she leave them? How could she walk away?

Meager moonlight streamed from the end of the tunnel. "Thank God," Leo mumbled.

They exited into the warm night air. "Get your stuff and get the hell out of here," one of the thugs instructed.

Emma nodded, starting across the sand to their gear and camels. Maggie hung back. "How could you do this?" Maggie cried. "How could you sell us out?"

"I didn't sell us out! I saved us!" Emma yelled. "They told me all I had to do was carry a locator and press a button when we arrived on site. They assured me we'd be free to go after they located the tomb."

"But we're not. Not all of us."

"I'm sorry, Maggie! I didn't realize that! Besides, it seems like your other friends are pretty damned used to this. They realized full well what they were in for."

Maggie crossed her arms, hot tears filling her eyes. "You're sorry? You're SORRY?" Maggie shouted. "You're a bitch!"

"Me? Are you kidding me? Who used me to get into the museum and steal an artifact? You lied to me. You nearly cost me my job! Almost got me sent to jail. When they told me they'd cover for me and I could keep my job and not go to jail if I did this, of course I accepted. What else could I do?"

"Maybe the right thing!" Maggie shouted back.

"Oh, like you? Saint Maggie! Who always does what's right! Always playing innocent and cutesy. Just as long as everyone loves sweet Maggie!"

"Oh, shove it, Emma."

"For the love of God, Mags, will you stop being so stupid? Emma's right! Let's go!" Leo joined the conversation.

"Unbelievable!" Maggie exclaimed. She threw her arms in the air. "Four people, one of whom is my uncle, are down in that tomb. They'll probably never see the light of day again and you want me to stop being 'stupid?'"

"We won't see the light of day again if we don't go now! Maggie, in the last week I have flown in a cargo plane to enter a country illegally, took part in a museum robbery, been kidnapped and held against my will and been dragged across the desert. I haven't showered in a week; I've barely eaten and being held captive has been no picnic. Now if you wouldn't mind, I'd like to leave this nightmare behind."

"Oh, would you? Would you, really, Leo? Don't you think that Uncle Ollie, Henry, Tarik and Charlie want the same?"

"No, Maggie, I do not. Emma has a point. Your new buddies are used to this. This is their lives. This is what they do. They are aware of the consequences. Now, please let's go!" he shouted at her.

"Go if you want to. And take the traitor with you. Seems you two think alike. I am not leaving!"

"Maggie!" Leo shouted.

"Save it, Leo. I'm staying," Maggie screamed. She turned to enter the pyramid again.

The two gunmen glanced at each other. "Should we stop her?" one said.

"Boss said to make sure they left, so I guess we should," the other answered. He shrugged. "I'll go."

Maggie stalked into the tomb's entrance. The gunman followed her. "Stop," he stated. "Get back here."

"No!" Maggie barked. The guard, focused on retrieving Maggie, wasn't careful with his foot placement. He stepped on one of the tiles, triggering an arrow to sail from the wall. It struck him in the neck. He gurgled as the arrow pierced his throat and the poison coursed through his artery. He dropped over dead in seconds. His body fell on another trigger, sending another arrow flying toward the opposite wall.

Maggie gulped, still not used to witnessing dead bodies.

She stood frozen, staring at the body for a moment, unsure how to proceed. A moment later, a shout emanated from the entrance. It must be the other man. Maggie squatted out of direct sight. His form loomed at the opening. The man entered the tomb. He spotted his companion sprawled on the floor. He rushed toward him, also forgetting the tiles on the floor. He trod on a trigger tile two steps into the passage. The arrow struck him in the shoulder. He writhed in pain, pulling the arrow from his arm. It clattered to the floor as he discarded it.

Maggie approached him, crawling on her hands and knees. He glanced down at her as she approached. "Sorry," she said. She winced as she pressed another tile with her hand. A new arrow shot from the wall, striking the injured man in the neck. It killed him within seconds as the poison coursed through his blood stream in an artery. He dropped to the floor as Maggie backed away.

She swallowed hard, staring at the two bodies in front of her. Two men dead. Leaving only four men downstairs. The odds weren't fantastic but if she could release Henry and Tarik, they may stand a chance. First, she needed a weapon. She grimaced as she approached one of the bodies. She slid the gun from his arm. She pulled it away from him, shouldering it. The man's arm thudded back to the ground with a sickening smack.

"Ugh," she moaned. Her stomach turned. For a moment, she reconsidered her decision. What could she do? She had gotten lucky with these two. The tomb had taken care of them for her. She wasn't cut out for this. She shook her head. No, she decided, she couldn't leave them. Determined, she turned around, facing the interior of the tomb. She picked her way through the trigger tiles and down to the antechamber outside of the large central chamber.

The large stone walls provided her a hiding spot as she

peered into the antechamber. Henry, Tarik and Charlie remained in the chamber with Ben, the group's leader. He paced back and forth in the front of them, his back toward the tomb's entrance.

"What a momentous day," Ben pronounced. "I will become richer beyond my dreams. The icing on this very rich cake is I will have the distinction to end the lives of the likes of you." He eyed each of them up. "Oh, which of you to end first? Decisions, decisions."

"Just do it already," Henry snapped at him.

"Oh, don't rush me, Taylor. I plan to savor this moment." He eyed them again. Maggie crept into the tomb. She slinked inch by inch, careful to stay out of his sight line as he turned to pace in the opposite direction. "Hmm. Yes, I think maybe you first." He pointed to Tarik. He considered it another moment. "Yes, that's appropriate."

CHAPTER 23

*B*en leveled his pistol at Tarik's head. Maggie snuck behind him, swinging the weapon she held at him. She struck him square on the head. The blow from the butt of the rifle knocked him unconscious. He fell to the floor in a heap. Maggie stood shocked for a moment, surprised her plan had worked.

"Maggie!" Henry cried.

Maggie rushed to Henry. She threw her arms around him. "I couldn't leave you."

"Aw, princess. I appreciate that. Although, you should have left. You're not safe."

"It doesn't matter. I couldn't leave."

"Since you're here, would you mind cutting me loose?"

Maggie smiled at him. "Not at all." Maggie glanced around. "I guess he has a knife, huh?" she asked, pointing at Ben.

"I'm sure he does. Give me that gun you've got." Maggie handed him the gun. He balanced it in his hands. "Now, careful, Maggie, kick that gun as far from him as you can before you approach him."

Maggie nodded and kicked the other gun across the room. "Good. Try his right pocket." Maggie stuck her hand into his pocket. She pulled out a Swiss Army knife, holding it up with a grin.

"Perfect, princess. Now cut me loose." Maggie cut Henry's zip ties, then Tarik's and Charlie's.

"Where are the other two thugs who escorted you out?" Henry queried Maggie.

"Dead," Maggie answered. Henry shot her a glance.

"I left Emma and Leo outside when I returned for you. They followed me, but they weren't careful in the first hall-way." Maggie shrugged her shoulders. Henry smirked at her.

"Good job, princess. You're one brave little lady."

"I knew you'd come back for me, chicky," Charlie said as Maggie cut him loose. Tarik scooped up Ben's discarded weapon. He searched Ben's pockets for any weapons. He found zip ties and used them to tie Ben's hands behind his back. Tarik dragged his body to the far corner of the room.

"Now, you need to leave, princess," Henry advised. "We'll take care of the rest."

"No way!" Maggie objected. "I'm not leaving! Not until my uncle is safe."

"Maggie…" Henry started. Maggie crossed her arms, standing firm. "Okay, you've earned it. I doubt the others will be much longer. You need to stay out of sight. Got it?"

Maggie nodded. "Got it. I'll wait behind the doorway to the ship room."

"Good. Oh, Maggie?" Henry said as she crossed the room.

"Yeah?" she asked, turning back.

"Thanks for coming back for us." Henry winked at her. Maggie smiled at him before racing across the room.

Maggie entered the ship's chamber. She hid herself behind the door, keeping the main chamber in view. Henry and Tarik kept their weapons trained on the doorway leading further into the tomb. Within ten minutes, movement appeared at the doorway.

"Drop the bags, toss your weapons to us," Henry ordered.

Logan and his associate appeared in the chamber. They dropped the bags they carried and raised their arms, startled at the turn of events. "Weapons," Tarik reminded them.

Their rifles were slung over their back. "Slowly," Tarik told them. They inched them over their heads, sliding them across the floor toward Henry and Tarik.

"On the ground, hands behind your back. Tie them up," Henry directed Charlie.

Charlie zip tied each of their hands. Henry and Tarik shouldered their weapons, approaching the others. They each hauled one of the men to their feet. "In here," Henry said, hauling them toward Maggie's hiding spot. They shoved them through the door, pushing each man to his knees.

He handed Maggie one of the weapons they collected from the men. "Keep an eye on them. If they move, shoot them."

"Okay," Maggie said. She aimed the gun at them.

"You know how to use that?" Henry inquired.

"Uh," Maggie hesitated.

Henry clicked off the safety for her. "Point, shoot. Don't stop shooting until they're down."

Maggie nodded. "Got it."

"Stay with her," he said to Charlie. He handed Charlie a weapon, too.

"Don't worry, chicky. I got your back," Charlie said. He raised his eyebrows over and over at her.

"Oh, now I feel so safe!"

Henry and Tarik disappeared into the passage leading further into the tomb. Within ten minutes they returned. The last of the tomb raiders marched in front of them. Henry, Tarik and Ollie came behind. They paused in the main chamber, Tarik staying with the other man, his gun trained on him.

"On your feet," Henry shouted at the two men Maggie and Charlie guarded. "Out here."

The two men climbed to their feet and were marched to the main chamber. As they entered the chamber, a groan emanated from Ben.

Henry squatted next to him, slapping his face a few times. "That's it, mate, wakey, wakey." As Ben's eyes opened, Henry dragged him to his feet. "Time to go."

They marched the entire team out of the tomb, passing the bodies of their dead colleagues. As they emerged into the night air, a droning noise pierced the silence. The noise grew louder and louder until it became the unmistakable thumping of a helicopter. Leo and Emma still stood near the tomb's entrance.

"Is that a..." Emma asked as she approached them.

"A helicopter, yeah. You weren't the only one who called for backup when we got here," Henry informed her.

"Backup?" Maggie asked.

Ollie answered, "We've got a lot to tell you, Maggie."

Within minutes, the helicopter was in sight, touching down several yards from them. Two men emerged, rushing over to the group. "Gentlemen," one shouted over the drone of the chopper, "I see you have the situation well in hand."

"Got a reputation to keep up," Henry answered. Two more choppers landed near the first. Men climbed from both.

The man from the first chopper shouted orders to them, instructing them to load the tomb raider team into one chopper and the others to secure the tomb site.

"Dr. Keene, Agent Taylor," the man shouted to Ollie. "If you'll follow me."

NELLIE H. STEELE

Ollie shook his head. "I don't want to leave the site. But please take my niece, Maggie, with you."

"It will be safe with my men. We'll have you back first thing tomorrow morning."

"Okay," Ollie agreed. "As long as we can take my niece, Maggie."

"Of course, sir."

"These folks will need an evac, too." Ollie motioned to Tarik, Charlie, Emma and Leo.

"Of course. If you will follow Captain Lewis," he said, signaling to his partner.

"Instruct your men to touch nothing in the tomb. They shouldn't even enter it. There are several booby traps that are deadly. In fact, there are two dead bodies in the entrance," Ollie said.

"Will do," the man answered. He spoke to one of his men. The man nodded, shouting instructions to his team. "Follow me." The man motioned toward the helicopters. After they retrieved a few items, Tarik, Charlie, Emma and Leo were led to one of the larger choppers that landed after the first. Maggie, Ollie and Henry followed the uniformed man to the first helicopter. They climbed inside, fastening their seatbelts.

Ollie sat next to the uniformed man, across from Maggie. Henry sat next to her. The helicopter lifted from the ground. "You've taken good care of my niece, Henry," Ollie shouted over the roar of the copter's blades. "Thank you."

"It was my pleasure, Ollie," Henry answered. "She's taken good care of me, too."

"I told you she was tough," Ollie said.

Maggie smiled. "Speaking of tough... did I hear him right? Did he say AGENT Taylor?"

"I told you we had a lot to tell you, Maggie," Ollie said, winking at her.

CHAPTER 24

*M*aggie sat at the street-side café, sipping her coffee. Ollie joined her, flown in from the tomb's site this morning to see her off before her evening flight home. "I just can't get over that fact that you work for the government!" Maggie exclaimed.

Ollie chuckled. "Didn't realize I had it in me, huh?"

"Who would have thought the government was invested in finding Cleopatra's tomb!" Maggie marveled.

"You'd be a wonderful addition to the team, Maggie," Ollie said. "Promise me you'll consider the offer to join our team."

"I promise," Maggie answered. "I'm just not sure. Like I told Henry, I'm not sure I can handle this turmoil in my life all the time. I need a minute to breathe."

"I understand," Ollie answered. "Henry will miss you though."

Maggie swallowed hard, recalling their conversation yesterday. She had told him she was going home, that she needed normalcy in her life. He hadn't argued, but his disappointment was clear. She recalled how stormy his blue eyes appeared when he told her he'd miss her. At that moment, she'd wanted to throw her arms around him and promise to stay. But she made her choice. She fought to stick to it. She needed routine and stability in her life. And her relationship with Leo was stable and solid. She needed that, she wanted that. She convinced herself to go. To return to normal life. The sting of that moment would pass once familiar things surrounded her. She'd force herself to focus on the upcoming Fall Ball as a distraction. It was only two days away. In past years, she'd been ecstatic at this time of the year, excited for the ball. This year it held little anticipation for her.

"I was hoping he'd come this morning," Maggie admitted.

Ollie smiled at her. "I'm not sure he could."

"Well, I guess there's no sense in delaying things. I'd better get going to the airport. That reminds me, thanks for setting up the flight. And dealing with my troublesome passport issues."

Ollie stood. "No problem. Is Leo still at the hotel?" he asked.

Maggie also stood. "He is," she answered. "I need to meet him there before we head to the airport."

Ollie wrapped Maggie in a hug. "Take care, Maggie," Ollie said. "Text me when you've landed. And if you change your mind... about anything... I'm just a call away."

"I know. I'll keep in touch."

Maggie stepped away from him, meandering down the sidewalk toward her hotel. She glanced back a few times, hoping to spot Henry. Ollie waved at her. She waved back, turning away for the last time, resigning herself to the fact that she wouldn't see Henry again. Perhaps it was for the best, she decided. It would have only made things harder.

She met Leo at the hotel. They went straight to the airport. With no luggage, they were at their gate with time to spare. Maggie was quiet as they waited to board. She skulked onto the plane, collapsing into her seat next to Leo.

"Why the long face?" Leo asked. "We're going home!"

Maggie faked a smile. "Just tired, I guess."

"Well, we've got a nice long flight to sleep." Leo seemed to be ecstatic to return home.

Maggie nodded in agreement, anything but convinced. Leo settled back into his seat as the plane taxied down the runway for take-off. Maggie found it impossible to get comfortable. She fidgeted in her seat, unable to settle. After a while, she glanced at Leo. His eyes were closed. She stared for a moment, hoping he'd wake up. He didn't.

She tapped his shoulder.

Leo didn't open his eyes. "What?" he asked.

"I can't get comfortable," Maggie informed him.

"Did you try leaning against the window? I gave you the window seat."

"Yeah, I did."

"Mmm," Leo mumbled.

"Can I lay on you?" Maggie asked.

"What?" Leo asked, his eyes popping open.

"Can I lay my head on your shoulder?"

Leo smiled at her. He pressed the call button. "Just a sec," he said.

The attendant arrived. "Can we get a pillow?" he requested. Within a moment, the attendant returned with a pillow. "Here you go."

Maggie grasped the pillow, confusion on her face. "I didn't need a pillow, I could…"

"No, come on, Mags! I'm trying to sleep too. I'll be uncomfortable with you laying all over me. My arm'll fall asleep. I just want to relax. The pillow will be more comfortable, anyway."

Maggie sighed. Leo closed his eyes again. Maggie

squashed the pillow into a ball and placed it against the wall. She laid against it, annoyed. She tried closing her eyes but found it impossible to fall asleep. She needed a distraction.

She turned back to Leo, poking him again. He sighed. "Now what?"

"I still can't sleep. My mind won't stop. I need a distraction."

"I told you you should have bought a book at the airport."

"I don't want to read. I want to talk."

"Maggie, it's the middle of the night. I haven't slept in days, I'm tired!"

"You could just listen, then."

"Listen to what?"

"Me. Listen to me."

"What's so important that can't wait until after I've gotten some sleep?"

"Nothing but it might help relax me."

Leo sighed. "Fine, fine. Okay. What do you want to talk about?"

"How about my dress for the Fall Ball?"

"All right." Leo acquiesced. "Tell me about it."

Maggie detailed her outfit. She finished her description with a question. "I wonder if we could get you a tie to match my dress. What color were you planning on wearing?"

"Uh, about that, Mags," Leo started. He paused.

"What?"

"Uh," he hesitated.

"What?" she repeated.

"The thing is… when we ended our relationship…"

"Yeah?"

"Cathy Simmons asked me to go to the Fall Ball with her."

"And you said what?" Maggie asked.

"I said yes."

"WHAT?!" Maggie exclaimed.

"We weren't together! You were gone! Off on some 'adventure' with another man! I was drunk, I said yes."

"Well, can't you explain to her it was a mistake?"

"Two days before? I'm not comfortable doing that. It's no big deal. Let's just get through it, put it behind us and move on. Okay?"

"No, it's not okay!"

Leo rolled his eyes. "Come on, Maggie. We were broken up. Forever, I assumed. You were off with some other guy. I was drunk. What did you expect me to do?"

"Not make a date with someone else. And I explained to you what I was doing with Henry."

"I'm sorry I didn't believe you. But you have to realize how the situation appeared to me. I was hurt. Was it a poor decision in retrospect? Probably. But it's done now."

"This is unbelievable. Just unbelievable!"

"Oh, stop. Don't make this a bigger deal than it is, it's not a big deal. I came after you, didn't I? Isn't that enough? Just go. We'll still have a good time."

"Myself? Just go myself?"

"Sure. I mean, it's not like you'll actually be alone."

Silence fell between them. Maggie crossed her arms, seething. "Come on, Mags…" Leo began.

Maggie fumed. "Go back to sleep, Leo," Maggie said.

"I'm sorry, Maggie. I am," Leo said. Maggie nodded in answer. He closed his eyes, wriggling in his seat to get comfortable. Maggie laid her head against her pillow. Things were already not starting out well. Their life-changing journey had done little to change Leo. But she made a choice, she would see it through. Leo had always accused her of being flighty. This time she would stay the course.

* * *

They landed the following afternoon at the international airport closest to Rosemont. Within forty-five minutes they were back in Rosemont. Maggie returned to her apartment. She paused as she entered. It seemed as though it had been ages since she'd been here. With no luggage to unpack, she tossed her purse on the counter and collapsed on the couch. Silence filled the room. She laid her head back on the pillows. She hadn't slept much on the plane. Despite being exhausted, she was too wired to sleep.

Her phone chimed from her purse. She rolled her eyes but retrieved it, remembering Uncle Ollie's request to text him when she was home. She dragged herself off the couch to get it.

As she collapsed again on the couch, she checked her display, expecting a message from Leo. Instead, she found one from Piper: *Heard you were back on the grid, boss lady.*

Maggie chuckled at the message. She answered, informing Piper she was home and safe. She sent the text, then sent another message to Ollie, informing him she was home and safe. Her hand hesitated over the send button as she typed her last message. This one informed Henry she was home. He had requested she send him a message, but she hesitated to send it. After a moment, she pressed the send button.

By the time she sent her last message, she already received a response to her first. Piper answered: *Home? You mean you didn't open the shop?*

Maggie laughed aloud. She responded she did not.

Piper responded: *Slacker... see you tomorrow? You're still going to that stupid ball, right?*

Maggie answered: *Yeah, I am... see you there, surprised you're going!*

Piper responded: *I want to see that dress you babbled on about for weeks... so I can confirm it's not as great as you said.*

Maggie answered: *Very funny, Piper... see you tomorrow!*

While Maggie finished her messages with Piper, two other messages arrived. She opened the first from her uncle, stating he was pleased she was home and would send her pictures of the tomb's excavation soon.

Maggie answered him before moving on to the next text. This one was from Henry. Maggie's heart skipped a beat as she opened it: *I'm glad you're home safe, princess... enjoy your ball, I'm sure you'll look beautiful.*

Maggie responded: *Thanks!* She closed her phone. She wanted to answer more, but she stopped herself. She meandered to her room. Her dress for the ball hung in her closet. She stared at it for twenty minutes. It brought her such joy to admire it before her strange adventure, now it evoked nothing in her. Perhaps she was tired. Perhaps she needed rest, real rest in her own bed.

After a dinner consisting of ice cream and jellybeans, Maggie stretched out in her own bed. Exhausted, she expected to be asleep in minutes. Instead, she tossed and turned, her mind churning over recent events.

She picked up her phone, intent on texting Henry, craving the comfort and reassurance he always provided her. Wait, she wondered, what was she doing? She made her choice. She should text Leo, not Henry. In the end, she decided not to text anyone, tossing her phone back on the night table and flopping back into bed.

Maggie awoke mid-morning the next day. Her phone chirped at her, reminding her of her hair appointment later in the day. Maggie climbed from her bed and made herself a cup of coffee. She checked her phone as she sipped it.

There were no messages from Leo. She had received several messages from Ollie with pictures of the progress at the tomb. Maggie studied them as she drank her coffee. Ollie also sent several descriptions of the pictures. He gushed about the findings, his enthusiasm obvious. It was infectious. Maggie found herself unable to stop staring at the pictures. She texted him back: *Looks like you're enjoying yourself! Have fun! I'd like to visit soon!*

Ollie answered her in minutes, sending two messages. The first said: *Anytime! You say the word, I'll arrange it!* The second message contained another picture with the message: *We miss you!* Ollie stood on the side of an enormous statue inside the tomb. Henry stood on the other. Maggie swallowed hard at the sight. She typed a quick message back: *Say hi to your new friend for me... and Henry!*

Ollie returned her text, telling her what she did not want to hear: *Tell him yourself... I'm sure he'd like to hear from you*

Maggie ignored the text, unwilling or perhaps unable to answer. She checked the time. "Shoot!" she exclaimed. "I'm going to be late!" She leapt from her bed, racing around to get ready for her hair appointment.

Maggie spent the better part of the afternoon at the salon getting her hair and nails done. When she arrived home, she did her makeup for the evening before dressing for the ball. She slipped the dress on, as she recalled detailing it to Henry. She zipped it and slipped on the shoes she had been so delighted to find.

She stared at her reflection in the mirror. She took a deep breath. Tonight would be her return to normal life. To the life she chose. She was happy, she would be happy. She smiled at her reflection. She would be happy.

* * *

The cool October air caressed Maggie's skin as she sat on the bench outside of the banquet hall. The day had been warm, its warmth lingering into the evening. But the slight breeze had the typical note of autumn coolness to it. She could still hear the music from the Fall Ball floating out of the hall to where she sat. Her auburn knee-length cocktail dress matched the color of the changing leaves on the tree she sat below. She smoothed the dress across her legs as she swiveled her high heels on the concrete below. She sighed as she stared into the cloudless evening sky. The stars shined back. She recalled her stargazing in the Egyptian desert with Henry. She remembered how relaxed she had been then.

Tonight had not lived up to her expectations. Leo had confessed on their plane trip home he was attending with someone else. But somehow she had assumed from their discussion the date was meaningless, that he would spend most of his time with her. Instead, she spent the night watching him gush over his new date. They had not even shared one dance together. Maggie guessed it was payback for her time with Henry. After a few hours, she had decided to get some air, heading out the front door and finding a nearby bench. Here she contemplated her next move: stay or go. The ball did little to excite her, soothe her nerves or comfort her.

The leaves rustled in the breeze. Maggie heard shoes moving along the concrete. She paid no attention, assuming it was other ball-goers seeking air, privacy or finding their way home. Out of the corner of her eye, she spotted a figure approaching her. Sliding her eyes sideways, she spotted Leo, standing there, hands in his pockets, staring down at her. She glanced away, sighing again.

"Not enjoying yourself?" Leo asked.

"No," Maggie answered.

Leo made his way around her, sitting down next to her on the bench. He leaned forward, his elbows resting on his knees, rubbing his hands together.

She was in no mood. "What do you want, Leo?"

"Just checking on you, I noticed you left and wanted to see if you were okay."

"Cut the fake concern," she barked.

"What? I'm being honest."

"Oh, really, are you? Would it matter to you if I wasn't okay?"

"Yes, Maggie, of course it would."

"Oh, well I wasn't sure. I mean, why would it? You seem pretty focused on your date. I'm surprised you even noticed I was gone."

"Oh, come on, Maggie. You're being ridiculous."

"Oh, I'M being ridiculous? Are you kidding me? Did you tell me I should come tonight so you could rub it in my face you are with someone else? Is this payback for rescuing my uncle with Henry?"

Leo leaned back. "No," he answered, "no, again you're being ridiculous. Come on, what would you have me do, ignore Cathy completely? She is my date."

"Yeah, she is your date. The woman you agreed to go with five minutes after we broke up. And refused to tell we were back together when we got home!"

"It was an impossible situation, Maggie. I told you that."

"And you could care less about correcting it! This isn't an impossible situation, Leo. WE are an impossible situation."

"I told you before this was one night and it's over. I owed her this. After tonight, we put this behind us and move on."

"What about what you owed me?"

Leo sighed. "Tell me, Maggie, what do I owe you? We're both at fault here. Let's just put it behind us and move on."

"How am I at fault?"

"Oh, come on, Maggie. You're the one who ran off around the world without even telling me."

"So, this is my fault? Your insistence on coming to THE event of the year in Rosemont with Cathy is my fault?"

"Why does it always have to be someone's fault, Maggie? Why can't we just start over fresh tomorrow? You stop blaming me for Cathy and I won't blame you for Henry."

"You've got to be joking! I have nothing to be sorry for. You have nothing to blame me for! Henry was helping me find my kidnapped uncle, remember? And, by the way, you didn't give a fig about the danger my life and his were in, you only cared about what I was doing with Henry!"

"And you have nothing to blame me for either, yet you will! I came to London for you! I picked you!"

"I came home with you! I picked you! And you failed to tell me about your date with Cathy until AFTER I decided to come home. I've finally realized the truth. We do not fit together, Leo. Our relationship is always work, it shouldn't be work. Cathy and Henry are not the reasons we don't work. They're just an example of the reasons."

Leo dropped his head back, throwing his arms up in frustration. Leo, intentionally or not, failed to be supportive to her. They didn't work. She had clung to the idea of the safety this relationship offered her when in reality it offered her nothing. He came to London for her. But he didn't come to support her nor to help her. He came to play the white knight, collect her and return promptly to their normal lives regardless of Uncle Ollie's safety. He came to London for her only because the action was expected of him, and she'd never hear the end of it. She rolled her eyes. Same old nonsense, always her fault. "Well," she said, standing and facing him, "this is it. I'm not angry, Leo. We look great on paper, but we just don't work in reality. This is finished." She turned on her heel and sauntered away. This time for good.

"Maggie," he shouted after her, "come on!" He waited for her to turn around. "You keep walking and we really are done this time," he warned. "I came to London for you and you're going to walk away from me? Well, that is IT!"

She kept walking and never looked back.

* * *

Maggie wandered through the streets of Rosemont. She expected to feel upset after her breakup with Leo. Instead, she felt free. She smiled to herself as she admired the changing leaves. She fished in her purse, pulling out her phone.

It was 11 p.m. in Rosemont. She converted the time to Egypt. It would be 6 a.m. there. Satisfied she wouldn't be waking her uncle, she dialed his number. After two rings he answered.

"Maggie!" he greeted her.

"Hi, Uncle Ollie!"

"How was the ball?"

"Eh," Maggie hedged.

"What happened?" Ollie prodded.

"Nothing," Maggie fibbed.

"Nothing, huh?" Ollie chuckled.

"I didn't say anything happened!" Maggie retorted.

"The Fall Ball is the highlight of your year, Maggie. Your non-answer makes it obvious something happened."

"Perhaps I've grown up and princess balls are no longer the highlight of my year," Maggie answered.

"And perhaps you called me at six in the morning because there's something specific you want settled."

"Okay, okay," Maggie admitted. "I called you because I need your help."

"Oh?" Ollie nudged.

"I may have flown home a little too early," Maggie confessed.

"You don't say," Ollie declared.

"I hoped you might get me on a flight back to Egypt. And get me to the dig site."

"Burning desire to see the progress on the excavation?" Ollie joked.

"Something like that," Maggie hedged.

"Why don't you take the night to sleep on it, Maggie? We can talk in the morning."

Maggie frowned. Why was her uncle hesitating to help her? Perhaps because she didn't admit her true intentions for the trip. Or perhaps because he felt she was being impulsive and childish. Within seventy-two hours she had left the country, and Henry, behind, returning to Rosemont with Leo, then reversed her decision. She sounded like a childish flake who didn't get her way and was lashing out.

Disappointment filled Maggie. "All-all right," she acquiesced.

"I have a feeling your situation may resolve itself, Maggie. Talk tomorrow?"

"Sure. Have fun with your artifacts," Maggie said. She ended the call. She stopped walking for a moment. She stared at the moonlit sky. Her uncle's last statement stung. He assumed after she cooled off, she'd change her mind again. He had reason to surmise that. She'd done it many times before with Leo. He was unwilling to help her because he feared she'd flip-flop on her decision again. He was protecting his friend. She understood his impulse. She hurt Henry when she walked away from him. Ollie wanted to prevent her from doing that again. She deserved that, she figured.

She continued down the sidewalk, turning the corner onto her building's street. A figure stood under the street-light across from her building's entrance. He held a bouquet of flowers. A smile crossed Maggie's face as she approached him.

"Hello, princess," Henry said as she approached. "Wow, you look stunning."

"Hello! Thank you. This is quite a surprise," Maggie answered.

"I'm sorry, Maggie. I couldn't stay away," Henry confessed.

Maggie smiled at him. "It's good to see you. I…"

"Just a second, Maggie," Henry interrupted her. "There's something I have to say. And this time you won't stop me. And I'm sorry if it makes you uncomfortable, or it ruins your night, but I have to say it. I realize you picked Leo, but I'm here to convince you that you were wrong. I missed you the moment you left. I couldn't think of anything but you. I love how tough you are and how smart you are and how beautiful you are." Maggie's smile grew broader. "Oh, these are for you." Henry handed her the flowers. "You mentioned carnations are your favorite."

Maggie was impressed at his memory. "Thank you. You remembered," Maggie said. "I have a confession to make, too," Maggie admitted.

"What's that?" Henry inquired.

"I called my uncle earlier. Asked him to book me a flight to Egypt. Told him I made a mistake by leaving."

"Did you now?" Henry asked. He grinned and pulled Maggie close to him.

"I did."

"What about Leo?" he asked.

"We broke up earlier this evening," Maggie confirmed.

"Oh, yeah?" he asked. "Poor bloke," he said. Henry kissed her.

Maggie wrapped her arms around him, returning his kiss. "There's one thing you left out earlier about me."

"Oh?"

"I can be difficult," Maggie tested.

"I love how difficult you are."

"Let's see how long that lasts." Maggie giggled, giving in to another kiss. It appeared Ollie was correct. Her situation had resolved itself.

"I hope you're prepared for a lifetime of adventures, because that's how long this will last," Henry promised.

"You promise?" Maggie asked.

"You bet and you know how seriously I take my promises."

The End

Continue the series with *Secret of the Ankhs*, Book 2 in the Maggie Edwards Adventures.

A NOTE FROM THE AUTHOR

Dear Reader,

Thank you for reading this book! *Cleopatra's Tomb* is my first foray into adventure novels and there's plenty more to come with Maggie Edwards! *Secret of the Ankhs*, Book 2 in the series, is now available!

I hope you enjoyed reading the story as much as I enjoyed writing it! If you did, please consider leaving a review and help get this book and series into the hands of other interested readers!

Keep reading for a sneak preview of *Secret of the Ankhs*, Book 2 in the *Maggie Edwards Adventures* series!

If you'd like to stay up to date with all my news, be the first to find out about new releases first, sales and get free offers, join the Nellie H. Steele's Mystery Readers' Group! Or sign up for my newsletter now!

All the best, Nellie

SECRET OF THE ANKHS
SYNOPSIS

Maggie is pitted against a powerful network of black-market dealers with an ankh is stolen. Does she have what it takes to survive?

Maggie Edwards is back in her boutique and she's landed a new government job after finding Cleopatra's tomb. So, when an undistinguished ankh is stolen from the local museum, Maggie is the first on the case. Especially when her archeologist uncle insists it could lead to a major discovery.

When Maggie's kidnapped, she learns firsthand the object's value. And the stakes have never been higher. The thieves will stop at nothing to keep Maggie from retrieving the object. From fires to boat chases and even another encounter with Cleopatra's deadly tomb, Maggie will have to brave it all to learn the secret of the ankhs.

If you love high-stakes adventure that takes you around the world, you'll love Secret of the Ankhs, book 2 in this female-led adventure series by Nellie H. Steele.

Get *Secret of the Ankhs* now.

SECRET OF THE ANKHS EXCERPT

"Money's in the register," Maggie choked out. "And let my assistant go, she doesn't need to be involved."

"I'm not here for the money, Ms. Edwards," the voice answered.

Maggie's brow furrowed. The man shoved her roughly toward the cashier's counter. "I want to know what you know about the location of the other two ankhs."

"What?" Maggie questioned as she stumbled to the counter. She spun to face him, grasping the counter behind her. She recognized James Michael Dean. Before he could speak again, she grasped Piper's arm, pulling her back and shoving Piper behind her.

"The ankhs, Ms. Edwards. I want the locations of the other two."

"I don't... I don't have the locations!" Maggie cried.

The man shoved his hand forward, leveling the gun at Maggie. "I don't buy that story," he growled.

"I don't!" Maggie insisted.

The man cocked the gun. "I'm going to ask you one more time."

Maggie breathed raggedly as her mind raced for a solution. She swallowed hard again, holding her hand out in front of her. "Okay, okay, wait," she breathed. "I don't know the locations of the ankhs, but I may have a lead for you. My uncle may have learned something about their location. M-Maybe he can help."

"The renowned Dr. Keene? Yes, Ms. Edwards, I expect he can. In fact, I expect he already did!"

"All right," Maggie stalled. "So, let's call him and..."

"Tell me what he told you!" the man insisted.

"He didn't tell me anything!" Maggie shouted.

The man raised his eyebrows at her. "You had dinner with him last night. He didn't tell you then? Come on, Ms. Edwards, I find that hard to fathom."

Maggie shook her head. Her mind spotted a temporary solution, and she took it. "No. No, I didn't have dinner with him last night," she lied.

"You're lying!"

"I'm not! I'm not. I can prove it." The man narrowed his eyes at her. "Check my phone," Maggie exclaimed, pointing with a shaky hand. "Check it. The code is 1753. Check the texts. You'll see, I told him I was running late. And then check the call log. I called him and we rescheduled. For tonight, actually! So, I haven't spoken with my uncle about anything."

The man squinted at Maggie before swiping through her phone. He fiddled on it for a few moments before he toggled off the display. He narrowed his eyes further at her. "See?" Maggie questioned. "I could call..."

"No!" the man roared. "No calls." His lips twisted into a gruesome smirk. "Let's pay dear Uncle Ollie a visit, Ms. Edwards."

Click here to keep reading *Secret of the Ankhs*!

OTHER SERIES BY NELLIE H. STEELE

Cozy Mystery Series

Cate Kensie Mysteries
Lily & Cassie by the Sea Mysteries
Pearl Party Mysteries
Middle Age is Murder Cozy Mysteries

Supernatural Suspense/Urban Fantasy

Shadow Slayers Stories
Duchess of Blackmoore Mysteries

Adventure

Maggie Edwards Adventures
Clif & Ri on the Sea

Made in United States
Orlando, FL
04 September 2022